PRAISE FOR *FE*

'In turns gripping and moving, as entrai
a consummate storyteller.' Kylie Ladd, au....... ....

PRAISE FOR *THE MOTHERS' GROUP*

'. . . it has that capacity that good social novels should have of creating meaning and intensity from what on the surface may appear to be ordinary . . . Higgins looks at the difficult moment of becoming parents with an unflinching but powerful humanity . . . Like its Allen & Unwin stablemate, *The Slap*, *The Mothers' Group* is a top-shelf novel about contemporary Australian life.' *Weekend Australian*

'. . . an enthralling read. Be prepared to burn the midnight oil, as it is impossible to put down.' *Sunday Herald Sun*, 4½ stars

'*The Mothers' Group* provides enough "aha" moments of recognition to make even the most sleep-deprived mum smile. And I should know: I read it while juggling my three-month-old daughter.' *Bookseller & Publisher*

'This heartfelt debut novel explores how challenging and bewildering motherhood can be—from postnatal depression and incontinence to loss of sexual desire—and how much empathy, reassurance and wisdom can be found in the shared experience of a support group.' *Better Homes & Gardens*

PRAISE FOR *WIFE ON THE RUN*

'Provocative, sharply insightful and wildly entertaining, *Wife On the Run* . . . is an engaging journey through love, heartbreak and self-discovery.' *Booked Out*

'Funny and sexy and briskly written, it's a page-turning domestic melodrama for the social media age.' *The Age* and *Sydney Morning Herald*

'The perfect home-alone read.' *Country Style*

Fiona Higgins is the author of two novels, *Wife on the Run* and *The Mothers' Group*, and a memoir, *Love in the Age of Drought*.

Fiona has qualifications in the humanities and social sciences, and has worked in the philanthropy and not-for-profit sector in Australia for the past seventeen years.

Having recently returned from three years in Indonesia, she now lives in Sydney with her husband and three children.

www.fionahiggins.com.au
www.facebook.com/fionahigginsauthor

Fearless

FIONA HIGGINS

ALLEN&UNWIN
SYDNEY·MELBOURNE·AUCKLAND·LONDON

First published in 2016

Allen & Unwin
83 Alexander Street
Crows Nest NSW 2065
Australia
Phone: (61 2) 8425 0100
Email: info@allenandunwin.com
Web: www.allenandunwin.com

Cataloguing-in-Publication details are available
from the National Library of Australia
www.trove.nla.gov.au

ISBN 978 1 76029 422 9

Set in 12/18 pt Minion Pro by Bookhouse, Sydney
Printed and bound in Australia by Griffin Press

10 9 8 7 6 5 4 3 2 1

For Stuart, the most fearless person I know.

FLYING

Janelle's eyes flew open as the aeroplane shuddered.

Not that she'd been sleeping, which seemed to be the preferred activity of most normal people on aeroplanes. No, she'd simply closed her eyes and succumbed to the numbing effect of the three vodkas she'd slammed down at Melbourne Airport before the flight. Followed by the sedative chaser prescribed by her doctor for emergency use only.

The fasten seatbelt sign pinged above her head. That was emergency enough.

Janelle closed her eyes once more and consciously attempted to slow her breathing. It was a technique she'd learned at university, a strategy for managing exam-time anxiety. With each outgoing breath, she counted backwards from ten to one, and imagined herself in a peaceful place. Typically a tropical island—not dissimilar to the photos she'd seen of her destination, Bali—with the rhythmic sound of waves lapping at the shore, the long fronds of coconut palms swaying in the breeze, and the lazy chirruping of crickets drawing her towards a calm core of inner stillness.

Except this time, turbulence was interfering with her serenity routine. The PA system crackled and the captain's voice addressed the passengers. *'Ladies and gentlemen, an update from the flight deck. We have some weather ahead and ask that all passengers and crew take your seats immediately and fasten seatbelts.'*

She resented the euphemism. It was never merely *weather*. Almost as soon as the captain had finished speaking, the aeroplane began to lurch.

Janelle stared at her lap, wishing she'd never booked the ticket. Remembering how she'd sat in front of her computer only a fortnight earlier, dithering about dates and departure times. Checking for ominous flight numbers divisible by the number thirteen, pondering if *this* or *that* flight might be an ill-fated one. In the absence of any available seats in the statistically safest tail section, she'd checked the emergency exit rows over the wing, but all had been occupied. Frustrated, she'd selected a row towards the rear, between two seats already reserved.

The plane pitched suddenly and several passengers cried out. The portly European man in the window seat next to her put down his newspaper. Tears of panic pricked Janelle's eyes.

It's just like driving on a corrugated road, she told herself. *The plane is designed to withstand this.*

'Excuse me.' The woman on her other side spoke to Janelle. She appeared rather agitated. 'I really need to go to the toilet. Would you mind holding my baby? I'll be quick.'

Janelle looked down at the tiny infant sleeping in the woman's arms. 'But the seatbelt sign is on.'

'Please?' The woman forced a smile.

Janelle was dismayed. It was hard enough holding herself together on a flight, never mind comforting a baby as well. Then, feeling sorry for the woman, she nodded.

The woman unbuckled the infant harness and secured it to Janelle's seatbelt, clipping the child in. The infant opened its eyes just as soon as its mother stood up. Janelle watched its lips quiver, but it was too late to call the woman back. She was already stumbling along the aisle, steadying herself against seats as she went.

'Madam.' A stern-faced flight attendant hailed the woman, moving after her. 'Sit *down.*'

The woman gestured to the toilet cubicle then disappeared into it, locking the door behind her. The flight attendant clawed her way back to her seat and sat facing the passengers, without looking directly at any of them.

Janelle glanced down at the baby. It stared solemnly back, perhaps searching for some recognisable feature. She couldn't guess its sex, nor how many months old it might be. She hadn't conversed with its mother at all; she'd been too focused on her deep breathing to engage in pleasantries. Yet here she was, holding a nameless, vulnerable infant during the roughest turbulence she'd experienced in her life.

The plane dipped and yawed. An overhead locker fell open, emptying its contents over the passengers below. A woman groaned and clutched her head, but Janelle couldn't see how badly hurt she was. A man nearby crossed himself, and the child next to him burst into tears.

'What's happening, Daddy?' the child screeched.

Janelle leaned towards the window, trying to orient herself, but could see nothing beyond a blanket of malevolent green-grey cloud. The engines whined, seemingly working at full capacity.

The plane jolted violently and Janelle felt dizzy, unable to determine if they were climbing or descending. A man across the aisle vomited, and some of it sprayed over Janelle's knees. She gripped the baby tightly, bile rising in her own mouth. An Indonesian-looking man several rows ahead began praying loudly, repeating the sames word over and over. *Allahu Akbar . . . Ya ampun . . . Allahu Akbar.*

The plane shook with unnatural, arrhythmic spasms, as if it was coughing. The seatbelt slashed across her waist, forcing her body against the seat. The baby wailed from its infant harness, connected to Janelle like a strange umbilical cord.

An almighty bang caused her to shriek with alarm and a sharp, pungent odour filled the cabin. Janelle looked around wildly, her ears ringing, but the lights flickered then went out. Passengers began to scream.

Oh my God.

A sensation of weightlessness, a nauseating pressure in her ears.

Suddenly, blinding sunlight speared through the window as the plane cleared the cloud. The turbulence eased immediately and air rushed out of Janelle's lungs.

'It's over,' announced the man next to her.

Janelle's heart was still pounding as if attempting to batter its way out of her body. 'What was that sound?' she asked, turning to him. 'Like . . . an explosion.'

'Lighting strike,' he replied evenly. 'It happens a lot in the tropics. That strange smell is ozone.'

Ozone? She stared at him, absently patting the baby in its harness. 'I hate flying,' she murmured. 'That was my worst nightmare.'

'No, it wasn't.' The man winked at her. 'We didn't crash.'

The lights in the cabin flickered on again. *'Ladies and gentlemen, apologies for the bumps,'* announced the captain. *'While I know it's uncomfortable, there is absolutely no threat to the aircraft. I've asked the crew to suspend cabin service for the time being, because we don't want you wearing your hot coffee in your lap.'*

Janelle didn't even smile. How could the pilot make light of the situation?

'We anticipate a smoother ride in around five minutes, at which point I'll be able to turn off the seatbelt sign and the crew will continue looking after you. Again, apologies for the inconvenience and thank you for your patience.'

The woman from the aisle seat returned from the toilet, her face flushed red—from embarrassment or fear, Janelle couldn't tell.

'Oh, sweetie,' she crooned at her baby, sitting down. She slid the harness off Janelle's seatbelt, secured it to her own, then cradled the infant in her arms.

'Thank you so much,' she gushed to Janelle. 'That was a wild ride, wasn't it?'

Janelle could barely nod. Instead, she pressed the call bell with a trembling hand. Deep breathing was useless now: she needed something stronger, and fast.

She closed her eyes, waiting for the five minutes to elapse, involuntarily thinking of her mother. How it had all started, when Janelle was just nine years old. They'd been travelling from Melbourne to the Gold Coast for the school holidays—Janelle, her brother, Kyle, and their mother—for their first ever family trip interstate. Her father couldn't join them, being unable to take leave from his work as a construction engineer, but Janelle had been thrilled all the same. As the aircraft started to taxi, she'd squealed with childish excitement. But her mother had gripped Janelle's arm and told her to shut up. Unusually harsh words, and her face was strangely white and contorted.

'What's the matter, Mum?' Janelle had asked shakily.

Her mother had whispered a reply. 'When I fly, I think I'm going to die.'

The flight to Queensland had been entirely uneventful, however. The plane had taken off and reached cruising altitude, the inflight entertainment was activated, an unexceptional snack was delivered, then the plane had descended and landed at the Gold Coast. And yet her mother's dire declaration—*when I fly, I think I'm going to die*—had impressed itself indelibly upon Janelle's mind, and carried disproportionate psychological weight ever since. Wasn't it always like that, with mothers and daughters?

Mercifully, Janelle had only had to fly infrequently since then. Mostly interstate within Australia, and once to Vanuatu on a university field trip. After graduating with double honours in sociology and anthropology, Janelle's first foray into full-time work—an entry-level market research role, for which she was thoroughly overqualified—had required little travel. Even so, her fear of flying grew, stoked by media coverage of major aviation disasters. Kyle had dubbed her a 'crash junkie' for her compulsive consumption of every harrowing detail: a clipped tail on take-off, a blocked Pitot tube, a disintegrating fan blade.

As her career progressed to more sophisticated consumer research, including political polling, Janelle had been relieved to remain grounded. But her flying phobia persisted and became a sticking point in her four-year relationship with Nick, her first serious boyfriend after a series of short-lived romances at university. A suave advertising account manager, Nick was almost certainly The One—a fantasy she'd held onto since adolescence, despite knowing better.

Every Christmas for the duration of their relationship, Nick had invited her to visit his parents with him in Perth. And each time, she'd staunchly refused to fly, suggesting they travel by car instead. Unprepared to commit to a week-long road trip, he'd finally stopped asking. Then, just over a year ago, he'd replaced Janelle with an adventurous redhead he'd met at a work conference—with whom he was now backpacking around Europe, posting nauseating Facebook updates:

Downing the biers in Dusseldorf!!
First time skiing in the Alps. Woo hoo!!!
Loving romantic Italy with Cherry. Pizza in
Pisa—that's amore!!!!

Life had turned into one big exclamation mark for Nick, it seemed, since he'd hooked up with Cherry. And judging from their Facebook photos, she was exactly as the name implied—glossy and luscious. The polar opposite of Janelle, whose life to date had been an exercise in mediocrity.

For as long as she could remember, Janelle had seen herself as Miss Average: normal height, regular weight, unremarkable features. Shoulder-length brown hair, a smattering of moles across her face. A modest bust, a curvy behind, too heavy-hipped for her liking. But the prettiest hazel eyes, Nick had said, a long time ago.

A high-pitched dinging sound made Janelle jump. The seatbelt sign had been switched off.

'Yes?' A flight attendant stood in the aisle nearby, the picture of coiffed composure. 'May I help you?' The woman's eyebrows were mesmerising: strong dark arches, perfectly plucked.

'Can I have a vodka, please?' asked Janelle. 'A double. On the rocks.'

The woman pursed her lips. 'In a moment. We're busy with injuries and vomit right now.'

'I'm sorry, I'm a . . .' Janelle began, but the flight attendant whirled away.

She returned ten minutes later with two plastic cups. Four ice cubes in one, some vodka in the other. She leaned across the woman with the baby and placed the items on the tray table in front of Janelle. 'Twelve dollars, please.'

As Janelle fished about in her purse—locating, inadvertently, another Xanax to take with the vodka—the man in the window seat glanced her way.

'That looks good.' He waved a hand at the flight attendant, who took Janelle's payment before turning her attention to him. 'Can I have one of those too?'

Janelle detected a flicker of irritation in the woman's eyes, before the polite mask returned. 'Certainly, sir.' The attendant moved off once more.

Janelle fumbled with the silver blister pack, discreetly popping a pill into her palm. Then, without glancing at either of her fellow passengers, she put the pill in her mouth and raised the vodka to her lips. She drank greedily, feeling the instant relieving heat cascading down her throat. Stifling a cough, she placed the cup back on the tray table.

A moment later, the flight attendant returned and delivered the man his drink.

'Thank you,' he said, before turning to Janelle and baring his yellow teeth in a smile more akin to a grimace. 'You like to drink vodka?' His accent was German, she guessed.

'Not usually,' she said. 'It just steadies my nerves in the air.'

It was blatant binge-drinking, Janelle realised, but she didn't do it at any other time. Nor did she usually take benzodiazepines; she'd only sought a prescription before the flight.

'I fly all the time,' said the man, unprompted. 'Domestic flights across Indonesia. Some of them are even worse than what we just went through. Do you travel for work?'

She toyed with the idea of divulging everything. *I just tossed in my job of five years. I'm almost thirty, reluctantly single and my life needs an overhaul. I lost my last boyfriend to my flying phobia a year ago, so I've booked myself into a fear-facing retreat in Bali. But after surviving turbulence like that, I might not need it now.*

Instead, she shook her head. 'I mostly do desk-based research. But I just resigned from my job, actually.'

In spite of spending the past five years progressing through the ranks at Preston Polls, Janelle had never felt terribly passionate about consumer research. Telephoning random numbers—ignoring the answering machines, the ring-outs, the hang-ups, the children who refused to fetch their parents—before seizing the moment when someone actually allowed her to speak.

Good morning, sir/madam, my name is Janelle from Preston Polls. Today we are conducting a survey about the buying habits of females aged eighteen to forty-four who use feminine sanitary products. Is there a female in your household of that age available to speak with me now?

It all came down to the tone of her voice, Janelle had learned. Sincere but not obsequious, friendly yet professional. But it was the nuances of interviewee psychology that had kept her engaged. Why had that mother with the colicky baby actually agreed to do a twenty-minute survey on global tobacco regulation? Whatever could have made that middle-aged man care so deeply about nonstick frypans? And was it loneliness that made that suspiciously elderly-sounding woman fudge her age—claiming to be within the required parameter of thirty-five and under—just to talk to someone, albeit about carbon sequestration?

'So why did you quit?' asked the man, pushing a packet of crisps in Janelle's direction.

Why indeed? She took a few and crammed them into her mouth. She wasn't hungry, but there was something comforting in their oily saltiness. Nick certainly wouldn't have approved of the extra kilos she'd gained since their break-up, but that was immaterial now.

'I've just had my twenty-ninth birthday,' she explained between mouthfuls, 'and I realised I'd been stuck in a rut for more than a year.'

Her persistent pining for Nick had been unproductive and unreasonable, given everything that *hadn't* been working for them. Like the way they'd sat across restaurant tables from each other, maintaining an aloof silence usually reserved for long-married couples. Or Nick's predilection for working from home at night and triathlon training on the weekends, which almost always trumped sex and sleep-ins.

After they'd parted ways, she'd fallen into a post-Nick pattern that somehow morphed into her daily life. Waking tired, having a shower, eating breakfast, taking her contraceptive pill—*for what, exactly?*—before heading in to work. Struggling through eight hours in an underwhelming job with a faux-impressive title—Senior Specialist, Business and Consumer Research—before returning from the office to her studio apartment in Moorabbin. Checking Facebook obsessively, eating too much, watching Netflix until after midnight, then falling asleep on the sofa. A routine interspersed occasionally with nights out with girlfriends, the odd exercise session, or catch-ups with her family.

She'd been marooned in this humdrum routine—like a modern-day Sisyphus—until the morning of her twenty-ninth birthday, when she'd been sitting at the kitchen table eating an unappetising breakfast of slightly stale Bircher muesli. Hunched over her mobile phone, senselessly scrolling through Nick's picture-perfect posts from Seville.

Suddenly, as if her fingers were possessed by an external power, she'd deleted the Facebook app. 'Yes, I *am* sure I want to remove it,' she'd muttered in response to the warning prompt. 'Enough is enough.' She opened her internet browser and typed into the search engine the words that had been roiling in her head for months: *How do I . . .*

The auto-prompt intervened with a convenient drop-down menu of most frequently searched terms: *How do I look? How do I get pregnant?* Then, strangely: *How do I get you alone?* A song title, Janelle could only assume, before continuing typing her own question: *How do I . . . change my life?* A link on the first results page drew her eye:

Change your life in Bali—join a Fearless retreat!

Clicking through to the homepage, Janelle had found herself transfixed by an idyllic scene of terraced rice fields. A granite statue of the Buddha dominated the foreground, surrounded by a carefully raked mandala of smooth white pebbles. Alongside it stood a tall, ascetic-looking man with intense blue eyes and an engaging smile. *New Fearless retreat starts 1 March in Bali—sign up now!* the website had urged her. The timing was perfect, allowing her just enough time to resign and work out her notice, but not enough to change her mind.

Janelle glanced sideways at the European. The double whammy of the alcohol and drugs—combined with the trauma of the turbulence—was loosening her inhibitions.

'I had to do something differently,' she continued, 'because I just couldn't keep going the way I was.' *With a boring job and a broken heart.* 'Facing my fear of flying seemed like a good place to start. I booked a ticket to Bali, even though I was scared stiff of getting on a plane. When I get back to Australia, I'll have to start looking for another job.'

She'd be okay for a while. Her mortgage was manageable, and she'd listed her studio on Airbnb for the duration of her month away, which made the entire exercise cost-neutral. Unless someone trashed the studio, she mused uneasily.

The man chuckled. 'But you know that flying is the safest form of transport? It's much more likely you'll be killed in a cab on your way into Kuta. Indonesians are crazy on the roads.'

'I'm not staying in Kuta,' Janelle replied, unsure if this technicality mattered.

'Wherever you're staying, they're *all* crazy,' the man said vehemently. 'I live in Seminyak with my wife. Very often we see blood on the road.'

'Blood?' Janelle flinched.

'They don't wear motorbike helmets, you see. When they do, they don't bother doing up the chin strap. They don't value life the same way we do.' He waved an index finger at her and Janelle was tempted to relieve him of any notion of 'we'. 'If you hire a motorbike, make sure they give you a helmet too.'

Janelle sipped her vodka calmly. 'I won't be riding motorbikes.'

The man clicked his tongue knowingly. 'That's what all the tourists say, but then they get excited seeing the Balinese on motorbikes. Where are you staying?'

'In Ubud for a week, on retreat. After that, I'm not sure.'

The man nodded. 'Ubud is nice, it's cooler in the hills. I have some business interests up there. A yoga retreat?'

Janelle shook her head. 'Actually, it's for people with phobias and . . . other anxieties.' Feeling a little embarrassed, she switched the conversational focus to him. 'What are you doing in Bali?'

'As little as possible,' the man joked. 'I live there. I am from Portugal originally, my wife is Balinese. Our sons are studying at university in Australia—I've just settled our second boy in Melbourne. My wife's family has land all over Bali. We have a few enterprises.'

Janelle nodded. 'And are they . . . doing well?'

The man sucked on an ice cube, then let it slip back into his cup. 'It depends on the enterprise. We have a handful of villas in Lovina, some adventure companies in the east, a wildlife sanctuary . . .'

Janelle blinked—she'd been enquiring about the man's sons in Australia, not his business concerns in Bali. But her interest was piqued. 'Your wildlife sanctuary—it's not orangutans by any chance?' she asked. 'I sponsor an orangutan in Borneo. It's terrible what's happening to their habitat.'

The man shook his head. 'Reptiles and birds, mainly. Some of the rarest birds in Indonesia. A nice little sanctuary, too, but my wife wants to sell it. There's talk of a second international airport being built in the area. We could get more money for the birds on the black market than from running the sanctuary.' He shrugged. 'Bali is one big black market, you know. Trust people at your own risk. They're usually not as nice as they seem at first.'

Just like you, thought Janelle.

'It's hard to find trustworthy staff,' continued the man. 'We pay them more than the minimum wage, but many times we have caught staff members stealing. That is how they repay us for treating them well.' He took another mouthful of his drink and winced. 'This is cattle-class vodka. Terrible quality.'

'I've heard the Balinese are very honest and gentle,' Janelle objected, motioning to her *Lonely Planet Guide to Bali*, tucked in the seat pocket in front of her.

'Gentle? Ha! You should see my wife on payday. Gentle is not the right word. No one screws with her. Except for me, of course.' He laughed at his own joke.

Do men like this go to Asia to find wives, Janelle mused, *because no one wants them in their home countries?*

'Have you and your wife . . . always lived in Bali?' she asked, skirting around her suspicion.

'Not always, but long enough for her to take everything I own and divide it among her family.' The man's belly shook as he laughed. 'Don't worry, I know what you're thinking: some old Portuguese man marries a young Balinese girl who doesn't know any better. Well, let me tell you—*she* is the boss of our family. Oh, yes, they all look so demure in their sarongs, so devout at the temple. But try marrying one, then you'll understand the real Bali.'

Janelle wished she could extricate herself from the conversation.

'I'm Diego, anyway,' he said, reaching out to shake her hand. 'I should have introduced myself earlier. It's a pleasure to meet you.'

'Janelle,' she said, nodding politely. She retrieved her phone from the seat pocket. 'I was just about to brush up on my Indonesian.'

She'd downloaded a language refresher course a few days earlier, and now seemed exactly the right time to begin. Her head was fuzzy, and Diego was grating on her. 'Excuse me,' she said, before inserting her earphones.

Selamat pagi. Good morning.

Apa kabar? How are you?

Baik-baik saja. I'm fine.

Mau ke mana? Where are you going?

Jalan-jalan saja. For a walk.

Terima kasih. Thank you.

It all came flooding back. Janelle hadn't heard the language since high school, when she'd chosen to study Indonesian in year nine, as an alternative to French. Her study of the latter had been disastrous—all those nasal vowels, uvular *r* sounds and gendered nouns—while Indonesian had seemed easier, with relatively uncomplicated grammar and phonetic pronunciation.

'*Siapa namanya?*' she whispered under her breath. '*Nama saya* Janelle. *Saya berasal dari Australia.*'

One of her earphones popped out; she moved to retrieve it and realised that Diego had pulled it out. He leaned close enough for her to smell his boozy breath—or was it hers?

'I was just going to say,' he said in a low voice, 'the only words you ever really need to know in Bahasa Indonesia are "*Suapnya berapa, Pak?*"—"How much for the bribe, sir?"' He pulled his thin lips back again into a smile. 'Those words will *always* get you out of trouble in Bali, so don't forget them.'

She nodded distantly, then turned up the volume.

⁓

Emerging from customs three hours later into stifling equatorial heat, Janelle stared up at richly sculpted red-brick gates marking the terminal exit. She screwed up her nose at the sickly-sweet scent of incense that hung in the air, and watched, daunted, as a mob of drivers jostled behind the barrier ahead of her.

Her hand moved to the small black pouch strung across her body, containing her passport and phone. She reread the email from Tony van de Jaager, the Fearless facilitator:

On arrival in Denpasar, you will be met by our English-speaking driver, Pak Ketut. He will bring you in our resort's air-conditioned minibus to Ubud, located a pleasant 1.5 hour drive from the airport.

Scanning the crowd again, her eyes settled on a fluorescent green cardboard sign inscribed with her name. It was held aloft by a diminutive man wearing a sarong, a collared shirt and an unusual hat—rather like a rolled-up silver scarf curled around his scalp—standing near the back of the mob.

Janelle waved to the man and he beamed at her, rushing forward and ducking beneath the barricade to greet her. 'Miss Janelle, welcome to Bali!' The skin around his eyes crinkled as he smiled. 'My name is Pak Ketut.'

'*Selamat sore*,' Janelle replied, allowing him to take command of her luggage trolley. '*Terima kasih*.'

'Ah! You speak Indonesian?'

'*Sedikit saja*.' Only a little.

'Very, very good!' His enthusiasm was infectious.

'I'm sure your English is better than my Indonesian, Pak Ketut,' she replied. 'I need some practice.'

'No problem.' Pak Ketut ushered her along a footpath, past a line of cars and towards a white minibus parked nearby. 'It is a long drive to Ubud, we can practise together. How was your flight?'

'Very rough. We flew into a storm.' Janelle still felt drugged, her tongue furry. 'I'm scared of flying, so I didn't enjoy it at all.'

'Oh, I am sorry. But you have come to the right place, to become *fearless*!' The driver opened the boot of the minibus and lifted Janelle's luggage inside. 'What are you afraid of, when you fly?'

'Crashing, primarily.' She laughed, which was much easier to do on the ground. 'Have you ever flown, Pak Ketut?'

'Me?' Pak Ketut looked amused. 'One day, when I am rich. Or maybe not.' He leaned towards her, as if to reveal a secret. 'There are many things to fear on the ground already, Miss Janelle. Enough for me, without adding things in the air.' He laughed again, but Janelle felt as though she'd missed the joke.

'Please,' he said, opening the minibus door and motioning her inside. A wave of blissfully cool air washed over Janelle as she sank gratefully into the seat behind him.

As they moved into the flow of traffic beyond the airport, Janelle gawked at something ahead. An entire family was perched on a single motorcycle: father driving, mother at the rear balancing bags on both knees, two children wedged in between them, and a sleeping infant with its head slumped on the handlebars, its tiny hands wrapped around the stem of the rear-view mirror. None of them wore helmets, and Janelle winced at the sight of their unprotected feet in thongs.

A moment later, she saw a long line of female workers at a construction site, carrying large tin buckets of rocks on their heads.

'Is that common here?' asked Janelle, horrified to see women her mother's age carrying such heavy loads. 'Women as labourers, I mean?'

'If you get the men to do it, they sit and drink coffee and smoke,' Pak Ketut said. 'Women are much stronger and cheaper.' He laughed again. 'Very different in Bali to your country?'

'Very,' said Janelle, feeling uneasy.

'*Ayo mari kita berbahasa Indonesia.*' Pak Ketut grinned at her in the rear-view mirror.

'Pardon?'

'You said you wanted to practise. Let's speak Indonesian!'

Over the next hour and a half, Janelle subjected Pak Ketut to her best linguistic efforts. She explained that she was an office worker from Melbourne, that she was *belum menikah*—not yet married—and that she lived not far from her mother, brother and niece in Moorabbin, a suburb near the beach.

When they stopped for a few minutes in heavy traffic, Janelle scrolled through her iPhone photos. She found a snap of her teenage niece, Arabella—the selfie they'd taken at Half Moon Bay two nights previously—then leaned forward to show Pak Ketut.

'This is my niece,' she said proudly. 'Her name is Arabella.'

'Very nice,' he remarked.

'Do you have family?' She attempted the words in Indonesian. 'Pak Ketut *punya keluarga?*'

The driver said nothing for a moment. 'My wife died eight years ago. She had *kolera*—what is that, in English?'

'Cholera, the same.' Janelle felt terrible. 'But it's . . . not something we have in Australia anymore.'

'No?' He looked surprised. 'In Bali, we have much *kolera.*'

Janelle stared out the window, feeling chastened. Food and water contaminated with human excreta was not a challenge she had to contend with in her privileged Melbourne existence.

He looked at her again in the rear-vision mirror. 'My wife was thin already,' he explained. 'The sickness took her quickly. Many people in our village died that year.'

'And you had no children?' She didn't attempt the Indonesian words.

Pak Ketut reached behind the sun visor above him and removed a faded photograph. A young girl with long black plaits and a shy smile, wearing a tan-coloured school uniform, sat side-saddle on a motorbike behind her father. Pak Ketut tapped the photo with his thumb, his eyes on the road. 'This is my daughter. Her name is Putri. She is fifteen here.'

Janelle smiled. 'Arabella is fifteen too. It's a nice age, isn't it?'

Pak Ketut nodded. 'Before the blood fever.'

Janelle blanched. 'What's that?'

'From mosquito bite. I think you call it dengue fever?'

'Oh no,' murmured Janelle. 'Did she . . . ?'

'Yes.' He continued to stare at the road. 'She would be eighteen now.'

Tears sprang into Janelle's eyes and she leaned forward in her seat, not knowing what to say. Wanting to touch Pak Ketut's forearm, but worried about the cultural appropriateness of this. To lose a wife *and* a daughter to preventable diseases—how could the driver even smile anymore? She opened her mouth but then, loath to trot out some useless aphorism, closed it again. She knew from personal experience that time did *not* heal all wounds. Things would *not* necessarily be okay.

Her own father had died when she was fourteen, after a short and unwinnable battle with stage four liver cancer, leaving a giant-sized gap in their family. Almost overnight, her mother had changed, filling the void he'd left behind with irrational, ritualised behaviour—from midnight cleaning frenzies and alphabetising the contents of their bookcases, to an unfounded dread of crowds and driving at night. Her mother's previously manageable fear of flying progressed to a severe phobia that grounded her permanently; she'd never flown since. Fifteen years on, Janelle could still recall the warm reassurance of her father's embrace, the comforting scent of his aftershave. Death changed *everything*, she knew.

'That . . . must have been terrible for you,' said Janelle, floundering.

Pak Ketut shrugged. 'I am Hindu, we believe in karma. You understand?'

Janelle wasn't sure that she did.

'When it is time to die, it is time to die,' he said. 'You must accept your destiny. This is what Hindus believe.'

Perhaps every culture had its neat, reductive adages to help the bereaved grapple with loss: destiny, fate, God's will.

'Many people in my village tell me to marry again,' Pak Ketut continued. 'They say, why are you waiting so long? There are many willing women. But it is not so easy to choose a wife.' He shook his head. 'It is not like going to a restaurant and choosing *nasi goreng* or *mie goreng*.' He shrugged again. 'I am waiting for the right one.'

'Me too,' said Janelle softly, staring out at the passing vista. The bland concrete sprawl of Denpasar had given way to patches of countryside; of rice fields and coconut palms, red-brick temples and golden-green bamboo fences, and tall, brightly coloured flags staked into the earth, fluttering about in the day's waning light.

'Then we understand each other, Miss Janelle,' said the driver. 'We must make good choices, because family is everything. Only twenty minutes to Ubud now.'

Family is everything.

She closed her eyes, fatigued by the trip and the tablets and the alcohol, recalling how she'd shared the news about her spontaneous trip to Bali with her family in Australia.

'But that's . . . so out of character for you.' Her brother, Kyle, had held his beer beneath his chin as if frozen. 'You'll miss Mum's birthday, too. She'll go off her rocker.'

Janelle winced, knowing he was right. They'd sat together on the sunken sofa, a dilapidated centrepiece in Kyle's weatherboard cottage overlooking Half Moon Bay. A view that he could only afford, Janelle knew, after more than a decade of hard work as the operator of his own plumbing business.

'Well, Mum will have to get over it,' Janelle replied, feigning boldness. 'I think I'm having a midlife crisis.'

'You?' Kyle snorted. 'You're a spring chicken, Nelly. Try being me—a divorcee dad, on my way to forty, with a teenage daughter who thinks I'm the biggest dag since dog turds.' He sipped his beer, pensive.

'Why?' asked Janelle. 'What's up with Bella?'

'No idea.' He shrugged. 'Maybe something's happening at school that she's not telling me about.' He ran his tradesman's hands through a mop of blond hair frayed at the tips. 'Girls, eh? I don't understand them.'

Janelle patted her brother's knee with mock sympathy. 'Oh, come on, we're just a bit complicated. Especially as teenagers. I hated being a teenager.'

'Did you?' Kyle looked at her with newfound interest. 'I didn't know that.'

'How could you? When I turned thirteen, you'd already moved out. You'd almost finished your apprenticeship.'

'Yeah, right.' Kyle looked thoughtful. 'An eight-year gap seemed pretty massive back then. But now it means zip, doesn't it?'

'That's because we're middle-aged,' she said.

'*I* am, Nelly. I'm thirty-seven. You've got your whole life ahead of you.'

She was grateful for her brother's optimism. 'Come to Bali,' she said suddenly, seizing his hand. 'You could bring Bella. We could all go together. Maybe even Mum, for her birthday?'

'What, just like that, in a few weeks' time? You're nuts.' The sound of the front door opening prompted Kyle to lean closer. 'Can you talk to Bella? She might open up to you.'

As his daughter walked into the room, Janelle tried not to gasp. She'd seen her niece barely weeks earlier for her fifteenth birthday, and yet Arabella's appearance had changed dramatically. She was wearing tight black jeans and an unseasonable black skivvy, with heavy kohl eyeliner traced around unsettled eyes. The happy rainbow girl that Janelle had spoiled rotten for years had been replaced by a surly Goth.

'Hi, Bella.' Janelle kept her tone unperturbed. 'Want to go for a walk?'

'What for?' Her niece's voice was flat.

'Don't speak to Aunty Nelly like that,' admonished Kyle.

Janelle glared at him, trying to communicate, *Don't push her.* 'There'll be a beautiful sunset.'

Arabella looked apathetic. 'Whatever.'

'Let's go then,' said Janelle, shooing her niece back towards the door.

Outside, they walked in silence for a few minutes, tracking along a well-worn path that led through grassy undulations to the near-deserted beach. The setting sun had turned the Red Bluff cliffs a rich, burnished gold.

Once on the sand, Janelle slipped her arm through Arabella's. 'Guess what I've gone and done, Bella?' she asked, playfully kicking water into the air. 'I've thrown in my job and booked a tropical holiday to Bali.'

Her niece looked surprised, then wistful. 'The year twelves are doing schoolies week in Bali this year,' she said. 'They're *sooo* lucky. They'll never have to go back to school again.'

Janelle watched Arabella closely. 'Is something wrong at school?'

Arabella shook her head. They continued to walk in silence.

'Well, if you ever want to talk about anything,' ventured Janelle, 'I'm always up for a chat with my special niece.'

'I'm your *only* niece,' Arabella said, rolling her eyes. 'There's nothing special about me.'

'Hey.' Janelle wheeled around and grasped Arabella's shoulders. 'Why are you saying that?'

Arabella lowered her gaze. 'I'm crap at everything. And I'm ugly too.'

'That's *not* true.' Janelle touched a hand under Arabella's chin. 'You're kind and funny and you're a great listener. Those qualities are going to get you much further in life than being . . .'

'Skinny and beautiful?' Her niece interrupted her. 'Then how come most successful women *are* skinny and beautiful? Miranda Kerr, Amal Clooney, Taylor Swift . . .'

'Taylor Swift is almost one-point-eight metres tall,' Janelle objected. 'She's literally a freak of nature. But she's *most* successful because of her songwriting skills.'

'Being skinny and beautiful helps,' said Arabella. 'Like, *a lot.*'

Suspecting that she was right, Janelle said, 'You're beautiful just the way you are, Bella.'

Her niece shrugged. 'At school, they call me Butt Ugly Bella. It's a joke, but it sucks.'

'*Who* calls you that?' Janelle was outraged.

'A few of the cool girls.' Arabella sniffed. 'They say I'm fat and ugly.'

Janelle exploded. 'Do the teachers know about this?'

Arabella shook her head.

'Oh, Bella.' Janelle reached out and stroked her niece's long, dark hair. Arabella *was* beautiful, of course, like most teenage girls. Glowing with the magnetic loveliness of youth; a power they possessed, ironically, at precisely the time in their lives when they felt most insecure.

'I know how difficult it is,' Janelle soothed. 'I went through it myself. Some of my so-called friends used to taunt me about my moles. They called me 'fly-shit face'. It was awful.'

Janelle could well recall the emotional carnage of the schoolyard; the crippling sense of her own inadequacy, the vindictiveness of a posse of pretty but hostile peers. Why did girls—and even grown women—so frequently criticise each other?

'Teenage girls can be utter bitches,' Janelle sighed, wrapping her arms around Arabella and wishing she could protect her from all of it. 'Hang on, did you feel that?' She put her hands over Bella's and squeezed the flesh at the sides of her own stomach. 'That's the waist of a real woman. Nothing wrong with a bit of wobble. Natural can be beautiful too, you know.'

Arabella smiled, but it seemed rather forced.

'Hey,' said Janelle, as they resumed their walk. 'Want to race to the end of the beach?'

She was relieved to see the return of Arabella's impish grin.

'Sure,' replied Arabella. 'Last one there is an *utter bitch*.'

Janelle laughed. 'Don't tell your dad I said that!'

Her niece smirked. 'Ready, set, go!'

They barrelled along together, their bare feet slapping the wet sand, jostling and puffing and giggling. At last, Arabella streaked out ahead.

'I'm done,' said Janelle, catching up to her niece and leaning against her, panting. 'And you can add "athletic" to your list of qualities.'

Arabella smiled, but as they followed the sandy track back up to Kyle's house, Janelle thought she saw her wipe her eyes. Or perhaps she'd merely brushed away a strand of hair.

If only Bella could see this, Janelle mused now, sitting taller in her seat as Pak Ketut manoeuvred the minibus into a pebbled driveway lined with frangipani trees. As they traversed its length, Janelle couldn't resist lowering the window and breathing in the heady fragrance.

Lush gardens stretched in every direction, spiralling tendrils and exotic blossoms and plants she didn't recognise, festooned with fairy lights. Mossy statues of dragon-like creatures, with bulbous eyes and protruding fangs, stood like sentinels marking the path towards a huge bamboo dome at the driveway's end. Colourful lanterns, glowing like stars, bobbed at intervals along the structure's thatched roof.

'It's beautiful,' she murmured.

'Welcome to Puri Damai,' said Pak Ketut, parking the minibus near the entrance. 'Your home for the next week.' He hurried around to open the door for her.

'Thank you,' she said, smiling at him.

As her foot touched the ground, a gong sounded nearby. Its deep thrumming reverberated in the warm night air, before fading into silence.

Henry zipped up his anorak under his chin, protecting himself against a wind that felt as if it was blowing directly off the Arctic tundra. He was only twenty-six years old, but eighteen years of birdwatching had rendered his body as stiff as an old man's. His neck ached and his arms were numb, a result of holding the same position for over two hours now. He peered through his binoculars, training them on the reed beds. The train trip back to London and his cosy flat in Twickenham beckoned, followed by a pint of Bridge Bitter at The Albany. But he was determined to see this one through. He'd been waiting two years for it.

And finally, there it was: a quick-moving, grey-headed beauty. With long black eye patches, like a cartoon bird bandit. A finely pointed bill, a chestnut mantle, a longish tail. It was, without a shadow of a doubt, a wintering Eurasian penduline tit.

He'd spotted all manner of delights around Rainham Marshes earlier: the water pipits flitting around relics of the Second World War armoury, the Caspian gulls under the long jetty, the skylarks fossicking on the grassed-over landfill at Coldharbour. But he'd seen all those birds before, on other weekends away from London. *This* was his day's prize, the moment of completion of his 'Birds of East Anglia' list. The Eurasian penduline tit was the last of two hundred and twenty-five targets he'd been checking off, bird by bird, over the past two years.

Henry lowered his binoculars and groped for his digital camera, sliding it cautiously from his pocket. He needed the photographic evidence to send to Bigfoot, his oldest birdwatching mate. He focused the camera patiently, ignoring the throbbing interference of his own heartbeat and the slight tremor in his hand. For one desperate moment the tit disappeared while foraging, only to re-emerge with a grub in its conical bill.

Hastily, Henry took the shot. Then he rolled onto his back and closed his eyes, listening in rapture to the bird's lilting call. Tits were great vocalisers, and this one was making a contact call, a friendly social feeding cue which probably meant there were other tits nearby.

He'd spent years lying on his stomach in inclement weather, watching and listening. Venturing into inhospitable forests and swamps across England, letting hours of his life slip past—the wild, inspired hours beyond his nine-to-five job as a software tester—for the merest glimpse of avian beauty. But it was always worth the wait for the sight of a curiously cocked head, a shining beady eye, a glorious fan of iridescent plumage. Birds, he'd decided long ago, were celestial messengers in a mundane world.

Not that he would have put it that way, of course, when he'd first started birdwatching. Then he'd been an ordinary eight-year-old boy from Derbyshire, with a predisposition for social awkwardness and flights of fancy involving dragons and centaurs. But when his sister, Pamela, fell critically ill with kidney disease and the transplant failed—rendering his parents grave and unreachable, and Pamela shrunken and fragile—such fantasy creatures proved utterly useless to Henry. Instead, it was the small birds in the back garden that helped to assuage his loneliness: the plovers, shanks and sandpipers, thrushes, wagtails and warblers that frequented the moors and heathlands around his Chesterfield home.

There were long hours of empty silence when Pamela was hospitalised. By the time he was nine, his parents assumed, quite rightly, that Henry was old enough to be left at home alone. But Henry didn't enjoy it, and when the lure of hours of television and books and Lego had faded, he took to watching the birds in the garden in earnest. Their quick movements and the noise of their gentle chattering through the kitchen window served to reassure Henry that he wasn't entirely alone.

As Pamela's condition worsened after a second transplant rejection, Henry progressed to constructing feeders and elaborate nest boxes. At precisely the time when his family stopped talking to him altogether, Henry's ears became attuned to the voices of feathered angels. Using a guidebook he'd unearthed at his local library—a slim tome published in 1978 entitled *Birds of Derbyshire*—Henry began recording in his notebook the first bird calls he heard every day upon waking. The dull quacking of a mallard, the chattering *ksi ksi* of a lesser grey shrike, the slow repeated *pew* notes of a willow tit (not to be confused with the sneezing *pitchoo* of the marsh tit), the loud, whinnying trill of the little grebe or, all too infrequently, the harsh *kak* of a peregrine falcon.

After his tenth birthday, using a scrapbook and a set of art supplies gifted by his aunt, Henry started drawing these birds. Recording their size and colour, their texture and distinctive markings, as well as any crests or ornamental feathers. He often attached rudimentary field notes describing their movements, unusual postures, vocalisations, and fighting or mating behaviours. By identifying one species at a time and carefully observing everything about them, Henry began to feel even more closely connected to the creatures he was studying.

His parents, naturally preoccupied with Pamela's precarious health, were unable to relate to his passion, and even seemed to find it rather shameful. They scanned Henry's detailed field notes with increasing bewilderment, dismissing his pastime to family and friends with flippant, sometimes hurtful words. *There goes Henry with his lists again.*

Pamela miraculously survived the various crises—albeit with long keloid scars across her abdomen and back—but she was pale, otherworldly, and utterly uninterested in birds. His parents endured too, but only just, becoming brittle versions of their former selves. They seemed to move through the world in a state of perpetual anxiety, badgering Henry to wear his windcheater, pack a scarf, eat his greens, mind his manners, turn off the computer, go to bed—and, above all, to be very, very careful.

Now a teenager, Henry humoured them, his thoughts caught up in endless speculations about the secret lives of birds. How were they affected by the flower varieties blooming in the garden? Those wintering flocks of finches and buntings that fed along the field boundaries at Carr Vale—where exactly did they go when spring returned? And what made the water rail, the secretive winter visitor that skulked above the marsh areas, announce its presence with such a surprising squeal?

Fortunately for Henry, in his high school years he found answers to these and many more questions at the fortnightly gatherings of his local ornithology chapter. The club's members included several other school-aged enthusiasts; a group of senior citizens with lifetime collections of leather-bound field notes; a widow of indeterminate age, Mrs Braithwaite, who chaired the meetings with Thatcher-like severity; and three generations of the Duffy family, who had been birdwatching in the area for sixty years.

It was at one of these meetings, in the summer after his sixteenth birthday, that Henry met Jim. Despite being shorter and slighter than Henry, Jim immediately assumed the mantle of authority associated with seniority. Apart from being twenty years old—*twenty!*—Jim had recently returned to Chesterfield from a six-month stint at the Onziebust Reserve in the Orkneys as a residential volunteer with the Royal Society for the Protection of Birds.

Henry idolised Jim. He was a fount of knowledge about island and shore fauna, including wading birds and divers, and had mastered an impressive set of bird calls. Jim's owl calls could fill the air with frightened finches, and he could tweet and whistle a nuthatch close enough to touch its quivering feathers. It quickly became clear that while Jim was a caller and a talker, Henry was a listener—in birdwatching *and* in life—and these complementary strengths made for a solid foundation for field trips and, in the years that followed, friendship.

In Henry's final years of school, weekend birdwatching with Jim was a merciful diversion from the terrors of school life. Like pimples and PSHE—a subject that involved, on one mortifying occasion, a teacher rolling a condom onto a banana—and Henry's tendency to feel breathless and dizzy whenever he delivered class presentations. Indeed, it was because of Henry's tendency to flush red while speaking at ornithology meetings that Jim had christened him 'Beets'. In turn, Henry affectionately called Jim 'Bigfoot'; their countless camping trips had etched into his mind not only the surprising size of Jim's feet, but also their putrid odour after a long day in the field.

Birdwatching with Jim was also a useful distraction from his unrequited passion for Penelope Elliot, who, despite living only two blocks from Henry's home, was easily more exotic than the legendary quetzal of the Rio Savegre Valley. He'd watched her for years and then, one serendipitous Saturday morning after his seventeenth birthday, he bumped into her at the corner store. Humiliatingly, he was holding a packet of rat bait in one hand— his bird feeders always attracted rodents, much to his mother's horror—and a twelve-pack of supersoft toilet tissue in the other.

Penelope Elliot stood waiting near the counter, luminous and perfect, in a tight white t-shirt emblazoned with a bright pink flamingo.

'I like your t-shirt,' said Henry, blushing.

Penelope folded her arms across her chest. 'That's really, really off, you wally.'

Henry's eyes widened: he hadn't meant her *breasts*.

'No, no,' he said, taking a step towards her as she edged away. 'I'm sorry. I mean, I like birds. I'm a birdwatcher. They're fascinating. And beautiful. A bit like you.' He couldn't believe what he'd just said. 'Do . . . do you want to come birdwatching with me tomorrow?'

He held his breath as Penelope paid for the loaf of bread she was holding.

Turning, she tossed her mane of flaming red hair over her shoulders. Henry could only imagine how soft that hair might feel beneath his fingertips.

'What, waste my Sunday with a Billy No-Mates?' she asked, her green eyes scornful. 'What kind of twat likes *birds*, anyway?'

Before he could say another word, she flounced off, the loaf of bread swinging from her right hand. Henry stood alone at the counter, wondering if he might vomit. He passed his money to the man behind it, refusing to meet his gaze, then hurried home.

In the privacy of his bedroom, he'd reefed his binoculars from their drawer and tossed them into a dusty corner beneath his bed. There they'd lain for an entire month before Jim's coaxing and reassurances—*Never mind her, Beets, there's plenty more birds in the air*—had finally prompted him to retrieve them.

Nine years on, Henry still had those binoculars, but pretty-faced Penelope was all but forgotten. In the intervening period, he'd completed a degree in information technology and achieved considerable success in the field of software testing. He had birdwatching to thank, too, for that particular career path: all those years of identifying, labelling, categorising and recategorising birds had taught Henry how to observe something while suspending all assumptions about it. He applied those skills daily now while attempting to anticipate and manage all possible error states in the software he tested.

The work was satisfying, up to a point, but Henry considered it merely a funding mechanism for his other life—the magical world of truth, beauty and birds. No woman could sustain his interest in the same way; he'd had three successive girlfriends with whom the relationship had petered out somewhere around the two-year mark, usually when they started griping about *quality time*. Birdwatching remained Henry's abiding passion, surpassing both women and a lucrative career.

He'd been doggedly pursuing his lists for years, focusing on 'Birds of East Anglia' for the past two. Finally, with just the Eurasian penduline tit remaining on that list, Henry had dared to draft a new one: 'Top 20 Birds of the World'. This list featured rare species across five continents, from the Bali starling to the Philippine eagle.

While not extinct, all were birds that Henry could barely hope to witness even once in the wild. They were ambitious targets, and their pursuit would inevitably entail adventure. Fortunately, Henry had been squirrelling away every penny of excess income for almost three years, and also accruing leave.

But when Henry had emailed this new list to Jim, only a month ago, his friend's response had been oddly lukewarm: *If you aim low, Beets, you can't fail. Twenty birds isn't the biggest target in the world.*

But these were no ordinary birds, Henry wanted to point out. It could take a lifetime to spot all twenty. Feeling wounded, he'd sent a sarcastic reply. *But size doesn't count, right, Bigfoot? You'd know that!*

Jim responded: *I'll hold the fort in Chesterfield while you gallivant around the globe.*

With a rush of understanding, Henry had called his friend immediately. 'Bloody come with me, Bigfoot,' he'd urged, meaning it. 'We can both do the top twenty world birds, starting in Indonesia. Why don't you take three months off work? Let's find the Bali starling together.'

After a pause, Jim muttered, 'Impossible on a ranger's wage. Not all of us have high-flying tech jobs. And Beth wouldn't like it.'

Henry knew he was right. Jim's long-term girlfriend would almost certainly veto any adventures that they might plan together. Beth barely even let Bigfoot go for a curry after a big day out bird-watching. With her ice-queen smile and precision logic that could never be argued down, she had a talent for subverting spontaneity.

And then there was Jim's tenuous financial position as a park ranger in Chesterfield, which seemed so much worse when compared to Henry's situation. As well as earning a decent salary, Henry had been offered equity in the software business before it was floated on the NASDAQ. And while Henry's boss and colleagues knew about and encouraged his plan to take three months of paid leave to tour the world identifying rare birds, Jim's job offered no such flexibility.

'Well, I'll send you my photos then,' said Henry, realising this was of little solace. 'I might need some help with species identification. Tropical birds aren't my forte.'

'I'm sure you'll have a blast, Beets,' said Jim, half-heartedly.

An awkward quiet had descended then, which hadn't concluded with their phone call; they'd not spoken since. For best friends who'd been in almost daily contact for ten years, the silence was deafening.

Silence.

The Eurasian penduline tit had gone quiet too, Henry realised now, its social feeding call subsiding into thin air. Jolted from his reverie, Henry glanced around and found himself still lying on his back at the edge of the icy marsh. The cold was seeping through his clothes, and his breath streamed out of his nostrils as vapour.

I've done it, Henry thought, grinning to himself. *I've completed the East Anglia list.*

He checked the photograph on his mobile phone once more, then sent it to Jim.

Bigfoot, I found it! he typed. *Now for the Bali starling.*

⁓

Henry couldn't decipher what the pilot was saying in his heavily accented English. But as the aeroplane's engines powered up and the plane began to climb once more, it was clear that they'd just aborted their landing into Denpasar. Some of the passengers tittered with alarm, and the man next to Henry shook his head in disgust.

'Bloody birds,' he drawled.

'I beg your pardon?' When the man had boarded the plane in Jakarta, Henry had wondered if he was Australian, based on the casual flip-flops and the tapestry of tattoos spiralling down his bulging biceps. His accent now confirmed this suspicion.

'Birds on the bloody runway.'

'Is that what the pilot said?' asked Henry. 'Well, I'd . . . er, rather have a missed approach because of birds than poor visibility. At least we've got a good chance of landing the second time around, because the birds will most likely move on. Mind you,' he peered out the window at the swirling haze, 'there's quite a bit of cloud out there. This *is* wet season on the waistband of the world, after all.'

It was the impulsive title he'd written on the first page of his travel journal while waiting to board at Gatwick: *Wet Season on the Waistband of the World.* From the sour expression on the man's face now, Henry realised he'd said too much. It was a habit he'd fallen into since childhood: maintaining a reserved silence for most of the time and then—when under duress or speaking in front of strangers—jabbering on without restraint, like a cork popping from a champagne bottle.

Embarrassed, he reached into the seat pocket and removed a copy of *The Jakarta Post* that he'd picked up at Soekarno-Hatta airport. The headline announced: *Salihin supporters call for his release before Lebaran.* In an effort to avoid further conversation with the Australian, Henry kept reading. A Muslim cleric from East Java had been detained for eighteen months under new national security laws, the article outlined, despite no evidence of his alleged involvement in terrorist activity.

The man next to him cleared his throat, and Henry glanced up warily.

'You're Pommy?' the man asked.

Henry didn't like the term, but nodded all the same.

'I could tell.'

Henry wondered what that meant. Nerdy-looking and a little pasty? Check. Spectacles and already thinning brown hair? Check. Tall and a tad pudgy around the belly? Check. The antithesis, at any rate, of this hulking great specimen of tanned antipodean manhood. He refolded his newspaper and, sliding it behind the laminated emergency procedures card, smiled uncomfortably at the Australian.

The aeroplane banked in a series of slow, broad turns, completing a circuit before lining up for its second approach.

'Hope they know what they're doing up there,' muttered the Australian, nodding towards the cockpit. 'Indonesia's got a shocking air safety record. One of the worst in the world.'

Henry looked at the man with interest. 'Is that so?'

He had a theory that every person you encountered in life could teach you something; it was just a matter of discovering what. Henry hadn't checked Indonesia's air safety record when booking his flight—he'd simply chosen the cheapest ticket from London to Denpasar, transiting in Jakarta.

The landing gear was lowered again with a loud *ker-thunk*, and the Australian didn't seem to like this. Watching his meaty fists gripping the armrest, Henry suddenly realised that Aussie Tough Guy might be afraid. The idea boosted his confidence to speak once more.

'Aeroplanes are incredible, aren't they?' he said, affecting a casual tone. 'They've got wings like a bird, but instead of flapping them around, the engine thrust creates the lift needed to fly. Have you ever seen a gliding bird, like a hawk—' he paused, considering the birds the man might have seen in Australia—'or a seagull hovering over one spot?'

The man nodded, still white-knuckled.

'Well, birds just point themselves into the wind and match their airspeed to the speed of the wind. It's not miraculous, it's science. Aeroplanes use the same principles of flight as birds, but to fly at much faster speeds.'

The Australian harrumphed. 'I'd trust a bird more than an Indonesian pilot, mate.'

'Ah, yes.' Henry smiled. 'There's always human error. Which is why I prefer birds to humans, too.'

The plane's wheels grazed the tarmac, and the man grinned back now. Henry wondered if it was the relief of touching down in Denpasar.

'I'm Matt,' said the Australian, extending a hand.

'Henry,' he replied, shaking it.

'You seem to know a lot about flying.' Matt unfastened his seatbelt prematurely, even though the aircraft was still taxiing.

'I know a lot more about birds,' said Henry. 'I'm here to find a Bali starling. And maybe a Sumatran ground cuckoo, if I'm lucky.'

Matt looked confused. 'Why?'

'I'm a birdwatcher,' Henry explained. 'The Bali starling's been on the endangered list since the early 1970s. I'm going to try to find one in the wild. They've got the most beautiful white plumage.'

Matt raised both eyebrows and Henry was reminded, strangely, of Penelope Elliot all those years ago. Wally. Billy No-Mates. Twat. Henry began to feel embarrassed all over again.

'What about you, Matt?' he asked. 'What brings you to Bali?'

'Same thing as you, mate,' Matt said, winking at him. 'All the pretty birds.'

⁓

Beyond the confines of the air-conditioned terminal, it was hotter than a sauna. Henry had no previous experience of tropical humidity—until now, the furthest he'd strayed from the British Isles was to southern Italy in the spring—and he felt as if he was wading, not walking, across the forecourt leading to the airport's exit. The cloying stench of human bodies assailed him as he picked his way through a motley crowd that brought to mind a squabbling brood of chickens.

The sweat slid down his forehead, accumulated above his eyebrows and began to drip onto the dusty tiled floor. He glanced down at his shirt, aware of the fetid sweat patches spreading out from his armpits, and wondered where he'd packed his handkerchiefs. Somewhere inaccessible, no doubt, among the industrial-strength insect repellent, antibiotic cream and water purification tablets.

Where *was* the taxi rank?

'Hello, mister. Where you go?' A smiling Balinese man waved him down.

'Oh, er . . . Pusat Burung.' Henry wasn't sure how to say it, so he pointed to the TripAdvisor summary on his iPhone.

'Pesta Burung?' The man ignored the screen. 'Legian?'

'No, I think it's Ubud,' Henry said, again uncertain of the pronunciation.

The man's eyes narrowed. 'You want to . . .' He waved his right hand in a rhythmic flapping motion.

Henry nodded, then thrust his iPhone forward again.

The man held up a hand. 'Wait. I ask my friends.' He turned away and spoke to several other drivers standing nearby. Henry understood none of it, except for the Indonesian word for bird—*burung*.

After a minute, the man turned back to Henry and smiled. 'Come,' he said. 'I know the way. My taxi is near.'

Henry followed the driver, gratefully allowing him to carry his large rucksack. The man looked like he would hardly weigh forty-five kilos dripping wet, but he didn't baulk at carrying a twenty-three-kilo pack. Arriving at the taxi, Henry climbed into the back seat and looked for two things: a working meter and an air-conditioning unit.

The driver started the meter and grinned into the rear-view mirror. 'Okay, mister?'

They were a friendly sort of people, Henry decided.

As they navigated their way out of the airport surrounds, Henry marvelled at a colossal white sculpture—a writhing mass of horses, serpents, and men brandishing bows and arrows—towering over an intersection.

'That is from the *Mahabharata*, ancient Hindu story,' said the driver proudly, taking one hand off the steering wheel to point at the statue. 'That is Ghatotkacha, warrior of the air. Balinese people believe this statue gives safety to all aeroplanes flying into Bali. Your aeroplane too.'

Henry smiled, wondering what Aussie Matt would have made of that story. He raised his phone to take a photograph of the statue, then found his view blocked by an enormous lorry, on the back of which sat at least ten men perched on long-handled shovels. Forgetting the statue, Henry snapped the men instead, and instantly sent it to Jim. *No birds yet, Bigfoot, just lads on lorries.*

Wasn't it dangerous, he asked the taxi driver, if the truck stopped suddenly?

'No, they go to work.' The driver's expression darkened in the rear-view mirror. 'They are from Java. Taking Balinese jobs, because of very low wage. Java workers not good for Bali.'

Henry wasn't sure how to interpret this, so he sat quietly watching the tide of trucks, cars and motorcycles moving along the road in a nautical fashion, flouting lane dividers. If any road rules were in operation, he couldn't discern them. Traffic lights were rare and, when present, appeared to be largely disregarded by motorists. Horns seemed to be used as the primary means of communication. Unlike the British inclination for rare but aggressive blasts, Balinese drivers issued regular, chirpy toots, which seemed to indicate: *I'm coming through!*

The driver braked suddenly behind a pick-up truck parked outside a shop, its tray protruding into the traffic. On the tray was a mountain of spiky-looking fruit.

'Durian,' said the driver. 'Last fruit of the season, so everyone is buying. You can smell?'

Henry's eyes were watering; the pungent aroma was over-powering. He found it surprising that a fruit could smell like sweaty gym clothes bagged up with caramelised onion.

The fruit were being sold by a young girl wearing a blue headscarf and a thick brown dress that fell to her ankles. She couldn't have been more than ten, Henry guessed, as her gloved hands carefully counted out change for a customer. Such heavy clothing seemed unnecessarily cruel in the stifling heat.

'Do many children wear the . . . ?' He gestured to the girl.

'Muslim only,' said the driver, rather tersely. 'Most Balinese are Hindu. Most Javanese are Muslim. Some come by boat in the old days, they make villages and join the community. But many Javanese come to make money now, they are *buruh*, workers. They cause trouble here.' He indicated the girl in the pick-up. 'Robbery, rape, murder in Bali—always Javanese to blame.'

Henry had never been to Java, but he found it difficult to imagine that all serious crime in Bali could be attributed to Javanese perpetrators.

'Traffic is very bad,' observed the driver, as he edged the taxi around the pick-up and into the ocean of vehicles once more.

The adjusted time on Henry's wristwatch read six o'clock in the evening, but his eyelids were growing heavy. The flight from Gatwick had been a punishing twenty-one hours, with a three-hour stopover in Jakarta. Everything seemed to be getting quite dark quickly.

Less than ten minutes later, they stopped again, this time behind a line of slow-moving cars.

'Ah,' said the driver. 'A ceremony.'

'What do you mean?' A moment later, Henry heard a metallic drumming, which seemed to be drawing closer. Suddenly a band of men appeared on the road, wearing polo shirts and red-and-black-checked sarongs. They began waving at the traffic with fluorescent batons and speaking into two-way radios.

'*Odalan*,' said the driver, as if the term was self-explanatory. 'It happens every two hundred and ten days. Birthday of the village temple.' He grinned at Henry. 'There are many temples in Bali, so every day there is *odalan* taking place somewhere on the island. The road is blocked now. We have to wait.'

'Every two hundred and ten days?' repeated Henry. 'Why that number?'

'We use three calendars in Bali,' said the driver, settling into the conversation. 'First, your Western calendar—three hundred and sixty-five days a year, yes?'

Henry nodded.

'This ceremony is for *pawukon* year, which has two hundred and ten days. It tells us when to plant rice or harvest, or store rice in the barn, or best time to cut hair or get married or propose a girl, you know?'

Henry couldn't imagine consulting a calendar to determine an auspicious day for visiting the barber.

'The third is *saka*, the moon calendar,' continued the driver. 'It starts with Nyepi, our day of silence. In a few weeks, after Nyepi, it will be saka new year.'

Henry shook his head, bewildered by the idea of three different calendars operating concurrently.

A mob of people in colourful attire suddenly surged into the road ahead, moving towards the taxi. A graceful group of women led the way, carrying soaring towers of fruit on their heads, chatting affably as if their loads were inconsequential. A group of teenage boys with percussion instruments followed, their hands pounding out a syncopated rhythm. Behind them came families, the women in glittering sarongs and sashes, the men wearing cloth headdresses cocked across their foreheads and loose white shirts flowing over gilt-edged sarongs. The elderly walked hand-in-hand with the children, a whole community moving as one.

Henry stared at the procession, overwhelmed by the splendour and foreignness.

'This is a big village,' said the driver, turning off the engine. 'We have to wait twenty minutes. Very important ceremony.'

Henry laughed at the beauty and absurdity of it all: never in downtown Twickenham would a religious procession stop traffic. Not without media coverage and copious letters to the editor from outraged citizens, at any rate.

After several minutes without the air conditioner, the heat in the taxi became unbearable and Henry opened the door for fresh air. Several children in the passing crowd spotted him and yelled, '*Bule! Bule!*' before laughing hysterically. Henry wasn't sure if they were making fun of him or being friendly, but he waved at them all the same.

Several young women turned their faces towards him then, flashing stunning white smiles beneath perfect almond-shaped eyes, their body-hugging lace blouses offering an alluring glimpse of corsetry beneath. He watched them pass, their thick dark hair undulating over smooth caramel necks and cascading down slim backs. He nodded in greeting and they looked away bashfully, giggling behind their hands.

Henry held up his phone to film the passing ceremonial crowd. Before long, lulled by the drumming, he found himself yawning again. Slumping down across the back seat, he closed his eyes, allowing the fatigue and jet lag to smother him to sleep.

———

'Pesta Burung is here, mister.'

Henry sat up, squinting at the neon lights blinking in his face.

'Where are we?' he asked, shielding his eyes to look down the alleyway in which they were parked. It was miraculous that the driver had managed to negotiate such a narrow thoroughfare.

'Pesta Burung,' the driver repeated. He motioned to a shopfront and helpfully translated: 'Bird Party.' A group of women were seated on large cushions inside the window, partially obscured by a white gauze curtain.

A hard-faced young man in black jeans and a denim shirt emerged from the shop and approached the taxi. He smiled, and Henry noticed that several of his teeth were missing.

'You want massage, mister?' he asked, thrusting a laminated menu at Henry. It was covered with thumbnails of women, each with a descriptor beneath.

Puspita, 18. Loves to give hand massage.
Ami, 25. Famous pick-the-mango technique.
Mitra, 21. Best BJ in Bali.

Appalled, Henry turned to the driver. 'There's been a mistake. This is not what I—'

'You no like my girls?' The man turned over the laminated card. 'What about my boys?'

Henry gasped at the young male faces on the card; some looked barely adolescent. 'No, no, you don't understand, I'm a *bird*watcher. I'm here to . . . watch birds.'

The man regarded him blankly for a moment, then smiled. 'I understand.'

Henry exhaled with relief.

'You like to watch,' the man said. 'Girl-on-girl, boy-on-boy, or threesome?'

'Please,' Henry appealed to the taxi driver, 'let's go.'

The young man laid a hand on Henry's arm and spoke sharply to the driver. Henry wrenched his arm away and, blushing, removed his iPhone from his daypack. He found the website entry and pushed it in front of the man's face.

'See here,' he said, pointing at the section called *Birdwatching in Bali*. 'These are the birds I've come to see. Starting at the Pusat Burung.'

The man studied the web page for some time. Then he threw back his head and cackled so loudly that some of the women sitting in the shop rushed out. They crowded around him, passing the iPhone between them, while he recounted the story in Balinese.

'Ahhh!' the driver almost shouted. 'You did not tell me you meant *burung* of this kind!' He laughed heartily.

'I tried to show you at the airport,' Henry said, his face still burning.

The driver looked as if he was going to pass out from sheer hilarity. 'In Indonesia, *burung* means two things,' he said. 'First, the thing with feathers, yes? Second is the thing between your legs.'

This made the group of women howl with laughter.

'I drive taxi for twenty years,' said the driver, wiping his eyes. 'Foreign men, the *bules*, they always come to Bali to use their *burung*.' He gestured to his crotch, then at the shop. 'This is what *you* want too, I am thinking. But you are first *bule* to ask for real birds.'

Henry nodded, trying to see the funny side. 'I see. It's been quite a misunderstanding then. Now, *please* can we go to Pusat Burung?' He retrieved his iPhone from the pimp and found the website once more. 'It says here that it's in, uh . . . Ubud.' He pointed at the word.

'Ubud is a very long way,' observed the driver. 'We stop the meter now and you pay me another three hundred thousand rupiah.'

'What, on top of the two hundred thousand already?' asked Henry. 'Why?'

'It is far away. I will take you to a hotel in Ubud tonight. You can go to Pusat Burung tomorrow morning.'

Henry sighed. The additional charge would take the cost close to twenty-five pounds, which seemed excessive. But marooned in a dark alleyway in the middle of Legian, he realised there was little scope for bargaining.

'Fine,' he said. 'But I haven't booked accommodation in Ubud.'

'No problem,' said the driver. 'There are many places. I will take you to a resort, my cousin works there.' He began reversing back along the alleyway.

'Come back next time, mister!' the pimp called out from the kerb, surrounded by the huddle of women he sold by the hour.

Henry couldn't bring himself to return his smirking smile.

To-kehk, to-kehk, to-kehk. A strange call roused Henry from his dream.

He'd been drinking a pint of ale at The Albany with Jim, surrounded by a swathe of dark-haired lovelies. Suddenly, the prettiest one—who was wearing Balinese ceremonial clothes—turned and asked him, *Why aren't you talking to me?* The whole pub fell silent, looking at him. With the crowd awaiting his answer, Henry felt the adrenalin flooding his body: the tingling extremities, the intense heat, the parched mouth, the panic. All he could do was stare at the woman, mumbling incoherently.

He sat up in bed. It took some time for his eyes to adjust to the soft light of dawn. Dozens of marigolds decorated his room, looped in garlands over mirrors, or arranged in delicate patterns on antique-style furniture. The previous night had been too dark, and his own fatigue too great, for him to notice much beyond the incessant whining of mosquitos.

He got out of bed and reached for the door, running his fingers across the ornate swirls carved in its wooden frame. Gripping the slider peg, he opened the door. He stepped onto the verandah in his boxer shorts, looking out over a broad rice paddy. Frangipani trees and coconut palms lined its perimeter, and neat rows of rice plants rippled in the breeze. He stood for a moment absorbing the beauty, noticing the warmth of the air, even at this early hour.

To-kehk. There it was again, the call, closer now. It sounded like a cuckoo—possibly channel-billed, a common species in this part of the world.

TO-KEHK, TO-KEHK, TO-KEHK.

Startled, Henry looked up. Clinging upside down to the verandah ceiling was an enormous gecko, at least ten inches long. Its olive-green body was speckled with orange spots, and its bulging eyes were an unblinking gold. It started up its strident call once more, and Henry instinctively backed away, accidentally bumping into someone. The man stumbled and dropped a small basket, which promptly rolled off the verandah, scattering a trail of colourful blossoms behind it.

'I'm so sorry,' Henry said, dropping to the floor to try to salvage the flowers. 'I didn't hear you there.'

The man stood up and adjusted his sarong. 'You were listening to the *tokek* talking.' His eyes danced, as if he found Henry amusing.

'A *tokek*?' Glancing up at the ceiling, Henry realised the lizard had vanished. 'I thought at first it was a bird.'

The man chuckled. 'And it probably thought you were a giraffe. You are very tall.'

Henry laughed too. He certainly did tower over the man, who was slim and fine-featured, with wrists and ankles that looked as though they might snap under pressure. There were crow's-feet around the man's eyes and streaks of silver in his neatly clipped black hair, but his smooth skin and boyish smile gave him an ageless air.

'Er, hang on,' said Henry, conscious of his bare chest. He'd read somewhere that Indonesians favoured modesty. He hurried back into his room, grabbed yesterday's t-shirt from the small pile of dirty washing on the floor, then pulled it over his head.

'I'm Henry,' he said, returning to the verandah and thrusting out his hand. 'From England, if it isn't obvious.'

'Pak Ketut,' said the man, bowing low and clasping Henry's hand for the briefest of moments, before touching his own hand to his heart. 'I thought you were American.'

'Oh, dear,' said Henry. 'I hope I don't sound like one.'

'Why?'

Henry didn't know what to say. 'Oh, I've just met a few loud Americans in my time.'

Pak Ketut continued to look steadily at him. When Henry failed to elaborate, he said, 'Excuse me, Mister Henry, I have to finish my prayers now.'

Henry groaned. 'You were *praying* when I bumped into you?'

'Not yet. I had not lit the incense, which is when the prayer starts. I will go downstairs and prepare another offering, then I will come back. *Tidak apa-apa*. No problem.'

Henry was intrigued. 'Do you mind if I watch you make the offering?'

'Wait here. I will come back.' Pak Ketut disappeared down the verandah stairs.

The sun was rising in earnest now, its golden beams transforming the rice field from shadowy grey to iridescent green. It was a fecund, vibrant colour that Henry had never seen in England. The field itself seemed to be pulsing with the promise of life and love in God's own garden.

God's own garden. Henry returned to his room to scribble the words in his journal. He didn't even *believe* in God. Well, not when he was in England, he didn't.

Returning to the verandah, Henry studied a map of the resort, Puri Damai, pinned on a noticeboard. He'd arrived here last night purely on the basis of a recommendation from the driver's cousin. Now, in the clear light of morning, he was relieved to find his expectations exceeded. He'd taken the cheapest accommodation available, in a block of single rooms, but the resort was far more expansive than he'd imagined. There were gardens, bungalows and at least two swimming pools. The map also indicated that there were several large bamboo outhouses and three restaurants on site. At the southernmost reaches of the property, perched on the edge of a gorge through which the Ayung River flowed, was an area designated for 'private retreats'.

Next to the map was a menu for one of the resort's restaurants. Henry scanned the list of unusual foodstuffs—from dragon fruit and cacao to tempeh and turmeric juice—all of which seemed entirely at odds with his regular British diet of oven chips, baked beans and Mr Brain's faggots.

His eyes moved further down the noticeboard, settling on a pink pamphlet:

Face your fears in Bali.
Join our popular 'Fearless' retreat at Puri Damai.
Next retreat begins 1 March: change your life!
What are YOU afraid of?

Reflexively, Henry answered the question: *public speaking.* Despite choosing an introvert's career, despite completing a Toastmasters course in his early twenties, despite rarely having to actually galvanise himself to *do* it, Henry still had nightmares about speaking in public. Even its most casual versions—speaking to a group of strangers at a wedding, asking questions at a business meeting, or delivering an impromptu toast at the pub—would turn him beet-red, breathless and bumbling.

Never mind more formal occasions, like the upcoming twitcher convention he'd agreed to address in London next month. *Why* had he accepted that invitation?

Henry glanced at his watch: the Fearless retreat commenced tomorrow.

'Are *you* afraid of something, Mister Henry?'

He jumped at the sound of Pak Ketut's voice, right behind him.

'Balinese men who sneak up on me,' said Henry, smiling.

Pak Ketut smiled too. 'What else?'

'Public speaking,' Henry admitted. 'I don't have to do it often, but I hate it when I do. And if I ever want a career apart from software testing, I'll have to deal with it.' He nodded at the noticeboard. 'Are these Fearless retreats any good, then?'

'Very good, guests say.' Pak Ketut's chest puffed out a little. 'I am the retreat driver.'

'How long have you worked here?' asked Henry.

'Five years,' said Pak Ketut. 'Before then I was a farmer, but it is hard to make much money from growing rice. When Puri Damai was built, the owner bought my family's land to make the resort bigger. My village is just over there, not far.' He waved a hand to the north. 'The owner employs us all now. My brother is a kitchen hand, my cousins are gardeners, I am a driver. It is work that I love.'

'That's important,' said Henry, realising that he had never ever described software testing as work he *loved*. 'And you have excellent English, I must say.'

Pak Ketut bowed slightly. 'I practise a lot with guests. Many hours in cars.' He motioned at the new offering he held. 'Excuse me, Mister Henry, I will pray first.'

Henry watched as Pak Ketut laid a small palm-leaf basket at the top of the verandah stairs. It contained white, yellow, red and blue blossoms, a wrapped sweet, a five-thousand-rupiah note, and several joss sticks, which Pak Ketut proceeded to light with a cigarette lighter. As the incense began to smoulder, Pak Ketut crouched in front of the offering, his right hand weaving in the air, tracing invisible symbols. Finally, he pressed his hands together in front of his forehead, a frangipani between his fingertips, his lips moving in silent prayer.

Only when Pak Ketut opened his eyes did Henry realise he'd been holding his breath.

'Is praying part of your job description?' Henry ventured.

Pak Ketut stood up. 'All the resort staff must pray. Not every day, but at least once a week. We are all part of Puri Damai, so we all want it to succeed.'

'Is that what you were praying for, success?' As soon as he'd asked, Henry wished he hadn't. Back in England, he would never have quizzed a churchgoer about the subject of his prayers.

Pak Ketut appeared unfazed. 'We say prayers of thankfulness for what we have and for . . . *tri hita karana*. "Balance" is the English word, I think, between God and humanity and nature. If we do not have that balance, life is not right. If we eat the wrong foods, or forget about God, or have too much fear, then we make bad choices.'

Pak Ketut's words were hardly audible above the tranquil babble of the irrigation channel running alongside the rice paddy, yet they prompted Henry to ponder, *Am I balanced?* A geeky software tester who doggedly pursued feathered fancies to the detriment of his ordinary life?

He stared at the potted hibiscuses lining the cobbled walkway below, mesmerised by their translucent white blooms. After a moment, without really knowing why, he declared, 'I like bird-watching. That is why I've come to Bali.'

Pak Ketut looked puzzled. 'Is that research of birds?'

'No, that's ornithology.' Henry considered the right descriptor, one that Pak Ketut would understand. 'Birdwatching is like hunting, but for . . . people who don't need to kill things. I watch birds in the wild. Sometimes I just get a sore neck from staring up into trees all day.' He rubbed the spot on his cervical spine that had been tender for the past few years. 'Sometimes I see a bird I've been trying to find forever, sometimes I see none for weeks. But that's the unpredictable nature of birdwatching. It's my escape.'

Pak Ketut nodded earnestly. 'From what?'

From everything else, Henry thought.

After a moment, he said, 'I'd like to go to Pusat Burung later today. Do you know where it is?'

'Yes.' Pak Ketut nodded again. 'But I am sorry, it is closed. There is a big funeral for the head of the village. Many preparations for the ceremony. No businesses open in that village for a week.'

Henry couldn't believe his bad luck. The prospect of waiting a further week to visit the birdwatching centre was more than unpalatable.

Pak Ketut smiled. 'Maybe God has brought you here, Mister Henry? You *think* you have come to see the birds.' He gestured out to the rice field. 'But there is a whole world you cannot see. In Bali we call it *niskala*. These are things that can only be felt in the heart, in the spirit.'

Henry smiled politely, but wasn't convinced.

'Maybe you should join the Fearless retreat?' Pak Ketut continued, motioning to the pamphlet. 'It will help your public-speaking. In the breaks between sessions, I can take you to see some Balinese birds. There are herons at Petulu, local bird markets. We still have many in the jungle. I know the right places.'

That's more like it, Henry thought. A local guide was exactly what he needed, until Pusat Burung reopened in a week's time.

'I can take you down to reception at nine o'clock if you would like to enrol?' Pak Ketut offered.

Ordinarily, Henry would have declined the invitation. He'd never been one for personal development courses, but on this first, glorious morning in an exotic environment—on the Island of the Gods, no less—he felt uncharacteristically disposed to try something new. The cost wasn't prohibitive and, with Pusat Burung closed for the coming week, he didn't have any alternative plans. Perhaps it would even help him to prepare for the twitcher convention. What harm could it do?

'Alright,' he said. 'I'll try it.'

'Good.' Pak Ketut nodded. 'I will come back at nine.' Henry watched him turn and pad noiselessly down the stairs.

The Bali starling could wait.

PUBLIC SPEAKING

Annie watched the awkward-looking young Englishman swaying on his feet. She'd had trouble catching his name when he'd introduced himself; he'd barely muttered it. Harry, wasn't it? She glanced at the others, seated on a circle of oversized cushions on the floor, dwarfed by the majestic bamboo pavilion overhead. There were only half a dozen in the group, and Annie was the oldest by a country mile.

After a distinguished teaching career in the San Joaquin Valley in California, Annie couldn't help but feel weary watching the Harrys of the world. Lord knows, she'd taught enough of them. All that wasted human potential: rational, coherent people— undiscovered geniuses, even—who were powerless to express themselves orally. There was usually someone to blame for it, if you dug deep enough: the individuals themselves (unmotivated, unskilful, unruly), their parents (neglectful, nasty, neurotic), or some half-witted teacher or half-baked school that had failed them early in life.

But her sixty-one years on earth had taught Annie that however severe or trivial the obstacles you faced, it was always possible to conquer them by deploying the 'Two Fs': focus and faith. She'd taped the words to her bathroom mirror some thirty-five years earlier, when she and Kevin were trying for a baby. After six barren years, the words had finally worked—and there they'd stayed ever since.

She'd met Kevin at church, just after he'd inherited his father's ranch; Annie had been twenty-five, Kevin twenty-nine. She'd been aware of his family beforehand, but it was only when he joined her Bible study group that she noticed him properly. His soulful brown eyes, in particular. Not to mention his wry smile and his gentle, affable nature that put everyone at ease. What he'd noticed about her, Kevin had told her much later, was the tinkling sound of her laughter—*like a lovely little cowbell*—and her hourglass figure. After a whirlwind romance, she'd gratefully swapped suburban Coalinga for the arid sweep of Oaktree Ranch.

Kevin's family had been farming Angus cattle in Fresno County for three generations; he'd learned everything he knew about ranching from his father and grandfather. He even insisted on using their ancient equipment—including a rough-running tractor, decrepit cattle yards, and a rickety feed wagon that always needed welding. Like his father before him, Kevin wasn't enamoured of modern farming technology, faddish science degrees, or the modern obsession with occupational health and safety. *I'm a graduate of the School of Hard Work*, he would say with a smile, *and that's good enough for me.*

His work ethic was unquestionable, but during some difficult cattle seasons in the first few years of their marriage, it was Annie's regular income as a secondary school teacher that had put food on the table. Then, after almost six years of trying and praying and hoping for a baby, they'd been blessed with a son. Baby Dennis seemed to take after his father temperamentally, liking nothing more than to lie on his bunny rug in the garden and gaze up at the cloudless sky.

Nine months after having Dennis, just when Annie was considering returning to teaching, she fell pregnant with Charlie. He was feistier than his brother, and refused to settle of a night unless he was comfortably nestled between his parents. Despite Charlie's intrusion into the marital bed, they'd somehow managed to conceive a third time. This final, sweet surprise for Annie, at the age of thirty-five, delivered a dreamy, golden-haired cherub named Natalie.

Of the three children, Annie had *enjoyed* her daughter the most—perhaps because she knew there would be no more babies— and she'd waited until Natalie was in her first year of elementary school before returning to work. Those eight years of stay-at-home child-rearing had been financially challenging, of course. But they'd been content, Annie often reflected now, with their shiny-coated cattle and their whippy working dogs and their three healthy children with sun-kissed noses and hearty appetites.

Kevin may have been rather too set in his farming ways, but there'd been a comfortable rhythm to their lives, a simplicity born of the turning of the seasons and the sweaty grind of physical labour. Kevin worked every day except the Sabbath, on which they'd all climb into their dual-cabin pick-up and drive to Coalinga for church. Always counting their blessings, tithing their income, helping out at Sunday school.

Until one unexceptional Saturday morning in an unusually windy August, not long after Kevin's forty-fifth birthday. He'd gone out to fix their tallest windmill at the furthest fence line on their property—a faulty vane he'd been meaning to repair for months—and not come back in for lunch. Ignoring the nervous pit in her stomach, Annie had insisted to herself that *he's just gotten busy*. She'd wrapped up Kevin's sandwiches and prepared a thermos of hot coffee and sent them off with Ralph, their part-time farmhand.

Ralph had returned half an hour later with a stricken expression on his face, holding the lunch bag in one hand and his Stetson in the other. Annie had watched his head shaking and his lips moving, but heard only one thing: *snake bite*. She'd crumpled onto the kitchen floor and the children had crowded around her in wonder, having never before seen their mother cry. When amazement turned to fear and they began to sob too, Ralph gently helped Annie to her feet and led her to the sofa.

He called the police, the pastor and her sister, in that order. Then he poured her a strong whisky from Kevin's liquor cabinet and read books to the children, while half of Coalinga wandered through their homestead. At sundown Ralph left, squeezing her hand and promising to return in the morning. Which he did, just after the sun had risen, and every day thereafter.

Somehow she'd managed to survive the funeral and those first wretched weeks after Kevin's death. But soon enough, when her bereavement leave ended and the well-meaning visitors carrying comfort food dwindled, Annie began to realise that she was, in all truth, alone. She had the children for company, but she had to be *their* rock, while also attempting to maintain the ranch.

Agriculture was not her area of expertise and she'd learned precious little by osmosis from Kevin. As the ranch became more rundown and she began taking days off school to do something about it, Annie realised that she needed to choose: her teaching career or the ranch.

By the grace of God, her dilemma was solved six months after Kevin's death, when Ralph arrived for work one Monday morning with an offer for Annie. He'd just completed his bachelor's degree in general agriculture and, having recently proposed to his college sweetheart, was looking for full-time work. He was only twenty-two years old and most of those years had been spent working on his father's walnut farm some eighteen miles west of Oaktree. But with the patriarch still reigning, and two older brothers jostling for succession, Ralph wanted to make his own mark on the world.

Ralph's aspiration aligned perfectly with Annie's need: he'd proposed a share-farming arrangement of twenty percent of net profits in return for full-time management of the property. Annie had agreed to this, then offered an additional incentive: an increase to thirty percent if he turned a six-figure profit. Ralph had contemplated her words for only a few seconds before smiling broadly and shaking her hand.

Over the next three years, Ralph had risen to the challenge. Reviewing ranch operations first, identifying areas of overspending (cattle feed) and underspending (infrastructure). He'd been scrupulous about day-to-day budgets, appraising all of Kevin's suppliers and, in most cases, replacing them with a more economical alternative. Finally, he'd spearheaded a joint venture with the University of California, Davis, enabling Oaktree to participate in genetic trials for Angus cattle and establishing a graduate internship program. Kevin would never have countenanced such innovation—exposing his farm to highbrow academics and the scrutiny of strangers—but fortunately, Ralph's strategy paid off.

Within five years, Oaktree Ranch was one of the largest private selective breeding sites of Angus cattle in California. Ralph was its operations manager, with equity in the business, and Annie's teaching career had become a source of disposable income for the family, not the mainstay. Within ten years, she'd achieved an enviable financial position that allowed her three children to attend colleges of their choice—quite a feat for a single mother. And when the farm started turning a profit of six figures, Annie finally stopped imagining she'd just heard Kevin's footsteps on the porch.

Nowadays, Oaktree homestead was plastered with optimistic proverbs:

When life gives you lemons, make lemonade.
God helps those who help themselves.
Live the Two Fs: focus and faith.

The Englishman clearly lacked both of the latter right now, Annie mused. He was muttering about his career in software testing, rocking on his heels like a nervous primary-schooler. Annie felt torn between the desire to stand up, seize him by the shoulders and shake some sense into him, or simply to pretend she wasn't witnessing any of it.

She looked to the facilitator, who'd just introduced himself as 'Pak Tony', wondering if he would intervene. A striking mane of salt-and-pepper hair cascaded over his tanned, sinewy shoulders.

His face was curiously wrinkle-free and the hollow in his throat glistened with droplets of sweat. He wore a powder-blue singlet that highlighted his eyes and white linen pants that tied around a slim, almost feminine waist. His toenails, Annie noticed, were smooth white discs without a trace of debris beneath.

'Alright, Henry,' Pak Tony said finally. His European accent was almost as hard to detect as his age. 'Can you tell us a little about what you are afraid of?'

'Well . . .' The Englishman dithered. 'My best friend calls me Beets because I go red when I . . .' Annie could see his throat muscles constricting at the collarbone. 'I . . . can't do this, sorry.'

Pak Tony nodded kindly, as if to a child. 'Many people don't like public speaking. It's one of the top three human fears, along-side death and flying.' He lifted both hands to the ceiling, as if stretching, and Annie caught sight of his toned, flat stomach.

'No, you see . . .' Henry tugged at the collar of his shirt now. 'Sometimes when I speak in front of people, I feel like I'm going to . . .' He looked stricken, then dropped to the floor.

Pak Tony sprang forward and cradled Henry's head in his hands, then rolled him onto his side. Several others in the group rushed forward to help. 'Give me that.' He pointed to a wooden stool near Annie.

She stood up quickly and moved to slide the stool beneath Henry's feet, while Pak Tony nudged Henry onto his back again and lifted up his legs. Within seconds of raising Henry's feet above his heart, his eyelids began to flicker.

'He's fine,' Annie observed, watching Henry's face. 'I've seen a few faints in the classroom. Do you get many on these retreats?'

'Not usually in the first session,' Pak Tony said dryly. 'It's more common when we go on our fear safaris.' He gestured to a water cooler in the corner. 'Could you please . . . ?'

Annie nodded and fetched a cup of water, then held it to Henry's lips.

The Englishman opened his eyes and blinked. 'Oh God, I didn't faint, did I?'

'Yes.' Pak Tony patted his arm. 'I'll call the resort doctor. It's just a formality, but best to have you checked.' He walked to a wall-mounted intercom and spoke into it in Indonesian, then turned to Henry. 'You have a history of fainting?'

Henry grimaced. 'Not for many years. It used to happen at school sometimes, if I was very nervous. It stopped me doing debating and musicals, those sorts of things. That's part of the reason I ended up in software testing—there isn't much of a need to talk in groups, you know? But even speaking in front of my own business unit is a problem.'

Pak Tony took a small towel from a wall cabinet, wet it under the water cooler, and then pressed it against Henry's brow. 'Avoidance only goes so far, and often brings its own problems.' He smiled down at Henry, as if they were the only two people in the room.

'But I'm not avoiding it. I've agreed to speak at a conference next month. I wish I hadn't.' The Englishman looked downcast.

'You'll be fine, after Fearless,' said Pak Tony confidently. 'Apart from public speaking, is there anything else in your life that might be holding you back, Henry?'

The Englishman's eyes roved across the curved bamboo struts in the ceiling. 'Well, my last girlfriend asked me if I loved birds more than her,' he said, in a matter-of-fact tone. 'That's been a bit of a theme in my relationships.'

Pak Tony arched an eyebrow. '*Birds*?'

Henry nodded. 'I watch and record them. Just for a hobby, not professionally or anything. But two of my girlfriends have given me ultimatums: *Is it the birds, or me?*' He shrugged. 'I tend to choose the birds.'

'I see.' Pak Tony smiled. 'We can explore that further when we have our private pow-wow. Henry, no—' He shook his head at the Englishman, who was attempting to sit up. 'Stay lying down until the doctor comes.'

'Of course.' Henry looked embarrassed. 'Sorry to disrupt everything. I guess I'm more of a mess than I realised. Push me out of my comfort zone and suddenly I'm on the floor.'

'Not at all,' said Pak Tony. 'It's given us a good insight into how physically powerful our fears can be.' He turned to Annie and smiled. 'Would *you* like to introduce yourself?'

Annie hauled herself to her feet again, conscious of the audible clicking of her ankles, and nodded to the others in the circle. 'They say age isn't important unless you're a cheese, but my feet don't agree.' She waved an admonishing finger at the group. 'Just you wait, kids. I'm the eldest here by at least twenty years and I can tell you, things get tougher as you age.'

It *was* harder to move her body these days. The excess weight didn't help, nor did the worsening diabetes—back in California, her doctor had ordered her to lose thirty pounds or risk a raft of nasty complications. She'd been forced to become more vigilant about environmental risks too, things she'd never paid much attention to before: narrow staircases, uneven flooring, loose pebbled surfaces. At Puri Damai, the slippery moss covering the cobblestones forming a pathway to her room was a potential hazard too.

These changes, Annie knew, were simply part of the landscape of growing older. But she didn't have to like them. She could still remember when her own mother had started slowing down, developing the rounded shoulders and shuffling gait of a stooped old woman. Annie could barely believe that she was now turning into that figure herself; how could she be, when she still *felt* forty? When the memory of Kevin's caresses still made her tingle with desire?

She blinked, sidelining these thoughts with her favourite 'F'—focus. 'Well, what can I say?' she began. 'I'm Annie from California. I live on a ranch west of a place called Coalinga that I can guarantee none of you have ever visited. But you'll smell it if you ever drive along the Interstate 5.' She laughed. 'It's cattle country, pretty flat and dry. It gets a good stink up when it hasn't rained in a while.' She fanned her face with her hand, feeling the sweat sliding down her chest.

'I was born and bred there, did my bachelor's in education at California State University in Fresno, then moved back to take a job at Coalinga High. I was an only child, so it was important to me to stay close to my parents as they grew older. But then I went and married a rancher, Kevin, and moved out to his farm.' She chuckled. 'I didn't come from a ranching family myself, so it was all very new to me. But I settled in after a while and we had three beautiful children together.'

Annie paused, mentally skipping over the two decades since Kevin's death; how she'd filled every empty week and month with sufficiently time-consuming activities so as to distract herself from the gap left by Kevin. Apart from her teaching career and the demands of Oaktree, Annie had embraced the roles of secretary of her local Lions Club, vice-president of the chamber of commerce, and lead alto in the church choir. Singing had given her enormous comfort, it turned out, when little else had.

'The kids are all grown up now, of course,' she continued. 'One of them, my daughter, Natalie, went backpacking around Asia last year. She came to Bali and fell in love with the place, and ended up staying much longer than she thought she would.'

She smiled. 'At the same time, I heard about the animal welfare work of an organisation called BAF. I was looking for something to do in retirement, so I researched volunteering opportunities, and, well . . . it all fell into place. I've been in Bali for six months now as a live-in volunteer at BAF. Natalie went back to California a month ago to start her master's in education. But I committed to doing a full year of volunteering, so I'm going to finish it.'

Scanning their faces, Annie could see that no one in the group was familiar with BAF's work. 'BAF stands for Bali Animal Friends,' she explained. 'We rescue domestic animals, mostly dogs, but sometimes cats and caged birds. A big part of what we do is try to educate the Balinese to treat their pets better.'

A young woman with stunning hazel eyes nodded eagerly. She was clearly an animal lover too.

'But how did you find out about BAF?' asked Pak Tony with interest. 'It's a long way from California.'

Annie smiled. 'Through my church, actually. One Sunday morning, our international outreach team showed us some shocking photos of the maltreatment of domestic animals in Bali, and truly, it was as if God spoke straight into my heart. Believe me, I'm not one of those Pentecostal types. But for the first time in my life, I felt God was calling me—to come to Bali and work against those atrocities.'

Annie found herself on the brink of tears, as she often did when describing this epiphany. She'd always had a healthy respect for God's creatures, especially the dogs and cattle on the ranch. To Kevin's bewilderment, from the earliest years of their marriage she'd let the working dogs sleep inside and given her favourite cattle names like Captain Red and Sir Steer. She'd even talked to them—and their expressive eyes had convinced her that they'd listened, too. Kevin had indulged her, for the most part, but when he saw her crying at cattle sales he had banned her from attending. His was a far more utilitarian view of life and death and the value of an animal.

'It's been a tough six months at BAF, to be honest,' she continued. 'At first it was a bit of a culture shock. I'm ashamed to admit that before I arrived, I didn't even know that Bali was part of Indonesia.'

'You're not alone,' said the young woman with the hazel eyes. 'My mother thought Bali was a country near Fiji.'

The other woman in the group, sitting opposite Annie, snorted derisively. 'I think a fair few Aussies consider it the ninth state of Australia.' She was pale and unsmiling, and Annie wasn't sure if she was joking.

'Well, a lot of people think it's a paradise on earth,' Annie continued. 'Which it is in some ways, but there are real issues here too. I mean, look at the trash. Why do the Balinese keep burning their rubbish or dumping it in rivers? Then there's all the preventable health problems, like endemic rabies—two hundred people die every year from rabid dog bites in Bali. And the level of human cruelty to animals here is appalling. I'm talking acts of violence and neglect that Americans would be prosecuted for.' She looked around the group, conscious that her lips had started to quiver. 'People routinely throw litters of puppies off bridges, or drown them in irrigation channels. For such a gentle culture, many Balinese have very little consideration for the suffering of animals. That's why I'm doing my small part to help them change their minds and hearts about the defenceless creatures around them.'

Pak Tony nodded, watching her. 'And what are you afraid of, Annie? What brings you to the Fearless retreat?'

'Oh, I haven't gotten to that yet, have I?' She chuckled. 'We Americans don't have any problems with public speaking.' She glanced at Henry, still lying on the floor. 'Well, it's kind of a long story. I've got a problem with snakes, you see . . .' Even now, twenty years on, she found it difficult to tell people about Kevin. 'That's one animal in this world I simply can't love. There are ten different types of rattlesnakes in California; let's just say there's a bit of history there, between me and them.' She fought back the lump in her throat. 'I used to have terrible nightmares about snakes; I was an insomniac for years. But it didn't stop me doing something with my life.' Involuntarily, she looked at Henry again. 'I kind of thought it was all behind me, but then last month, something awful happened. I was doing the breakfast shift at BAF and I opened one of our cages and almost stepped on a fourteen-foot-long reticulated python. It was sleeping, because it had just eaten one of our dogs.' She shivered. 'It triggered a really paranoid response in me. I started having my old nightmares again, and I didn't come out of my room for a week. Until one of the other BAF volunteers showed me a brochure for this course.'

She glanced around the group. 'I realised then that I can't have my fear of snakes compromising BAF's work—what we're doing there is too important. So Fearless seemed like a great chance to tackle my fear, once and for all, before heading back for my final six months of volunteering.'

Several members of the group spontaneously clapped and Annie nodded in acknowledgement. Remembering suddenly the last time she'd been applauded, at the special assembly marking her retirement from Coalinga High. All the touching student tributes and affectionate farewells from colleagues—the bouquets and chocolates and even a gold paperweight inscribed with the words *Happy Retirement, Annie!*—that had filled her with a quiet dismay.

'Thank you for sharing, Annie,' said Pak Tony. 'That must have been quite a confronting situation for you. Your work at BAF can't be easy, either. Oh, here's the doctor now.' He stood up and greeted an Indonesian man carrying an oversized black satchel, who immediately began tending to Henry.

Annie resumed her position in the circle, next to the pleasant young woman, and watched the doctor work through his standard checks: taking Henry's temperature, pulse and blood pressure, then shining a light into his eyes, testing for concussion.

Snakes aside, the past six months *had* been difficult, Annie reflected. Many of her Balinese 'adventures'—as she often called them in cheery emails to her children and church—involved the most prosaic aspects of life. Like the hazards of navigating the squat latrine in the volunteer living quarters at BAF. The first time she'd entered the bathroom, she'd been forced to seek out a staff member to translate the handwritten sign stuck to the door: *Jangan buang air besar di lantai.*

The woman she'd consulted, an office secretary, had blushed a deep shade of red. 'Er . . . please do not do your . . . poo-poo on the floor,' she explained.

'On the *floor*?' Annie replied, goggle-eyed.

Is that what Indonesians do? Annie wondered, as the woman began backing away.

'Wait,' said Annie, and pointed to a large tiled tub filled with water in the corner of the bathroom. 'Is that where I take my bath?' It looked as though it might accommodate a petite Balinese person, but certainly not Annie.

The woman repressed a smile. 'No. That is for the toilet.'

Annie stared. 'Do people . . . go in *there*?'

The woman shook her head and picked up a small bucket floating in the tub. She scooped up a pail of water and pointed at the latrine. 'After you go to toilet . . .' she threw the bucket of water into it, 'wash it away.'

'Oh!' Annie smiled, understanding. 'It's the flush. And where is the toilet paper?'

The woman looked confused. 'Use the water only.' She motioned at the bucket, then pointed at her bottom with her left hand.

Annie grimaced. *I signed up for this?*

'Use it for shower too,' continued the woman. 'Stand here and . . .' She mimed tipping water from the bucket over her head.

'I see,' said Annie. 'There's no hot water, then?'

'Maybe next month,' said the woman.

Annie doubted she could survive four weeks without a hot shower. 'Will there *definitely* be hot water next month?'

'After Galungan holiday,' the woman replied, backing away again.

Only recently had Annie come to realise that this was her first experience of a cultural specificity she better understood now: the Balinese habit of never saying 'no' outright. Instead, the locals used circuitous or abstract rebuffs, avoiding confrontation at all costs.

Can you take me to the supermarket? *It's raining.*

Are you able to work this weekend? *I have a ceremony.*

Would you like to come over? *The traffic is terrible.*

But in her first week in Bali, Annie had yet to understand this. So she'd waved the woman off, heartened by the promise of hot water in the not-too-distant future. With her stomach cramping, she'd closed the bathroom door, desperate to use the toilet.

It was a disastrous first ablution. After dealing with the diarrhoea, Annie somehow managed to saturate her pants with the water scooper. Then, having squatted down to relieve herself, she had trouble standing up again. Lacking the strength in her thighs to push herself up, Annie spent several excruciating seconds suspended in a half-squat, before, finally, sinking forwards and landing heavily on her knees. She crawled across the wet floor towards a towel rail affixed to the wall, then used that to lever herself up.

It wasn't just toileting that proved challenging in Bali, Annie soon discovered. Simply walking down the sidewalk—when there was, in fact, a sidewalk—involved a minefield of high steps, sudden holes and open drains. Not to mention trays of rice drying in the sun, rancid dog vomit and slippery, half-rotten banana leaves just waiting for a foreign foot. It was astounding to Annie to see how the dainty Balinese women seemed to move effortlessly around the chaos, laying out their offerings with infinite poise, often in the most treacherous places—on rickety bridges, at the intersections of busy roads, near precipitous edges of plunging gorges. Offerings were made wherever human beings were at risk of meeting an untimely death: to appease evil spirits, gratify good spirits, and maintain the cosmic equilibrium of *tri hita karana*.

It was an elusive equilibrium, Annie had concluded after her first six months at BAF. For every good she encountered, there seemed to be twice as much evil. She'd started out working long days—and often nights—for the animals rescued and rehabilitated at BAF, but the operating conditions had slowly eroded her enthusiasm. For starters, the two paid veterinary staff—a young, slightly chubby vet named Putu, and his giggly vet assistant, Kadek—were unreliable at the best of times. On the days they did show up, the pair spent most of their time chatting and flirting and doing little more than the bare minimum required to keep BAF's doors open.

The two other foreign volunteers at BAF weren't much better. One was Nathan, a young Australian taking a gap year before commencing his veterinary studies. He was gregarious and laid-back and lived only a short distance from BAF in the village of Kumbuh, but was almost entirely preoccupied with the state of the surf break at Keramas, or with the demands of his insecure Balinese girlfriend.

Then there was Gabriela, an older Spanish woman, one of the facility's founding donors. She seemed to spend much of her day holed up in the volunteer bedroom next to Annie's, writing a memoir. Gabriela spoke only Spanish, which delighted the Balinese staffers, who'd adopted phrases including *hola!*, *adiós* and *no comprendo*. Gabriela's lack of fluency in both English and

Indonesian seemed to create an impenetrable linguistic bubble around her and she simply glided through the day, unbothered by many of the things that kept Annie galvanised.

Such as the soiled litter trays, or animals being kept—even temporarily—in cages too small for them. Or the neonates that needed handfeeding first thing in the morning—a task that simply couldn't wait until someone wandered in late. Or the necessity for quarantined animals to be kept in their quarters with the door closed—*no exceptions!*—and that dogs be walked twice daily. Not to mention that the floors be swept and mopped, the soap dispensers filled, the towels washed daily and the dogs fed quickly at mealtimes to minimise the brain-shattering barking.

Within weeks of her arrival at BAF, Annie had drawn up a comprehensive daily timetable that divided responsibilities between paid staff and volunteers—a timetable that was subsequently ignored by everyone at BAF. The junior staff would only take orders from 'Doctor Putu', as they called him, and a roster was difficult to enforce with Nathan mostly absent (even when he was physically present) and Gabriela unreachable. The Spaniard cared little for tasks and lists; she spent most of her irregular shifts lifting animals from their cages, greeting them with an effusive embrace, then cooing at them in Spanish.

In her first month of volunteering, Annie spoke tactfully to Doctor Putu about the desirability of maintaining a Western-style facility, if for no other reason than that BAF derived most of its funding from Western sources. He'd nodded and smiled and warmly concurred with her position, but his actions didn't follow. He failed to observe even the simplest preventative measures for maintaining animal health—like basic hand-washing and autoclaving—while continuing to overprescribe the donated medicines sent in Styrofoam boxes from overseas. He was particularly zealous with a superseded pentobarbital product—branded 'the green dream' by Nathan—supplied by an anonymous pharmaceuticals company in Australia.

In Annie's second month on the job, a distressed German tourist had walked into BAF carrying a squirming hessian bag that she'd found in a stream behind her hotel. The tourist set down the bag, her eyes moist, then blurted, 'I have a massage booked,' before walking out again. With some trepidation, Annie opened the bag. A sable-coloured puppy looked up at her, curled on top of a pile of others. It didn't growl, despite the fact that its leg was obviously broken. From behind her shoulder, Doctor Putu murmured, '*Kasihan*. Give them the green dream.'

'Why?' Annie demanded. 'Some are alive.'

'The ones underneath look unconscious.' Doctor Putu shook his head. 'The one on top has a broken leg. It will be hard to recover from that.'

'*I'll* nurse her then,' said Annie, taking the puppy from the bag and cradling her protectively.

Doctor Putu shrugged. 'She is *untung*. I'll take the others through. Kadek!' He called for the vet nurse, then lifted the bag and carried it into the procedures room.

As Annie nuzzled the puppy, a single tear slid down her cheek. The dog whimpered and licked it up, then managed to wag its crazy little sickle tail. Annie laughed to see it move, like a trembling handle attached to its furry bottom. The puppy would need surgery, a plaster cast, possibly eight to ten weeks in recovery.

It would be a miracle if she made it through at all, Annie knew, in such substandard conditions.

Several minutes later, the vet nurse returned, holding the empty bag. 'They feel no pain now,' she murmured.

Annie's heart heaved. 'Kadek?' she asked. 'What does *untung* mean in English?'

'Lucky,' replied Kadek, carrying the sack towards the door.

Annie hugged the puppy to her. 'Untung,' she breathed, inhaling the scent of the damp fur. 'I'll look after you.'

Annie and Untung had been inseparable ever since. Not only had the puppy survived her operation, she'd recuperated more rapidly than anyone could have anticipated. Within weeks, Annie moved Untung into her bedroom, where she slept on a flat rattan basket and was handfed milk from a bottle. Then the puppy started eating strips of chicken and, after regaining some movement in her hind legs, began skidding playfully around BAF in her cast. When the cast finally came off, Annie instructed all BAF staff that under no circumstances was this dog to be placed in the 'For Adoption' cages in the front window.

Untung was, Annie had often reflected since, the best thing that had happened to her in Bali. Whenever the humidity and pollution and general mayhem of life in the tropics became intolerable—and whenever she lay alone under the mosquito net in her room, missing her children, and especially Natalie—Annie would take Untung in her arms and remind herself that *this* was why she'd come to Bali. Her God-given mission was to protect the defenceless and speak for the voiceless. She'd become so attached to Untung that it had been a wrench to leave her in the care of

Nathan for the Fearless retreat. Already Annie felt like stealing back to BAF to check on her.

'Could we go and visit it?' A female voice penetrated Annie's thoughts. 'During Fearless?'

Annie turned, confused; it was the young woman who'd been smiling at her earlier.

'Your animal shelter,' the woman continued. 'BAF, isn't it?'

'Oh yes, of course.' Annie laughed. 'That's my early-onset dementia, sorry. I'd be thrilled if you'd visit.'

Pak Tony saw the doctor off at the door and walked back towards the group. Annie noticed that Henry was sitting up now, with more colour in his cheeks.

'That's a great idea, Janelle,' said Pak Tony, rejoining the group. 'But Annie, I've just noticed something else that we might explore in your personal pow-wow.'

'Oh?' Annie felt vaguely concerned.

'Did anyone hear how Annie mentioned her age three times while she was talking?' Pak Tony didn't wait for an answer. 'First, she said that she was much older than everyone else. Then she complained about how her body feels as she ages. Now she's just made a joke about dementia. None of this is very positive self-talk, is it? Do you think perhaps Annie is afraid of getting older?'

Annie laughed dismissively.

'Or maybe,' he said, looking directly at Annie, 'she's afraid of what happens *after* getting old. Death is a very common fear. It's the ultimate human conundrum. Why do we have to die, and what happens when we do? Does consciousness exist outside the body? Or does everything we've worked for, experienced and achieved in our life simply disappear when we do? These are questions we all need to answer for ourselves, or the fear of death may constrain our life.'

Annie frowned, mildly offended. She was a person of faith: she didn't fear dying. She knew exactly where she was going in the afterlife. 'I'm sorry,' she began, 'but that's not—'

'Your fear of snakes could be masking a deeper fear of dying, Annie—which is what might happen if you get bitten by a snake.'

Annie felt her ire building. How dare he put words in her mouth?

'Consider it, anyway,' Pak Tony said. 'We'll revisit it in your pow-wow.'

Annie was indignant. Pak Tony was canvassing territory well beyond his remit. Did this self-styled guru really believe he had answers about eternity?

Pak Tony turned his attention to the woman sitting next to Annie. 'We have some downtime built into our schedule, Janelle. I'm sure we can manage an excursion to BAF.' He smiled at her. 'Now, why don't you introduce yourself?'

The hazel-eyed woman stood up. She had a symmetrical face framed by long, light-brown hair, and a smattering of sweet-looking beauty spots across her cheeks. Annie guessed she was in her late twenties.

'I'm Janelle, from Moorabbin, in Melbourne, Australia,' she started. 'I've worked in consumer and business research since university, but I'm not really . . . fulfilling my potential, I suppose.' She spoke clearly and deliberately, which was a welcome departure from the sibilant mumblings of Henry earlier.

'And if I'm honest with myself,' Janelle went on, 'I'm not very *happy* a lot of the time. So I came on this retreat to find out why.' As she spoke, the colour deepened in her cheeks.

'There are many methods of change-making, Janelle,' said Pak Tony. 'Why Fearless?'

Janelle glanced around the group. 'Well, one of the reasons my last relationship ended was my fear of flying. It's a full-blown phobia, and in the past it's stopped me doing certain things. The only way I can force myself onto an aeroplane is to drink alcohol beforehand—and lots of it.' She looked embarrassed. 'When I turned twenty-nine recently, I realised I was at a crossroad. I could stay stuck in a rut and let fear rule my life, or I could start making changes. When I read about Fearless online, I booked in straight away.' She laughed nervously. 'My family and friends think I've gone crazy.'

Pak Tony smiled. 'Well, congratulations on getting yourself to Bali.'

The group applauded politely.

'Apart from your fear of flying, how else do you think your life might need changing, Janelle?' Pak Tony asked. 'As I said to Annie, sometimes phobias or fixations mask much deeper fears.'

The Australian hesitated. 'I'm not sure. There's nothing *wrong* with my life in Melbourne, really. I go to work, come home, spend my weekends with family and friends.' She shrugged. 'It's pretty good, most of the time.'

'Too predictable, perhaps?'

'Not now I've turned my life upside down.' She grinned. 'But ordinarily, yes.'

'We'll explore that further in your pow-wow, then. You've started a journey of change, and that's wonderful, but we don't want you slipping back into old habits when you go home. Thank you, Janelle.'

She sat down, and Pak Tony nodded at the man on her other side. 'Your turn.'

The man was tall and athletic, with a neatly clipped goatee and a grin almost as broad as his shoulders. His tousled fringe kept falling across his chocolate-brown eyes. Annie had initially imagined that he might be a Canadian Mountie, but decided that he was a tad too dishevelled for that.

'I am Remy,' he announced, with a European accent that surprised her. 'You can probably hear that I am French. I have never been to Asia before, so I am feeling extremely hot right now.' He turned his back on the group. 'Look at my shirt, wet all over. My friends would be disgusted.' Remy held out his t-shirt and flapped it back and forth, as he turned to face the group.

'I will tell you what I am afraid of. I have a *big* problem with heights. Since I was small, I have been getting vertigo. I am thirty-one now, and it is still the same. When it is very bad I fall over, like Henry.' He motioned to the Englishman. 'This would be no problem if I stayed on the ground, *n'est-ce pas*? But for seven years I am working in the finance industry. Where do all the banks have their headquarters? The investment firms? The brokers? *Pfff!*' Remy closed his eyes and shook his head slightly. '*Always* in tall buildings.'

Annie smiled, quickly warming to him.

'Lucky for me, I am Parisian,' he went on, 'so we have mostly old buildings that can only be six storeys high. My office is on the fourth floor. But two months ago, my boss asked me to do a presentation in one of the towers at La Défense. They are very ugly and hard to find your way around.' He glanced around the group. 'Has anyone been there?'

No one had.

'The meeting was in the tallest tower, two hundred and thirty-one metres high. I told myself I could do it. Maybe it would get me the promotion I am wanting for three years? I prepared well, I did my research. But when I caught the elevator to the forty-second floor, the doors opened and there were big glass windows in front of me and—' He lowered his chin to his chest, looking glum.

'Suddenly there was an emergency inside of me. I tried to ignore it . . . a colleague was with me, and I could not let him down. I kept away from the windows and started my presentation, but soon I was feeling sick and imagining terrible things . . . a tsunami of pictures in my brain. First I am seeing the windows blowing out, then the building collapsing. Then in real life, everything went dark at the edges of my eyes, and a moment later—' he slapped his hands together—'I am looking at the ceiling from the floor.'

'It was a *catastrophe*. For me, my colleague, the whole company. We did not win the bid and certainly there was no promotion for me. *Bof!*' Remy shrugged. 'Not only that, my boss told me to take time off and see a doctor. He prescribed anxiety tablets, but I do not like putting chemicals in my body. So I asked the doctor for something else, and he told me to try desensitisation therapy. I looked that up online, and found Fearless.'

Pak Tony grinned. 'Ah! My website keywords are working, then.'

Annie frowned, troubled by this flippant comment.

'Actually, I like that phrase you used, Remy,' the facilitator continued. '*An emergency inside of me.* This is true for all kinds of phobias and fears. It is definitely how we feel when we are in the grip of something irrational. But the good news is, we can train our minds to manage the emergency.'

'Remy?' Janelle piped up. 'Are you afraid of aeroplanes too, or just heights?'

Remy turned to Janelle with interest. 'That is a very good question. It is strange, actually. On aeroplanes, I do not worry. It is like I am sitting in my apartment in Saint-Germain-des-Prés, only it is much smaller and the chair is uncomfortable and the food is *'orrible.'* His French accent emphasised the word, and the group laughed. 'The problem is when I'm in the open air, or near a window, or sometimes in an elevator or stairway. I have never been up the Eiffel Tower. But on aeroplanes, I can take an aisle seat and watch movies. I feel like I have no control, and that is liberating.'

'But that's exactly why I *hate* aeroplanes!' said Janelle, giggling. 'I feel totally out of control.'

Remy laughed too, a deep, infectious rumble. 'We are like the sun and moon, then,' he said, grinning back at Janelle. 'Opposites.'

Pak Tony cleared his throat. 'Phobias can feel very controlling, but they're actually much easier to treat than some other fears. We'll discuss phobia management strategies in your pow-wow, Remy.'

The Frenchman inclined his head in a little bow, then sat back down.

Pak Tony turned to the only member of the group who had not yet spoken, seated on the other side of Remy. 'Cara. Would you like to tell us about yourself and why you're here?'

The woman rose to her feet. Her frame seemed gaunt beneath loose yoga clothes, and her honey-coloured hair was uncombed. Her skin was pallid and flaky, her eyes a milky blue. Annie guessed she was in her early forties.

'Thank you,' the woman said softly. 'I'm Cara. From Sydney originally, but Bali's been my home for the last four years.'

Annie was surprised she hadn't seen Cara in any of the cafés frequented by the expatriate community in Ubud.

'I'm a print journalist by trade,' Cara went on, 'but I only write online content now. I heard about Fearless a few years ago through a yoga studio, but I've never quite made it along. This year, I decided . . .' She seemed to lose her way mid-sentence, and stopped, pondering a spot just above Pak Tony's head. 'I'm joining now because . . .' She trailed off again, her gaze floating further up towards the ceiling. Annie began to wonder whether Cara, like Henry, was afraid of public speaking.

After a long pause, Cara said, 'I lost someone four years ago and my whole life just . . . disintegrated. My yoga teacher thinks it's made me afraid of intimacy, of letting others in. She seems to think that this retreat might help.' Her expression remained impassive.

'And do you think your yoga teacher is right?' Pak Tony asked.

Cara sighed. 'Probably.'

Pak Tony nodded sympathetically. 'Loss is the shadow side of love, and one of life's hardest lessons. When we lose someone, we often respond by shutting ourselves off from the rest of the world, for fear of losing others. But we can't stop loving for fear of loss, just as we can't stop living for fear of death.'

'I'm not sure I'm even capable of love anymore,' said Cara softly. 'I'm numb, even after four years.'

Annie found herself nodding. She'd felt the same way after Kevin's death, trapped in an emotional limbo. It had taken years for her to start feeling anything at all. And even when the feelings had returned—the thrill of business success on the ranch, the joy of her children's graduations, or the quiet pain of her parents' passing—they had felt strangely muted. She'd kept her emotions in check, somehow, since Kevin died; but she'd never labelled it a fear of loss, as Pak Tony described it. Annie had simply understood it as the way things were *after* the dissolution of her world *before*.

Pak Tony smiled at Cara. 'But your yoga teacher seems to think differently. She believes you have the capacity to love again, Cara.'

The woman sighed once more. 'I still have family and friends back in Sydney, and I love them, of course. But I could never start a relationship again. Not without ruining it.'

'Because you ruined things in the past?' Pak Tony prompted gently.

Cara's facial expression briefly conveyed such self-contempt that Annie felt like leaping up and hugging her. *Something terrible had happened to this woman*, Annie thought; her face seemed to reflect the same ravages of grief that Annie had observed in the mirror for years after Kevin's death. *How had it happened for Cara?* Annie wondered, but didn't dare ask.

Pak Tony gestured at Cara to sit down. 'There's no need to push things now. We have plenty of time to go deeper. Thank you, Cara.'

The Australian resumed her cushion, her head bowed.

It was Pak Tony who stood now to address the group. 'You have all given something of yourselves this morning, thank you. That takes strength of character, especially when we're all so new to each other. If you forget anyone's name, here's a list.' He indicated a small board affixed to the wall, on which their names and nationalities were written:

Annie—United States
Remy—France
Janelle—Australia
Cara—Australia
Henry—United Kingdom
Lorenzo—Italy

'Look at those countries—all red, white and blue flags.' Pak Tony smiled. 'Except for Lorenzo, whose plane has been delayed. He'll be joining us at morning break. We have a nice balance of men and women too, and a good spread of countries—with an extra Australian, of course.'

Of course, Annie mused. That was typical of Bali, where Australians outnumbered every other foreign nationality by at least two to one. In fact, not long after her arrival, Nathan at BAF had told her that there were eighty thousand Australians in Bali on any one day. She'd dismissed this figure as grossly inflated, until the first time she'd visited Kuta Beach. There, around every poolside bar or sunset barbecue, were garrulous mobs of Australians downing bottles of Bintang, basting themselves in the sun, or watching Aussie Rules football on huge flat screens. They were friendly enough, Annie had discovered, despite their sometimes incomprehensible accents.

'So let's get started,' said Pak Tony, spreading his arms wide. 'Welcome to Fearless! Thank you so much for committing to arrive today, a Sunday. We always like to start these retreats on the first day of the month, there's a certain magic about it. I also find it takes a day or so for participants to settle in and get to know each other a little, before commencing the retreat more intensively. For the past ten years, Fearless has been helping people from across the globe to transform their lives. By the end of our week together, you will all be embracing your innate gifts and potential. You will be far less fearful, and considerably more *life-full*.'

Annie heard a voice from beyond the pavilion; a woman sounded upset outside. What language was she speaking?

'The fears you have shared this morning are among what the research tells us are the top ten human fears,' Pak Tony went on. 'These include flying, heights and public speaking—which covers Janelle, Remy and Henry. Then there's the fear of intimacy and the fear of death, for Cara and Annie. These are very common fears; millions of people around the world are going through exactly what you are. To fear is human.'

Annie raised her hand. She wasn't afraid of death, she wanted to point out.

'Just a moment, Annie.' Pak Tony's piercing blue eyes moved across the group. 'Over the next few days, you may find that new fears bubble up inside you, some of which you weren't aware of before. If this is the case, don't be too concerned. We will help you to face them in a constructive, life-affirming way. Yes, Annie?' His eyes settled on her.

'I'm afraid of *snakes*, Pak Tony,' she observed crisply. 'And I'd like to know what made you become a Fearless facilitator?'

Pak Tony smiled. 'It's all on the website.'

'But I can't remember much,' she said. 'Isn't that *terrible*?' The truth was, she'd been so desperate to get away from BAF after the snake incident that she'd barely scanned his biography.

The facilitator looked momentarily pained, before his smile returned. 'I'll give you the abridged version,' he said. 'We have a lot to get through this morning.'

Annie nodded.

'I grew up in Rotterdam in the Netherlands,' he started, 'but it wasn't a pleasant experience. I was the classic overweight, pimply kid who no one liked. I spent my school years running away from bullies, hiding behind bushes and trying not to get noticed by the cool kids. University wasn't much better. I was quite interested in campus life and I did well in my business degree, but I'd developed such severe acne by then that I avoided most social situations. It was crippling for me.'

Annie scanned the facilitator's smooth jaw; it was difficult to imagine pustules there.

'I tried everything—from prescription drugs to Chinese herbs and magic honey from New Zealand—but nothing helped. The acne turned me into a recluse. By the time I graduated, it had killed my self-esteem. I took a junior job in sales, an obvious role for a business graduate, but I felt like I couldn't face the world. I started taking more and more days off work . . .'

Pak Tony's expression suddenly lightened. 'And then one miraculous day in my mid-twenties, I was at the library when I stumbled across a Dutch translation of *You Can Heal Your Life* by Louise L. Hay. That book was a turning point for me. It was the moment I realised that toxic thoughts and fears were at the root of my skin problems. In fact, they're the cause of almost *every* problem. Once I understood that, I began to reclaim my power. I started to use my thoughts for good. Not only did I heal my acne, but I started having a positive effect on others too.'

Annie pressed her lips together, fighting the urge to thrust her hand into the air again. Having watched her own elderly parents become sick, deteriorate and then die—while maintaining forebearance and good humour throughout—Annie had little time for the idea that sickness was somehow a reflection of a person's interior world.

'I retrained in executive coaching,' continued Pak Tony, 'and then I started running positive psychology courses in Kralingen. I did that for almost ten years until I was lucky enough to meet my wife, Etna, on one of those courses. She's a homeopath and an entrepreneur. It was a true meeting of minds and hearts for us. Etna's father is Balinese and her mother is Dutch, so we straddle both cultures now.' He smiled again, too triumphantly for Annie's liking. She thought she detected a timid knock from the direction of the door, but Pak Tony didn't waver.

'We designed the Fearless retreat together about twelve years ago. We also offer two-week retreats for people with specific health issues and a three-day program called Manifesting Your Best Life. So we are kept very busy all year round.'

Pak Tony pushed his silvery hair behind his shoulders, before continuing. 'After experimenting with a few different venues in Bali, we based ourselves here at Puri Damai. We've got an international reputation now, and we're growing exponentially. I do the facilitation and Etna runs the administration. Obviously we have a great team of local staff too, and the results speak for themselves. Whatever fears people arrive with—and I've seen some unusual ones—we've never failed to guide our clients towards their higher truth by their departure.'

And how would clients know they'd attained their *higher truth*? Annie wondered dubiously. It wasn't like a tourist destination, helpfully signposted.

There *was* a knocking at the door, Annie was certain now. Pak Tony's face twitched, but he made no move to respond.

'Excuse me, Pak Tony,' said Janelle. 'What are some of the unusual fears you've seen?'

Pak Tony smiled. 'Well, we had a young man who suffered from somniphobia, the fear of falling asleep. Then there was the chaetophobic lady, she was afraid of body hair . . .'

'She would not like me, then,' said Remy wryly, pushing his fringe out of his eyes.

An abrupt, loud knocking made them all turn towards the door.

Pak Tony pursed his lips. 'I do apologise, friends. Sometimes the staff forget that we are not to be interrupted. Wait a moment, please.'

He strode to the door and opened it with a flourish.

Lorenzo had tried to divert her, but Lavinia would not be dissuaded. The driver—a stoic Balinese named Pak Ketut—stood outside the retreat venue, shuffling from foot to foot. He pointed repeatedly at a wooden plaque attached to the door, carved with an image of a man sitting cross-legged in meditation pose, one finger pressed against his lips. It was an incontrovertible sign for 'do not disturb', but Lavinia kept disputing this.

'Just knock, please,' she insisted. 'We are only a little bit late.'

The driver knocked, but barely made a sound, then turned to Lavinia. 'Mrs Lavinia, I am very sorry. Pak Tony has a rule, we must never interrupt his retreats in progress, unless it is an emergency.'

Lorenzo looked at Pak Ketut with growing pity. His three-year marriage to Lavinia had taught him that her juggernaut of righteousness could rarely be repelled.

'This *is* an emergency,' said Lavinia, flicking her dark tresses over bare, sun-kissed shoulders. 'I was supposed to be at the Shakti

Centre three hours ago for an important appointment. I won't wait any longer—please tell Pak Tony we're here. It will be my interruption, not yours.'

She stood with her arms crossed, glowering at the driver. Even in anger, she was exquisite. As a teenager, she'd been plucked from obscurity in her native San Gimignano and thrust onto the catwalks of Milan. Now aged thirty-two, Lavinia still drew attention in their home suburb of Navigli, where the locals gaped at her as if she were a celebrity. She wasn't—after retiring from modelling at twenty-eight, Lavinia had been only moderately successful in her new career in fashion design. Yet she always carried herself with such an air of entitlement. It was one of the traits that had attracted Lorenzo in the first instance; he'd described it to his friends as magnetism, charisma, assurance.

Pak Ketut fidgeted with his wristwatch. 'Pak Tony has asked me to bring Mister Lorenzo into the workshop at the morning break,' he said. 'That is only thirty minutes to wait.'

'No!' Lavinia shook her head in frustration, then looked at Lorenzo with her palms turned upwards. '*Coglione!*'

Lorenzo could only assume that Pak Ketut's knowledge of Italian expletives was limited. 'Lavinia . . .' he murmured, trying to placate her. 'Surely we can wait?'

'Knock on the door again,' she demanded.

Lorenzo lowered his eyes, noticing the granite pavers on which they stood and the fine green moss leaching out between them. Over the past three years, he'd grown used to the sensation of staring earthwards while Lavinia held forth from her own personal podium.

After a moment's silence, he looked up again. The driver's hand was trembling, poised above the polished teak handle of the elaborately carved door. He tapped lightly, but louder than before, then took three steps backwards. He waited for several minutes, imploring Lavinia with his eyes. Detecting no movement on the other side, he raised his hand and rapped once more, louder this time.

The door swung open and Tony van de Jaager strode out. Lorenzo recognised him instantly from the Fearless website; in person, there was a sleek, leonine quality about him. Tony smiled, his flawless white teeth almost blinding Lorenzo, then turned and spoke to the driver in Indonesian. Looking increasingly cowed, the driver nodded. When Tony had finished, Pak Ketut promptly disappeared down a path leading into the gardens of Puri Damai.

'So this must be Lorenzo and Lavinia? I am Pak Tony. It is *so* nice to meet you both,' he said, shaking their hands. 'I do not speak Italian, I'm sorry. But you two have very good English, I'm sure.'

'We speak no Dutch either,' said Lavinia, smiling.

Lorenzo noticed Pak Tony's eyes lingering on Lavinia's face a little longer than decorum would ordinarily allow. He was used to this kind of reaction: when exposed to Lavinia's beauty for the first time, people simply had to stare awhile, before affecting nonchalance.

'We are very sorry to disturb the session,' Lorenzo began, gesturing to the pavilion door. 'Lavinia is due at the Shakti Centre for an appointment, before her workshop starts tomorrow. She wanted to meet you before she goes, because this is . . . a joint commitment for us, as you know.'

'Of course.' Pak Tony smiled. 'The Shakti Centre has such wonderful healers, you will be in good hands. Let us know how you are doing there, Lavinia. There may be some resonances between Shakti and Fearless. Or you may choose to attend some of Lorenzo's sessions here, to keep things flowing for you as a couple.'

'Oh, that is *exactly* what I was thinking,' gushed Lavinia, clasping Pak Tony's hand for a moment as if poised to embrace him. 'I'm so happy to meet you, but I should find a taxi now.' She motioned at her suitcase, a flamboyant pink colour, which sat alongside Lorenzo's muted grey duffel bag.

'Allow me,' said Pak Tony, moving towards a large bronze gong suspended from a bamboo strut. 'Ketut can take you there, it is no trouble at all.' He lifted a small mallet and struck the gong.

Before the vibration had ceased, the driver materialised from the garden again. He listened to Pak Tony's instructions and then, placing his palms together, bowed to Lavinia. 'This way, Mrs Lavinia.' He took up her suitcase.

'Yes, but I must do this first.' Lavinia flung her arms around Lorenzo, pressing her lips to his. The driver averted his gaze. 'I love you,' she murmured, her dark eyes moist. 'Remember why we are doing this.'

Lorenzo nodded, a little embarrassed.

'*Ciao.*' She pulled away and blew him another kiss.

Lorenzo watched his wife follow Pak Ketut down a cobbled path leading to the resort lobby. She turned and waved to him once more, before disappearing behind a row of snow-white hibiscuses.

'Well, Lorenzo,' said Pak Tony, nodding towards the door, 'are you ready to face your fears?'

Lorenzo picked up his duffel bag and conjured a smile. He followed the facilitator into the airy pavilion, where a handful of people sat in a circle on the bamboo floor.

'Everyone, this is Lorenzo,' announced Pak Tony. 'The missing Italian piece of our puzzle. All the way from Milan.'

'*Ciao*,' said Lorenzo, raising a hand at the group.

Some of them smiled and nodded, while others murmured a greeting. A large, jovial-looking woman called out 'Hi there!' and Lorenzo contemplated fleeing immediately.

Pak Tony motioned to a board hung on a wall nearby. 'There's a list of everyone, but let's do some brief introductions. Take a seat, Lorenzo.' He nodded at a space in the circle next to the woman who'd just called out.

As he sat down, she extended her hand. 'I'm Annie,' she said in an American accent. He couldn't help staring at her strawberry blonde, bouffant hair.

'Lorenzo,' he replied, shaking her hand.

The others introduced themselves in turn: a pale Englishman called Henry, an amiable Australian named Janelle, a hirsute Frenchman called Remy, and Cara, another Australian, who looked thin and rather unkempt.

'For your benefit, Lorenzo,' began Pak Tony. 'Among us we have a fear of flying, a fear of public speaking, a fear of heights, a fear of intimacy, and a fear of death—I mean, *snakes*.' He smiled at the American, who did not smile back. 'And those are only the fears we have labelled. There may be others we don't recognise, or don't want to acknowledge, deep inside us.' He looked pointedly at Annie again, then turned back to Lorenzo. 'So, could you please tell us a little about what brings you to Fearless?'

Lorenzo felt suddenly light-headed. It had been an exhausting series of flights from Milan, transiting in Rome and Doha for several hours apiece; he felt as though he could sleep for two days. Still, he stood up, noticing for the first time a gap on the other side of the pavilion where a wall should have been.

The windowless space framed dense jungle that fell away into a gorge beyond. Insects hummed and finches flitted between twisted lianas. A branch moved beneath the weight of a small, squirrel-like creature which stood up on its hind legs for a moment, as if listening. Lorenzo watched its bushy caramel-coloured tail swirling from side to side, before it darted up the curved trunk of a coconut palm. He resolved to take out his camera later, when the heat receded, to capture some of this tropical beauty.

Pak Tony and the group were waiting for him to speak, he realised.

'I am Lorenzo.' He hesitated. It had been difficult enough explaining the issue to family and friends in Italian back home, never mind describing it in English to a group of strangers in Bali. 'I am here with my wife, Lavinia, because . . . we are having trouble making a baby. We have tried for three years already, since we were first married. We have had all the medical testing. I am thirty-eight, she is thirty-two, and the doctors can find nothing wrong. Now they suggest IVF, but Lavinia does not like these interventions. She prefers a natural process.'

He cleared his throat. 'Two months ago we went to Vatican City to see a priest we know, Monsignor Fattori. He is friendly with my family for many years. You may not believe . . .' He glanced around the group. 'Many people in Italy say Monsignor Fattori has the gift of spiritual insight. When we visited him, he laid his hands over Lavinia's womb and said, "There is fear in your relationship." He told us to go away and consider our fears, because perhaps they are stopping our pregnancy.'

Lorenzo exhaled, feeling awkward about speaking of such issues in public. 'We did some research. Lavinia found the Shakti Centre here in Ubud, which helps women prepare for childbirth. Then she found Fearless, to help me face any fears about fatherhood.' He stopped, hoping he'd said enough.

Pak Tony gazed at Lorenzo with his unsettling blue eyes. 'And *do* you have any fears about fatherhood, Lorenzo?'

Lorenzo suddenly realised that until now, no one had actually asked him that question. Lavinia had simply planned their trip to Bali and booked them into the retreats, presenting it to him as a fait accompli.

'Friends say that having a baby is magnificent,' he said, 'but that it also changes your relationship.' He could still remember the words of his best friend, Nico, a year after his daughter was born: *A baby relieves you of your wife's love and your manly dignity.* 'So maybe I am afraid of these changes.' Would *that* be sufficient? he wondered.

'Are you?' Pak Tony's steady gaze continued to bore into him. 'Or do you think you might have other subconscious fears about fatherhood?'

Lorenzo glanced out at the jungle again, and then, finding the glare oppressive, averted his eyes. It was not a light conducive to photography after all, he decided.

'Well, if I *do* have subconscious fears, I don't know about them yet, do I?' he said. 'That is why I am here.'

The facilitator nodded but clearly wasn't finished with him. 'And could it be, Lorenzo, that you don't fear fatherhood itself, but that you fear *failing* as a father? Many competent people feel overwhelmed by the prospect of parenting. It's a big responsibility and it can make you feel very out of control. And to some extent, you are—you can't predict anything about this new little person who comes into your life, and once they're there, you can't send them back.' Pak Tony smiled again. 'Particularly given that you've been so successful in your professional life, Lorenzo, perhaps you fear failure as a father?'

'Maybe,' said Lorenzo. Pak Tony's gaze encouraged him to say more, but he remained silent.

Eventually the facilitator said, 'Well, thank you, Lorenzo. Let's get started with our introduction to mindfulness. Every morning for the duration of the retreat, we will commence with a group meditation. I will guide you through our first visualisation now, as a practice session. Please lie down.' He motioned to a set of yoga mats laid out in a sun pattern, encircling a small wooden stool. 'Heads in the middle, feet at the edge.'

Lorenzo hung back for a moment, watching the rest of the group take their places. Then he lay down on the last mat available, between the hairy Frenchman and the overweight American. Pak Tony moved into the centre and sat down on the stool.

'Close your eyes now, please,' he said. 'Let's take some deep breaths together. Inhale, one . . . Exhale, one . . . Inhale, two . . . Exhale, two . . .'

Lorenzo closed his eyes willingly, despite having no prior experience of meditation. The nature of his work had always seemed antithetical to mindfulness: the photographic glorification of branded accessories, within frenetic deadlines and for exorbitant fees. He had shot for all the major fashion houses and magazines in Europe—iconic wristwatches, signature sunglasses and dazzling jewellery, framed against smooth canvasses of flawless skin. These professional labours afforded Lorenzo the financial buffer to pursue his real photographic passion, a far more whimsical photography of inference. Of timid eyes, half-closed and averted, of buttons drifting open at the chest, of porcelain-white thighs partially exposed in fields of wildflowers. The beguiling curve of a neck or the sensual allure of a scapula captured by a timeless, hazy lens.

Pak Tony's voice slowed as he counted, and Lorenzo felt his breathing settle into an easy, circular rhythm.

'Imagine there is a shining sphere of light entering the room above you,' began Pak Tony. 'Warm and comforting, it is a sphere of love, and it is hovering above you, gradually descending.'

A sphere of love? Lorenzo's rational mind objected. Then, in the grip of extreme tiredness, he abandoned all resistance.

'The light is golden and soft, it can never harm or burn you. It is moving closer and touching the top of your head . . .'

Lorenzo could almost feel his scalp tingling beneath the glow.

'It is entering your head now,' Pak Tony continued, his voice somnolent, 'and this sphere is carrying warmth and love down through your body, relaxing all of your muscles as it passes along your neck and spine, into your arms and fingertips, through your chest, heart and abdomen, then into your hips and pelvis.'

His body felt weightier against the floor, Lorenzo noticed.

'Now you can feel the sphere's warmth at the base of your spine and flowing down into your legs. Your thighs are heavy against the floor, your knees have surrendered. Your ankles, your feet, even your toes are heavy . . . And now your whole body is totally relaxed. You are enfolded in the pure light of love. Stay with that feeling for a while.'

Lorenzo floated in comfortable silence, carried by his breath.

After a while, Pak Tony spoke again. 'I want you to imagine that you are in a completely safe place. A place where no one is judging you, where there is no risk of failure in some way. A place where you are accepted for who you really are. It might be a real place you have visited in your life before, or a place in your imagination. What does this place look like? What does it smell like? Who is with you in this place—or are you alone? What is the nature of this place where you are recognised and loved for who you really are?'

Lorenzo found himself in his grandmother's kitchen in San Cristoforo. Sitting on nonna Marisa's lap, his back pressed against her soft, generous folds. Watching the long-handled knife she held—his small hand resting on top of hers—as it sliced cloves of garlic on a large wooden chopping board. The pungent smell of oregano and basil hung about them as she regaled him with fanciful tales—of potatoes that sprouted legs, picked up their peelings and bolted out of the kitchen; of acrobatic sausages that turned somersaults, as she stuffed their skins with pork; of tomatoes and olives that constructed an elaborate catapult using her skillet, a soup ladle and a can opener, then launched themselves out of the kitchen window to freedom.

Lorenzo could hear a child's high-pitched laughter, his own delighted giggling at her stories. Her warm flesh wobbled as her arms enveloped him, her lips smattering his cheeks with damp kisses. He heard again the pet names she'd showered upon him long ago: *tesoro, piccolo, cucciolo.* He could even taste the titbits she'd fed him as she cooked: slabs of freshly baked bread dipped in olive oil, crumbling hunks of *stracchino* cheese that melted as she put them in his mouth, smooth strips of chargrilled eggplant lying like ripe purple tongues on a greasy cooking tray.

'Now I want you to stand up in that special place.' Pak Tony's voice made Lorenzo's eyelids flicker, and a feeling of longing lodged itself as a dull pang in his chest. 'And I want you to imagine that you have a small glass bottle hanging on a string around your neck. This is a magic bottle that can capture the beautiful feeling of being truly cherished. I want you to reach out now and take a bit of that wonderful feeling into your magic bottle. As you put the lid back on, consider what that feeling looks like. Does it have a colour, or a smell?'

Lorenzo slid down from his grandmother's knee and turned to look up at her kindly heart-shaped face. Her long white hair was secured at the nape of her neck with a mother-of-pearl hairpin, her cocoa eyes twinkled with a light reserved for Lorenzo alone, and she nodded approvingly as he showed her the small glass bottle hanging from the sandalwood rosary beads slung around his neck. He waved the bottle in front of her ample bosom and noticed, as he inserted the cork stopper again, that the vapour inside was a pale pink colour. A fruity perfume emanated from it, the scent of the delicate climbing roses that grew rampant across her garden walls.

'*Grazie, nonna,*' he murmured.

She nodded again, beaming at Lorenzo and cupping his cheeks with her soft hands.

'Now,' Pak Tony continued, 'I want you to take that bottle and carry it with you into a different place. A place you fear in some way. It might be a place where something frightening has actually happened, or a place where you fear something might happen. I want you to hold fast to your magic bottle as you enter that place of fear, because it gives you protection and immunity . . .'

Lorenzo felt his nostalgia for nonna Marisa turn into a cold, hard lump wedged at the back of his throat.

It was one of his father's worst rages. He was standing in the kitchen of their run-down apartment in Salario, untastefully decorated in country style by his well-meaning mother, listening to the sound of his parents arguing. As his father's fury intensified, Lorenzo turned and fled to his parents' bedroom, running past the hunting trophies framed along the hall: the mournful-eyed doe, the magnificent stag, the massive Sardinian boar.

He threw himself into the tall mahogany closet, burying himself at its base, trying to conceal himself beneath his mother's shoes. Piles of winter boots, moccasins, high heels; if he lay like a corpse, Papa mightn't see him. Papa's rages were unpredictable, only erupting occasionally. But when incited—fuelled by a long afternoon drinking *grappa* with his friends—it swept through the house like a tornado, leaving behind it a trail of wreckage and Mama's inconsolable tears.

Their voices moved closer and Lorenzo closed his eyes.

'Faith?' his father bellowed at his mother. 'You have pine cones in your head! *Faith* won't help our bank balance!'

The closet door was wrenched open and Lorenzo held his breath. But when he felt his father's iron grip around his ankle, he couldn't help but cry out. Shoes flew in every direction as Papa pulled him out of the wardrobe. Lorenzo's head connected with the cold tiled floor; dazed, he let go of the magic bottle. It rolled into the dark void underneath his parents' bed.

'Papa,' he whimpered, covering his face with his hands. He needed to stay quiet, he knew, to prevent his mother from intervening. The last time she'd done that, she'd lain motionless in bed for three days afterwards, her bruised eyes staring unseeingly at the ceiling.

His father seized him by the seat of his trousers and tore them down, leaving his underwear hanging at his hips. Then Papa pulled off his underpants, too, the elastic snapping painfully at his skin. Lorenzo tried to crawl away, but the steel-capped boot slammed into his bare buttocks, once, twice, three times. As the pain ploughed into his hips, his thighs, his lower back, Lorenzo screamed and tried to cover himself.

He heard his mother's wailing, and then the blows stopped. After a moment of quiet, Lorenzo gingerly pulled himself up onto all fours and looked around for his father, just in time to see his purplish face and swinging boot. There was a bolt of excruciating pain to his testicles, and he fell face-first to the floor.

'Now, I want you to open your magic bottle and throw its loving contents all over your fear . . .' Pak Tony's voice hauled Lorenzo back into the room, and he sat up, his heart thumping wildly.

Pak Tony was sitting on the yoga stool, his eyes closed. Everyone else lay obediently supine, presumably dousing their fears with bottled love, but Lorenzo could not return to the place the meditation had taken him. There were some things magic bottles couldn't fix. As it was, Lorenzo had been fortunate that only one of his testicles had been removed and his fertility remained unaffected.

When Lavinia hadn't fallen pregnant as quickly as she hoped, it had been the first test they'd taken. To Lorenzo's surprise, his result had returned normal.

Pak Tony opened his eyes now and Lorenzo felt dangerously exposed, certain that the facilitator could discern, somehow, the years of denial, flashbacks and fear. That he could intuit, too, how Lorenzo's carefully constructed life was as flimsy as a silken spider's web strung across a busy thoroughfare.

'As you smother your fear with love,' Pak Tony continued, gazing at Lorenzo, 'you will notice that it becomes weaker, or disappears altogether. This bottle of love is infinite; it recharges with every use. All you have to do, whenever you feel afraid, is to open the bottle and douse your fear. You can inhale the scent, feel its healing power, and use it to help yourself and others. Your fear may be very old, and it may be very strong, but it cannot last forever. Love is *always* stronger than fear.'

Lorenzo lowered his gaze, dismissing these glib words. In the real world, it was not so easy. His beloved nonna Marisa, his maternal grandmother, had never witnessed his father's 'passions', as Lorenzo's mother had obliquely called them. Even when Lorenzo was hospitalised and an orchidectomy performed, his mother had concocted a tale about him climbing a tree and falling spreadeagled onto a fence—telling the hospital staff, the surgeon, nonna Marisa, Lorenzo's teacher and even Lorenzo himself.

Aged just six, Lorenzo couldn't understand why his mother told a story that wasn't true. When he'd found himself alone with his mother, he gazed at her, the question in his eyes. His mother had looked away, mumbling that some truths cannot be spoken in public.

From this, Lorenzo had concluded that the adult world was an ugly, contrary domain, to be avoided for as long as possible.

He'd certainly avoided his father, who'd seemed shaken by Lorenzo's injuries at first and sworn off alcohol. But then, as Lorenzo had recovered and the lure of *grappa* proved too great, Papa's rages returned. Only once or twice a year, his mother insisted, never enough to be habitual.

As a teenager, Lorenzo had sometimes wondered what nonna Marisa might have done had he told her what really happened in their home. He'd even fantasised about it, picturing how, on reading Lorenzo's letter, she would burst into outraged tears, immediately pack her battered leather suitcase and catch a connecting train to Milano Centrale, sit fuming all the way to Roma Termini, then arrive in a late-night taxi at the door of their apartment in Salario. How she would barge in like a whirlwind and call his father all the names Lorenzo could not—like *bastardo* and *schifoso* and *farabutto* —and then assume calm command of the family.

First, she'd send Papa to Monsignor Fattori in Vatican City for a lengthy dose of penitence. Then she'd send Lorenzo's mother on holiday to Cinque Terre, where the briny ministrations of the sea would repair her body and soul. Finally, Lorenzo and nonna Marisa would sit together in the kitchen, making *pasta fresca* and *ajo* with chopped garlic and dried red peppers in olive oil. They would live like that for weeks, cooking and laughing and conspiring, until Papa returned all haggard with contrition, and Mama returned tanned and relaxed, and the three of them would thank nonna Marisa, their angel of intercession, and put her back on the train for San Cristoforo.

But that childhood fantasy had never come to pass. He'd never written the letter, and nonna Marisa had died when he was fifteen.

His relationship with his parents had limped along. Until finally, after marrying Lavinia, he'd dispensed with pretence altogether and abandoned contact with his father. He'd remained in touch with his mother, however, catching up with her whenever he passed through Rome. Always on neutral territory outside the family home.

'I want you to imagine something different now,' Pak Tony said, drawing Lorenzo's attention into the room again. 'I want you to think of a time in your life when you have succeeded.' The facilitator gestured to the yoga mat, and Lorenzo decided to lie back down. As an international leader in fashion photography, Lorenzo wouldn't have trouble imagining success, and he needed to expunge from his mind the other painful memories.

Closing his eyes once more, Lorenzo conjured a very different version of himself, now in his early twenties. Some fifteen years ago, in his final year of an interior design degree at the Istituto Superiore di Architettura e Design in Milan. Living a student's life, far enough away from his parents' home in Rome. Managing to support himself with the money nonna Marisa had bequeathed him and a part-time internship at *Fashion Milan*.

It was an ordinary Monday morning in the magazine's office. Lorenzo was busy putting the final touches on the lighting of the indoor set for a ten-page spread on youth haute couture when he heard the editor approaching.

'*What* did you say?' she bellowed. 'Ginevra is *sick*?'

Lorenzo heard the editor's assistant murmuring in her best placating tone.

'Ginevra is a *dog*!' exclaimed the editor. 'What about Martino then?'

More low murmuring, followed by an explosion, nearer now. 'And what do you propose, *porco*?' the editor screeched. 'The shoot is tomorrow. Three of Italy's leading labels are involved. We can't just get any miserable piece-of-shit photographer!'

Calmly, Lorenzo stood up from behind the chaise longue where he'd been adjusting the fill light. 'I can do it,' he announced, looking the editor in the eye.

For a moment, she stared at him as though a bug had just spoken. In the silence, he opened his satchel and boldly passed her his portfolio.

'Shot over three years with a fifty-millimetre lens,' he explained as she leafed through the images. He had nonna Marisa's bequest to thank for his fancy camera, too.

The editor raised an eyebrow. It was an audacious suggestion, but Lorenzo noticed her face changing as she scrutinised his photos.

After several minutes she said, 'Alright. But if you fuck it up, you'll be making coffee for the rest of your career.'

'*Certamente*,' said Lorenzo, unintimidated. Professional success was secondary, after all, to the visceral thrill of the work he loved best.

The following day, when Lorenzo lifted the camera to his eye, he felt omnipotent. The lens transformed his prepubescent models—an eleven-year-old girl named Valentina and a twelve-year-old boy named Pietro—into seraphim of the firmament. Their perfection was breathtaking: the dimple at the corner of Valentina's mouth, the blonde mane that tumbled down her back and billowed about her slender hips; Pietro's tanned limbs covered in fine, downy hair, and an enigmatic smile that hinted at the possibilities of manhood. Despite being draped in ostentatious accessories, their purity outshone all.

The shoot continued for six hours, until the models' minder intervened; a grandmotherly woman wrapped Valentina and Pietro in white fluffy robes and bundled them off into a hire car with tinted windows. Lorenzo collapsed into a chair, exhausted yet elated and curiously titillated.

The labels were delighted with the results, as was the editor. 'I'm changing the terms of your internship, Lorenzo,' she told him a week later. 'You're wasted in design. You're doing photography from now on.'

That was Lorenzo's first taste of success, and it hadn't stopped there. He'd stayed at *Fashion Milan* for a further five years, widely touted as a rising star of fashion photography. Not long after his twenty-eighth birthday, he accepted a job at *Vogue Italy*. There, it was everything he'd heard and more: the untenable hours, the volatile egos, the extravagant cocaine parties. Lorenzo loitered at the edges as an interested observer, eschewing the drug-induced highs in favour of weekends spent developing his first private exhibition.

'Take a nice deep breath now.' Pak Tony's droning voice penetrated Lorenzo's awareness once more. 'What does success *feel* like? Who is there with you?'

Lorenzo exhaled, remembering it well. After two years of preparation, his private exhibition—titled *Initiation*—had opened. His parents had travelled from Salario for the launch party; Lorenzo's eyes turned watery as he watched them move woodenly through the chic crowd. They listened politely to the speeches, to the professor of modern art gushing over Lorenzo's work with words like *liminal* and *avant-garde*. Then they shuffled along the gallery's walls, stopping before each image, their heads tilted at various angles, trying to understand.

Eventually, when there were no more photographs to examine, his father approached and shook Lorenzo's hand. He kissed both of Lorenzo's cheeks, but refused to meet his eyes. Lorenzo's mother mumbled something about being too old and ignorant to truly appreciate contemporary art. They were going back to their hotel, she told him.

Lorenzo had dutifully waved them off outside the gallery. Promising to visit at Easter, wondering if his father still flew into rare but terrifying rages and manhandled his mother. Blowing his mother a kiss, he told himself, *It's not your role to protect her.* But a voice inside his head demanded, *Then whose is it?* As he stood there, the sense of success that had filled Lorenzo before the launch began to deflate, like a leaky balloon.

His parents weren't the only ones bemused by Lorenzo's work, it turned out. Three days later, a stinging critique appeared in *Metro Milan*: 'Lorenzo Ricci's photography is visually arresting, but the ambiguous age of his models, typically half-naked or otherwise vulnerable in floating outdoor landscapes, positions this *Vogue* photographer's private work in dubious territory.' He'd paid it no heed, assuming that few people took notice of a free newspaper distributed in the underground, until the same review was syndicated across the *Metro* newspapers in Padua, Rome, Bergamo, Bologna, Genoa, Verona, Turin, Venice and Florence. Interest surged on social media, with high-profile bloggers posting commentaries entitled 'Porn or Art?', 'Teen

"Initiation" Controversy' and 'Making Purity Explicit'. National and international attention followed, with critics comparing Lorenzo's natural studies of adolescents to the work of controversial photographers Sally Mann, Irina Ionesco, David Hamilton and Bill Henson.

When Lorenzo's exhibition was mentioned in *The New York Times* just a week after the opening night, the editor-in-chief of *Vogue Italy* invited him into her office. Not to rebuke him, as he initially feared, but for a celebratory drink.

'*Salute!*' she bleated. 'You're a disruptor brand now, Lorenzo.' She raised her glass of cognac and clinked it against his. 'Did you plan it all behind our backs?'

Lorenzo stared at her for a moment, confused. 'I just . . . followed my passion,' he explained.

'For what?' asked the editor, lighting a Toscano. 'Virginal eros?' She guffawed into her cognac.

Lorenzo shook his head, loathing her. 'For everything that you and I have ever lost.'

They chitchatted for an interminable fifteen minutes before Lorenzo set down his glass. 'Thank you for the drink,' he said. 'I have plans this evening.'

Not long afterwards, encouraged by a flood of professional enquiries and his growing international reputation, Lorenzo left *Vogue* for a freelance career. The editor still wanted to employ him as a freelancer, which was eminently satisfying—and created a springboard to other lucrative contracts.

The following year, while shooting for *Velvet* magazine, Lorenzo met a costume design consultant named Lavinia. She was elegant, fiery, and possibly the only person in the European Union who didn't have an opinion on his work. When he fished for her views over their first lunch together, she simply said in a bored tone, 'Why is there so much discussion about it? It's beautiful. Of course youth is alluring. I don't understand the controversy.'

Lavinia's indifference was a blessed relief, and perhaps one of her more attractive qualities—alongside her sultry good looks, lively personality and brazen lack of concern about anyone else's opinion. As their friendship morphed into a relationship, Lavinia never once queried Lorenzo's photographic preoccupations: the angular elbows and androgenous faces and enticing moles in unseen places. Lavinia was unmoved by it all, assessing it only in terms of its aesthetic value. Which prompted Lorenzo to wonder, for the first time in his life, if this might be the woman to wed. Indeed, from the perspective of many of Lorenzo's friends, romancing the beautiful Lavinia Argento was proof of success in itself. Lying on the yoga mat, Lorenzo floated in his warm feelings of pride and comfort in having married Lavinia.

'And now we will start returning to our physical selves,' announced Pak Tony. 'I'm going to count back from ten to one; when I reach one, our meditation will be over. You will be fully present in your body, but feeling deeply relaxed.'

Lorenzo slowly resurfaced, becoming aware of the space and people around him once more.

When everyone was back in a seated position, Pak Tony asked, 'Does anyone have any feedback on our first meditation session?'

The Australian woman with the agreeable face raised her hand. 'I went to a completely different place.'

'Me too,' enthused the American. 'And I sure need that bottle of love for my work at BAF.'

Pak Tony smiled. 'You can take that bottle mentally with you anywhere and use it to extinguish your fear.'

'I had trouble imagining that part,' admitted the Frenchman. 'When I am up in a high place, my body takes over. I am sweating and shaking. No imaginary bottle of love is going to stop that.'

'Really?' Pak Tony countered, his eyes dancing. 'You might surprise yourself. Tomorrow we have our first fear safari, at Jimbaran Beach. You will have the chance to use your bottle of love while parasailing, Remy, and we will see if you are stronger than you think.'

'Parasailing?' Remy turned a pale shade of green. 'Above the sea?'

'Yes,' said Pak Tony cheerfully. 'Tandem parasailing behind a speedboat. Here is our updated itinerary.' He took up his clipboard and began distributing the papers inside it. 'Subject to change, of course. We're moving with spirit, so we should expect the unexpected.'

Lorenzo studied it with some trepidation. Tomorrow's schedule included *fear safari*, *parasailing* and something called *passion talks* in the afternoon. The next day featured a *water cleansing ceremony*, *personal pow-wows*, then an evening timeslot entitled *group dinner: your odyssey*.

Lorenzo grimaced at the idea of a group dinner. He was thirty-eight years old, with a well-developed social network; he didn't need any new friends. But like it or not, for the next seven days he would be forced to coexist with five strangers, joining them for eclectic activities such as *neurolinguistic programming*, *harnessing the collective unconscious* and *spiritual sexuality*.

'Any questions?' asked Pak Tony. 'You will be familiar with most of it from the materials you received on booking.'

Not Lorenzo; it was Lavinia who had pored over the Fearless literature.

'I have a question,' the Englishman said, a little shakily. 'I was a last-minute booking, so I haven't read much about the program. Can you please explain what a "personal pow-wow" is?'

'I was hoping someone would ask,' said Pak Tony, rubbing his hands together with evident glee. 'Here in Ubud we have a renowned spiritual healer, Littlefish, living among us. He is native Alaskan from the Yup'ik tribe, and usually he is booked up months in advance. But all of you will have the chance to spend forty-five minutes with him for a personal pow-wow, or consultation. It's the launchpad for your odyssey, an individual challenge that will be set for you for the rest of the retreat. Your odyssey is designed to confront you and shift you into a space of deep transformation.'

'Oh.' Henry's baffled face mirrored Lorenzo's feelings exactly. 'Is it essential? I was thinking of going birdwatching with Pak Ketut tomorrow afternoon.'

Pak Tony chortled. 'It *is* essential.'

Henry looked crestfallen. Lorenzo wasn't at all sure he was ready to discuss his 'shadow side' with a Native American healer.

The dishevelled Australian woman raised her hand. 'What's a passion talk?'

'Passion talks are a chance for you to share something that puts fire in your belly, using a creative method. You can sing, dance, draw pictures; it's all about expression of the soul. It's not a professional presentation, so please don't get nervous about it,' Pak Tony smiled at Henry. 'It shouldn't be longer than five minutes.'

'What's this on day four?' asked the American woman now, pointing at the schedule. 'The intimacy workshop?'

'It's a wonderful opportunity to explore the healing power of touch,' said Pak Tony, 'and to get really comfortable with our bodies. Afterwards, we'll break into two groups, for powerful manhood and womanhood rites. Releasing fear in the body is a precursor to letting go of it mentally and spiritually.'

It sounded like one of Lavinia's sessions at Shakti; his wife had been in raptures over the prospect of a week-long bonanza of fertility yoga, spiritual decluttering and ecstatic dance. When she'd described the final night's sweat lodge with other prospective mothers, Lorenzo had been forced to repress his laughter. He dared not even smirk, given Lavinia's mood around the topic of baby-making lately, which routinely made her snap at him or dissolve into tears or both.

'After the intimacy workshop,' Pak Tony continued, 'we will head out for our second fear safari, at Paradise Animal Sanctuary. Home to the largest collection of birds and reptiles in Bali.'

Annie blanched. 'Reptiles, like snakes?'

'Let's just say it's a great opportunity to challenge our reptilian brains,' said Pak Tony. 'The part of us that's responsible for our fight-or-flight responses.'

Annie still looked concerned. Lorenzo didn't much like the sound of it either. His only prior contact with snakes was as accessories: skinned for handbags and belts.

'Any other questions?' asked Pak Tony. 'Remy? You seem quiet.'

The Frenchman shrugged. 'I am thinking about parasailing.'

'Oh, please don't,' the facilitator replied. 'Overthinking is the antithesis of action. You will have Janelle for support tomorrow.'

The pair looked shyly at each other.

'If there are no further questions, let's take a short break,' said Pak Tony, motioning to a door at the side of the room. 'You'll find all kinds of fresh juices and natural treats at the buffet. I highly recommend the chai-spiced energy balls.'

Lorenzo glumly followed the group to the door. He would have preferred coffee and *cornetti*.

A verandah outside was shaded by bamboo thatching, offering some relief from the blazing sun. Remy bounded towards the buffet and began piling food onto a plate.

'I am *starving*,' he said, dipping a handful of carrot sticks into a tub of hummus. He leaned towards Lorenzo and muttered, 'It is only day one, and already I am eating more vegetables than I eat in a week in Paris. Raw carrots are for rabbits.'

'Tell me about it,' chimed in Janelle. She took a crisp stick of red capsicum from a bowl and bit into it. 'Yum, yum.' She and Remy laughed together.

'Where is the coffee?' asked Lorenzo, staring at a bowl of brown powder. 'This is not coffee.' He pinched some between his thumb and forefinger and sniffed it, flinching at the aroma.

'It's chicory root powder,' said Cara, pointing to a handwritten sign behind the bowl. 'A bit like dandelion coffee.'

Lorenzo wiped his fingers on a serviette. 'You cannot make proper coffee from *flowers*.'

'Lucky I'm a tea drinker then,' said Henry, riffling through a basket of tea bags next to the hot water urn. His face fell. 'They're all herbal.'

'See? *Everything* is good for us.' Lorenzo walked to the far end of the buffet, where a range of fruit was displayed. 'I am looking for something sweet.' He selected a waxy red fruit from a large silver bowl.

'*Jambu*,' said a voice behind him, and Lorenzo turned to find Pak Ketut, the driver.

'*Ciao*,' he said. 'You are back already. Lavinia made it to Shakti?'

'Yes, it is not far,' said Pak Ketut, watching Lorenzo bite into the *jambu* and screw up his face at the tartness. He laughed. 'It is sour?'

'A little.' Lorenzo threw the fruit into a thicket of bushes beyond the verandah.

Pak Ketut followed it with his eyes. 'Very special to our children,' he said. 'We call them temple apples. After important ceremonies, the priest will give *jambu* to the young ones. They are like candies.'

Lorenzo felt awkward now, for throwing the uneaten portion away.

Annie appeared beside them, holding a piece of the same fruit. 'What did you call them?' she asked the driver. '*Jembut*?'

'Missus Annie!' The driver's eyes widened. He took a step towards her and lowered his voice, looking furtive. 'Please, do not say that word again.'

'*Jembut*?'

The driver flinched.

'What does it mean?'

Pak Ketut leaned towards her and whispered, 'The hair . . . down there.' He gestured at his sarong.

Annie stared at him for a moment. Then she threw back her head and laughed. 'Oh, I'm so sorry,' she said. 'Lordy, I need some language instruction! Do you think you could help me, Pak Ketut?

I've been meaning to take some Indonesian lessons for months. I'd be happy to pay you.'

The driver thought about this. 'There is no need for money. I will teach you some Bahasa Indonesia in the break times. But you must promise never to say that word again.' He grinned. 'You shocked me, Missus Annie.'

As the pair continued to chatter, Lorenzo drifted back towards the buffet. He selected a rice paper roll; it was floppy and cold, filled with unappetising vegetables, but he was ravenous, so he shovelled it into his mouth anyway. As he chewed, he checked his phone and saw a message from Lavinia: *Please call me as soon as you can.*

He moved away from the group and stood under a frangipani tree, holding the phone to his ear. After six rings he was on the verge of hanging up, when Lavinia answered.

'Oh, Lorenzo, I can hardly breathe,' she wept.

Lorenzo didn't panic. Lavinia was emotional at the best of times. 'What's the matter?'

'The kinesiologist did some muscle testing on me this morning. She told me *exactly* why we're not getting pregnant.' Lavinia's voice sounded strangled with tears. 'My core minerals are depleted because I was so thin as a model. I starved myself for *years*. It was good for my portfolio, but ruined my fertility.'

'You're not as thin as you used to be,' he observed. It was true; since concluding her modelling career, Lavinia had gained almost eight kilos.

'I know, I know,' she wailed, 'but the damage was done a decade ago. I am so *angry*. Why didn't anyone tell me that being a model might *murder* my future babies?'

'Now, *amore mio*,' he consoled. 'I am sure there is something we can do.'

'Maybe.' She sniffed. 'I am eating a banana right now.'

He smiled.

'I have a nutrition plan,' she continued. 'Maca, cacao, coconut oil, almonds, bananas . . . these are fertility foods to help create a supportive internal environment for our baby. You will have to help me, Lorenzo.'

'Of course,' he said. 'I am a banana specialist.'

She didn't laugh. 'I *really* want a baby, Lorenzo.' Her voice wavered. 'More than anything I've ever wanted my whole life.'

He didn't know what to say.

'Did you hear me?' she asked.

'Yes, Lavinia,' he replied. 'I understand.'

But he didn't understand, he'd come to realise. He'd never been struck to the heart by the charms of other people's babies, never been visited by paternal pangs. Life without children seemed an entirely palatable prospect: a life of artistic pursuit and purpose without having to perpetuate his genetic imprint. There was nothing distinctive about having children, he'd decided; the whole world was doing it, like a pack of rutting dogs. Perhaps it was more courageous *not* to do it, in fact. But Lorenzo could never say that aloud. Certainly not to Lavinia, and not even to his closest friends.

'Thank you,' said Lavinia, calmer now. 'I have to go, it's time for my belly blessing. There'll be flowers and holy water and a Balinese priest.' He could hear that she was smiling.

'I'm sure it will be perfect,' he said, smiling too. 'Everything will turn out exactly as it should.' Such sentiments could soothe her, he knew. '*Ciao, amore.*'

He slid his phone back into his pocket and stood for a moment, transfixed by the fallen frangipanis carpeting the earth. Pure white stars, once perfect on the tree, their edges now brown and curling in the heat. Nothing in life remained unblemished. Everything was subject to the inexorable cycle of birth, degradation, death and rebirth. He stooped down and plucked a large white bloom from the ground. For a moment he held it to his nose, breathing in its fragrance. Then turning back towards the pavilion, he tossed it away.

HEIGHTS

We are going to die, Remy thought, trying to ignore the burning sensation in the soles of his feet. Standing on the scorching wooden jetty, resisting the urge to urinate in his swimming trunks. He wasn't sure which was more disconcerting: the rusted metal harness into which he'd just been strapped, or the Australian woman who'd been clipped in next to him.

'Would holding hands make you feel better?' asked Janelle, laying a hand on his arm. 'I'm not sure I agree with desensitisation therapy. You must be terrified.'

'*Non.*' He shrugged her hand away, too nervous to explain himself in English.

A smiling Balinese man on the boat, presumably the skipper, was attempting to start the outboard motor. The man next to him, with a zoom-lens camera slung around his neck, tried to help. When their vehement yanks yielded nothing, a third man stepped down from the jetty to assist, a cigarette clenched between his teeth.

Instantly, tsunami-mind assaulted Remy, black and white images bombarding his brain like a manga cartoon. He watched the slim sheaf of cigarette ash drift in slow motion into the diesel tank and, a moment later, the Vesuvius-like eruption that spewed their bloodied body parts across Jimbaran Bay.

Remy gasped and closed his eyes, just as the engine sputtered into life. The smoker climbed out of the boat and stood next to them. 'Going soon, boss,' he said. 'Okay?'

'Not okay,' Remy replied. But the man paid him no heed; he was too busy talking to Janelle in Indonesian. She was clever too, apparently. Watching her converse, Remy wondered absently why she hid her shapely figure in such an ugly long-sleeved top and board shorts.

The Balinese man nodded at the boat, which was now puttering away from the jetty. 'Good luck,' he said. 'Smile for photos.' He pointed at the photographer on the boat.

'*Terima kasih*,' Janelle replied.

'I feel betrayed,' said Remy tersely, watching their towline unravel as the boat moved further away from the jetty. 'You are supposed to hate flying. Why are you so relaxed?'

Janelle threw back her head and laughed, exposing the smooth flesh of her neck. It made a disproportionately strong impression on Remy, perhaps because of how little he could see of the rest of her.

'Parasailing isn't flying. And it's very safe, on the whole,' she said. 'There aren't that many accidents. It's not like skydiving or hang-gliding.' She adjusted her helmet, prompting Remy to fidget with his. 'I've done the research.'

He grunted. 'But that towline is flimsy. And our harnesses are worn.'

'True. But most parasailing accidents involve on-shore landings and high winds. We've got neither today.' She waved a hand at the aquamarine bay, sparkling like an exotic jewel before them. 'Just look at that.'

Remy could barely appreciate it. 'Why do you . . . ?' He gestured at the thick white substance on her nose, mimicking applying sunscreen.

'Oh, it's zinc. Not very attractive, I know. But it's the only sunscreen that totally blocks out the sun's rays. If I get sunburnt, I just turn a nasty red and peel. I don't have that lovely European skin of yours.'

Had she just told him his skin was *lovely*?

The towline was taut and completely extended now. Remy glanced nervously at the two Balinese crew members standing on the jetty behind them, holding up the red-and-white striped chute between them. The wind was making it billow in places and Remy scanned it anxiously, checking for holes.

'I suppose Europeans don't wear zinc?' Janelle laughed self-consciously and, with her index fingers, began to smooth the clay-like substance on either side of her nose.

'*Non*. French women never wear it. And they do not wear . . . what is *that*?' He pointed at the navy-blue long-sleeved top she wore over her swimsuit.

'We call them rashies in Australia,' she said. 'It keeps out the sun.'

Remy shook his head. 'French women, never.'

'Oh, I'm sure,' she said, wiping her fingers on the back of her hands. 'And French women don't get fat. *And* their children don't throw food. That's what the books say, right?'

He couldn't tell if she was poking fun or annoyed. 'But that is not . . . *Oh mon dieu!*'

His words were drowned out by the thundering of the boat's engine as it accelerated away from the jetty and out towards the open sea.

'Pull back!' yelled one of the crew members behind them.

Remy and Janelle leaned back together, resisting the pull of the towline. Remy also tried to resist the darkening tunnel encroaching on his peripheral vision.

A man bellowed in his ear, 'Three, two, one. Go!'

Janelle tried to take a few steps towards the edge of the jetty, as they'd been instructed in their pre-flight briefing, but Remy was immobilised. A second later the towline dragged them both towards the edge and they tumbled off, their legs entangled. Remy felt his left foot touch the water, then suddenly they lurched up.

He screamed and gripped the rubber handlebars of his harness, screwing his eyes shut as they rocketed skyward. From some faraway place, he noticed he sounded like a girl. Janelle whooped gleefully and Remy was reminded of what a girl really sounded like. Even so, he couldn't open his eyes.

'Wow,' said Janelle, after a while. 'Remy, it's so beautiful. Take a look.'

Remy was aware that they were no longer shooting upwards, and now that neither was screaming, a curious quietness had enveloped them. The boat's engine was a distant purr. Little else was audible beyond the occasional rustling of the canopy stretched above them. It was a curious sensation, floating blind and almost silent, buffeted by the sea breeze.

'Are you alright?' Janelle asked gently.

'I can't open my eyes,' he said through gritted teeth.

'Well, don't look out *there*.' Her voice was close and kind. 'Just look at me.'

'I'll . . . try.' Remy turned his head in her direction and opened his eyes.

The blue sky framed her face, strands of hair clung to her zinc-covered cheeks, and her eyes were wild with exhilaration. The breath emptied from his lungs; she was the most natural beauty he'd ever seen.

'You're okay, aren't you?' She beamed at him.

He nodded and, tentatively, looked down. His hairy, stubby toes dangled side-by-side with her perfect pedicure. Below them, white-winged seabirds wheeled in slow circles, riding invisible eddies. Further down, symmetrical wrinkles moved across the great blue span and a foaming wake stretched behind their boat, like a long lace bridal veil.

Janelle extended her hand again, and this time he gripped it gratefully. '*Merci*,' he murmured. '*Merci beaucoup*.'

They dipped suddenly as the boat turned, but ascended again when it sped into a straight. Remy's heart thumped faster with the altered sensation, but he no longer felt as though he might faint. On the contrary, he was beginning to feel energised. He was seventy-five metres above the sea and actually starting to *enjoy* himself.

Grinning at Janelle, he flapped his arms. Then he threw back his head and howled, like a wolf at the moon. She copied him, and they exploded into laughter. They carried on like this for some time, yowling like teenagers.

After a while, when their laughter quietened, they simply floated together in wonder, suspended above the sea. The light reflected mirror-like off the water, but if he squinted, Remy could just make out the hazy forms of distant islands. The splendour of the day was upon him—or perhaps it was the endorphin rush of drifting so high above sea level—and Remy felt as if his body was comprised of sunbeams.

Exhaling with a long sigh, he stopped resisting altogether. Sinking into the harness, he released his grip on the handlebars and let his hands dangle at his sides. The boat began carving out figures of eight beneath them and Remy soared serenely through the long, languid curves.

After several minutes, the boat turned back towards the jetty.

'You're alright, aren't you,' said Janelle, more a statement than a question this time.

Remy nodded, surprised too.

'Looks like we're landing soon,' she said. 'Which is a shame, since you're doing so well.'

In a moment of insanity, Remy felt like kissing her. Instead, he simply nodded, mute with euphoria.

The driver reduced the throttle and they drifted gently downwards. Remy drank in the moment. The unblemished sky stretching to the horizon, the golden arc of beach dotted with cheerful umbrellas, the coconut palms standing like sentinels along the coastline. And, close enough to touch, an intriguing Australian woman with eyes like rare gemstones.

A second boat, manned by land crew, shadowed them as they descended further. It pulled alongside just as their feet touched the water. The engine was cut completely, and Remy and Janelle splashed down into the sea. Two crew members leaned into the water, unhooked them from the chute, and helped them clamber aboard.

The crew members chattered in Balinese as the boat puttered back to the jetty. Remy and Janelle sat together in the prow, dripping and ecstatic.

Over coffee at a small *warung* on Jimbaran Beach, the group's parasailing stories gained new embellishments with every iteration. The six of them sat on long wooden stools, watched by a wizened old woman behind the counter.

'It was incredible,' enthused Annie, sipping on her Diet Coke. She nudged Henry, who was hunched over a coconut, sucking out the juice with a bamboo straw. 'I didn't really want to do it at first, not that I'm scared of heights, or anything. But Henry talked me through it the whole way, didn't you? And while we were up there, we spotted a . . . what was it?'

'A great crested tern,' said Henry. 'Common as mud around these parts, but fascinating to observe from above. I've only ever birdwatched from below. I wish I'd got a photo of it for my mate Jim. He'd be green with envy.'

As if summoned, a slight Balinese man approached their table. 'You want photos?' He pushed a flip album in their direction. 'Only fifty thousand rupiah.'

Lorenzo leaned over to inspect them, smiling at the expressions of shock and elation on the parasailers' faces. 'I'll buy one for my wife, to prove I'm working just as hard as her.' He felt for his wallet, then passed the man a crisp blue note. The seller slipped Lorenzo's selection into a commemorative frame.

'Is it cheaper if we buy a few together?' asked Annie.

The man tilted his head to one side as if confused.

'What about thirty thousand each, if we all buy one?' she proposed.

The man shook his head. 'No, ma'am, that price is too low.'

Annie frowned. 'There's supposed to be a culture of bargaining here, right?'

Remy shrugged. 'But thirty thousand rupiah is . . .' he did the mental calculations, 'only two or three euro? That is still a good price.' Especially since the scrawny-looking photo seller had a desperate air about him. Even more so than the beggars Remy encountered outside the stairs descending into the Paris Métro, who called out to passing commuters from beneath their tattered blankets.

Remy turned to Janelle. 'Today's memories are priceless! I will buy one, too. Actually, two.' He held up two fingers at the seller, then leaned closer to Janelle. 'You choose the one you like best, it is my gift to you.'

'Oh.' Janelle looked surprised. 'You don't have to do that.'

'I want to. They would be resuscitating me on the beach right now if you weren't there earlier.'

'I didn't help *that* much.' Janelle giggled. 'But thank you, that's a lovely thought. This one's funny . . .' She pointed at a photo of them landing in the water, their faces a mirror of each other. Eyebrows arched in surprise, mouths open, hands clasped.

Annie and Henry followed suit, each selecting photos and paying the seller.

Then the man turned expectantly to Cara, the only member of the group who hadn't yet purchased a photograph, but she shook her head.

'You must buy a souvenir too,' urged Remy. 'To remember this moment together, *n'est-ce-pas?*'

Cara surveyed him coolly. 'I live here. I don't need a souvenir.' She waved the seller away.

Why was Cara so bristly? Remy wondered, observing her over the rim of his lukewarm coffee. She certainly didn't have Janelle's friendly manner, which Remy had come to consider an Australian trait. But cultural stereotypes were dangerous, he reminded himself: he was not quite the Frenchman he was born to be, after all.

He could still remember the evening he'd realised that, aged twenty-four. He'd been sharing a meal with his parents on the fourth floor of his spacious apartment in Saint-Germain-des-Prés, bequeathed by his great-grandparents. Despite living in the same building commissioned by their forebears in the nineteenth century—his parents occupied *l'étage noble*, the second floor, while renters occupied the rest—they rarely shared a meal together beyond weekly Sunday dinners. But on this particular Friday evening, Remy had just completed his first week as an entry-level investment officer at the historic Société Paris bank. He was feeling slightly overwhelmed by his new responsibilities and his mother had offered to cook.

'Well,' his father had declared with satisfaction, as he decanted a bottle of St-Estèphe Bordeaux into a Dansk crystal flask, 'we couldn't have predicted *this* in your younger years, could we?'

Remy instantly understood the inference. Compared to his confrères at the exclusive private school he'd attended, Remy had always been a little too goofy, a little too outdoorsy, and a little too slovenly for his father's liking. A threat, of sorts, to their conservative pedigree.

'I was concerned in your last year of university,' his mother added, in a veiled reference to his former girlfriend, a professor in gender studies at the Sorbonne. 'It's a responsibility, being a Brive. You've chosen well, Remy. Claudine de Croix works in finance too, doesn't she? You two should catch up.'

He'd acknowledged her words with a compliant nod, while his stomach churned. *Claudine de Croix?* His mother had been trying to matchmake them since childhood, and Remy could understand why: Claudine was pretty, poised and intelligent. But with a dangerously inflated sense of her own self-importance, as far as Remy was concerned, which his mother somehow failed to see. This wilful or ignorant blindness by his mother to the follies of her own social class was a hazard, Remy decided, and a trait he didn't wish to emulate.

As he looked across the vast polished dining table at his parents, Remy felt a growing panic. Tsunami-mind was filling the room with spectres of their noble ancestry; not quite part of *les 200 familles*, but traceable still to the Revolution. The figures began milling about the table, peering down their Gallic noses at him, moving closer and closer until Remy clamped his eyes shut and blurted, 'Arrête!' When he opened his eyes again and observed the alarmed look on his parents' faces, Remy felt even more keenly aware of his departure from the mould of *being a Brive*.

After his parents left that evening, Remy had sat alone in the living room long into the night, staring at the glowing embers in the fireplace. He was expected, he knew, to marry and populate this very apartment building with children who could run between the floors. His sister, Camille, three years his senior, would have been up to the task—*she* was a classic Brive. Practically a carbon copy of their mother, she was already married into a family of lineage in Neuilly-sur-Seine. Her privileged world as a wife, mother and part-time solicitor was a natural extension of her upbringing.

But Remy? He was a messy aberration within his well-bred family. He could think of nothing worse than procreating with Claudine de Croix and herding their children for the holidays to Brive-la-Gaillarde in the Corrèze region. He was not looking forward to inheriting his parents' draughty chateau there; in fact, he felt largely undeserving of all the bounty accompanying his genealogy. His hefty bank balance alone embarrassed him, speaking only of the efforts of his forebears and describing nothing of himself. Remy resolved that night to remedy this situation through personal exertion.

Over the next few years he'd done just that, working ridiculous hours and rising steadily through the bank's hierarchy until, finally, he had twenty-two staff members reporting to him. But even when his astute investment decisions allowed him to purchase a studio apartment in the exclusive Marais precinct, which he then rented out for a princely sum, Remy's uneasiness never receded. Tsunami-mind still accosted him at inopportune moments, running twenty-second brain clips of stern uniformed officers—the career police—bursting into meetings and interrogating him in front of clients. *Did you, or did you not, receive your first career break on the basis of ancestry alone?*

Even after a decade at the bank, Remy felt frightened by what the answer to this question might be. And perhaps, he reflected now, it was this self-doubt, in addition to his crippling fear of heights, that had contributed to his faltering in the tower at La Défense. Remy stared into his cup of bitter Balinese coffee, his face burning at the memory of how he'd destroyed any chance he might have had of promotion to the revered role of General Manager, Investment.

A gust of wind whipped a blast of sand into the *warung*, interrupting the others' conversation, and Remy looked up from his reminiscing. Ominous-looking clouds had gathered above the beach, like a puffy grey blanket trapping the baking heat below.

'We were lucky this morning,' said Annie, just as the first drops of rain began to sprinkle across the sand. 'There won't be any parasailing this afternoon, I'd say.'

Pak Tony poked his head around the *warung* door and motioned towards the car park. 'A storm's coming. Pak Ketut is here with the minibus. Time to make our way back to Ubud.'

After paying for their drinks, the group filed back to the bus. Remy was grateful for the cooling rain, a temporary respite from the oppressive heat.

Inside the minibus, Annie and Henry sat together. *They seem peculiarly well matched*, Remy thought: the consummate American talker and the quintessential English listener. Even the chic Italian and spiky Cara had evidently created some kind of bond while they were in the air, taking a seat together at the front of the bus. Pak Tony's parasailing tactic was clever, throwing together individuals who might otherwise avoid each other.

Janelle boarded the bus in front of Remy, but paused to talk to the driver. Pak Ketut greeted her like an old friend. It was a habit of Janelle's, it seemed, to converse with any Balinese person she encountered: retreat staff, the parasailing crew, even the old woman in the *warung*. This dashed Remy's hopes of following her to a seat, so he walked nonchalantly to the rear of the bus. Pak Tony bounded on a moment later, prompting Janelle to move along the aisle.

'You've all done some serious fear-facing today,' Pak Tony exclaimed, as they pulled out of the car park. 'Especially Remy. Great work!'

Remy grinned as the others applauded; then he waved at Janelle and patted the adjacent seat. To his delight, she continued down the aisle and sat next to him.

'Hello,' he whispered, resisting an outrageous impulse to squeeze her knee.

'Hi,' she whispered back, her eyes trained on Pak Tony. Remy tried to follow suit, but her physical presence was distracting. He could smell her, he was sure; a heady combination of coconut, citrus and sea salt.

'Are you wearing perfume?' he murmured. Just then, a repulsive stench filled the minibus, the foul odour of rotten fish, overripe watermelon and rancid butter.

'That's not nice, Remy.' Janelle pinched her nose between her thumb and forefinger.

'I didn't mean . . .'

'Close the vents,' Pak Tony ordered the driver, as the bus passed by a mound of rubbish spewing out of a huge concrete receptacle onto the road, on which several dogs and a brood of chickens were scavenging.

'Remy,' Pak Tony continued, when the smell began to clear, 'what did you learn today about facing fears? Did you use your magic bottle of love up in the sky?'

'Actually . . .' Remy glanced at Janelle. 'I didn't have to. I tried to relax and focus on the beauty around me.' He stole another glance at Janelle. 'Having someone with me helped a lot.'

Pak Tony smiled. 'You're right, Remy. Those techniques are helpful, especially sharing the experience. You embraced your fear, which is exactly what desensitisation therapy is all about. I'm proud of you.' He led the group in another rousing round of applause.

Remy nodded, quietly proud too. A month ago, if someone had told him he'd be parasailing off the coast of Bali—with an enticing Australian woman at his side—he simply wouldn't have believed it.

'Just a brief reminder of what we're doing now,' Pak Tony went on. 'We're heading back to Ubud for the first of our passion talks. Janelle and Annie are doing theirs today. Tomorrow, it's Henry and Lorenzo, right after our Balinese water cleansing ceremony. Then, on day four, we have Cara and Remy.'

Remy was privately glad he'd been scheduled for the final round of passion talks. Even with two more days to prepare, he was struggling to identify a suitable topic. He enjoyed chess, Greco-Roman wrestling, and hiking in green precincts within a short train ride of Paris. But could any of those be branded a *passion*?

'Are you ready for your talk?' he asked Janelle.

'I think so,' she said. 'I changed my mind about my topic this morning, though. I redid the whole thing before breakfast.'

'Why?'

She shifted in her seat. 'It's a long story.'

'I love long stories.'

Her eyes narrowed, as if weighing him up.

'Only if you want to tell me,' he added.

After a moment, Janelle said, 'Okay. Well, I've been sponsoring an orangutan in Borneo for a few years now and I was going to talk about the role of palm oil in destroying habitat, because that's what big corporates usually plant after they knock down the rainforest. It's happening all over the world, not just in Indonesia. I'm a member of Global Forest Watch.' Her earnest eyes made Remy's stomach somersault. 'Did you know that the word orangutan actually means "person of the forest" in Malay?'

Primates were a subject about which Remy was almost entirely ignorant. 'I think I saw something about that once when I was little,' he said, trying to dredge up a distant memory. 'A film with Sigourney Weaver in it.'

'*Gorillas in the Mist*?' Janelle laughed. 'That was about gorillas in Rwanda.'

Wrong species, wrong continent. *What a fool I am making of myself*, Remy thought. He turned to the bus window and watched the tropical downpour, trying to conceal his embarrassment. The rain was spearing down, causing traffic chaos. Motorbikes lined the roadside while drivers scrambled to remove raincoats from panniers. Poorly drained parts of the road were awash with floating leaf litter, plastic bottles and other rubbish.

The minibus stopped at a busy intersection, next to a convoy of other vehicles. Remy noticed a large electronic timer attached to a traffic light, its red numerals counting down the seconds to green. A Balinese melody blared out of a speaker, a jarring jangle of xylophones, gongs, chimes and cymbals, audible even over the deluge. Remy could only presume the music was for the entertainment of waiting motorists.

'How can they call that music?' he muttered.

'Well, it's about five hundred years old, for starters,' said Janelle. 'It's called gamelan. Almost every village has a set of instruments and anyone can learn to play them, as long as they're prepared to practise. It's like every suburb in Melbourne having a community orchestra, or in Paris . . .'

'Every arrondissement,' said Remy. He felt boorish for dismissing the music so readily. 'You seem very knowledgeable about . . . gamelan,' he observed. 'Is that the topic of your talk?'

'No.' Janelle laughed rather guiltily. 'I just read about it in the *Lonely Planet*.'

Remy smiled. 'What *is* your topic then?'

Pak Ketut turned his head and hailed Pak Tony. 'I take a detour,' he called, steering the bus onto a narrow side street. 'Too much water.'

The road was partially flooded, but Remy was surprised to see most motorbike riders simply standing out of their seats and riding on through the torrent. He glanced back at Janelle to gauge her reaction to this sight, and was horrified to see tears in her eyes.

'What's the matter?' he asked. 'Did I say something wrong?'

She shook her head, composing herself. 'Are you ready for my long story?'

Remy listened quietly as she told him about her family. A father who'd passed away prematurely when Janelle was fourteen, leaving behind a mother who'd become permanently afraid of life beyond her home—especially of flying. She described her close relationship with her older brother, Kyle, and his teenage daughter, Arabella, and the last time she'd seen her niece. How they'd walked along the beach together, a few weeks after Janelle's twenty-ninth birthday, and talked about the cruel comments Arabella had been subjected to in the schoolyard. And then the contents of the email Janelle had received only yesterday from Kyle that had shocked her to the core.

'The doctor thinks Bella's bulimic,' she explained, her voice quivering. 'I mean, I knew she was getting thinner, but I didn't realise she was sick. They're taking her to an eating disorders clinic. The worst thing is, on the night I saw her, Arabella told me that she was being bullied at school about her body. She told me how it made her feel. But all I did was offer a bunch of stupid words that didn't help at all.'

A single tear trickled down Janelle's cheek and Remy lifted up the edge of his t-shirt to wipe it. 'It is all I have, sorry,' he said.

'Thank you,' she said, letting him dab her face. 'Good thing we're up the back of the bus. I feel so powerless. I'm livid with all those bloody fashion magazines spreading ridiculous expectations about women's bodies. Young girls like Bella are impressionable. They try to conform to these stupid ideals of skinny-as-a-rake women with big boobs. Can't we contemplate a bit of diversity?'

Remy didn't understand all of Janelle's words, but he saw the distress in her eyes.

'And it's not just young girls,' she continued, 'it's women of all ages. Did you see the cosmetic surgery centres we passed today on our way to Jimbaran? Full of Western women paying for new breasts or a designer vagina.' She stopped and looked at Remy apologetically. 'I'm sorry, Remy, I'm ranting.'

'You are very upset for your niece,' he said. 'That is reasonable. Will you talk about this at your passion talk?'

'I wouldn't call it talking, but yes,' she replied. 'I'm dedicating my passion talk to Arabella. Pak Ketut took me to the markets this morning to get a few things for my . . . outfit.' She looked briefly terrified, then her expression returned to normal. 'Could you possibly film it for me? I want to send it to Arabella afterwards in a private YouTube link.'

'Of course,' said Remy, impressed by how much Janelle seemed to care. About the orangutans of Borneo, the world's rainforests, the gamelan orchestras of Bali, teenagers with eating disorders and, naturally, her own family. He considered what *he* cared about. The last time he'd cried was after the defeat of Paris Saint-Germain to archrivals Montpellier in round 32 of the Ligue 1 football season. *Janelle's compassion is more than refreshing*, he thought. *It's intoxicating.*

Catching himself staring at her, he turned away. Outside the window, he saw a woman squatting in a narrow irrigation ditch running alongside a small shop signposted *Bengkel*. Inside, two mechanics were hunched over a motorbike, a mass of tools and wire coils strewn around them. The woman was within their line of vision, but neither of them paid her any attention. She simply crouched in the ditch barely two metres away, holding a newspaper above her head with one hand, and cradling a baby in the other.

She shifted her position slightly, to hitch her long sarong above her knees and turn her face away from the road. Only then did Remy realise she was defecating.

Mortified, he looked away. He had suffered humiliation, he'd thought, in the tower at La Défense. But *this* was the definition of true humiliation, a life with no choice but to relieve yourself in public. Remy's eyes began to sting with the burgeoning realisation of his own privilege. He'd lived his entire life in the seventh arrondissement of Paris, fortunate enough to be born into a moneyed family. No opportunity had ever been denied him, except for the ones he sabotaged himself—as he'd done so comprehensively two months earlier.

'Where I come from,' Remy said quietly, turning back to Janelle, 'there is no trash in the street. Everything is so . . . orderly. The Métro arrives on time, we don't have to wait for anything. Except maybe for fresh baguettes at the bakery, but that is easy because everyone stands nicely in queues, you know? Not like here.' He waved a hand at the motorists surging forward en masse. 'I can see now how lucky I've been all my life. Without ever really truly appreciating it.'

Janelle's eyes shone with recognition. 'I feel that too.'

'What I have in Paris, compared to what the people have here is . . .' *Indecent*, he thought, shaking his head.

He cast a sidelong glance at Janelle, wondering how she might react if she knew the extent of his affluence. If he told her how, when he'd graduated with honours in economics from Dauphine a decade back, his parents had given him an entire floor of their apartment building in Saint-Germain-des-Prés. Just as they'd done for Camille when she'd completed her law degree. Remy had since acquired the Marais studio with the proceeds of his own hard work, but in all those years of striving, he'd never had to worry once about how to feed himself. In the world beyond the bus window, Remy could see, nothing came easily: food, shelter, work, or even basic human dignity. The poorest people of Bali were battling far more pressing problems than trifling aversions to heights or flying.

'Janelle,' he murmured. 'I look out there, I see people just surviving. While we Westerners are worried about first-world problems. How many Balinese have ever gone parasailing or flown in an aeroplane?'

'Hardly any, I imagine,' Janelle said. 'It's too expensive.'

'Exactly,' said Remy, his disquiet growing. 'People like us, we're just wasting time. We should save up our fear for when something really goes wrong. We need to start living again.'

And caring again, he thought, watching Janelle nod in emphatic agreement. *Why did I stop caring?*

When he was at Dauphine, he'd harboured all manner of undergraduate dreams for a better world and thoughts as to how he might contribute to it. But these public-spirited goals had been increasingly sidelined during his decade of career development, his focus redirected from social equity to company equity schemes. The shift had gone unchallenged, he realised now, by a network of family and friends whose life philosophy was, for the most part, oriented towards the pursuit of security and comfort. It was a common and understandable desire, especially when children were involved, but did that make it right?

Remy stared out the minibus window at the potholed roads, dangerously low powerlines and newly built Western-style villas advancing like cancer across rice fields. Pak Ketut had told him that most of these villas were actually foreign-owned, the tyranny of Western wealth encroaching on prime agricultural land. What might this unstoppable advance of globalised growth be doing to local people and cultures?

Remy sighed, unable to answer his own questions. Being in Bali was reminding him of an uncomfortable truth: that the pursuit of wealth rarely occurred in a vacuum. That the very action of getting ahead invariably meant that others were left behind.

―⸝

Janelle stood in front of the group, fidgeting with the cuffs of her blouse. She wore unusually warm clothes for the tropics: a long-sleeved shirt, blue jeans and, oddly enough, white cotton gloves, a beanie, a scarf, and a pair of fluffy boots. Remy was struggling to keep his t-shirt on in the heat, but this layered outfit was obviously part of Janelle's passion talk. Positioned next to her, facing the audience, was a standing easel with a ring-bound set of laminated cardboard sheets resting on it. Handwritten in large letters on the cover sheet were the words *For Bella.*

Janelle nodded at Remy, and he bent down and activated an MP3 player placed beneath his chair, with speakers attached. Then he held up his iPhone and pressed record.

As the opening bars of Taylor Swift's 'Fifteen' sounded, Janelle looked directly at the phone. 'You're fifteen, Bella,' she said, over the strumming of country guitar. 'Let me show you what I've learned at twenty-nine.' She moved to the easel and turned over the first cardboard sheet, revealing the words:

The brain inside my head outshines the style of my hair.

Smiling shyly at the group, she removed her beanie and shook out her long hair. Annie gave a little cheer, but Remy wasn't exactly sure why. Then, moving her head in time to the music, Janelle turned over the next cardboard sheet.

Sometimes a girl has to stick her neck out to be true to herself.

She started unwinding her scarf, a tinge of pink creeping up her cheeks, and tossed it aside. Then she began peeling off the gloves, one at a time. She turned over the next sheet, then held up her hands and fluttered her fingers.

*These fingers aren't manicured, but they've held
the hands of the dying.*

Cara clapped, and several others joined in. Janelle's eyes glistened, and Remy wondered if the hands she'd held had been those of her father.

She fumbled with the buttons of her blouse and Remy's eyes widened as she tugged it open. It fell to the floor, revealing a flimsy white camisole.

My heart is so much fuller than these breasts will ever be.

Henry whooped and whistled and Remy stared at him, hard. Janelle closed her eyes, as if to block out her audience, and began to sway rather stiffly. But slowly her face relaxed a little, and her movements became freer too. When she opened her eyes again, Remy beamed at her, trying to communicate the extent of his admiration. To his great relief, she smiled back, ignoring Henry altogether.

After turning over the next sheet, she lifted the edge of her camisole, revealing the luscious curve of her waist.

This belly's not a washboard, but it can grow a miracle inside it.

Remy's mouth went dry and he had to concentrate to hold the phone steady. The camisole floated to the floor and she stood before them in a white bra. Then she reached down and unzipped her jeans.

Why analyse the size of thighs—yours or mine?

She waggled her hips a little; then, turning her back on the group, slid the jeans down over her thighs. She playfully poked out her bottom and flipped over the next sheet.

If my butt looks big in this, the earth will keep on spinning.
(Because it's not a race for winning, those magazines
I'm binning, and I'll just keep on grinning!)

Remy forced himself to chuckle along with the rest of the group, watching Janelle gyrate in white knickers.

She sat down on the ground, kicked her feet up in the air and wrenched off the jeans and fluffy boots. Pitching them to one side, she stood up and began to dance around the room. The group cheered her on, as she flipped over further pages at intervals:

Your body is a friend, I've learned, and one worth treating well.
Starvation is punishment, a type of living hell.
Does the world need thinner bodies, stronger muscles,
whiter teeth?
Whatever's on the outside, it's always you beneath.

As the final bars of 'Fifteen' echoed around the room, she looked straight at Remy and the camera and formed a heart shape with her hands.

A stunned silence followed. Still standing in her underwear, Janelle lowered her eyes.

Suddenly, Annie leaped up and hugged Janelle, enthusiastically congratulating her. Cara followed, smiling broadly and murmuring appreciation. Pak Tony stood up next, moving towards Janelle as she hurriedly pulled on her jeans and blouse. When she was dressed, he enfolded all three women in his tanned arms.

'That was truly inspiring, Janelle,' he said, then turned to the men of the group. 'Wasn't it wonderful?'

'*Stupendo!*' said Lorenzo, stepping forward to kiss her on both cheeks, while Henry shuffled forward and muttered, 'Good job.'

Remy simply stood gazing at Janelle, not trusting himself to speak. When she looked at him, he pretended to check the video on his phone and then, rebuking himself as a coward, propelled himself forwards. But before their bodies could connect, he aborted the embrace. If he actually *touched* her, the whole room might know. He shook her hand clumsily instead. 'I'll upload it to YouTube from my phone, if you like.'

'Oh, yes, please,' she replied. 'For Arabella to see.'

She smiled at him and her mouth kept moving, but he couldn't take in the words, distracted as he was by her dazzling eyes, her bewitching beauty spots and the comfortable weight of her hand in his.

Suddenly it occurred to Remy that he had spent years—no, decades—of his life preoccupied wih banalities. But within thirty-six hours of meeting this spirited Australian woman—who not only cared about social issues but was courageous enough to try to change them—the extent of his own inaction had been exposed.

With a shiver of recognition, Remy dropped Janelle's hand. He would never be indifferent again.

Later, after Annie had delivered her passion talk, entitled 'The Dogs of Bali Matter', Remy followed the others back to their accommodation block comprised of six adjacent rooms. All on the ground floor, with individual balconies overlooking an expanse of landscaped garden.

'I'm off to Petulu with Pak Ketut now,' announced Henry, as they crossed the neat lawn towards their rooms. 'Does anyone want to join me? It's only a twenty-minute drive.'

'What's interesting about it?' asked Annie.

'Well, apparently at sundown every day about five thousand wild herons fly along the main street. It's supposed to be amazing and incredibly noisy.' Henry shook his head. 'In England a heron is a rare sight. I can't imagine five thousand of them at once.'

'I'm in, then,' said Annie. 'Do I have time to freshen up first?'

'Of course,' said Henry, stopping outside the door to his room. 'But I daresay the birds won't care what you look like.'

'It's not the birds I'm concerned about,' said Annie, with an enigmatic smile. 'I'll meet you in the foyer in fifteen. Have a nice night, everyone,' she called, before disappearing into her room.

'Would anyone like to . . .' Remy glanced at Janelle, then at the remaining members of the group, 'have a drink on my balcony?'

Lorenzo looked apologetic. 'I am visiting Lavinia at Shakti tonight for a couples ceremony. Tomorrow maybe?' He opened his door. '*Ciao*.'

Cara shook her head too. 'I'm tired. I'm just going to order room service and go to bed early. See you tomorrow.' She retreated into her room.

Remy looked hopefully at Janelle.

'I'm sorry,' she said, 'but I need to call my brother and find out how Arabella's doing today.' She inserted her swipe card and pushed her door open.

Remy tried not to look disappointed. 'I will upload your clip to YouTube tonight.'

'Oh, thank you. Remember to . . .' Remy could hear Janelle's mobile phone ringing in the room beyond. She glanced over her shoulder. 'Excuse me.'

'No problems,' he called, as the door slammed in his face. Remy stood there a moment, staring at the beige-coloured paint peeling in places around the doorknob.

Imagining, for a ridiculous few seconds, following Janelle inside.

What are you afraid of? Lorenzo's words were audible over the tinkling of the holy man's silver bell, but Cara continued to feign deafness. Staring into the deep pool of murky water into which she was supposed to slide, fully clothed, for a Balinese water cleansing ceremony, Cara heard the Italian repeat his question, louder this time.

They were the last two scheduled for the water cleansing. According to the presiding priest, the ritual would cleanse them of any residual fears from past lives and unnecessary anxieties in the present. Already they'd watched Remy then Janelle being blessed and submerged, followed by Henry and then Annie. When Lorenzo was midway through his ceremony, a tropical downpour caused the priest's attendant to send the others away.

'*Hujan deras*,' she explained from under the plastic canopy shielding herself, the priest and their holy objects. 'Heavy rain will make you sick. Go now.'

This had prompted the others, already wet and shivering, hurrying towards the changerooms for hot showers and dry clothes.

'We will wait on the bus with Ketut,' Pak Tony had called, before following them.

For reasons unclear to Cara, Lorenzo had stayed on after the completion of his ceremony to watch hers.

He lingered next to her now on the uneven, stony edge of the pool. His t-shirt was plastered across his chest, still wet from his submersion. The sarong tied at his waist showcased sculpted abdominal muscles, and his hair was slicked back into artful waves above designer aviator sunglasses. His entire body—as far as Cara could tell—was tanned and hairless. Were they born that way in Italy, she pondered, or did Lorenzo wax it all off? Whatever the answer, the Italian evidently engaged in far more personal grooming than she did.

A young Balinese woman, the priest's attendant, materialised beside Cara and commenced the blessing. The woman's elegant hands weaved around Cara's face, setting flowers behind her ear, flicking holy water across her hair; she then poured a little of the water into Cara's hands for her to sip from, and finally pressed uncooked grains of rice against her forehead.

Cara closed her eyes, tense and overwhelmed by the memories bombarding her. Locals said the pool's depth was unknown, that it changed according to the whim of the *tonya*, a community of spirits who inhabited the river area that fed the sacred pool. The *tonya* were responsible, it was said, for the disappearances of at least a dozen children in the vicinity of the ravine.

How convenient, Cara mused, to be able to blame a supernatural cause for your child's death. Rather than having to endure the crushing weight of your own guilt, like a prison sentence, for the term of your natural life.

She opened her eyes and stared at the swirling waters, wondering for the umpteenth time why she'd agreed to enrol in Fearless at all. She'd been pestered into it by Jasmine, the vivacious Canadian yoga teacher who'd become one of her few friends in Bali. If 'friendship' was even the right term for it. More than once, Cara had wondered if every expatriate connection she made here was merely a relationship of convenience, a camaraderie born of mutual foreignness.

'Miss Cara,' announced the Balinese attendant, 'it is almost time to enter the water.' The sound of the ceremonial bell grew louder.

'Ready?' Lorenzo asked Cara. 'It's colder than the ocean.'

Yesterday's parasailing splash-down had been shock enough, but this murky, brown pool mimicked Manly Dam itself. The place where her beautiful one-year-old baby girl, Astrid, had accidentally wandered into the water. When would Cara ever be ready? She turned towards the Italian, ignoring her heaving stomach. Feeling drawn towards the water, as if by invisible hands.

'You look unwell,' said Lorenzo, frowning. 'What are you afraid of?'

There it was, that question again.

'Is it the water?' he persisted.

Until four years ago, Cara had simply viewed water as a basic element of human life. She'd written extensively about droughts and water crises in the developing world, particularly in Africa, where she'd spent several years early in her journalistic career.

Beyond that, she'd enjoyed water as a benign gift of nature, packaged in inviting forms like misty rain or cascading waterfalls, plump cumulus clouds or delicate snowflakes. How radically this easy relationship with water had changed forever, on the day of her daughter's first birthday party.

Cara closed her eyes again, shutting out the malevolent pool in front of her. The rocks, the mud, the reedy vegetation were all evocative, somehow, of that terrible day. She could remember, too, all the busy preparation beforehand, the idle worries about the weather and the last-minute discussion of alternative venues in case of rain.

But then a perfect day of sunshine had dawned, so bright it expelled all concerns. Hours of delight had followed, of champagne and laughter and photographs of giggling children, and flippant conversations about imagined futures. Little had Cara known that beneath that shining mirror of a day, danger lurked. Until it was too late.

She opened her eyes, but the image of that day didn't disappear. Instead, the rustling sound of the steady rain in the jungle canopy above became the billowing of Astrid's party skirt as she wandered into the water. The mossy rocks on the river bed were the last things Astrid saw before she slid into the incomprehensible gloom. The insistent, buffeting wind around her was Astrid's final, gasping breath. The cloudy ripples on the water's surface became a shroud of death that spirited away her rosy-faced daughter, returning instead a cold, blue-lipped corpse.

Unaware of anyone around her, Cara plunged forward. The water rose up to meet her, slapping her face and soaking her sarong, scarf and kebaya. She was sinking in her clothes, but she did not resist. She merely opened her eyes and blinked at the amorphous shapes beneath the surface. Bubbles rushed from her lungs with a queer, distorted sound, grazing her ears as they streamed past. When the bubbles finally stopped, she simply hung in the aquatic calm, her limbs drifting apart, as if disconnected from her body.

A splashing sound shattered the peace and hands grabbed her waist, hauling her upwards. They broke the surface together and Cara gasped for air. The priest and his attendant rushed forward, their faces alarmed.

Lorenzo pushed her to the side of the pool. 'What happened?' he demanded.

As she filled her lungs with oxygen, the words tumbled out of her mouth. 'My daughter drowned four years ago. I haven't been near water since. Except for yesterday, parasailing with you.'

Lorenzo gaped at her. 'What?'

'I'm sorry.' She turned her face away, feeling the tears start.

The priest beckoned to them. 'Please, come out of the water now.'

Lorenzo helped Cara to clamber out of the pool, then pulled himself up next to her. The attendant draped towels around their shoulders as they sat on the pool's edge, catching their breath.

At length, Lorenzo placed a hand over hers. 'I'm sorry.'

Cara shrugged, but did not remove her hand.

The priest approached them again. 'We fear it is the *tonya*,' he said. 'They are displeased. We must prepare extra blessings now.'

Cara nodded. There was no point contesting this, of explaining that yet again, *she* was to blame.

Lorenzo looked at her. 'Are you alright?'

'I'm fine now,' she lied. She glanced at the Italian and saw that his hair was dishevelled and his sunglasses were missing. 'Sorry about your sunglasses. They looked expensive.'

Lorenzo shook his head. 'I have several pairs. They're just part of my job.'

'Oh.' Then, automatically, she asked, 'What do you do?' As if they were strangers at a party, exchanging small talk.

'Fashion photography. I specialise in accessories. But my real passion is the photography of the young.'

What did that mean, Cara wondered, *the photography of the young*? Since arriving in Bali four years ago, she'd developed a mistrust of self-appointed labels. Ubud was full of people describing themselves as healers, visionaries or spiritual masters. But the bulk of them, Cara had come to conclude, were charlatans or delusional.

'I capture things that cannot last,' Lorenzo went on. 'Youth is always on its way out, to something grosser and baser—the awareness and self-consciousness of adulthood. But in a photograph, innocence is eternal.'

Cara nodded. Eternity in a photograph was something she understood; the things she held dearest now were the photographs preserving Astrid's imprint on earth. Even the blurry images Richard had taken by accident—shots that other parents would simply delete—had, after Astrid's death, become precious archival material.

Cara's hand began to stiffen under Lorenzo's and she winced, at both the ache and the realisation that she hadn't had such physical contact with a man since Richard. Since fleeing Sydney after the inquest, when the coroner had found that Astrid's death had been caused by *accidental drowning*. But Cara hadn't required a formal finding to confirm her negligence. The fact that others were there that day—family, and people she'd once called friends—was irrelevant. As Astrid's mother, she alone was responsible for safeguarding her daughter.

They sat for a while, watching petals floating on the surface of the sacred spring. Then Lorenzo asked, 'So, why did you decide to come to Bali after your daughter . . . ?'

Cara sighed. The truth was, she hadn't really decided anything. She'd covered the Bali bombings as a journalist in 2002 and, since then, Bali hadn't been on her list of must-see destinations. But after Astrid's death, she had been faced with two possible choices: suicide, or self-imposed isolation. Strangely enough, Bali had emerged as a viable third alternative.

'It was unexpected,' she explained. 'When Astrid was alive I was close to the other women in my mothers' group, and one of them was originally from Bali—a woman called Made. After the accident, I was a mess. Made offered to take me to her family's compound, in a little mountain village not far from Kintamani, for a break away from all the attention in Australia. I needed some time alone. It felt like my only chance to get away.'

She closed her eyes, remembering how quickly she'd realised her mistake. Living in a Balinese family compound was not the balm she'd hoped. After an uncomfortable week, during which every well-meaning member of Made's extended family—and a steady influx of neighbours—attempted to console or befriend Cara, or simply to practise their English with her, she had fled to a budget hostel in Ubud. In her usual kindly fashion, Made had taken no offence, quickly recognising that Cara needed anonymity and space, not dozens of people scrutinising her every move.

But the crowded hubbub of Monkey Forest Road made Cara claustrophobic, with its street hawkers and sprawling markets and swarms of overweight Westerners downing cocktails and beer. Or even the svelte, virtuous ones with yoga mats strung across their backs, picking at raw mezze plates and drinking green juices. After more than a week of roaming the streets and trawling through accommodation websites, Cara was almost ready to give up on Bali altogether.

Then one afternoon while sitting in a café in Penestanan village, drinking gritty Balinese coffee and wondering if she would ever sleep at night without sedatives, Cara spotted a colourful flyer pinned to a noticeboard. In the centre was a photo of an airy-looking double-storey villa perched in the middle of a verdant rice field. The few sentences beneath the photo promised privacy and peace at Villa Gembira.

When she rang the number on the flyer, a pleasant-sounding Indonesian man answered. He offered to show her around the villa immediately. 'Just wait at the café,' he told her. 'I'm on my way.'

Fifteen minutes later, she found herself climbing onto the back of a motorbike driven by Indra, a tall thirty-something man with a cheeky smile and long black hair tied back in a ponytail. She kept her body carefully separated from his, holding onto the rear of the seat and bracing her abdominals. They drove along winding back streets that Indra called *gangs*, and through a picturesque patchwork of rice paddies.

As they pulled up outside Villa Gembira, Cara knew instantly that this was the place for her. Indra ushered her inside. On the ground floor was a small kitchen and lounge, and a high-walled outdoor bathroom with a huge marble bath at its centre.

Up a narrow, uneven staircase to the second floor, she found a comfortable-looking four-poster bed draped in a filmy white mosquito net. The balcony faced west, overlooking the rice fields, and suspended from its ceiling was a rattan swing chair lined with plush cushions.

'Perfect for a couple,' said Indra, motioning to the oversized chair.

Cara looked at him blankly.

'Or just for one,' he added quickly.

They descended the stairs once more. 'How much?' she asked when they were outside.

'Six million a month, or sixty-five million a year.' He smiled. 'For you, five million a month or sixty million a year.' Were Indonesian teeth actually whiter than the Western variety, Cara wondered, or was it simply the contrast against treacle-dark skin?

She did the mental calculations: it was only six thousand dollars a year, a little more than their monthly mortgage repayment in Australia. Not that she would own the Sydney house for much longer; she'd already composed the email to Richard, seeking a formal separation. It was saved in her drafts folder, waiting for her to push the button, literally.

'I'll take it,' she said.

'For how long?' Indra asked.

'I don't know.' Then, looking up at the balcony and the rattan chair rotating slowly in the breeze, she made a snap decision. 'A year,' she announced. 'With first right of refusal on renewal, please.'

Indra looked a little taken aback. 'I will ask the owner to prepare the lease. The year will need to be paid in full in advance, you understand.'

Cara nodded. She had more than enough in her Australian account, and a longer-term lease made sense. After all, she didn't have a definitive return date in mind. Slowly, Indra extended his hand to shake hers and, squinting against the rays of the late-afternoon sun, Cara reciprocated. As their hands touched, a tingling sensation caught her by surprise.

Now Cara lifted her gaze from the water and blinked. Her wrist was beginning to hurt from holding the same position, and the wet sarong was cold and clammy on her skin.

Lorenzo looked at her. 'Is your husband here in Bali?'

'We're separated.' How could a couple's relationship survive the death of their only child?

'Have you been lonely?' asked Lorenzo.

Cara looked away. She'd had Indra, at least.

Soon after moving into Villa Gembira, she'd learned that Indra was Javanese, not Balinese. He'd left Yogyakarta, the cultural capital of Central Java, some ten years before, seeking work on the more prosperous island of Bali. Lucky for him, he'd found work with a Belgian property developer, for whom Indra now managed five villas in the Penestanan and Sayan regions, including Cara's. Apart from looking after general maintenance on the villa, Indra delivered Cara market produce in the mornings and her post in the afternoons. She'd never asked for these small attentions—they were included in the villa service fee—but she appreciated them all the same.

A fortnight after she moved in, Cara had opened her front door to find a basket of oranges sitting on the doormat, a little card placed on top with the word '*jeruk*', and an Indonesian–English dictionary lying alongside it. Tucked into its cover, she found a note from Indra, in neatly penned English: *You are staying in Bali for a year, so you need to learn Indonesian. We can start tomorrow at eleven o'clock.*

Cara recognised the truth in his words; her career in journalism had taught her that understanding language was a prerequisite for comprehending culture. For the first few months, she spent an hour a day with Indra, six days a week, learning the basics of Indonesian. Gradually their conversations became more complex, about politics, history and current affairs. She insisted on paying him the market rate for such lessons, despite his apparent reluctance to accept a fee.

'It is not work for me,' he murmured at the end of every lesson, before stuffing the notes into his pocket.

Six months into their tutorials, Indra started arriving on Saturday evenings to collect Cara on his motorbike to '*jalan-jalan*' to nowhere in particular. 'It is an important part of your language learning,' he insisted.

Invariably these evenings involved a meandering, scenic route, and often a meal of *nasi goreng* or *sate ayam* at a roadside *warung*. If Cara didn't feel up to the outing, Indra simply went away again; but he always reappeared the following week to *jalan-jalan* once more.

It was an easy, casual, comfortable friendship. Convenient for them both, Cara realised, once Indra had divulged more about his background. As the youngest of eleven, he was destined to fend for himself in the world. He'd done well by local standards, and the earnings from Cara's language lessons were helping too. But their relationship was more than commercial. With only a handful of other acquaintances in Bali—met mostly at Friday prayers at the mosque in Denpasar—Indra considered her his friend.

'We are both foreigners in Bali, Cara,' he'd said to her on more than one occasion. 'The Balinese hate the Javanese. You like me more than they do.'

And he accepted her. She'd never told him about Astrid, but he didn't seem surprised by her experimentation with multiple healing modalities. She tried so many healers, she lost count of them; including a Swiss woman who used Tibetan singing bowls in her lengthy 'soul adjustment' sessions, an American raw foodie who claimed Hawaiian *lomilomi* massage could cure everything from sadness to cancer, and an old Balinese priest who advertised as clairvoyant but failed to intuit anything at all about Cara's situation.

When people didn't work, Cara turned to products. Everything from conventional Western psychiatric therapies—antidepressants and anti-anxiety drugs purchased readily without a prescription—to alcohol, magic mushrooms and ganja sold in dark alleyways by young men with glassy eyes.

As Cara's linguistic skills expanded, she found herself increasingly enjoying Indra's company. Perhaps due to his status as the *anak ragil*—the youngest child—of such a large family, Indra was hardworking, funny and unfailingly buoyant. As the months had turned into years, and Cara had moved from taking drugs to yoga classes, her fondness for him grew. And she fancied she sometimes caught him looking at her longingly as he strummed his guitar on her balcony. But never once in more than three years of friendship had he tried to touch her. Nor had she ever acted on the fleeting impulse to stroke his long dark ponytail.

Cara moved her hand uneasily beneath Lorenzo's, discomfited by this stranger's touch.

'Let's go,' the Italian said. 'You must be cold.'

They stood up, leaving the priest and the attendant to their task of appeasing the *tonya*. The rain had all but stopped, and as they walked along the cobbled path towards the car park, peddlers popped out from behind stalls proffering fruit, ice cream and souvenirs. Lorenzo waved them away, gently steering Cara through them.

Suddenly grateful for his thoughtfulness, she said, 'Thank you, Lorenzo. For helping me back there.'

'Please, get changed.' He motioned at a set of changerooms the others had used earlier. 'Then let us drink coffee. You are shaking.' Cara realised he was right. The sky was still grey and a light breeze tugged at their wet clothes.

'Meet you there,' he said, pointing at a nearby stall where two middle-aged women were selling coffee in the shade of a coconut palm.

Cara nodded, then carried her bag of dry clothes into the changerooms. It was a relief to peel off the sodden fabric.

Several minutes later she emerged to find Lorenzo sitting on a wooden barrel next to a squat table. He motioned at another barrel for Cara to sit on.

'But surely the others will be ready to go?' said Cara.

'They can wait. They are dry at least,' Lorenzo said. 'What would you like?'

She smiled, relenting. 'Black coffee, no sugar.'

Lorenzo greeted one of the attendants—a tall, thin woman wearing a brown batik sarong—and ordered two Balinese coffees.

They sat in slightly awkward silence now.

Cara was unsure what to say to the Italian. She wondered what would have happened if he hadn't been there earlier, and she hoped he wouldn't ask. She listened to the ladies' idle chatter behind the stall; they were speaking Indonesian, not Balinese, presumably because they hailed from different parts of the archipelago. The taller woman was fixing their coffees, while her plump friend grated a turmeric bulb over a small sieve. The woman's hands were stained yellow from the liquid, which she siphoned into plastic bottles to sell as a medicinal *jamu* drink.

'Why does a *bule* need a water ceremony, anyway?' asked the woman preparing the *jamu*. 'They're not Hindu, so why bother?'

Cara's eyes widened.

'Why do they do anything?' asked her friend, pouring hot water over the coarse coffee powder. 'They're strange. No sugar in their coffee. Milk in their tea. How revolting.' She pulled a face. 'But they're the rich ones, right? Just do as they ask.'

The ladies tittered and Cara's cheeks reddened. She was tempted to turn and shock them by responding in Indonesian, but she remained silent, riveted by their candid assessment of *bule* idiosyncrasies.

The taller woman brought over their coffees and set them down. 'Twenty thousand,' she said in English.

Lorenzo fished a green note out of his pocket, the exact amount, and passed it to the woman. '*Terima kasih*,' he said, with his rolling Italian accent.

'You're welcome,' the woman replied, smiling at him. She lingered at the table, looking from one to the other. Lorenzo smiled back at her.

After a moment, the woman turned and headed back behind the counter. 'Miser,' she muttered to her friend. 'So rich, but he won't even give five thousand for a tip.'

Oblivious to this reproach, Lorenzo sipped his coffee, then turned to look at Cara.

'My wife, Lavinia, wants a baby,' he said abruptly. 'She would be the best mother in the world, I am sure. But she is very frustrated that pregnancy hasn't happened yet.' He swallowed another mouthful of coffee. 'Maybe if she met you, she would realise there is something much harder than not getting pregnant.' He shook his head. 'I cannot imagine how terrible it must be, Cara, to lose a baby. Or how you can rebuild your life afterwards.'

Disarmed by his empathy, Cara squeezed her eyes shut, fearing the onset of more tears. When she opened them again, Lorenzo's earnest gaze was still trained on her.

Something in her gave way. For the first time ever, she found herself trying to explain what it felt like to lose a child. She told Lorenzo how it wasn't truly living, existing with a baby-shaped gap in your life. How poisonous hindsight could be, like salt rubbed into a festering wound. How guilt sometimes visited her in the night as an invisible supernatural force that crushed her chest. How she'd tried to expunge the nightmares with sleeping tablets, but even now she still woke to find herself reaching for Astrid.

She described how senseless it seemed, robbed of her only child, to watch expatriate parents so readily outsourcing theirs to a battalion of Balinese babysitters. Or the cringing fear she felt when she saw young parent-yogis, bedecked in lycra on their trendy Vespa scooters, casually strapping babies to their chests, with nothing but a flimsy layer of fabric to protect their infants from the road. How she longed to confront these New Age fools as they zoomed past, sequined scarves trailing behind them. *Oh yes, it will never happen to you!* she wanted to scream. *I thought that once, until it did.*

Lorenzo sat in silence as she relayed the pain she felt on passing a schoolyard, a playground, a toy store. The grief that still randomly flattened her when pushing her supermarket trolley past shelves of baby products, receiving baby-related email spam, or scanning jovial Facebook posts about other people's children. The peculiar sorrow of watching families with multiple children; Astrid's death had deprived Cara not only of her first child, but also of the possibility of having more—because how could she ever sufficiently recover from losing her first baby to properly love a second?

She described, too, the melancholy she felt when she watched Balinese children running barefoot through the streets under the care of grandparents, cousins or older siblings because their parents were too busy making a living elsewhere. And how she'd cried in the street outside Ubud Palace one day, after meeting a ragged beggar woman holding a limp-looking infant in her arms, who told Cara she couldn't feed her baby anymore.

'I *could* care for Astrid,' she told Lorenzo now. 'I devoted myself to her, but she was taken away. Why is life so unfair?'

Lorenzo drained his coffee, his face sombre, evidently considering the question. Cara looked down at her lap, shocked by how much she'd divulged, and exhausted by the telling. Her two closest friends in Bali—Indra and Jasmine—had never been privy to such an outpouring. No one had, in fact.

'Why is life unfair?' murmured Lorenzo. 'It is hard to say, Cara. But I know from personal experience that sometimes parents do and say things that they don't mean, or that they live to regret. Sometimes these things are within their control, but many times they are not.' His voice was a little shaky.

'I have known a mother's love,' he continued. 'They do their best to protect their children and keep their family together. But sometimes mothers, too, make mistakes. Sometimes they don't have everything they need in their lives to make better choices. Whatever happened to your daughter, Cara, I can see that you loved her deeply. When she was alive, she would have known that. She would have felt that, deep inside her. And that is all that counts, in the end.'

Cara's eyes smarted as she remembered how she'd soothed Astrid off to sleep with old-fashioned lullabies, or danced her around the kitchen to ballet music. How she'd fretted incessantly about Astrid's body temperature, her appetite, and even changes in her bowel movements. How she'd celebrated her first smile, her first commando-crawl, her first tentative steps. How she'd sat beside her crib after midnight feeds, watching Astrid's tiny chest rise and fall, enthralled by her sheer perfection. Did Astrid feel all that love? And had it been enough for her, when the time came for her to leave?

The tears spilled over and she gripped Lorenzo's hand, searching for the right words. 'How do you know?'

He nodded sympathetically. 'Pain understands pain.'

Cara saw the hurt in his eyes and wondered who or what had wounded him so badly.

'We should go,' he said, standing up. 'Before they really do leave us behind.'

Cara got up too, hastily wiping her eyes. They hurried along the path to the car park and onto the waiting minibus. Sarcastic cheering greeted them.

'What took you so long?' asked Remy. 'Something foul to cleanse from your soul, Lorenzo?' He grinned cheekily.

'You'd have to ask the priest that,' Lorenzo replied. 'We got lost in the moment, I think.'

'Excellent!' Pak Tony exclaimed. 'When we are fully present in the moment, fear is pushed from our minds.'

The man has a maxim for everything, Cara thought, as the minibus nudged its way out into the traffic.

'Did you get a souvenir photograph at the sacred spring?' asked Janelle, waving hers.

Lorenzo shook his head. 'Some things cannot be captured by camera. As a photographer, I know this.'

Cara gave Lorenzo a quick, grateful smile. Life's most precious moments couldn't be memorialised, she knew. Joy and suffering inscribed upon the soul were remembrance enough.

—⁓

The day seemed to drag for Cara. Back at the resort, after another vegan lunch, they watched Henry deliver a faltering but heartfelt passion talk about citizen-driven science, entitled 'Not just a hobby: how birdwatching can help humanity's future'. This was followed by a crisp, rather intellectual delivery by Lorenzo on the topic 'Is the camera a medium of art?' Cara cringed at the conclusion of these talks, knowing hers was due for delivery tomorrow. With little other inspiration, she would have to talk about her freelance work as an online social justice reporter, mostly on issues affecting women and girls. It *used* to be a passion, before her world imploded.

In the late afternoon, Cara followed the hulking figure of Littlefish, the Yup'ik spiritual healer of whom Pak Tony had spoken so warmly, into a dimly lit outhouse for her 'personal pow-wow'. A massage table was set against one wall, positioned beneath a rainbow-coloured dreamcatcher. Four recliner chairs were clustered around a low table in the centre of the room, on which an eclectic array of mystical objects was laid out: a collection of quartz crystals, a deck of tarot cards, a drum with a fish-shaped handle, and a jagged dagger that Cara recognised as a *keris*—an Indonesian blade believed by many to possess magical powers.

For a moment, Cara wondered what an Indo-European divination method like tarot, or New Age crystal therapy, had to do with Native American beliefs. The past four years had rendered her sceptical. Practically any rite was purchasable in Ubud, from pre-Christian European bonfire ceremonies and the chalice rituals of Celtic Wicca, to the incense and chanting of Hindu *puja*. Cara always felt troubled by this mixing and matching across multiple traditions, seemingly at the practitioner's whim. While some expatriates embraced it as spiritual universalism—a kind of friendly global fusion declaring *your God is my God*—she often wondered if it wasn't the worst type of appropriation, disrespecting all of the traditions involved. This was one of the reasons that she had ultimately embraced yoga as her daily practice. It promised nothing divine or eternal, but simply a space in which to nurture a hollowed-out body and a grief-numbed mind.

'Please, sit down,' said Littlefish, his voice strangely high for a man of his size. He motioned to a chair.

Cara obeyed, avoiding his gaze. Littlefish was an unnerving sight, his bulky girth arrayed in an animal-hide kaftan. He wore a headdress, too, in the shape of a bear's claw. His hair was greasy and dreadlocked, his skin chalky—unusual for a resident of Bali—and his huge jowls quivered when he spoke. When she'd first seen him, she'd stifled a giggle. He looked like an Anglo-Saxon imposter dressed up as a medicine man for Halloween. And now that he'd spoken, his voice had a southern twang that didn't sound Native American at all.

'You doubt I'm a Yup'ik man, don't you?' said Littlefish suddenly, his brown eyes boring into hers.

Cara's mouth dropped open. 'I . . . I don't know much about Yup'ik culture,' she stammered, horrified that he'd read her mind. 'You . . . don't look as I expected, I'm sorry. In Australia there are many people who identify as Aborigines but sometimes they don't look very indigenous either.'

Littlefish stared at her a moment longer. Then he smiled, apparently unoffended by her answer. 'You are Australian,' he observed. 'But you don't really feel at home anywhere, do you?'

I used to, Cara thought, determined not to disclose anything. She was sick of supposed healers who conversed their way through a session, gleaning important titbits of information to help them flesh out a picture of their client's life.

'I can see there is nowhere you feel at peace,' he went on. 'There is no refuge for you anymore.'

In spite of her cynicism, for a moment Cara felt as if she might burst into tears.

'Have some tea,' said Littlefish, gesturing to a steaming mug of brown liquid on the table. 'The herbs will help you relax.'

She dutifully lifted the mug to her lips and sipped, before screwing up her nose at the bitter taste. She replaced the mug on its saucer. 'What kind of herbs are these?' she asked.

'I am going to channel Great Spirit now,' Littlefish said, ignoring her question. 'Don't be alarmed if I burp or sneeze, or move around the room as the energy works through my body. I may have to lay hands on you, and you may feel some warmth when I do. If there is anything you are not comfortable with, please tell me straight away and we will find another path.'

Cara nodded, swallowing hard.

Littlefish picked up the drum from the table. He began to strike it with a long thin stick, alternating between the head and the rim, creating two distinct sounds.

'Close your eyes now,' he commanded. 'Breathe slowly and deeply.'

Obeying him, Cara listened to the deep resonance of the drum, noticing how the sound changed. Littlefish began to sing, and his voice was surprisingly sonorous. The rhythm sped up, but just as Cara began to recognise some of the song's repeating forms, Littlefish stopped drumming.

He snickered. It was a high-pitched giggle, followed by a long, deep burp.

'My tummy hurts,' he announced in a strange falsetto. 'I swallowed too much water.'

Gooseflesh rippled across Cara's neck.

'Mummy?' he whimpered.

The fine hairs on her arms stood on end. She shook her head, willing the voice away, while feeling compelled to keep listening.

'You're so sad, Mummy.' It was a peculiar voice, accentless.

Cara's lips parted. The air left her lungs in a sharp exhalation. *He has to stop*, she thought. *Whatever he is doing, he has to stop it now.*

'Don't worry, Mummy,' said the diminutive voice. 'It's alright.'

Hot tears pooled behind her eyelids. She was paralysed between the desire to call an instant halt to the session and risk missing out on . . . what exactly? Or to allow it to continue, and risk being torn apart.

Littlefish made a guttural sequence of clicking and popping sounds. Cara's head felt fuzzy, but she was certain that she detected an aroma in the room: of mashed potato and mince, the meal she had often cooked when Astrid started taking solids.

The soft, girlish voice said, 'I am safe here.'

'Where?' Cara whispered. 'Where *are* you?'

'With you,' the voice replied. 'I never left. You must know that, Mummy.'

Cara's chest began to heave. 'I . . . I'm sorry,' she whispered. 'I should never have let you . . . wander off.'

Littlefish began to whimper, then gave another loud burp. 'It wasn't your fault, Mummy. It had to be that way.'

'*No.*' The word blasted its way out of her constricted throat. 'It *didn't* have to be that way. I could have stopped it from happening. I should never have handed you over to someone else. I could have saved you, if I hadn't been so selfish . . .'

Cara moaned, catapulted back to Astrid's final minutes. How she'd toddled through the colourful chaos of bouncy balls strewn across picnic rugs, giggling and clapping her hands. How she'd called out 'Du-du-du!' in excitement as she spotted the ducks paddling in the distance. How she'd stood on tiptoes to reach the

172

low trestle table laid with party food, stuffing her little fists with fairy bread, before turning and spotting a large dog belonging to one of the partygoers. How Cara had whisked Astrid up into her arms, deeming the animal a danger, and passed her instead to Miranda, a trusted friend from her mothers' group. How the last words she'd ever spoken to her daughter had been utterly banal—*Stay here with Miranda, honey, I'll be five minutes*—before she'd trotted away to talk to Ravi, an old flame from university. And how Astrid had called out 'Mummy!' one last time, before Miranda had distracted her with bouncy balls.

If only she could touch Astrid again. Shivering, Cara stretched out her hand.

'Mummy, be careful where the ducks are,' said the voice.

Cara winced, remembering the coroner's report—and the media coverage that ensued—outlining that Astrid, in all likelihood, had followed the ducks into Manly Dam. 'Astrid?' Cara's fingers fluttered in the air, searching for her daughter. Suddenly, she felt small, soft fingers pressing back against hers. 'Astrid!' she gasped, goosebumps cascading down her arms.

'There is no failure, Mommy. There is only forgiv—'

Involuntarily, she opened her eyes.

Littlefish's enormous hand was touching hers. Cara wrenched it away and covered her mouth, sobbing. The healer blinked and stared blankly for a second, before refocusing his eyes.

'She was here,' he said. 'Your daughter. But now she has reverted. She is never far from you.'

Tears cascaded down Cara's cheeks and she shook her head, overcome. 'How do you . . . how could that *happen*?'

Littlefish lifted a glass of water to his lips. 'I cannot explain it. Great Spirit comes and goes. I am just the receptacle. I am sorry she died. Your daughter loved you and . . . the red-headed man I saw.'

'My husband, Richard,' Cara whispered. 'Astrid's father.'

Littlefish nodded. 'Did you understand your daughter's message about your safety?'

Cara shrugged. 'There were ducks . . . on the day she died.'

'No matter,' said Littlefish. 'In time you will understand. Come.' He gestured to the massage table. 'You must be exhausted. I will lay hands on you and sing to Great Spirit, to rebuild your energy. Lie down and rest.'

She walked robotically to the massage table, her limbs leaden, and climbed onto it. Littlefish placed one hand between her shoulder blades, the other over her sacrum, and within seconds she began to feel a soothing warmth through her clothes.

Littlefish began crooning, a warbling, affecting song. Her body melted into the table, her ankles rolled inwards, and within seconds, she felt saliva collecting beneath her tongue.

Suspending all scepticism, she surrendered to the song.

An hour later, at the southern reaches of the resort, the group assembled for sunset drinks on a bamboo balcony overlooking the Ayung River gorge. They stood together next to a long timber bar, behind which two Balinese attendants offered them drinks and canapes.

A long wooden table was laid out for seven nearby, decorated with swirling trails of rose petals and tall white candles that flickered in the breeze. Cara was groggy, weary and acutely emotional. It was only because Pak Tony was joining them—and perhaps there would be a penalty for truancy—that she hadn't boycotted drinks and dinner altogether.

'What *I* want to know is, how does an Alaskan Eskimo end up in Bali?' said Annie, moving closer to the women of the group.

'Isn't the term Eskimo considered a bit offensive these days?' asked Janelle quietly.

'Maybe,' said Annie, rolling her eyes. 'But he was a bit offensive to *me*, too. A real nineteenth-century spiritualist with all the trappings . . . burping and farting and spooky voices. There were probably magic mushrooms in that tea he gave us! After five minutes, I'd had enough and stopped the session.'

'Did you really?' Henry joined the conversation. 'You're much braver than me. Why, what did he do?'

Annie pressed her lips together. 'It isn't possible to speak with the dead.'

'He *didn't*, did he?' Henry looked shocked. 'What, with *Kevin*?'

Cara remembered that this was Annie's husband, who'd passed away under tragic circumstances.

Annie's eyes grew teary. Suddenly she looked vulnerable and rather old.

'Oh, dear.' Henry patted her arm. 'How awful for you.' He glanced around the wider group, his eyes stern behind his spectacles. 'When I decided to join this course, I thought none of it could do any harm. But taking advantage of people's vulnerability—that's despicable.'

From his position seated on a bar stool, Remy nodded. 'Maybe I am cynical, but I have been thinking . . . did Littlefish access our personal records?' He spun the bar stool towards Lorenzo, seated on his other side. 'All that information we wrote on our application forms, about major life traumas. Maybe Pak Tony shared it with Littlefish?'

Cara hadn't considered that; there certainly had been sufficient media coverage for Littlefish to develop a good understanding of the circumstances surrounding Astrid's death. It was all in the public domain, plastered across the internet: the coronial findings, the events leading up to the tragedy, photographs of Manly Dam, Astrid, Richard and even the members of her mothers' group. Still, Remy's theory jarred with Cara's sense of her session with Littlefish, which had felt very real.

'I doubt it,' said Lorenzo. 'That would be a breach of privacy.' He stared out across the gorge. 'Littlefish channelled my grandmother. It was all very accurate.' Cara noticed that Lorenzo's hand shook a little as he drank from his glass.

'For me too,' she murmured, catching his eye. 'It felt like my daughter was in the room.'

Annie's face flushed red. 'Well, even if it was accurate, what he's doing is dangerous. I don't think it's real, but just say it was, then he's messing with the occult. How do we know for sure that he's channelling our loved ones? He could be contacting spirits who are *pretending* to be our loved ones. Did anyone think of that?'

Henry put an arm around Annie's shoulders, attempting to soothe her. 'It all sounds very distressing,' he said. 'I'm glad I didn't meet any spirits in my session.'

'So what happened in yours?' asked Annie.

Henry chuckled. 'Oh, Littlefish just put some crystals over my body, then I took a short nap on his massage table. He used some tarot cards, and the King of Cups is my big thing apparently, because it's all about emotional maturity. He said I couldn't grasp the feminine until I'd embraced the masculine.' He glanced heavenward. 'Then he told me to follow the truth in my heart or I'll never fulfil my potential, which I fancy I've heard before . . . like, a thousand times.'

'He used tarot with me too,' said Remy, his face slightly more earnest than Henry's. 'I drew Lady Justice, with the blindfold, the scales and the sword. Littlefish said that justice was like love; blind to wealth and power. He told me not to fear heights, because that's where the angels fly.' He paused. 'I didn't know whether to laugh or leave.' His expression turned wry. 'Then I drew the Temperance card, reversed, which wasn't good news at all. He warned me about imbalance and excess. And I say *salut* to that!' Remy raised his glass and swallowed another mouthful of red wine, then turned to Janelle. 'What happened in your session?'

Janelle winced. 'He chanted loudly, which was a bit bewildering. Then he used crystals and talked about Great Spirit, which I guess is God for the Yup'ik people.' She paused, her expression circumspect. 'He said that I didn't have to honour my mother's fear anymore, that it was time to live my own life.' Her voice was a little wobbly. 'Right at the end of the session he told me, *Your anger marks the path to love.* I've got no idea what he means by that.'

Annie shook her head emphatically. 'It's all quackery. I wonder how much Littlefish is being paid by Pak Tony? An authentic healer wouldn't take money for his work.'

'But don't healers have the right to earn a living?' Janelle replied. 'It doesn't mean they're dodgy just because they accept payment for their services.'

Annie sniffed. 'Jesus never sought payment for his miracles.'

'True,' said Janelle, in a placating tone. 'But I don't think Littlefish is holding himself out as the Son of God. He told me he was just a messenger of Great Spirit, and that religions have different names for God, which is actually a huge cosmic source of love that knows what's best for us, even when we don't.'

'Well, I for one am confused,' said Annie, quite worked up now. 'On the one hand, God is a huge, impersonal source of love. On the other, He knows what's best for us as individuals. I'm sorry, honey, but God can't be both impersonal and personal.'

'Why not?' Janelle countered. 'God is God, right? Maybe God defies our limited human understanding. He—or She, or It—exists beyond the constraints of theology, because God is everything we can imagine *and* everything we can't.'

'Ah, yes,' said Annie, her tone barbed. 'The relativist's pipe dream. Your God is my God, and He's bigger than our pea-brains can grasp. Never mind that He's left us some pretty good signposts called scripture and liturgy. When God equals everything, honey, He stands for *nothing*.' She turned away towards the gorge, beyond which the sun was quickly setting.

'Well, friends,' said Lorenzo, breaking the uncomfortable silence. He seized a bottle of champagne from an ice bucket on the bar. 'Let us celebrate our . . . diversity! Dissent is healthy because it leads to change. Look, we are watching a very beautiful example of change right now.' He pointed at the deepening sky. 'Let us toast this beautiful sunset.'

'What a good idea,' said Pak Tony suddenly, stepping through the doorway leading out onto the balcony. 'But before we do, I would like to announce your individual odysseys for the rest of the retreat. I have talked with Littlefish about your pow-wows.

As you can imagine, he had many insights.' He removed a small notebook from the tan-coloured leather bag slung across his body.

'Let's begin with Remy.' He smiled at the Frenchman. 'For the rest of the retreat, your odyssey is to perform a daily act of service for someone else.'

Remy nodded, looking relieved.

'*And* you must drink no alcohol and eat no meat for the rest of the week,' Pak Tony added. 'To learn to moderate your excesses.'

'What?' Remy's face dropped. 'But I am *French*. We drink wine like water, and we do not have . . . *vegetarians*.'

'Exactly,' said Pak Tony. Remy began muttering, but the facilitator held up a hand. 'Wine and meat are privileges, as I am sure you are aware, Remy. It's only a few days.'

The Frenchman looked rather embarrassed at his outcry and fell silent.

'Now, Annie.' Pak Tony turned to the American. 'Your odyssey is to say nothing at all for the rest of the retreat, except when you're asking a question.'

Annie opened her mouth and then closed it again, clearly flabbergasted.

'That was easy.' Pak Tony chuckled. 'On to Lorenzo now.'

'May I ask a question?' Annie interjected.

'Certainly.'

'Is this some kind of punishment on me for the forthright opinions Americans are famous for?'

'I'm happy to discuss the rationale in the correct forum, Annie. Tomorrow one-on-one, if you would like?' Pak Tony replied evenly. 'Is that your only question?'

Her face turned almost scarlet with outrage. 'No. Is there someplace nearby where I can inject insulin? It's been a long day. Between the water cleansing and the passion talks and the pow-wow, I got caught up and forgot . . .'

'Of course.' Pak Tony snapped his fingers and one of the Balinese attendants stepped out from behind the bar. 'Ari, please show Ibu Annie to the ladies' room,' he ordered. 'And please help her down the stairs.'

Watching the older woman leave, Cara felt a nervous flutter in her stomach. What would *her* odyssey be?

Pak Tony turned to the Italian now. 'Lorenzo, your odyssey is unusual. You must help run a children's art workshop on Friday afternoon at the Bali STAR foundation. That's short for Survivors of Trauma and Recovery. It's a registered charity helping Balinese orphans and foster children who have survived physical or mental abuse.' The facilitator's face was earnest. 'You will work alongside the trained counsellors there, as a volunteer, and perhaps make contact with your own inner child in the process.'

Fleetingly, Lorenzo looked anxious, then he simply nodded in acquiescence.

'Now for Henry,' said Pak Tony. The Englishman shrank down on the bar stool. 'Your odyssey requires discipline. You must speak your truth—exactly what comes into your mind—at any given moment. However uncomfortable or dangerous that might feel.'

Henry looked aghast.

'Let's have a short practice now,' said Pak Tony. 'How do you feel about your odyssey, Henry?'

The Englishman blinked. 'I'd rather poke out my own eye than do it.'

'Good!' said Pak Tony.

'But what if my thoughts are bad?' asked Henry. 'Like, *Pak Tony, those psychedelic yoga pants are a bit naff?*'

The rest of the group stared at the facilitator's trousers.

'Then you're off to a flying start, Henry,' said Pak Tony, with a fixed smile. 'Right, who's next?' He scanned his notebook. 'Ah, Janelle, yes. For the remainder of the retreat, you must seek out a new experience daily. The more unusual or challenging, the better—be expansive and visionary!'

Janelle nodded eagerly.

'And finally, Cara.' Pak Tony smiled at her.

Cara wasn't at all sure she liked that smile; there was something forced about it. On the surface, Pak Tony seemed the typical guru, with gleaming teeth and a supremely healthy lifestyle and a thousand positive aphorisms for every silver-lining moment. But all this perfection had made her wonder, for reasons not entirely clear to her, what might happen if Pak Tony ever got *drunk*.

'Your odyssey, Cara, is to be in someone else's company for the remainder of the retreat.' He winked, as if sharing a humorous secret. 'Except when you're asleep or using the bathroom. Otherwise, you must have a companion with you always.'

Cara frowned. The idea was deeply unappealing; she carefully guarded her solitude. *Why had he given her this challenge?* she was tempted to demand, while already knowing the answer. She'd kept everyone at a distance for the past four years, including herself. *It's only for a week*, she told herself. *I'll just have to go to bed very early.*

Annie reappeared from the restroom, her face returned to its normal hue. She took a glass from the bar and served herself some water from a jug.

'Well,' said Pak Tony gleefully. 'You all have your odysseys, so let's make a toast.'

'But what's *your* personal challenge, Pak Tony?' interjected Annie, in a slightly abrasive tone. 'You're part of this group too, aren't you?'

'Good question, Annie.' His smile didn't waver. 'Perhaps you should all set me an odyssey. Why don't you each consider that tonight, then talk it over as a group tomorrow? No group has ever suggested that before. I'm impressed.'

He scanned the contents of the ice buckets on the bar. 'This is the one I like,' he said, pouring himself a glass of organic grape juice. 'I'm glad you're all enjoying the local wine and beer. Does anyone need a top-up?'

Janelle held out her empty wineglass. 'Yes, please.'

'*Non,*' said Remy, theatrically swooping on Janelle's glass. 'This is my odyssey in action. I am here to serve you.'

'Why, thank you.' Janelle giggled and smoothed her hair. Were they flirting with each other, Cara wondered, or was it just the work of the alcohol?

Remy topped up her glass, then passed a beer to Henry and another red wine to Lorenzo.

'Let's all take part in the toast. I will start,' said Pak Tony. He raised his glass. 'To the heights of fearlessness! No pun intended, Remy.'

'The heights of fearlessness,' Remy echoed, turning to the others. 'And to . . . the vegetables of the world!'

The group cheered.

'Oh Lord, how can I turn a toast into a question?' asked Annie.

'Inflection,' said Lorenzo. 'Like this . . .' He raised his glass and pulled an inquisitive face. 'To the big questions?'

Annie laughed.

'And to the children,' he added softly.

Henry raised his glass now. 'And to . . . all the offence I'm going to cause over the next few days as I 'speak my truth'. My apologies in advance.'

'And to new experiences,' said Janelle, looking pleased.

'And to close companions,' added Cara, forcing the words out through clenched teeth. 'Whether you're willing or not.'

'Don't worry, Cara, we're willing,' said Annie, smiling kindly at her. 'Whoops! Sorry.' She shot a guilty look at Pak Tony. 'I've just breached my odyssey. May I start again, please?' He nodded. 'What I mean is . . . we're all in this together, right?'

'Alright,' said Remy, bounding across to high-five Annie. 'Except that I am the only vegetarian in the group. That is my bad luck.'

Henry groaned. 'Well, if eating vegetables is the toughest thing in your life, Remy, you're a bit of a princess.' He stopped and looked horrified. 'Just popped into my mind, sorry.'

Remy looked rather taken aback, too.

Annie laughed. 'Ooh, what's happened to our English gentleman?'

'Radical honesty,' said Henry, blushing. 'I must've caught it from you, Annie.'

The American laughed heartily.

'Look,' said Pak Tony, indicating the nearby table with a flourish. 'A marvellous Balinese feast awaits us. Please, bring your drinks.'

Cara cast a longing look at the darkening gorge behind them. The small bamboo outhouse, the site of her earlier session with Littlefish, stood at a distance like a solitary cocoon in the light of the setting sun. Had Littlefish really channelled Astrid, or was it all a sham as Lorenzo had suggested? And how *would* she endure constant company for the next four days? The last time she'd actually savoured the presence of others, she'd been part of a trio that she'd thought would last forever.

At the table, Lorenzo pulled out a chair for Cara and politely motioned for her to sit down. It reminded her of Richard, somehow; all his countless, chivalrous attentions, which she'd invariably taken for granted.

'Thank you, Lorenzo,' she said. *And thank you, Richard*. He'd always been there, Cara realised, lurking in her consciousness. Always a faithful companion, since years ago.

The table was laden with hot coconut curries, several whole baked fish wrapped in banana leaves, trays of sweet-and-spicy tempeh, satay tofu, steaming bowls of vegetables, several colourful salads and platters of exotic fruits.

'*Bon appetit!*' cried Pak Tony.

'Let's try it in Indonesian,' Cara suggested, raising her glass. '*Selamat makan!*'

'*Selamat makan!*' the group echoed her.

And for the first time in months, Cara realised she was actually hungry.

INTIMACY

Janelle glanced up from her breakfast bowl of coconut, quinoa and slabs of fresh pineapple. Remy was looking at her again, his gaze lingering on her lips. She wiped them discreetly with a serviette, in case they were smeared with food. Like Henry, who had a smudge of Greek yoghurt across his chin—but who was talking about the Petulu herons again with such animation it didn't matter. Annie was nodding enthusiastically as he spoke between doughy mouthfuls of buckwheat pancake. Remy was pushing some overripe watermelon pieces around his plate, while Lorenzo was valiantly ploughing into an omelette—but judging by the look on his face, he wasn't relishing the experience.

'No herbs,' he said, exasperated. 'Someone should take these Balinese cooks to Europe.'

'At least you have some bacon and sausage.' Remy looked despondent. 'Already I am losing weight.'

'Good morning!' said Pak Tony, striding up to the table carrying a colourful bag. 'Are you ready for day four?' He began distributing the contents of the bag: six orange sarongs. 'When you finish breakfast, please take off your clothes and change into these for our intimacy workshop. Wrap the sarong around yourself, a bit like a towel, so your shoulders are exposed. You can use the bathrooms in the pavilion for changing, if that is easiest.'

'*All* of our clothes?' asked Annie, putting down her fork.

'Yes, please,' said Pak Tony blithely. 'I'll meet you at the pavilion shortly.'

Janelle had harboured misgivings about this intimacy workshop from the beginning: six virtual strangers expected to massage each other? Now her reservations ballooned. The flowing, gauzy fabric of the sarongs brought to mind a tantric orgy, an idea that might have been hilarious if they hadn't been in Ubud—global hotspot for ecstatic coupling, genital ozone, and pelvic chakra realignment. And while it was one thing to remove *some* of her clothes for a choreographed passion talk on teenage body dysmorphia, it was quite another to abandon *all* of them for an intimacy workshop.

Fighting the urge to run away and hide in her room, Janelle stood up from the table and walked the short distance to the pavilion. In a cubicle in the ladies' toilets, she changed out of her clothes, donned the ugly orange sarong and tied it in a tight knot across her chest. Then she went out and sat down on the floor of the pavilion for their regular morning circle, watching the sunbeams slant through the glassless window, her heart beating unnaturally fast.

Fifteen minutes later, Janelle realised that she'd overreacted. As was often the case in her life more generally, her improbable fears had not come to pass. The group was merely sitting in their circle, slightly closer than usual, their bodies turned in the same direction, giving each other an innocent shoulder massage. To substantial effect, Janelle had to concede, as Lorenzo's fingers began to release the painful knots in her neck.

'To gain maximum benefit from the intimacy of massage, you must allow yourself to *let go* and be vulnerable,' crooned Pak Tony, who was being massaged by Remy. 'But when it comes to human touch, to give is to receive. Give everything you can.'

Janelle dutifully focused on working the bare shoulders in front of her: Remy's. She again dipped her fingers into the small ceramic bowl of coconut oil; being hairier than average, his shoulders had required several applications of oil. Involuntarily, Janelle recalled her ex-boyfriend Nick. How fanatically hair-free he'd been, waxing, shaving and plucking his way to a personal best. It hadn't been a turn-on, Janelle realised, looking at Remy's shoulders now. There was something quite masculine about body hair. Sexy, even.

'Keep your eyes closed at all times,' said Pak Tony, his tone low and reverent. 'It will keep you in an intuitive state.'

Janelle closed her eyes again, wondering if he'd seen her ogling Remy.

'Now, I'd like you to find a point under your fingers that is extra tight,' Pak Tony went on. 'Focus on that area. Give it all your love and try to relieve the pressure.'

Janelle felt Lorenzo rotating the pads of his fingers around a knotty lump in her neck. In turn, she pushed her thumbs deeper into the fleshy crest of Remy's right shoulder, then slid her knuckles back and forth over it.

After several repetitions, she whispered to Remy, 'Is that okay?'

'Yes,' he answered, his voice a little hoarse.

'Good work, Janelle,' chimed Pak Tony. 'Communication is crucial for intimacy. We need to convey our needs and wants, so let's check in with each other now. Moving around the circle, please tell us how the massage is feeling for you. Remember, keep your eyes closed. We'll start with Cara.'

Janelle was tempted to peek at Cara, who was being massaged by Pak Tony himself, a position she'd been relieved to avoid.

'It feels . . .' Cara's voice trailed away.

Janelle waited, listening. When Cara said nothing more, Pak Tony intervened. 'Sometimes it's hard to find the words,' he said. 'Massage can unlock the inner wounded child, hurts that have been buried out of sight, sometimes for years. We should not fear this physical release, we should welcome it.'

After a short silence, he said, 'Henry, can you tell us how you're feeling?'

'I want to marry Cara,' Henry replied in a leisurely tone, and everyone laughed.'

'And Annie?' said Pak Tony.

'Why haven't I had more massages in my life?' asked the American. 'Why did I leave it until my sixties to start?'

'Great questions,' Pak Tony said. 'Whatever your age, the positive effects of massage are universal. What about you, Lorenzo? How are you feeling?'

The Italian exhaled audibly. 'The parasailing strained my shoulders, but Annie is fixing it. *Grazie*, Annie.'

'Ah, well done!' Pak Tony almost shouted. 'You have said the magic words, Lorenzo. Intimate touch should be respectful and gracious. When we give words of appreciation, we create a virtuous circle of positive reinforcement.'

Janelle knew it was her turn, and didn't wait for a prompt from Pak Tony. 'This shoulder massage feels like it's helping my whole body,' she said. 'Even my feet.' She wished she had something more profound to say.

'Great,' said Pak Tony. 'Tiny body parts can be trigger points for enormous pleasure. The earlobes are a case in point. Try massaging your partner's earlobes now.'

Janelle reached for Remy's earlobes and tugged at them gently, feeling rather self-conscious.

After a minute, Pak Tony asked, 'Remy, how does Janelle's massage feel?'

'Like being touched by an angel,' he murmured.

Janelle felt her cheeks flush, and several members of the group snickered. She was glad the entire group still had their eyes closed.

'Thank you for your feedback, everyone,' said Pak Tony. 'Now, it's time to return the favour for the person behind you. No need to open your eyes. Just turn around and find them with your hands.'

Janelle spun herself about on her bottom and reached for Lorenzo's shoulders, accidentally clipping his ear. 'Sorry,' she mumbled, mortified by her clumsiness.

She touched the Italian cautiously, noticing that his shoulders were devoid of both hair and bulk. Unlike Remy's brawny back, Lorenzo's felt loose and supple. *Almost like a woman's shoulders*, she thought.

At that moment, Remy's hands reached her. He cupped the base of her neck, and instinctively, she leaned back into his hands. He began moving his palms in a languid circular motion, sliding his fingers through her hair. All her life, she'd loved having her head touched; at the hairdresser, during facials, or at any other time she'd been lucky enough to receive a head massage. She felt the muscles in her face slacken and her lips drift apart.

After a while, Remy's fingers moved to the front of her neck and slid along her collarbone. He stroked its bony protrusion so tenderly, she could barely stay focused on Lorenzo. Gripping the flesh at the tops of her shoulders, Remy rolled it firmly between his thumb and fingers. She sighed, surrendering to the gentle rocking motion. And then, feeling the warmth of his breath on the back of her neck, she felt an overwhelming desire to turn around.

'Alright, please conclude your massages now.' Pak Tony's voice catapulted Janelle back into awareness of the group. 'Open your eyes and face the centre of the circle.'

When Janelle turned, timidly glancing in Remy's direction, he seemed distracted. He kept shifting his weight from side to side, as if his cushion was lumpy.

'Thank you,' she murmured, holding his gaze. Imagining, for a moment, stroking his jaw with the back of her hand.

'You're welcome,' he said, looking towards the door. 'I'm sorry, I need to . . . I had too much Balinese feast last night.'

'And that's too much information, friend,' said Henry, with a wink.

'I will be back,' Remy announced brusquely, before stalking out of the room.

Watching him go, Janelle wondered if he had even been aware of the impact of his touch. Not likely, she concluded, remembering their parasailing experience together. How he'd derided her use of zinc and a sun-safe shirt, telling her that French women would never wear either. Even worse, how he'd cracked a joke on the minibus about her unsavoury smell. Not to mention his cool reaction to her passion talk for Arabella. While the rest of the group had been full of congratulations, Remy had made no comment whatsoever, except to offer to upload it to YouTube.

I must send that link to Arabella today, she thought.

Pak Tony stood up and addressed the group. 'It is time for the second part of our intimacy workshop. Remember when you went on school excursions as a child? After boring history classes, your teacher would take you to the museum and make it all come alive?' He smiled. 'Well, we are doing the same for your intimacy learning. We are separating the women from the men for an experiential session.'

Pak Tony took up his clipboard. 'Lorenzo and Henry and . . . Remy has gone to the bathroom, hasn't he? Your manhood morning is taking place in Pak Ketut's home village. In the developed world, we often fail to mark important transitions in our lives, including the vital evolution from boy to man. But where this transition is not acknowledged, men can get stuck in the mentality of boyhood—which causes all kinds of problems for intimacy, commitment, and even fatherhood. Here in Bali, the way the locals mark the transition to manhood is with tooth filing.'

'Pardon?' said Henry.

'Tooth filing,' repeated Pak Tony. 'It's an important rite of passage in Bali.'

'Oh, Jesus,' muttered Henry.

'It's *symbolic*, Henry.' Pak Tony laughed. 'It won't hurt.'

The door opened and Remy re-entered the room, looking sheepish.

'Feeling any better?' asked Pak Tony.

'You'd better be,' Henry piped up. 'Because you're about to have some dentistry.'

Remy looked momentarily alarmed, then resumed his place in the circle without looking at Janelle.

'Now for the ladies,' Pak Tony said.

Janelle waited anxiously. She didn't like the sound of tooth filing at all.

'The three of you will be participating in a traditional Balinese vagina spa, assisted by Balinese facilitators.'

Janelle frowned; she couldn't have heard Pak Tony properly.

'A . . . what?' Cara turned a shade paler than usual.

'You're joking, aren't you?' said Annie.

'Vagina spas are very common in Indonesia,' Pak Tony went on lightly, as if he were discussing a manicure and pedicure. 'The locals call it *ratus*. Many Balinese women fog their vaginas after menstruation, to reduce stress, or to improve fertility.'

'And how exactly does one . . . *fog* one's vagina?' Janelle heard herself asking. She glanced sideways, sensing that Remy was stifling laughter, but his eyes remained doggedly focused on Pak Tony.

'The facilitators will explain it all,' Pak Tony replied. 'I'll call them now.'

'Do we have to do it?' persisted Annie.

'I assume that question is rhetorical.' Pak Tony went to a corner of the room and struck a small bronze gong.

Several seconds later, three impeccably groomed Balinese women filed into the room. '*Om swastiastu*,' said the tallest of the three, pressing her hands together and bowing slightly. 'I am Ayu. Ladies, please follow us.'

Janelle's eyes met Cara's across the room and, for a moment, Janelle glimpsed mutiny there. Then, with a nod of acquiescence, Cara stood up. Janelle followed suit but almost toppled over in her tight sarong. She held out a hand to help up Annie, whose face had a grim set to it.

'Goodbye,' said Pak Tony, waving them off.

'Enjoy,' said Henry, with a wicked glint in his eye.

Falling in behind the three Balinese women, they walked the short distance to the resort's spa, comprised of four wooden *joglo* cabins connected by a wide verandah. Ayu gestured to the colourful wooden door of the largest *joglo*, emblazoned with a giant blue swastika. Janelle stared at the symbol.

'It means "all is well" in Hinduism,' Cara explained.

'Oh,' said Janelle. 'For a moment, I thought . . .'

'No Nazism here,' said Cara. 'Hitler appropriated the swastika and misused it.'

Inside the darkened *joglo*, three trays of glowing charcoals were positioned in the centre of the room, each topped with a clay pot. An aromatic scent of herbs filled the air.

'Please change into these,' Ayu said, passing them each a loose white robe with an elasticised hole in the centre. 'Your head goes in there.'

'Do we have to get changed?' asked Annie. 'We're already naked under these sarongs.'

The woman smiled at her. 'But we need to get into there,' she said, motioning in the direction of Annie's pelvis. 'Without you catching fire.'

'Oh dear God,' muttered Annie, seizing the white robe, turning her back to the others and letting her sarong drop to the floor.

Janelle hesitated and then, seeing Cara begin to undress, she took a robe and did the same, careful not to look at anyone else.

When she turned back, Ayu was sprinkling a fine brown substance over each of the clay pots. 'This is the *ratus* powder. Traditional secret of Javanese princesses.' Her eyes were trained on her task. 'It is made from *jamu-jamu*, special herbs.'

The attendants took three wooden stools, each with a circular hole in the centre, and placed them over the pots.

Janelle had barely managed to get her head through the robe, when Ayu said, 'Sit down, please. We will keep your robes away from the fire.'

Annie eyed the stools nervously. 'How many Javanese princesses have gone up in smoke?'

'The vagina *drinks* the smoke,' said Ayu, evidently misunderstanding the question. 'It returns vitality there. It will feel like virginity again.'

Cara snorted. 'After delivering a four-kilo baby, *nothing* feels like virginity ever again.'

Janelle giggled, disarmed by Cara's uncharacteristic candour. But the circumstances were exceptional, she realised: standing half-naked together in the semi-darkness, preparing for a communal vagina spa.

'So, are we going to do this?' asked Annie doubtfully.

'I guess so.' Cara pulled a face. 'But what happens on vagina spa stays on vagina spa.'

'In that case,' said Annie. 'I won't be talking in questions anymore. And you won't tell Pak Tony, right?'

'Your secret is safe with us,' said Janelle, as Ayu motioned at them to sit down.

The three women carefully lowered themselves onto the stools, helped by the attendants who tucked their robes around their shins, then stoked the coals beneath them with hand-held fans.

Janelle wasn't sure which was more perturbing: the sensation of hot smoke wafting across her privates, or the proximity of a stranger fanning the coals. Feigning nonchalance, she counted the number of bronze bobbles adorning the head of a nearby Buddha statue. Finally, she couldn't ignore the discomfort any longer.

'It's getting a bit . . . warm, isn't it?' She winced and shifted on the stool.

Ayu instantly moved to Janelle's side. 'Too hot?'

'A little,' she replied, through gritted teeth.

'I fix.' Ayu lifted Janelle's robe and began adjusting the pot and coals below. 'Very good!' she exclaimed suddenly. 'Already you have the mucus coming out. That is fighting infection.'

Janelle died a thousand deaths.

'Oh, my!' Annie guffawed. 'And why aren't the men of Fearless off on a penis cleanse together?'

'Who says vaginas are dirty, anyway?' Cara sniffed. 'And how exactly is vagina fogging supposed to help with so-called intimacy issues?'

'Well, as the social scientist in the room,' said Janelle, repressing a smile, 'the only way we could properly test the benefits of vagina fogging would be to have sex *beforehand* as the control, then *afterwards*, to test for changes. We'd also have to repeat the experiment multiple times, for statistically significant results.'

'Oooh!' Annie hooted. 'Where can I sign up for the trial?'

'Your Miss V is important,' chimed in Ayu, from her position near Janelle's feet. 'She deserves special attention. You sit here for fifteen minutes, I will bring herbal tea. Good for cleansing inside.' She stood up and spoke to her colleagues in hushed tones, then left the room.

Turning to the others, Janelle whispered, 'Did Ayu just call our vaginas "Miss V"?'

'Why, yes. Doesn't *your* vagina have a name?' asked Cara, sniggering.

Janelle giggled. 'Actually, I struggle with the word vagina. It sounds like an angry queen ... *Her Royal Highness Vagina the Third is indisposed this evening.*'

They all laughed.

'But isn't vagina better than some of the other names for it?' observed Annie.

'You mean like *muff* or *box* or *beaver*?' asked Cara.

The American flinched.

'My brother's a tradesman,' said Janelle. 'So I grew up with *cock pocket*, *stench trench* and *beef curtains*.'

Annie's mouth dropped open.

'But not all Australian men use those terms,' Cara explained hurriedly. 'In fact, I've never heard an Australian *woman* use them, besides Janelle.'

Annie stared at them both goggle-eyed. 'I guess I'm just an old-timer country gal, but why do we even *need* a name for it?'

'Of course we do,' said Janelle. 'Think about it—there isn't a casual word for it, like "dick" for men. Vagina is really anatomical. The c-word is taboo. My mum used to call it "your flower". I mean, really.' She turned to Annie. 'What did your mum call it?'

Annie hesitated, her face flushing red. 'A *foo-foo.*'

The Australians looked at one another, their mouths curling upwards. Then all three of the women burst into laughter; it was a raucous, tension-relieving cackle.

When their laughter faded, Janelle said, 'Seriously, it's like the great unmentionable body part. Little boys talk about their *pee-pees* or *wee-wees* or *dickie-birds*, but with girls it's often . . . nothing.' She looked at Cara. 'What word did you use with your daughter?'

Cara stayed silent, and Janelle felt instant remorse. 'Oh, I'm sorry. That was insensitive of me.'

'That's okay.' Cara shook her head. 'I guess I need to learn to talk about her. Astrid was only one when she died, so genitals weren't on the agenda. She'd just started saying words like *du-du* for ducks, or *bicca* for biscuit.'

Janelle felt awkward. 'You don't have to—'

'I want to,' said Cara, rather forcefully.

The rhythmic fluttering of the attendants' fans punctuated the quiet.

After a moment, Cara sighed. 'I loved being a mum. Nothing prepares you for the passion you feel. It's fierce and intoxicating and no one else ever comes close, not even your partner. That's the big unspoken truth between parents: *you were the most important thing to me, until . . .*' She shrugged. 'Suddenly there's someone else on earth for whom you'd willingly lay down your life. They enslave you and you embrace it, because you suddenly see how little your life actually meant before.'

Janelle tried to imagine loving someone so fiercely.

'I know what you mean,' ventured Annie. 'Before I had kids, I used to worry about ridiculous things like whether teaching was the right career for me, or if I could lose ten pounds by Christmas.

After children, those sorts of worries became trivial. So much energy spent on absolutely nothing. No offence, Janelle.'

'None taken,' said Janelle, but on some level, she felt like a novitiate among the sisterhood. Would there ever come a time when she, too, would experience such an all-consuming passion? She loved her niece, but how much more strongly would she feel about her own child?

'Before I had Astrid,' continued Cara, 'I had this crazy life as a social justice reporter. I worked in the toughest places on earth. Liberia, the Sudan, Congo—I ended up managing the South African headquarters. I was fluent in French and Afrikaans and doing something really *useful* with my life. I spent a decade convinced I wasn't ready to have children, that I loved my job too much. I waited until my mid-thirties to even start thinking about babies. But when Astrid was born, my career finally met its match.'

Annie nodded vigorously. 'I was almost fluent in French, too. I had this big dream of teaching in Paris. But after kids, I decided *les enfants sont la priorité.* I didn't begrudge giving up years of teaching to look after them either. It's the most important thing I've ever done.'

'*C'est vrai,*' agreed Cara.

Janelle's grasp of high school French was sufficient to understand this exchange, but she still felt grossly inadequate. She was fluent only in her mother tongue, she hadn't travelled the world, and she didn't have a clear vision for her career. In fact, in some of her darker moments, Janelle wondered if her hopes and dreams of family life—of a husband, children, a pet and a picket fence—were actually a result of her lack of ambition. If her life didn't feel so aimless, would children really seem so appealing?

'I don't even have a career to give up for children,' she confessed. 'I tossed in my job before I enrolled in Fearless and I've got no idea what I'll do when I get back.' What had seemed like an act of courage in Melbourne just a few weeks earlier now kept her awake at night in Bali.

'You're a clever girl,' soothed Annie. 'Look at your passion talk—funny, sassy, contemporary. Leaving the wrong job will open doors to the right one. And if it doesn't, you can always retrain.'

Janelle nodded.

'At least a job's replaceable,' said Cara. 'Some things are irreversible.'

Tears filled Janelle's eyes and she reached for Cara's hand. 'I'm so sorry about what happened to your daughter.'

'It's remarkable you survived at all,' said Annie.

'Well, I didn't, really, for the first couple of years.' Cara shrugged. 'I was taking antidepressants, alcohol and anything else I could get my hands on. It stopped the sadness, and every other feeling too. Then one day I wandered past a yoga studio in Pengosekan and I just went in and did a vinyasa class. It was the first time in my life I'd done yoga.'

She smiled. 'Suddenly I was in my body again, and it helped calm my mind too. I started doing yoga every day, then twice daily. There's this pose called *savasana*—the corpse pose—where you have to slow down your body and mind, but not go to sleep. It's quite difficult to achieve, even though it looks easy; there's no thinking or hoping or wishing or striving for anything except stillness. In *savasana*, I can accept Astrid's absence somehow.'

Cara said nothing for a while. 'Of course, when *savasana* is over and I stand up from my yoga mat, my mind goes back to all the usual places. The grief, the loneliness, the anger. But yoga gives me a break. Every day, just for a little while, I've got no history and no future. I am who I am: Cara, right now, in the breath. And that's how I've survived in Bali these past few years.'

She glanced at the others. 'Fortunately, my husband just accepted this as part of my grieving process. He keeps my bank balance topped up with what my freelance writing doesn't, no questions asked.' She smiled weakly. 'Obviously I try to live frugally. But I realise how generous Richard has been. I also know I can't keep doing this forever. I'll have to start doing something more than just surviving. But it's so hard to move on.'

Cara's expression was difficult to read in the dim light. After an extended silence, she turned towards Annie. 'Do you ever think about what Kevin would want you to do, without him?'

'All the time,' replied Annie. 'Especially when I consider . . . going on a date or something, with another man in a Stetson.'

'What actually happened to Kevin?' asked Janelle, emboldened by the darkness. 'Was he sick?'

'Lord, no,' said Annie. 'He got bitten by a rattlesnake. I spent years feeling angry with him for being so stupid—I mean, he must've done something to aggravate it. The venom load it injected was huge. It killed him before he could even drive back to the homestead for help. Our farmhand found him sitting upright in the pickup.'

'No wonder you're afraid of snakes,' observed Cara.

Annie nodded. 'Kevin became a statistic, and my life changed overnight. It's never been the same since—I've been mourning him for twenty years. So I know how you feel, Cara.'

'And you haven't . . . had another partner at all, since Kevin?' ventured Janelle.

'I've kept myself too busy for a relationship.' Annie smiled. 'This vagina spa is as intimate as I've been in years.'

They all laughed once more.

'A few men have sniffed around at church,' Annie continued, 'but I've never felt ready. Kevin was a good man, a kind man—and they're hard to find. It's a cliché, but it's true. Probably a bit like your Richard, Cara.'

Janelle nodded, thinking of Nick. The epitome of an advertising executive—driven, handsome and funny, but devoid of that crucial quality, kindness.

'I'd like to meet a kind man,' she blurted. 'And have a baby.' Inexplicably, she thought of Remy, then castigated herself for it. She barely even knew him.

'There's still plenty of time for that,' said Annie. 'How old are you?'

'Twenty-nine,' Janelle replied. 'But it takes time to get to know someone, right?'

'Not necessarily,' said Annie. 'Kevin and I only courted for three months before we tied the knot. That was decades ago, of course. But sometimes you've just got to take a risk and follow your heart.'

Janelle smiled wistfully. 'So the fairytale does exist?'

'Until your handsome prince gets bitten by a snake,' said Annie.

They watched the smoke curling around them.

After a while, Janelle spoke again. 'Do you still miss him?'

Annie grunted. 'Of course. Here in Bali, I'm surrounded by so many people, but I still feel isolated. Maybe it's the fact that I can't speak Indonesian, maybe it's because they're strangers, mostly. I don't know.' She sighed. 'I could go home to California, but I'm an empty-nester; there's nothing to keep me there, really. At least the animals at BAF need me.'

Janelle felt suddenly sorry for the older woman. 'There's got to be love out there for you somewhere, Annie.'

'Love's overrated.' Annie laughed. 'Unless you know of any fellas who want to cosy up with a fat American?'

'You've got truckloads of charisma,' said Cara.

'And your hair is beautiful, Annie,' added Janelle. 'You always look like you've just stepped out of a salon.'

'Well, I'm a bit of a fixer-upper.' Annie sounded as if she didn't know quite how to handle these compliments. 'So, what happened to Richard? Are you still in touch?'

Cara hesitated. 'After the accident, he wanted us to stay together. But I needed space, so I . . . ran away, I guess, to Bali. He tried to call me regularly, but every time I heard from him, I started grieving all over again. After I got into yoga, I rang him. We had an honest conversation, and I asked him to stop contacting me. To his credit, he respected that. Now he only makes contact for things he can't avoid—insurance renewals and that kind of stuff. It's been working well for a year now.' She sighed. 'Then last month, someone from my mothers' group emailed me. She told me he's started dating again, which probably means he'll be looking to . . . formalise the separation soon.'

'Ouch,' said Annie. 'That's gotta hurt.'

One of the attendants looked at her. 'Your Miss V is sore?'

'No, no.' Annie chuckled uneasily. 'It's fine.' She turned back to Cara. 'How do *you* feel about divorce?'

In the light of the glowing embers, Cara's eyes were shiny with tears. 'Well, there's no other way, is there? Too much history between us. To be honest, I don't even know if I'm sad about Richard, or if I'm just grieving the idea of happily-ever-after. Which is rather lame, isn't it?'

'It's not lame,' said Janelle quietly. 'Everyone's looking for the same thing. Love, connection, happiness . . .'

'Contentment,' corrected Annie. 'Happiness is fleeting. But contentment, well, that's achievable in a relationship with the right person. I had that with Kevin.'

Janelle nodded, deep in thought. She'd been infatuated with Nick, dazzled by his success and desperate to please. But he'd never been content with her, always encouraging her to lose weight, get fit, be more ambitious in her career.

'That's a good way of describing it,' said Cara softly. 'I was content with Richard, but we weren't wildly passionate, so I used to think there was something wrong. I took our relationship for granted and always compared it with other couples.' She shook her head.

'Is it really too late with Richard?' asked Janelle. 'I mean, surely it's possible for two people to survive a tragedy? Not to forget about Astrid, but to—'

Cara cut her off. 'I doubt it.' After a moment, she said, 'But what I do know is that *you'll* find love and have a baby, Janelle. You'd make a great mum.'

Janelle beamed. 'That's one of the nicest things anyone has ever said to me.'

'Really?' said Cara gently. 'You must be keeping the wrong company, then.'

I have been, Janelle thought now. *Nick was never good for me.*

The Balinese attendants sitting at their feet in the shadows began waving their fans faster, relentlessly pushing the smoke upwards as they chatted away.

Annie turned to the others. 'I think there's only one thing worse than *having* a vagina spa, and that's *giving* one.'

They all laughed again, then sat together in comfortable silence. *Remarkably comfortable*, Janelle thought, *given they were strangers just four days ago*. Perhaps there was a method in Pak Tony's madness, after all.

The door swung open and Ayu entered, carrying a tray set with steaming glasses of tea. 'Ladies,' she said, 'the vagina spa is over. Please take your bath.' She motioned to a large privacy screen on the far side of the room.

Janelle stood up first, a little shakily, and walked after Ayu. Annie and Cara followed, stepping gingerly across the damp slate tiles. Reaching the wooden screen, Janelle stared at the huge clawfooted tub beyond. Tea lights lined its rim and petals floated on the surface of the water.

Ayu gestured at the water. 'Please, your bath.'

'Er . . .' Janelle cast her eyes about the bathing area. 'Is there only one?'

Ayu smiled. 'Yes, but very deep. Big enough for all of you.'

'*What?*' Annie was evidently exasperated. 'First we have our vaginas fogged. Then we're supposed to take a bath together?'

Ayu nodded.

'Well, that's it for me,' said Annie, resolutely. 'My intimacy experience is officially over.'

'But what happens if we abscond?' asked Janelle.

'Who cares?' said Annie.

'Hear, hear. I'll tell Pak Tony myself,' said Cara. 'Can we go back now, please, Ayu?'

The Balinese woman bowed and showed them to the door.

Ten minutes later, back at the bamboo pavilion, they found Pak Tony sitting on a yoga mat. His eyes were closed and his legs tucked up in lotus pose.

Cara cleared her throat to speak, but Pak Tony raised his right hand for silence. 'Don't say a word,' he urged, his eyes still closed. '*Ratus* creates a sacred female space. Whatever transpired between the three of you should not be disclosed to me—or to any other male—at any time, because together, you were manifesting the Divine Goddess.'

Janelle raised an eyebrow. She caught Cara's eye, then Annie's, and the three of them struggled to suppress their laughter.

Pak Tony opened his eyes and smiled at them. 'Do you feel transformed?'

They all nodded, poker-faced, but Janelle was certain her nostrils were flaring.

'The men will come back from their manhood morning soon,' he continued. 'Why don't you have some lunch? You'll need your energy for this afternoon's fear safari at Paradise Animal Sanctuary. They have the largest snake collection in Bali, and some very rare birds.'

The women walked together towards the door and the buffet beyond.

'Well, even if *I* don't love this fear safari,' said Annie, 'it sounds like Henry will.'

After their meal, Pak Tony herded the three women into the minibus, where they sat waiting for the men to return. They'd been delayed, Pak Tony explained, on account of an unexpected invitation to lunch after the tooth-filing ceremony in Pak Ketut's family compound. When the trio finally appeared, on foot, with frangipanis tucked behind their ears, they seemed buoyant.

Pak Ketut boarded the bus, looking penitent. 'I am sorry, very long ceremony. Big feast.' He glanced rather fearfully at the facilitator. 'We go now to the animal sanctuary?'

Pak Tony nodded and the driver started the engine while the other men climbed aboard. Henry took a seat behind Pak Ketut, and immediately engaged him in earnest conversation. Lorenzo followed Remy halfway down the minibus, where they stood for a moment, Lorenzo's arm slung around the Frenchman's shoulders, talking to Pak Tony about their manhood morning.

Annie leaned across the aisle to Janelle. 'Maybe they *did* have a penis cleanse,' she whispered. 'But, then again, Italians *are* demonstrative.'

Janelle giggled. As the bus began to move off, Lorenzo sat down in a seat to himself several rows ahead of them.

Cara turned towards the other two women. 'You know, it's totally acceptable in Bali for men to touch each other. It's touching the opposite sex that's taboo.'

'What, no touching?' Remy sat down next to Janelle. 'Dare I ask about your . . . vagina spa?'

'Nooo,' said Janelle, feigning prudishness. 'Pak Tony has forbidden us to talk about secret women's business.'

'I knew you were up to no good.' His eyes wandered over her face and then lower, straying towards her chest—making her stomach flutter—before returning to her face. 'You look fresh, Janelle.'

The way Remy pronounced her name, with a soft *J*, made her heart sing. All her life, she'd been a harsh, larrikin-sounding *Ja-nelle*. But Remy had transformed her into an exotic, Continental-sounding *Zsa-nelle*.

'And you seem to have all your teeth,' she replied. 'How was the tooth-filing?'

'*C'était incroyable!*' enthused Remy. His arm lay casually across the top of the empty seat in front of them and, inspired perhaps by the massaging earlier, Janelle imagined palpating his bicep.

He leaned even closer. 'Janelle, it was strange. When I was lying on my back in the ceremony, I thought of you.' He lowered his voice. 'Suddenly I realised something very important. I would rather lose a tooth—'

'Remy!' Lorenzo called, waving his mobile phone at the Frenchman. 'Have you seen the number of views on the YouTube clip already?'

Janelle squinted, curious about what Remy was about to say. 'What . . . YouTube clip?'

'Yours,' said Remy. 'The one you told me to upload, *For Bella.*'

'I didn't tell you to upload it.' She stared at him. 'Not for the public. You uploaded it privately, didn't you?'

Remy's face fell. 'No, I . . . uploaded it to the main platform.'

'*What?*' Janelle snapped. 'My niece hasn't even seen the clip yet. I wanted to check it first, then send her a *private* link. I remember telling you that, Remy. How could you just go and—'

Lorenzo flopped down onto the seat in front of them. 'Janelle, see for yourself.' He turned his phone towards her. She stared at the image on the screen—a thumbnail of herself, mid-striptease—then at the number of views listed beneath: 1,978,566.

'That's not possible,' she gasped. '*When* did you upload it?'

'Two days ago,' said Remy. 'Straight after your passion talk.'

'It's been syndicated by Noteworthy and Speakout,' explained Lorenzo. 'It's all over social media. You're a heroine to many young girls now, Janelle. Congratulations.'

Janelle was struggling for breath. She read the description beneath the YouTube listing: *An average Australian woman takes a provocative stand against unrealistic beauty ideals imposed by the fashion industry and pop culture. Dedicated to Bella, her niece, and to girls affected by eating disorders everywhere.*

Part of her was impressed by how well Remy had captured her intentions, the other part was outraged at being labelled 'average'—even though it was true. But she could barely believe that almost two million people had watched her do a striptease.

She turned to Remy and exploded. 'What were you thinking?'

He looked contrite. 'I didn't hear you tell me not to upload it publicly.'

'I find that hard to believe,' Janelle hissed. 'My instructions were clear. Do you need your ears cleaned out?' She realised suddenly that she was screeching like her mother.

'But this is great,' said Lorenzo, pushing the phone towards her again. 'Marketers dream of this sort of success. Two of the biggest content creators have picked it up. You've had a real impact, Janelle.'

'But not on the person I was trying to reach,' she protested. 'That clip was meant for my family, not the whole bloody world.'

She stared at the numbers on the screen once more. What would her extended family and friends say? Maybe everyone she knew had already watched it? The thought made her feel faint.

'I want you to take it down,' she said to Remy. 'Right now.'

'I can't do that from my phone,' he replied despairingly. 'I need access to my laptop. I'll do it as soon as we get back from the animal sanctuary, I promise.'

'Think about it, Janelle,' said Lorenzo, standing up and sliding his phone back into his pocket. 'The clip is out there already, you've touched a lot of people. You're supposed to do something new every day for your odyssey, aren't you?' He looked at her pointedly. 'So leave it online.' He turned and picked his way back to his seat.

Not like this, Janelle thought, feeling overwhelmed. She'd only been in Bali for five days, four of them at Fearless. She'd spent the time absorbed in quirky activities with almost-strangers, situations contrived to mimic intimacy, but were any of these interactions authentic or meaningful? Her niece was struggling in Australia, and now Janelle's privacy had been compromised. Was choosing Fearless a huge mistake?

Pak Tony cleared his throat. 'Just a little warning,' he said, standing at the front of the bus. 'Many of you appear to be very attached to your devices. But it's a delusion to believe that using social media constitutes a relationship. Be prudent with your use of technology on this retreat, or I might confiscate your phones.'

Lorenzo made a derisive sound, and Pak Tony levelled his gaze at him. 'Are you a nomophobe, Lorenzo?' he asked. 'Many people can't go an hour without checking for electronic affirmation of their existence.' He smiled. 'One of your challenges at the animal sanctuary will involve *real* communication with someone important to you, using an old-fashioned method like a phone conversation or a handwritten letter.'

The Italian shrugged as if this didn't faze him. Pak Tony stared at him a little longer before he took his seat once more.

Sensing that Remy was about to speak to her again, Janelle stood up quickly.

'I am sorry, Janelle,' said Remy, his tone plaintive.

You can stuff your 'Zsa-nelle', she thought, stepping into the aisle.

'Please.' He reached out and caught her hand.

Shaking it free, she found a seat elsewhere.

Henry looked out the bus window at the neat-looking village through which they were passing. It was evidently a centre for stonemasonry, with almost every roadside stall filled with lava-stone statues, granite planters, or intricate sandstone reliefs. He reached forward and tapped Pak Ketut on the shoulder.

'Does *your* village have a trade specialty?' he asked, motioning to the stalls beyond the window. 'I didn't notice anything earlier.'

The driver shook his head. 'Before Puri Damai was built, our village was a centre for woodcarving and farming. Now we have tourism. Some of our old people still do woodcarving, like Pak Polos.'

Henry nodded. He'd met Pak Polos, the village elder, at the tooth-filing ceremony. Along with almost every other member of Pak Ketut's extended family of sixty.

'The villagers were happy you visited,' said Pak Ketut now. 'This morning also, when I took Ibu Annie for her Indonesian lesson. She made them very happy by asking many questions.'

'But I had to,' Annie called out, grinning. 'My odyssey gave me no choice, right?'

The driver returned her smile in the rear-view mirror. 'Your questions mean you are learning more about Balinese culture, Ibu Annie.'

The American seemed to sit taller in her seat.

'It was nice to meet everyone in your village,' said Henry.

Though nice isn't exactly the right word, Henry thought; perhaps *intense* and *confronting* were more appropriate terms to describe Henry's first contact with Balinese people who weren't serving him in some way.

They'd set out for the village on foot from Puri Damai, escorted by Pak Ketut. Arriving at the sprawling family compound, they were immediately introduced to three young men—Oka, Gede and Kadek—all of whom were having their teeth filed that morning. They had recently turned seventeen, although their slight frames and boyish grins made them seem much younger. Dozens of family members and neighbours milled about wearing flamboyant ceremonial garb reminiscent, in Henry's eyes, of the bright plumage of Amazonian macaws.

Pak Ketut guided the three Westerners to a guest room and distributed their ceremonial clothes, all freshly laundered after the water ceremony the previous day. Henry marvelled at the flat squares of precision-ironed clothes wrapped tightly in plastic. The ironer had even pressed his underpants, he noted with some mortification as he unwrapped them.

'Oh,' said Pak Ketut, handing Henry a one-hundred-thousand-rupiah note. 'The laundry lady found this in your shorts.'

'Thank you,' said Henry, impressed by her honesty.

Once changed, they were escorted to a courtyard festooned with decorations handwoven from pandan leaves and coconut husks and other natural materials. Dogs sniffed around a table of lavish offerings placed in front of a simple ancestral temple where a white-clad priest and his grey-bearded attendant were leading prayers. Henry soon found himself on his knees in the hot sun, pressing a petal-filled offering to his forehead, trying to mimic the synchronised movements of the Balinese around him.

As soon as the prayers were concluded, Henry rose to his feet, cursing his clumsiness in a sarong. Turning to look for a bathroom, instead he'd found a wall of Balinese well-wishers waiting to greet the Westerners. After Henry had shaken hands with at least forty people, an ancient-looking man had approached, offering small glasses of steaming, fragrant tea.

'I am Pak Polos,' the man said in English. 'Welcome to our village.'

Henry instantly sensed his status. 'Thank you,' he replied, accepting a glass. 'I'm Henry. It's a great honour to be here. We have nothing like tooth filing in our home countries.'

'Then you have not grown up,' observed Pak Polos.

Henry considered this as he watched wave after wave of villagers submitting their offerings at the shrine. His former girlfriends would probably agree with the old man's assessment, he decided. One of them had even told him that he had Peter Pan syndrome, a term he'd had to google. It echoed Littlefish's view of him, too: *You're still a child inside.*

'Your friends don't drink tea?' asked Pak Polos, nodding at Lorenzo and Remy.

Fearing that they'd caused offence by not taking a cup, Henry replied, 'They're enjoying talking to new friends.'

A gaggle of Balinese girls had encircled Remy, taking selfies with their mobile phones. The towering Frenchman—sweating profusely in his too-tight sarong—appeared baffled by all the attention. Lorenzo stood several metres from Remy, aloof in his reflective sunglasses. His arms were slung casually around the shoulders of two young men, mimicking the stance of the locals.

'You are from England?' asked Pak Polos.

'Yes,' said Henry, surprised. 'How could you tell?'

The old man laughed. 'Many tourists come here, almost every day. I learn your language. I know your accent.'

A prolonged metallic ringing prompted Pak Polos to relieve Henry of his teacup. 'Go now,' he commanded, pointing towards the family shrine.

The priest's attendant shepherded them towards a raised bamboo platform near the shrine. There, they lay down side by side in pairs—Henry with Gede, Remy with Oka, Lorenzo with Kadek. A crowd gathered and a small gamelan orchestra, which Henry had somehow previously failed to notice, struck up a discordant arrangement. Sitting on his heels at the edge of the orchestra was a shrivelled old man playing a small bamboo flute. His fingers flew deftly over it, his eyes closed and his expression rapturous.

Henry stared up at the thatched ceiling, feeling distinctly nervous. *But you wanted to see how the real people live*, he reminded himself.

A moment later, the priest appeared carrying a long metal rod. 'The teeth will be killed first,' announced the attendant, causing Henry to gasp. 'Open your mouth.'

'Nothing hurting,' whispered Gede, lying next to him.

To Henry's relief, the priest only lightly tapped their teeth with the rod, using its end to inscribe invisible Sanskrit symbols on each tooth. The attendant followed behind, chanting ancient mantras and flicking holy water over their faces, then slipping small cylinders of sugar into their mouths.

As Henry sucked the sugar, the attendant approached him once more. 'You first,' he said amiably. 'Open your mouth wider now.'

Henry shook his head, as if in sympathy with his knees.

The attendant crouched down. 'I will file four times, one for each dog tooth,' he explained.

Gede placed a hand on Henry's arm and whispered, 'You will not feel much.'

Henry screwed his eyes shut and opened his mouth. He sensed a gentle pressure against his upper right canine, then heard a scraping sound. This occurred again on the left, then on the lower canines.

'*Sudah*,' said the attendant, with a finality in his tone that prompted Henry to open his eyes. The attendant grinned down at him. 'Finished. When you die, the gods will now see you are a human, not a dog.'

Henry raised himself up onto his elbows to watch Remy and Lorenzo, who were subjected to only a few light strokes, too.

'Thank you,' he whispered to Gede, as the ceremony proceeded. 'You were right. Not too bad.'

The Balinese, however, were subjected to far more forceful treatment, he saw now. The three youths grimaced under the pressure, sweat pouring off their foreheads, but none of them recoiled. To Henry's great dismay, the gamelan orchestra played louder to drown out the unnerving sound of the file being drawn back and forth across their teeth. Finally, when Henry felt he could watch no longer, the youths were helped up into a sitting position to spit their tooth filings into a small silver bowl. The attendant siphoned these filings into miniature yellow coconuts, which the priest then took away for burial in the family temple.

With the ceremony now complete, the women of the village began passing around trays of *jajan*: deep-fried spring rolls, stuffed tofu, banana cake, green honey-soaked pancakes, red bean rolls, and a range of colourful jelly treats that the children seemed to love.

'Stay and eat now,' said Pak Polos, clapping a hand on Henry's shoulder. 'There will be yellow rice and fried eel. Join us.'

Henry looked to Pak Ketut for direction. Judging by the driver's expression, this was not an invitation that could be refused.

'We'd love to,' said Henry. 'But we may not be able to stay very long, I'm afraid. We are going to Paradise Animal Sanctuary this afternoon.'

Pak Polos looked unconcerned and beckoned to a young boy, speaking to him in Balinese. The boy hurried off, and soon returned with four white chickens dangling upside down from one hand and an enormous knife in the other. Obviously a late addition to the feast, the birds were alive but strangely silent, with rolling, frightened eyes. The wire with which they were bound was rubbing against the scaly flesh of their legs, making it bleed. Henry winced at the sight.

'You don't eat chicken?' asked Pak Polos, his eyes narrowing. 'We make for you.'

'No, it's not that,' Henry replied hurriedly. 'It's just I . . . feel a bit sorry for them. Back in England, we use—' he realised he couldn't backpedal now—'slightly more humane practices with animals.'

Pak Polos hooted as if Henry had just told a tremendous joke. Then his face turned deadly serious. 'Where are your grandparents?'

Henry hesitated; three of them had passed away. 'Er . . . my nan lives in Cornwall.' He thought of his kindly grandmother, with her slightly bewildered pale blue eyes, sitting in a wheelchair alongside the other residents of Leighton Gardens Aged Care Facility.

'With you?'

'In a nursing home, actually.'

'I know about those.' Pak Polos motioned around at the bustling compound. 'Here, eight families live together. Three generations. The oldest have the best rooms—highest off the ground—because they have earned our respect.' He looked at Henry. 'In your country, you send your elders away. No family is living with them in a . . .'

'Nursing home,' Henry repeated.

The old man shrugged. 'You think we are unkind to our chickens. We think you are unkind to your elders.'

Henry stared at the man.

'Come and eat,' said Pak Polos. 'We talk too much.'

But after he'd eaten his fill and talked some more, thanked the villagers and taken his leave with Remy and Lorenzo, Henry kept pondering this discomfiting truth.

And as their minibus pulled into the crowded car park of Paradise Animal Sanctuary and he resolved to write to his nan for the first time in years, Henry realised that the old man's words would stay with him forever.

⟳

Forty-five minutes later, with a sugary welcome drink sloshing about in his stomach, Henry found himself sweating profusely at the front of the Python Pit. It was a cavern-like space designed for small groups, with three low benches facing two glass cases. Each case contained an outlandishly long snake, spotlit from the ceiling. Standing next to Henry was Pak Nyoman, an exuberant snake handler.

'Now,' said Pak Nyoman, nodding at the python coiled on the end of his handling pole. 'Here are the rules. Don't turn Shanti upside down or dangle her in the air. Use your whole hand when you touch the snake, not two fingers. Don't make abrupt movements; move calmly and smoothly. And don't have any food on you when you handle her, or she might slide into your pockets. And one last thing.' He grinned at Henry. 'Don't worry, be happy.'

Chuckling at his own joke, the handler moved behind Henry and carefully lowered the snake's midsection across the Englishman's shoulders. The head and tail were still visible, which Henry found vaguely reassuring, but he couldn't bring himself to look the creature in the eye.

Annie waved at Henry from the rear bench. 'How does it feel?' she called nervously, her own forehead glistening with sweat beneath the lights. As the three-metre-long reticulated python entwined itself leisurely around his shoulders, Henry found himself lost for words.

Heavy, he wanted to reply, *and rough*. He'd always imagined snakes to be slippery, lightweight creatures.

'Henry, no!' admonished Pak Nyoman. 'Shanti can read your body language. If you don't relax, she will grip your arms more tightly. She doesn't like those shaking branches.'

It was true: Henry's arms were trembling. He was breathing rapidly too, as if poised to deliver a speech. He needed to remember one of Pak Tony's fear-facing strategies, and quickly.

Exhaling deeply, Henry closed his eyes and pictured himself lying in the Rainham Marshes, watching a handsome family of blue tits. Their yellow and blue-grey plumage was exquisite, rivalled only by their trilling calls. It was a warm spring day, all sunshine and flowers and bumblebees, and there was music on the breeze—his second-grade scripture teacher's adaptation of 'All Things Bright and Beautiful':

All things sweet and frightening,
All stampeding herds,
All the slimy, slippery things,
And all the pretty birds.

Snakes are just like birds, Henry told himself now. *Flightless, featherless birds.*

He opened one eye. Shanti was still lying heavily across his shoulders, but he'd stopped trembling. He opened the other, realising with relief that he wasn't going to faint. Janelle smiled jubilantly at him and Remy gave him a theatrical thumbs-up.

'You're a natural,' said Pak Nyoman.

Henry snorted, prompting the python to rear back into a sharp S-curve.

'Oh, Jesus,' he gasped.

Pak Nyoman thrust his handling pole between the snake and Henry's face. 'Okay, Shanti,' he crooned, guiding the python onto the pole.

Once the snake was curled tightly around it, he turned and glared at Henry. '*Never* make sudden sounds like that.'

Henry mumbled an apology, relieved to be rid of Shanti.

'Never mind, Henry!' called Pak Tony, stepping forward and beaming at him. 'You seemed to struggle with that fear safari, even though you've not had a problem with snakes before.'

'I've not been that close to one, have I?' objected Henry. 'We don't get bloody great big pythons like that in England. I thought I was going to pass out.'

'But I saw you deploying a relaxation technique. That is a much better outcome than fainting.' The facilitator slid his hand over Shanti's scales, in the direction of her tail. 'Today's fear safari is actually an extension of this morning's intimacy workshop. The snake is a powerful archetype and a common symbol of sexuality.'

Henry looked at him askance. There was *nothing* sexual about this.

'But the real challenge today is not handling a python.' Pak Tony turned to the rest of the group and smiled. 'It's never that simple with a Fearless exercise, is it?'

Henry grimaced in anticipation.

'Your challenge is to answer an intimate question while holding Shanti,' Pak Tony continued. 'I will whisper a question in your ear, and you need to think of the answer. Holding the snake will engage your reptilian brain—which is all about instinctive responses—and help keep you honest. Please don't tell me your answer—keep it to yourself.'

Pak Tony turned back to Henry. 'Since you've held Shanti already, Henry, you can be our first guinea pig.'

An unfortunate metaphor, Henry thought, considering the normal course of relations between snakes and guinea pigs.

Pak Nyoman moved towards him again, his expression mildly disdainful. Slowly he settled the snake across Henry's shoulders once more.

Pak Tony leaned into Henry and cupped his hands around his ear. 'Who do you wish was next to you right now?' he whispered.

A mental image appeared instantly, and Henry smiled. *Jim.* His oldest friend, his birdwatching partner, the brother he'd never had. A man going through the motions of his ranger's existence in England, while Henry indulged in an equatorial quest of parasailing, intimacy workshops and tooth-filing ceremonies. What on earth would no-nonsense Jim make of it all?

'Good,' said Pak Tony, observing Henry's face. 'You can sit down, Henry.'

The snake handler lifted Shanti off Henry, who at once felt elated with relief.

'Now, who's next?' asked Pak Tony.

Annie raised her hand at the rear of the pit and turned to Pak Ketut, who was sitting next to her. 'Better get it over and done with, right?' She moved to the front, visibly shaking, and faced the group. Just by the look of her, Henry worried she might faint.

Pak Tony laid a hand on her arm. 'It's not a venomous snake, there's nothing to fear. This is radical desensitisation and it can work wonders, if you relax with it. If it becomes too difficult, just say "stop" and we will.'

Annie nodded, steeling herself as the snake handler approached from behind. Henry heard her draw in a long sharp breath, which she seemed to hold for an extended period. She swayed a little on her feet and Pak Ketut suddenly rose from his bench and took several steps towards her, clearly worried.

'It's alright, Ketut,' said Pak Tony, motioning at the driver to return to his seat. 'Nyoman's got it all under control.'

'Oooh,' Annie half giggled, half squeaked, as the handler draped the snake across her. 'Is this how Eve felt, I wonder?' Despite her apparent jocularity, she was still deathly pale.

'You're doing so well,' said Pak Tony. 'Using humour and curiosity to negate your fear. Now . . .' He leaned forward and whispered his question in her ear.

'Oh, that's easy,' she said softly. Closing her eyes, she appeared to be concentrating, then she opened them once more and nodded at the facilitator.

'Right then,' said Pak Tony. 'You can sit back down.'

Pak Nyoman lifted the python from Annie's shoulders. The colour rushed back into her cheeks, spreading right up to her ears. As she moved back to her seat, Pak Ketut rose again from the bench and took her arm, patting her on the back as she sat down.

One by one, each member of the group held Shanti with varying degrees of anxiety and discomfort while Pak Tony whispered his question to them.

Finally, only Lorenzo remained. Unlike the others in the group, he didn't appear remotely concerned by the python. But when Pak Tony whispered the question into his ear, he looked confused.

'I am sorry,' Lorenzo said. 'I do not understand.'

Pak Tony spoke into his ear again, but Lorenzo shook his head.

'Is it still not clear?' asked Pak Tony, in a vexed tone.

'I heard the words.' Lorenzo glanced around the Python Pit, seeming mildly disoriented. 'I need more time.'

He screwed up his eyes, as if in deep thought. After a minute or so, he said, 'I failed.'

'What do you mean?' asked Pak Tony.

'I cannot answer the question.' Now it was Lorenzo's turn to sound vexed.

'Why, Lorenzo?' Pak Tony had slowed and lowered his tone, as if speaking to a difficult child. 'Would you like to try again?'

Lorenzo shook his head, stroking the snake absently. 'Already I have tried. There is no solution to my problem.'

'*What* problem?'

Lorenzo eyeballed Pak Tony, and Henry felt as if he was witnessing a battle of sorts. A moment later, Lorenzo lowered his gaze and signalled to the snake handler. 'Please,' he said. 'Take her back.' He lifted his arms confidently to help Pak Nyoman shift the snake onto the handling pole.

'What happened, Lorenzo?' Pak Tony persisted. 'Please share?'

The Italian looked blankly at Pak Tony. 'I simply cannot think of anyone who would enjoy being this close to a snake. I know Lavinia wouldn't.'

Pak Tony watched Lorenzo return to his seat, a concerned expression on his face. Henry had the distinct impression that the facilitator was about to challenge him further. He didn't, however, and instead turned back to the group.

'Right. For all of you who *did* answer the question, the final component of this challenge is the intimacy bridge. Over the next thirty minutes, you are going to reach out to the person you pictured.' He motioned to a large box of stationery filled with notepads, pens, envelopes and Indonesian postage stamps. 'If the person is living, please write them a letter or call them directly. No emails, please. You must tell this person what they mean to you.

'If the person is no longer alive,' he continued, 'you can still write them a letter. Explain what they meant to you and how you plan to honour them in the future. We'll discuss later what to do with that letter. But for the time being, just write it, then keep it in a safe place.' He smiled. 'Any questions?'

Henry raised his hand. 'I want to call someone in England, but it's quite early in the morning there. What time are we meeting up again?'

'Four o'clock at the bird show. But don't concern yourself with time zones, Henry. Take a chance.' Pak Tony grinned. 'Risk waking someone up, tell that person exactly how you feel. Be authentic and vulnerable, because that is how love thrives in the world.'

Henry was not at all convinced that Jim would appreciate an emotional declaration before sunrise on a Wednesday morning.

Pak Tony glanced around the group. 'If there are no more questions, please complete your intimacy bridge and we'll meet again in roughly thirty minutes for the Bali Birds of Prey show. Think of it as a reward for all your hard work today.' He waved a hand towards the exit of the Python Pit. 'It's a spectacular demonstration of instinct. I've seen it dozens of times before, but I never get sick of it. The amphitheatre is a short walk from here. All of you may leave now, except for Lorenzo.' He nodded at the Italian. 'You and I will stay in the Python Pit a little longer.'

As the rest of the group began filing out of the Python Pit, Henry saw the Italian shake his head. 'Are you alright?' Henry asked in a low voice as he passed.

Lorenzo turned and, for a second, Henry saw untrammelled fury in his eyes. Henry recoiled, surprised to see the relaxed, cool Italian so unsettled. Why was he so angry? Then the Italian shrugged aimiably and Henry was left wondering if he'd simply imagined it.

Emerging from the Python Pit, Henry squinted in the glare. The afternoon was shimmering and cloudless, with a steady line of tourists still streaming through the iron gate at the entrance to the animal sanctuary. The Fearless participants began wandering in different directions across the grassy concourse.

Janelle and Cara moved towards a gift shop, pausing near a pond to watch a raft of brown and white ducks, with unusual crests on their heads, waddle out of the water and across their path. Remy headed to the public toilets again—Henry could only assume he was suffering from Bali belly—while Annie followed the signposts down a path leading to the amphitheatre, *mushola* and owl house. Henry pondered what a *mushola* might be, then spotted a drinks stall. A wiry young man sat behind the bright red wooden trolley; two large cooler boxes were perched on top of the trolley, shaded by a frilly-fringed umbrella. As Henry approached, the seller stood up and lifted one of the lids to display its contents.

'*Selamat siang*,' Henry said, inspecting the drinks. It was a greeting Cara had taught him.

The seller smiled. 'You speak Indonesian?'

'Hardly,' said Henry, selecting a bottle of iced tea. Withdrawing a handful of coins from his pocket, he opened his palm to the seller. 'I don't know much about your money, either.'

He let the seller pick out the required amount, then glanced at the man's name tag. '*Terima kasih*, Yanto,' he said, and noticed the man's eyes for the first time. One was slower than the other and partially closed. Henry wondered if it was a birth defect or the result of an injury.

'You're welcome,' said the man, smiling again.

The Balinese are always smiling, Henry thought, *but how can they be happy? People like Yanto, standing all day in the scorching sun, selling drinks to sweaty Westerners.*

Henry looked down at the remaining coins in his palm and held them out to the seller. 'Here,' he said. 'I don't know how much it is, but you can have it.'

The seller looked confused.

'Take it,' said Henry, placing the coins in a pile on the second cooler box. 'Consider it a tip.' It couldn't be much, he knew, and *he* certainly wouldn't miss it.

'*Terima kasih*.' Yanto slipped the money into his pocket.

'*Kembali*,' said Henry, mimicking Cara's pronounciation. *You're welcome.* He began fumbling with the cap on his iced tea. *Why are products wrapped in layers of impenetrable plastic? What has happened to old-fashioned screwtops? The world's gone security mad*, Henry thought.

'I can do it,' said Yanto helpfully, reaching forward to assist. With a single wrench, he broke both the outer and inner seals.

'You are strong,' observed Henry. 'Stronger than me. Which part of Bali are you from, Yanto?'

The man shook his head. 'I am from East Java.'

Henry recalled the words of the taxi driver who'd driven him from Denpasar airport some five days earlier, and his indignant tone when describing Javanese workers taking Balinese jobs.

'Do you like Bali?' Henry asked, swigging on his tea. It was far too sweet, but deliciously cold.

Yanto's smile remained fixed. 'I go back to Java soon.'

'For work?' Henry swallowed another few mouthfuls, then proffered the drink in Yanto's direction. 'Would you like some? You must be hot.'

Yanto shook his head. 'I am fasting. I go to Java next week for Lebaran. At the end of Ramadan, our fasting month.'

'You're fasting now?' Henry didn't think he could survive a single day in the tropics without eating or drinking. 'That must be quite a challenge.'

A tourist approached the drinks stall and Henry took a step back. She was dressed skimpily in a neon orange bikini top and tight denim shorts. Her skin was burnished copper, and her flat abdomen was studded at the navel with a glitzy green stone. So much of her flesh was exposed, Henry hardly knew where to look.

'Coke,' she said brusquely, thrusting a ten-thousand-rupiah note at Yanto.

He opened his cooler box, retrieved a well-worn glass bottle and passed it to her. 'Fifteen thousand, please,' he said, averting his good eye.

'What?' The tourist's voice was indignant. 'I'll give you ten thousand.' It was difficult to identify her accent: Russian, perhaps.

'I am sorry, madam. It is fixed price.'

The woman sniffed. 'That's convenient.'

Henry couldn't contain himself; his odyssey wouldn't allow it. 'It's one American dollar,' he said, smiling at the tourist. 'You'd be hard-pressed to buy a soft drink for that price where you come from, wouldn't you?'

The woman harrumphed and fished around in the pocket of her shorts for the additional five thousand rupiah. Finding it, she tossed the note onto the cooler box and turned to leave.

'Excuse me, madam,' Yanto said, his tone apologetic. 'Please bring back the bottle when you finish, for recycling?'

The woman looked disdainfully at him. 'That's the most expensive Coke I've bought in Bali. *I'll* decide what I do with the bottle.' She flounced away, the curve of her buttocks visible below her tiny shorts.

Overcome with a desire to apologise on behalf of all Westerners, Henry held out his empty iced-tea bottle. 'I'm sorry about that,' he said. 'She was very rude to you.'

Yanto took the bottle and placed it in a plastic vat behind him, waving away the flies that swarmed around the receptacle when he opened it.

'We're not all like that, you know,' Henry continued. 'Some of us just shouldn't be given passports.'

Yanto turned back to Henry. 'That lady has much money, but no modesty.'

Henry stared at him for a moment, imagining the inclusion of a human decency test in the issuing of passports. 'Quite right,' he said. 'Well, enjoy your trip back to Java. If I keep going this way—' he nodded at the path that Janelle and Cara had taken—'is it very far to the Birds of Prey show?'

'No, very close.' Yanto seemed to hesitate. 'But the show is . . . not so good. The birds do not always obey their trainers.'

'Really?' Henry recalled Pak Tony's gushing assessment. 'I've heard it's spectacular.'

'Better somewhere else, like Keramas Beach.' Yanto nodded towards the park's exit. 'Only twenty minutes from here.'

Perhaps Yanto has seen the show too many times, Henry thought. 'Thanks for the tip, but I'm meeting friends there. Goodbye, Yanto.'

He waved to the seller and followed the path, humming to himself. Feeling refreshed by the iced tea, relieved to have escaped the Python Pit, and buoyed by the prospect of speaking to Jim, he peered with interest at the enclosures he passed: eclectus parrots, wreathed hornbills, palm cockatoos, Pesquet's parrots, and birds of paradise. None of the birds were particularly animated in the heat, but they seemed to be well cared for, with large perches and lush foliage for shade. Their feeder boxes were overflowing with papaya, banana and sweet potato, as well as protein sources such as eggs, crickets and caterpillars. Water was provided in small pools on the floor, mimicking ponds or puddles in the wild.

Then suddenly, he saw it, perched on a knotted branch at eye level. He checked the information plaque on the enclosure, just to be sure. He was right: it was a Bali starling.

He stood motionless, marvelling at its loveliness. A mere tuft of white, smaller and finer than he'd expected, and with a long drooping crest, black-tipped wings and graceful tail feathers. A fetching diamond of bare blue skin framed its eyes, giving it an ethereal look; he understood now why the Balinese considered it a symbol of purity and royalty.

He stepped forward to read more of the plaque. Less than forty Bali starlings remained in the wild, it said, despite recent releases from captive breeding programs. Poachers remained a major threat to the birds, whose gentle, trusting nature made them prized catches both locally and internationally. An additional handwritten note was affixed to the sign: *It is breeding season. Bonzo and Rozina may be antisocial at this time.*

Henry looked around the cage to try to spot the other member of the pair, but clearly the bird had hidden itself out of sight. Perhaps mating season wasn't going so well then, he mused. Reaching for his mobile, he took a shot of the Bali starling and sent it to Jim. Then he checked the time: it was almost eight o'clock in Derbyshire now. Not too early for an intimacy bridge, he decided.

He dialled Jim's home number. Within three rings, his friend answered.

'Bigfoot!' said Henry, grinning. 'Guess what? I'm standing a metre away from a Bali starling. And he's having about as much luck with the ladies as I do.'

'Beets?' Jim cleared his throat. 'Where are you?'

'Not in the jungle,' Henry replied. 'In an animal sanctuary. Some lovely birds here, too.'

'But . . . *why*?'

Henry knew exactly what Jim was thinking: that bird sanctuaries gave non-birders access to the world's avian exotica without them having to work for it.

'I'm stooping to new lows. It's actually part of this thing called Fearless, a fear-facing program I'm doing. Believe it or not, I've just held a three-metre python in my bare hands.'

232

'Jesus, Beets.' Jim sounded genuinely impressed.

'And this morning, I had a tooth-filing ceremony.'

'A *what*?'

Henry laughed. 'Actually, I'm ringing because I . . .' He faltered. 'Been redecorating anyone's place lately, Bigfoot?'

They laughed. Jim had a habit of rearranging items in Henry's flat just to annoy him. The last time Jim had overnighted in Twickenham, Henry had found his neat canister of pens secreted in the vegetable crisper—two days later.

'How are you, anyway?' asked Henry.

'Fine. Nothing to report. Nothing like what you're up to, anyway. Just about to head in to work. Boring as shite.'

Henry hesitated, trying to summon the courage to say what he'd intended to. Yanto appeared on the path, pushing the unwieldy drinks trolley towards the amphitheatre, clearly pursuing the crowds. Henry nodded at him as he passed, but the seller didn't respond.

'Bigfoot, I've got something to tell you. It's part of this Fearless program, so don't worry if it sounds a bit odd.'

A streak of white behind some bushes caught Henry's eye. An ivory peacock was scratching in the soil, its lacy tail feathers cocked in a magnificent fan.

'It happened when I was holding the snake, you see,' Henry continued.

'When you were . . . holding your snake?' Jim sounded incredulous.

'Not *my* snake.' Henry chuckled nervously. 'They gave me a big python to hold, you see, then they asked, *Who do you wish was next to you right now?* And I didn't think of Mum or Dad or Pam, or even Tessa the Titan.' This was the frivolous name they'd invented for a buxom cashier at their local cinema, before Henry had moved away from Derbyshire to Twickenham. 'I thought of *you*.'

Jim said nothing.

Henry listened hopefully into the silence. A group of Asian tourists strolled along the path, and he flattened himself against an enclosure to let them pass. Then he followed the peacock into a small garden with hedge-lined paths that led circuitously back to the concourse.

After an excruciating minute, Henry spoke again. 'You there, Bigfoot?'

'Yes,' Jim replied.

'Look, the thing is . . .' Henry swallowed hard. 'My family life was a bit off when I was young, with Pam's kidney disease and everything. My parents weren't really there for me—they couldn't be, you know? Then I started birdwatching and you came into my life and it was like *oxygen* for me, Bigfoot. I could finally be myself. What I'm trying to say is . . .' He took a deep breath.

'You fancy me?' Jim's voice was tremulous.

'No! Jesus, Bigfoot.' Henry was mortified. Then he was struck by an appalling thought. 'Why . . . do you fancy *me*?'

Jim snorted. 'You're too hairy for my liking.'

They both laughed.

Wandering back onto the concourse, Henry saw Lorenzo striding out of the Python Pit, carrying an envelope in his hand. Pak Tony had evidently forced the issue of the intimacy bridge.

'You had me worried for a moment, Beets,' said Jim.

'Why?' protested Henry. 'Why can't a man tell his best friend how he feels without being accused of wanting to sleep with him?'

Jim sniggered. 'I'm used to the stiff upper lip, I suppose. Men don't normally . . . talk like this, do we?'

'Why not?' asked Henry. 'Women do it all the time. Telling their friends they love them and all that guff. No one assumes they're lesbians, do they?'

'Good point,' said Jim.

Pak Tony emerged from the Python Pit too and began jogging in the direction of the amphitheatre. Spotting Henry, he grinned and waved before disappearing down the path leading to the bird show.

Henry paused next to an enormous, ancient-looking fig tree and lowered his voice. 'You're my best friend, Bigfoot. I love you, in a totally asexual *bromance* kind of way.'

'Alright, that's enough.' Jim guffawed. 'I feel the same way about you, but I *never* want to sleep with you.'

'Understood,' said Henry. Standing in the shade of the fig, he peered along the path after Pak Tony. Only a solitary Asian tourist remained, taking photographs of the albino peacock.

'I've got an idea, actually,' said Jim, with a mischievous edge to his voice.

'Uh-oh.' Henry wondered what was coming.

An excitable announcement over the PA system signalled the commencement of the bird show. Music blared in the background, punctuated by rousing applause. Henry didn't want to be late for the show, but surely Pak Tony wouldn't begrudge him a heart-to-heart intimacy bridge with his best friend?

The peacock turned around on the almost empty path and began walking towards Henry, pursued by the Asian tourist. Lifting a foot and pausing a moment, as if testing the earth's solidity, before replacing it carefully on the cobblestones.

'I'm thinking of joining you in Bali, if you'll have me,' declared Jim.

'Really?' Henry was surprised. 'But . . . what about Beth? And your job?'

A crackle of interference rasped in Henry's ear and he jerked his head away from the phone.

In that same instant, it flew out of his fingers.

The sky pulsed with savage yellow light and a series of dull cracking sounds reverberated around the concourse. The earth rippled and a wall of flying debris slammed into him, hurling Henry behind the fig. He lay there in the dirt, stunned and winded, staring up at the dark green leaves and eddies of white feathers billowing around him. Plumes of dust clouded his vision, settling on branches and buttresses and his own motionless body.

Breathe, he told himself, realising that his mouth was wide open.

A pall of dark smoke descended. All was eerily silent, bar a faint high-pitched ringing in his ears.

Breathe. His eyes were streaming. He closed his mouth and tried to swallow. An intense pain stabbed at his left shoulder, on which he'd fallen heavily. For a moment he fancied that Jim was standing in the curling smoke beyond the fig tree.

For God's sake, breathe.

His chest heaved, and with a wheezing shudder, air and smoke and dust rushed into his lungs. A pungent, sickly-sweet smell filled the air, of scorched human hair and firecrackers on New Year's Eve.

All at once, sound stampeded into his ears. The wild screeching of birds, the demented whooping of gibbons and the cries of human distress. And coughing and gurgling noises, of which *he* was the source. Suddenly he realised he couldn't feel his limbs.

Whimpering with fear, he wiggled his fingers and toes. Warm fluid seeped down his legs.

I'm bleeding.

He lifted his head but could see very little without his glasses, which had flown off his face. He tried to scan his flattened body, his breath rasping. Seeing no obvious blood, he realised it must be urine he could feel. Judging by the dreadful screaming he could hear, others were not so lucky.

What the hell just happened? An earthquake?

He pushed himself onto an elbow, then rolled onto his right side. Panting heavily, he curled his legs under him, dug his shoes into the dirt and pushed himself up onto his haunches. He lurched, crablike, to the front of the fig tree. Blackened fragments of metal were embedded up and down its sides. He stared at the shards, uncomprehending.

An unearthly shriek prompted him to wheel around.

In the middle of the concourse, the Asian tourist lay writhing in the dirt. Her camera still hung from its strap around her neck, but her clothes were ragged strips. The rest of her was a bloodied, charred mess. She was still alive, her hands pressed against her abdomen, barely stemming the flow of blood. Clutching the tree, Henry began pulling himself up to standing, determined to help. He heard voices calling out nearby.

Thank God, someone is here.

Two men rushed onto the concourse, pressing handkerchiefs against their faces and carrying long sticks. One of them darted the short distance to the iron gate separating the concourse from the ticket booth and car park beyond. The man tugged at the great gate, sliding it closed. He tapped a wall-mounted keypad next to it, then shouted, '*Sudah!*'

Henry stared blankly. Why were they *locking* the only exit?

The other man approached the woman writhing on the ground and prodded her casually with his foot. Henry squinted in confusion, before all at once realising that the stick he carried was a rifle. The man pointed it at the woman's head.

Henry gasped and threw himself behind the tree again. He crouched there, terrified. He looked around desperately for an escape route, but saw only the twelve-foot stone wall that surrounded the sanctuary on every side. A sickening bang reverberated and the woman's wailing stopped.

Henry screwed his eyes shut, appealing to a God he'd thumbed his nose at long ago. *Dear Jesus, have mercy . . . help me now in my hour of need . . . do not forsake me.* Childhood prayers, long dormant inside him, tumbled forth.

Footsteps moved in his direction. Henry shrank back against the trunk of the fig, pressing himself into its lichen-filled furrows. *I didn't even say goodbye to my family, or to Jim.* All the precious hours he'd squandered. The callous jokes, the unsaid words. He closed his eyes, whispering a prayer.

The footsteps moved closer, then stopped in front of him. Something nudged his leg. Shaking violently, he opened his eyes. Brown feet with white soles in orange flip-flops stood in front of him, and the butt of a rifle rested in the dirt. Henry looked up, into the mismatched eyes of Yanto the drinks seller, who lifted his rifle and pointed it at Henry.

'Please,' Henry begged. 'Don't.' He cowered against the trunk, covering his face.

God help me.

Random images accosted him. Zeroes and ones on a computer screen. Snowflakes falling across a field of bracken. Jim lying next to him on the heath, laughing.

And Yanto the smiling drinks seller, pointing a rifle at his head.

There was an earsplitting crack and dirt exploded around him. Henry lay face down, his whole body twitching. Then, inconceivably, the footsteps began to move away. Yanto called out, '*Sudah!*' and the two men were gone.

Henry sobbed into the dirt.

Then, with his gut cramping in terror, he hauled himself to his feet again.

I have to get out.

He stumbled onto the concourse, turning his face away as he passed the woman's corpse. He ran to the exit and tugged at the gate, but it held fast. Moving to the keypad, he began pressing random combinations.

Think, think.

At the base of the opposite wall, just inside the gate, he spied a fire hose. Affixed above it was a glass cabinet containing an axe. A sign on the cabinet read: *Break in case of fire*. If nothing else, the axe was a weapon.

He scouted for something with which to shatter the glass, and decided his foot would do. Then he noticed the heavy bronze coupling on the end of the fire hose. He pulled a lever to release the hose, which unwound rapidly. Hauling a length over his shoulder, he aimed the coupling at the cabinet and swung it as hard as he could. It barely dented the glass.

Sweet Jesus.

He looked around the concourse again. Spotting a thick bamboo stake in the remains of the labyrinth garden, he raced towards it, fell to his knees and wrenched it out. Then he noticed something lying beneath a nearby bush. It was the limp body of a man with matted, silver hair.

'Pak Tony?' Henry whispered, scrambling towards him. The facilitator blinked.

'Wait here.' Henry bolted across the concourse and hurled the bamboo rod at the glass cabinet, smashing it. He pulled out the axe and began to hack maniacally at the lock on the gate. The blows made a loud clanging noise, and the action jarred his injured shoulder, but he kept swinging all the same. A moment later, he heard Indonesian voices in the distance.

'Oh, dear God.' He threw down the axe and ran back to Pak Tony, then dragged him out from under the bush. 'Can you stand up?'

Pak Tony lay unmoving, his eyes glassy and his lips working silently.

'Get up!' Henry yelled. His eyes roved to a large black skip bin not far from the fire hose, trash bulging against its lid.

'Right.' Henry pulled Pak Tony to his feet and shunted him over his good shoulder. Then, stumbling under the man's weight, he carried him to the skip bin and sat him against the wall. The facilitator sagged forward, his eyes fixed on the ground. There was no evidence of bleeding; Henry could only assume he had internal injuries.

With a grunt of exertion, Henry climbed onto the bin. The rubbish inside helped to reinforce the lid, and the top of the wall—set with a loose coil of barbed wire—was now within reach. He gripped the edge of the wall with both hands and, with one almighty pull, scrabbled upwards. The unevenly hewn stones provided several natural footholds, and he managed to raise his head over the wall. In the several seconds he kept himself suspended there, his arm muscles screaming with fatigue, Henry saw three things: a small crowd gathering outside, a precipitous drop into the car park below, and Pak Ketut pacing at the locked gate.

'Ketut!' he called. The driver looked up in astonishment, just as Henry's arms gave out.

He dropped back onto the skip bin, panting hard. The Indonesian voices behind him were moving closer, coming from the direction of the amphitheatre.

Henry leaped down off the bin and snatched the fire hose, unravelling its entire length as quickly as he could. He coiled it into large loops in one hand, with the heavy coupling dangling at one end, then threw it at the top of the wall. It clattered back down to the ground.

He tried again, coiling the loops more evenly this time, restraining his natural urge to rush. Then, rocking back and forth on his heels, he let go of the coupling. This time it soared like a lasso—up and over the wall—taking several metres of hose with it.

Turning now to Pak Tony, Henry spoke into his ear. 'I'll get you to the top of the wall. Stand up.'

Pak Tony mumbled something in Dutch. His knees buckled as Henry pulled him up to standing.

'Stay there,' said Henry, jumping up onto the lid of the skip bin once more. Reaching down, he hooked his arms under Pak Tony's armpits. 'Now, push!' he said, hoisting him up as best he could. 'Use your legs.'

Pak Tony obeyed, groaning in pain. He slid up the side of the bin, then flopped face-first onto it.

'Stand up,' Henry urged again, hauling Pak Tony onto his knees and then into a precarious standing position. The facilitator collapsed against the wall, pale and trembling.

'You're doing well, Tony,' he said, crouching down. 'Step onto my back, I'll give you a leg-up.' He felt the bin wobble a little under their combined weight, but Pak Tony didn't move.

The garbled Indonesian voices came nearer. If they found Henry and Tony here, Henry knew, they'd shoot them.

'Plan B,' he announced. 'I'm going to climb up first, then I'm going to pull you up onto the wall after me. Just don't sit down, okay? Stay standing.'

Henry bent his knees and, aiming at the top of the wall, sprang off the bin. He grabbed the edge of the wall and hung there for a moment, his legs dangling, seeking a foothold. Finding one, he pulled himself up. Rusted barbed wire pierced his flesh as he swung a leg over, straddling the wall. It wasn't razor wire, he told himself, it was survivable. Breathing heavily, he extended his right arm, his strongest, towards Pak Tony.

'Henry!'

He glanced down over the other side of the wall. Ketut was already there, propping a flexible bamboo ladder directly beneath him, assisted by a group of Balinese men.

'I've got Tony,' Henry called down. 'He's injured.'

Ketut nodded and spoke urgently to the other men. Then he slipped off his sandals and began to climb the ladder.

Henry turned back to Tony now. 'Reach up,' he urged. 'Give me your hand.'

Pak Tony looked up, his face contorted. Slowly he raised a hand and Henry grasped it. Then, gripping either side of the wall with his feet and bracing his abdominals, he called, 'Push up, Tony!'

Pak Tony's feet scrabbled at the wall, but it barely helped. Henry groaned aloud, pulling with all his might. His left shoulder was numb and his muscles were burning, but slowly, Tony began inching up. Expelling the last of the air in his lungs, Henry thrust his other arm under the man's armpit and dragged him onto the top of the wall.

The facilitator screamed as the barbed wire sank into his flesh. Then he lay prone and heaving, his legs dangling on either side of the wall, his eyes closed.

'Tony, stay with me,' said Henry.

Pak Tony opened one eye, then closed it again.

'Sit up.' Henry pulled Tony up by the back of his shirt, and they sat astride the wall like men on horseback.

Alerted by loud voices, Henry looked down into the animal sanctuary. Two men with bandanas over the lower half of their faces were sprinting down the path from the amphitheatre, rifles pointed.

Grabbing the hose dangling over the wall, Henry thrust it into Tony's hands. 'Hold on!' He pushed him over the wall, towards Ketut, who stood at the top of the ladder less than a metre below.

Pak Tony swung out wildly, knocking into Ketut and unbalancing him. The pair slid down the ladder, tumbling onto several men at its base. Then the ladder fell, too.

There was a thunderous crack and something grazed Henry's earlobe.

Dear Jesus.

He didn't turn to look. There was no time to wait for the ladder. With the sound of his own heartbeat hammering in his ears, Henry flung himself out over the expanse of grey concrete below.

A giddy moment of weightlessness, his arms outstretched to touch the edges of the sky.

Like a bird, poised to fly.

DEATH

Annie arrived fifteen minutes early, trying to secure the best vantage point for the bird show. The amphitheatre descended in tiers and was already filling fast. Tour groups had occupied the best seats at the front and centre of the stage, but then she spied two empty benches. One was on the right-hand side of the stage, in the very first row. The other was on the left, some six rows back, but shaded by a large tree that grew, somewhat crazily, between rows five and six. The Balinese were superstitious about certain trees, Annie knew, and could not be convinced to cut them down. This one was significant, it seemed, with a black-and-white checked *poleng* cloth stretched around its trunk. *The owners of Paradise Animal Sanctuary probably had to ask the spirits permission to build the amphitheatre around it. Lucky for me they agreed*, she thought, desperate for some shade.

After carefully navigating the steps, she positioned her gear at intervals along the bench to save places for the others, and then sat down. For her intimacy bridge, she penned a letter to

Kevin, shedding some tears as she wrote the final sentence: *You're irreplaceable, Kevin, but I'm getting to know someone special.* Then she sealed her letter in an envelope and stood up to hail her friends.

Cara and Janelle arrived first, shortly followed by Remy. They joined her in the shade of the tree as many more tourists, of predominantly Asian extraction, filed into the amphitheatre. As they exchanged small talk and waited for the show to begin, Annie admired the Asian women, their petite figures and flawless complexions shielded by dainty parasols. Their impeccable clothes and slender hands in white cotton gloves. Asian women were femininity and grace personified, she decided. At least in comparison to clammy oversized Westerners such as herself.

Just before four o'clock, as an enthusiastic Balinese compere took to the stage and announced the imminent commencement of the bird show, Annie noticed Lorenzo picking his way along the row towards them. She lifted a bag off the bench to make room for him, keeping the remaining space for Henry and Pak Tony. *Where have they gotten to?* she wondered, feeling rather lightheaded, and realised that she'd forgotten her insulin again. The theatrical sound of trumpets drew her attention back to the stage, where three smiling bird trainers took their places.

Two men in khaki uniforms, and a woman in a surprisingly short pink skirt, bowed in a choreographed fashion to the opening bars of Avril Lavigne's 'Fly'. The trainer in the miniskirt hurled a handful of raw titbits into the sky and launched a Javan hawk off her thick falconer's glove. The bird swept into the air, did several tight somersaults, then snapped the falling meat into its beak. The crowd *ooh*ed and *aah*ed and applauded.

And then, a deafening explosion hurled her sideways.

When Annie opened her eyes, she was lying face down and quivering, the taste of dirt and blood in her mouth. Another blast shook the earth, further away. After some time—she didn't know how long—she pulled herself up onto her hands and knees and began to crawl, trying to find a way out. Almost immediately she encountered the trainer with the pink miniskirt, her legs a mottled, gelatinous mass, her face unrecognisable. Crying out, Annie turned away and bumped into Lorenzo, also on all fours. Blood trickled down his temple and she reached out to touch him, but he disappeared behind a choking cloud of dust.

Suddenly she felt his strong arms lifting her up, and she wept aloud with gratitude. Gripping each other, they staggered across the rubble and timber and twisted metal and scattered possessions. A baby's blackened soother, a blood-stained smartphone case, shattered bodies she couldn't bear to look at. As the dust began to settle, Annie thought she detected Cara ahead of them and called out. The woman turned as if in slow motion. She was pale and limping, but it *was* Cara! Annie's relief was inordinate. *There are three of us, at least.*

They continued through the ruins together. It was slow-going and treacherous and Annie was terrified of further explosions. There had been more than one, after all, and soon it became clear that the rear wall of the amphitheatre, where dozens of audience members had been sitting, had collapsed. Some survivors were clambering over the dead and wounded amid the pandemonium, trying to find their way to an exit. Others were forming a human chain over the wreckage, helping one another to the top.

'Up that way,' Lorenzo said, pointing to a stairway which was still partially intact. Cara suddenly gasped and dropped to her hands and knees. She began pulling frantically at the rubble, where a small brown arm protruded from beneath a large piece of timber. Now Annie could hear a child's whimpering.

She and Lorenzo fell to their knees too, working frenziedly to move the debris. Finally, Lorenzo called out, 'Stand back!' and prised up the piece of timber.

A little boy cringed in the cavity below, his right arm jutting out at an unnatural angle. A woman was curled around his body, her hijab stained with blood, her lifeless eyes trained upon him.

Cara bent down and carefully scooped out the little boy, draping his unbroken arm around her neck. 'You're okay,' she murmured, patting his back. 'It's alright.'

Lorenzo went to help her.

'It's okay, he's light,' Cara said, cradling the boy to her chest.

They started out again, the sounds of suffering humanity all around them. As they guided each other over the jagged wasteland that only minutes earlier had been an orderly amphitheatre, Annie began to hope that help was near. That an emergency services crew would descend at any moment and pluck them out of the mayhem.

But as they drew closer to the top of the amphitheatre, Annie saw armed men barring their way.

Fresh fear seized her heart. 'Who are *they*?'

'Just do as they say,' Lorenzo whispered.

The armed men stood blocking the route to the park's exit, rounding up survivors. On the ground nearby was a huddle of the sanctuary's staff members, sitting with their hands on their heads. Some of the women were crying, and the men looked stunned and fearful.

The armed men barked monosyllabic orders in English—*Stop! Move! Now!*—as they shepherded non-staff survivors down a path signposted *Birdsong Café* and *Owl House*. Annie focused on Lorenzo's feet as she followed him, feeling strangely disconnected from her surrounds. As if she were acting in a Hollywood movie with bandits and bombs and brutality and at any moment, the director would yell, '*Cut!*'

Reaching the Birdsong Café, Annie stared at the unusual-looking building, with its three polished concrete walls. In lieu of a fourth, wide bamboo panelling covered most of the façade. An understated entranceway marked the centre of the façade, set back behind three steps and a small bridge spanning a water feature. It was impossible to discern the café's interior from the outside.

They were herded inside and forced to surrender any personal effects that hadn't been lost in the blast—handbags, backpacks, electronic devices—then instructed to sit on the floor. The chairs and tables were stacked at the rear of the room. As Annie lowered herself onto the white tiles and scanned the café for other exits—rapidly realising that there were none—the word *bunker* sprang to mind. There was a drinks bar on the left side of the room, and, behind that, a door leading to the kitchen. But there were no doors beyond, Annie saw, and even the kitchen windows were so high as to be inaccessible.

To soften the effect of the windowless concrete, the internal walls were lined with fabrics from across the Indonesian archipelago, but in the absence of any skylights, the room could well have been underground. The usual lighting—comprised of both downlights and uplights—was not in operation, presumably to intimidate the captives or to conserve energy. There were at least twenty people in the room now, with more trickling in as the minutes passed.

'Do not move or speak,' a guard instructed every new arrival.

Annie, Lorenzo and Cara obeyed. But others didn't, to Annie's disbelief. Almost immediately after they sat down, a burly Russian man who'd hidden a mobile phone in his underwear was summarily outed when it rang. The guards pushed him to the floor, bound his hands behind his back, then marched him from the café. Two others—an injured Korean man who moaned too loudly, and an Indonesian man who asked too many questions—were ordered to dig a toilet trench outside using small trowels. Neither of them returned. Not long afterwards, a fidgety Australian man was told by those seated around him to *sit still or you'll get us all killed.*

The majority of captives sat rigid and silent. Some wept quietly, their faces drawn with fear. Many were injured, lying beneath tables stacked at the rear of the room, propped along walls, or slumped against strangers.

When some time had passed—Annie couldn't guess exactly how long—and no further captives were delivered to the café, Annie counted sixty-eight people, including Remy and Janelle. Her joy at spotting them in a far corner was moderated only by concern for Janelle, whose head was lolling about like a rag doll. The Frenchman had used his ceremonial sarong to cover her and his shirt as a makeshift bandage on the back of her neck. He wore a running singlet and gym shorts now. Only once had Remy acknowledged Annie, blinking in recognition before quickly lowering his head to avoid the guards' scrutiny.

While pins and needles crept across her legs and lower back, Annie kept waiting for something to happen. What was going on outside the animal sanctuary? Would they be rescued soon? How would she run, if she had to? She cursed her own tired, defective body.

After several tense hours, the light at the café's entrance began to fade. With the darkness, Annie's sense of desolation grew. It must be too difficult or risky, she realised, to try to get them out. Or perhaps there was some other reason, one she couldn't fathom from inside the park, why it was impossible to rescue them.

Not long after sunset, the little boy Cara was holding cried out in pain, and one of the guards whirled around. Cara looked stricken as he approached.

'*Lengannya patah*,' she explained, before he even reached them.

The guard looked surprised at Cara's fluency, then leaned over to inspect the boy's arm. After a moment, he nodded and moved away.

As he did, an agitated elderly man called out to him in German, while his daughter tried to quieten him. The old man paid her no heed, pointing at the guard and speaking in an accusatory tone.

'Keep your father quiet,' commanded the guard in English, but the old man kept haranguing him.

Finally, after several more warnings, the guard dragged the old man up by the arm and escorted him to the entrance. When his daughter burst into tears and ran after him, the pair of them were marched away by another set of guards who materialised, seemingly out of thin air. *How many guards are there?* Annie wondered despairingly.

She watched the two guards patrolling the café's entrance now, with their long rifles and filthy bandanas obscuring their faces. Stopping sometimes to share a cigarette, or to check their mobile phones. There must have been more of them stationed elsewhere in the animal sanctuary, and they seemed to be taking turns to guard the hostages in the café. *Hostages.* As much as she didn't want to admit it, this was the only word to adequately describe their situation.

Lorenzo sat against the wall on Annie's left, his eyes closed. He was not asleep, however; he kept crossing and uncrossing his legs, evidently uncomfortable on the hard floor. The spasmodic sound of helicopters overhead prompted him to open his eyes at intervals, perhaps anticipating a rescue. She wanted to talk to him, but dared not disturb the silence.

On Annie's right, Cara sat cross-legged, holding the Indonesian boy in her lap. He couldn't have been older than three, Annie guessed, and made no further sound, despite his injured arm. Cara sat stroking his face, waving away mosquitos, and watching the guards through half-closed eyes. The position of her head suggested that she was attempting to listen to their brief, softly spoken exchanges.

After hours of sitting deep into the night, Annie's limbs were leaden and her bladder bursting. She tried to ignore this, along with the relentless refrain in her head that taunted, *You'll never see your children again.* Dennis and Charlie and Natalie, her beloved babies who'd once clung to her as if their lives depended upon it, but for whom Oaktree Ranch held little appeal now. She'd served out her major purpose in their lives, Annie knew. If she didn't make it out alive, they were more than capable of surviving without her.

Yet even as she attempted to reconcile herself to that idea, a quiet tear of protest slipped down Annie's cheek. She was *not* done with her children, her dream of being a grandmother one day, her farm, her church, or her circle of friends in Coalinga. She was not done with Bali, or BAF, or her dog Untung.

If Kevin were next to her now, she knew exactly what his exhortation would be. *Keep your head down and it'll be alright, Annie.* She could almost feel his presence, as the dimly lit café became blurrier before her eyes. It was surely after midnight, more than sixteen hours since her last insulin injection. She'd never gone so long without it; her tongue was swollen, her head was thumping and her eyelids were beginning to droop.

'Are you okay?' she heard Cara whisper.

Annie mumbled something about a diabetic coma. Cara instantly raised her hand.

'Yes?' a masked guard asked, keeping his distance.

Cara gestured to Annie. 'My friend is sick. She has diabetes and needs her medicine. It's in her bag.' she translated her own words. *'Ibu ini sakit, Pak. Dia kena penyakit gula. Obatnya di tas. Boleh diambil, Pak?'*

The guard's eyes widened; he was just as surprised by Cara's linguistic skills as his colleague had been earlier. He contemplated them both before motioning to Annie to stand up. She couldn't quite manage it.

'Quickly,' urged the guard.

'I'm trying,' said Annie, feeling tears welling in her eyes again.

'I'll help her.' Cara passed the little boy to Lorenzo. He barely stirred, nestling against the Italian's chest.

Even with Cara's assistance, Annie struggled to stand. She gripped the edge of a table to pull herself to her feet.

'You are fat,' said the man, his eyes sneering over his bandana.

'Yes,' she murmured. 'I am.'

The man prodded her in the stomach with his rifle, and she thought she might wet herself. 'Walk,' he ordered.

They picked their way to the mound of personal items heaped in a pile at the front of the café. Cara lowered Annie onto a chair, then turned and spoke to the guard in a placating tone. He nodded once, and she began rummaging through the pile until she found the small BAF satchel with its distinctive doggy paw prints. As a deterrent to petty theft, Annie had been wearing it all day under her clothes.

This morning I was afraid of pickpockets, she thought.

Cara passed her the syringe kit. 'Do you need help, Annie?'

'No more help,' snapped the guard.

Annie's vision swam as she unzipped the small black case. Luckily she'd been injecting insulin for years and could practically do it blindfolded. She reached under her kaftan dress, exposing the flesh of her stomach.

'*Menjijikan*,' muttered the man, turning his eyes away. 'No see. You go there.' He pointed in the direction of an amenities block that stood against the park's boundary wall.

In Annie's dazed state, it looked far away. Cara rose to accompany her, but the man barked, 'You not go.'

Cara negotiated respectfully with the man in Indonesian, until finally he muttered something and walked away. She turned to Annie. 'I can take you to the entrance of the toilets.'

Annie leaned heavily on Cara as they made their way out the café entrance, across the miniature bridge and down three uneven steps. A cobbled path led to the amenities block, some five metres away.

At the entrance, Cara whispered, 'Call me if you need me.'

Annie shuffled cautiously into the ladies' block and across the tiles to the first cubicle. Mercifully, it was a Western-style toilet. She pushed her knickers to her knees; the stream of urine began before she'd even sat down.

On the toilet, Annie exhaled with relief. Then, sitting taller, she squeezed a roll of skin at her midriff between her thumb and forefinger and, removing the lid of the syringe with her teeth, pressed the needle into her flesh. Afterwards, she let the syringe drop to the floor and she slumped back against the cistern.

When she opened her eyes again, a few seconds later, the bathroom seemed much brighter. She stared at the back of the cubicle door, plastered with some kind of public health message about HIV/AIDS. Standing up to flush, she noticed a high, glassless window above her. Large, rectangular and spanning the rear wall of her cubicle, it was an economical way to deliver light and air into the lavatory. Annie had seen such windows before in many Balinese public toilets, and even in the retreat pavilion at Puri Damai. This one, she noticed, was covered in flimsy chicken wire hung on a few thin nails around its edges. Without hesitating, she climbed up onto the toilet seat and inspected the grille. There was no glue, no staples; she pulled gently at the grille's edge and it peeled back easily.

Suddenly she heard footsteps outside the amenities block.

'Already?' called the guard.

'Oh.' She squatted down on the toilet seat. 'Er . . . not quite.'

Annie heard Cara talking to the man in Indonesian, her tone conciliatory. *Thank God for Cara.* There was no time to lose.

Annie stood up again and, murmuring a quiet prayer, climbed up onto the cistern itself. Would it hold her weight? She gripped the edge of the window and peered through the gap. There was a short span of foliage outside the amenities block, and behind that, the top of the boundary wall.

She heard footsteps stalking into the bathroom. The man rapped on the cubicle door. 'Why you take so long?'

She slipped to the floor with a clatter and pressed the flush. With burning cheeks, she opened the door. *'Buang air besar,'* she said. *I defecated.* Applying the first phrase she'd ever learned in Indonesian, signposted on the BAF bathroom wall: *Don't defecate on the floor.*

'Menjijikan,' the man repeated, pushing her out of the bathroom. She didn't need a translation to detect his mood.

Cara moved to Annie's side. 'How are you feeling now?'

'No talk,' said the man. 'Go back.'

They walked in silence to the café, where they were met at the entrance by another guard. He held up a mobile phone for his colleague to view. After scanning its contents, the guard nodded.

He turned to Cara and Annie, looking back and forth between them. 'You come,' he said to Annie. Then, waving a hand at Cara, 'You stay.'

Annie winced. Where were they taking her?

'Now,' he ordered. 'No bag.'

Annie glanced down at her BAF satchel, her eyes filling with tears. *This is it*, she thought.

Passing her bag to Cara, she murmured, '*Il y a une fenêtre dans la salle de bains.*'

Cara gave no indication that she'd heard, or understood, Annie's words. But Annie knew that Cara was fluent in French, and had used it in the hope that neither of the guards would understand. *There is a window in the bathroom.*

'*Merci,*' Cara called, as the second guard shoved her back towards the café.

She *had* understood, Annie realised, with a rush of relief. She watched Cara go, feeling suddenly more afraid than she'd ever been. *I'm not ready to die.*

The guard marched Annie away from the café, past the rubble of the amphitheatre, and along a short path lined with cages that had been blown open by the explosive force. Eerie nocturnal bird calls filled the night air.

'Faster,' said the man, nudging the rifle at her back.

It was difficult navigating the cobbled path in the dark. Finally, a large shape loomed ahead, a two-storey domed structure that Annie thought must be the owl house. The guard called out a brief, clipped greeting, and someone responded from the second floor.

Annie's breath came in short, terrified gasps. Where were they taking her? Was she going to be executed, presumably the fate of the captives who'd been marched away earlier? Would the guard stand her up against a wall and shoot her? She should never have lingered in the toilet scouting for an escape. The guard had guessed what she was doing, and now she would be punished.

The guard pushed in front of her and thrust something into her hand. She stared at it dumbly: a mobile phone.

'Here.' He clicked on a torch and shone it onto a piece of paper. 'I call media. Read the words.'

The guard dialled a number and held the phone to her ear. The words on the page swam before her eyes and her mouth went dry. A woman answered and said something in Indonesian.

'I am an American citizen.' Annie began, her voice quaking. 'I am a hostage at Paradise Animal Sanctuary. I call on the government of the Republic of Indonesia to release Muslim cleric Abu . . . Marfu'ah . . . Salihin—' she stumbled over the name—'who has been wrongfully detained without charge for eighteen months. It is a violation of human rights and the rule of law in a democratic society. Please consider my request, to spare my life.'

She began to cry, and the woman on the other end started speaking in rapid Indonesian. The guard snatched the phone from Annie and listened for a while, before speaking into the phone himself. His tone was agitated, and Annie's dread mounted. After a while, a voice could be heard speaking English on the end of the line, but the guard simply hung up.

'Walk,' said the guard, tucking the phone into his pocket.

Tears leaked from Annie's eyes as she lumbered on in the darkness. Why had she survived the amphitheatre explosion only to be executed now? She began reciting Psalm 23 under her breath. *Yea, though I walk through the valley of the shadow of death* . . .

But there was no solace in recitation. Her two Fs, faith and focus, recoiled like beaten dogs in some unreachable corner of her mind. There *was* no divine plan for her life, she realised now, no rationale for human suffering. If God actually existed, he wasn't at Paradise Animal Sanctuary.

'Stop,' ordered the man.

Annie obeyed and looked up at a solid iron gate. Two more men appeared out of the shadows, also wearing bandanas. The three conversed in whispers, looking at a mobile phone. Then one of them approached the gate while another moved into position at one side. Suddenly she understood what they were going to do: execute her and throw her body beyond the gate.

'Why me?' she sobbed, appealing to the guard next to her.

'Because you are old and fat and useless.'

The gate slid open, barely half a metre. Annie felt the cold muzzle of the rifle behind her left ear.

Kevin.

'Walk on,' the guard ordered.

Annie shuffled forward.

Let it be quick.

A sharp blow between her shoulder blades thrust Annie out through the gate, and she stumbled and almost fell. Straightening up, she stood rocking on her feet, squinting against a thousand brilliant lights trained upon her. She glimpsed a cavalcade of vehicles and a sea of lanterns, yet everything was deathly quiet.

Instinctively, she raised her hands above her head. The iron gate slammed shut behind her and she jumped.

Seconds later came a blaze of blinding flashes and a hundred hands jostling her. As she swayed on her feet, a familiar face moved into her dazed view.

'Kevin?' she murmured.

'Ibu Annie!' he said.

It was Pak Ketut, flanked by men in uniforms pressing themselves into a human ring around them both.

Ketut's arms caught her as she fainted.

'Ibu Annie?'

Dark chocolate pools peered at her, beneath an anxious brow. *How kind those eyes are*, she thought.

'Pak Ketut.' Her own voice sounded otherworldly.

A stinging sensation in the back of her hand made her look down; an IV drip protruded from it. Reality rammed into her consciousness then; the animal sanctuary, the explosions, the men in bandanas. The anticipation of execution, followed by her inexplicable release. She looked down at the rest of her body, covered by an off-white bedsheet. With a trembling hand, she lifted it up; every part of her seemed to be intact. Relief flooded her, tinged with a creeping sense of guilt. She had survived, but others had not.

She tried to sit up.

'Please, do not move,' said Pak Ketut. 'You have had a big shock.'

She smiled weakly at this understatement.

Pak Ketut returned her smile, and suddenly she began to weep. Great breathless sobs that made Pak Ketut frown in concern. He reached out to pat her arm, and she took his hand, gripping it tightly. As if to check that he was real, that she truly had escaped. Except that she hadn't, she reminded herself. Her captors had let her go.

'What day is it?' she asked, looking around the room. How long had she been in hospital?

'Still Thursday.' His tone was soothing. 'Just after midday. They released you this morning, around three o'clock. You have been asleep all morning.'

'I need to call my children,' she said.

'I have already,' said Pak Ketut. 'They know you are safe. I found some contact numbers at Puri Damai. Natalie called back straight away.'

'Oh, thank you,' she said, tears still trailing down her cheeks. 'Pak Ketut, tell me everything you know.'

He looked uncertain. 'The doctors said . . .' He glanced over his shoulder as if one of them might burst in.

'Please,' she said. 'Is it over yet?'

He shook his head. 'There has been contact between police and the terrorists,' he began. 'It is on television and the internet. They are workers at the animal sanctuary, six of them, from East Java. Three are brothers, from a very poor area. They came to Bali for a better life.'

'Then why are they doing this?'

'Publicity.' Pak Ketut's face was grave. 'They went to a *pesantren*, an Islamic school, when they were young. Some of the teachers there are members of Jemaah Islamiyah—you know this group? They planned the Bali bombings years ago. Many people died.'

Annie nodded. She could still recall the horror of watching it unfold from her lounge room in California, only a year after the World Trade Center attacks.

'About eighteen months ago, one of their teachers, Abu Marfu'ah Salihin, was arrested,' Ketut continued. 'It was part of a government operation to destroy terrorist networks in Indonesia. The problem is, they put him in prison on Nusakambangan Island before they had proven his guilt. So there has been a big campaign for his freedom, with many supporters. Even foreigners are involved, the human rights activists. The campaign has received much support over the last year.'

Pak Ketut held up his mobile phone to show her a Facebook page entitled 'Free Salihin', with tens of thousands of likes. Annie had heard of the case; it had been all over the local news.

'The brothers have been involved in the campaign too,' he continued. 'Three weeks ago, their posts started calling for *jihad* and purification of the world by fire. Two of the teachings of Salihin.' He shook his head. 'It looks like they are acting this out at the sanctuary. This bombing attack has attracted the world's attention. Now they are demanding the release of Salihin, in return for hostages. You were the sixth Western hostage released, Annie, to show their goodwill.'

Goodwill? Annie suddenly realised just how fortunate she'd been. Literally standing in the right place at the right time—and sufficiently *useless*, as one of the guards had told her—to be readily jettisoned.

'What is the Indonesian government doing?' she asked. 'The police?'

Pak Ketut sighed. 'Not much, when the hostages keep coming out. I think this is the terrorists' plan to delay a rescue. There is much media discussion, foreign governments are involved. It is very sensitive.'

Annie frowned. 'But it's been almost twenty-four hours, and people are injured in there. Something has to be done, before something worse happens.' She thought of the young men patrolling the animal sanctuary. Products of long-term poverty, marginalised and susceptible to grandiose calls to action within a radicalising religious movement. Prepared to do anything to deliver meaning to their otherwise obscure lives.

'Our army and police are . . . not very experienced with this,' said Pak Ketut. 'We had the bombings years ago, but it was not like this, not many hostages. Not *any* hostages, Annie.'

'But the injured need medical attention,' she said, thinking of the little boy Cara had rescued and poor Janelle, limp in Remy's arms.

'The whole of Bali is praying,' said Pak Ketut. 'Let us be grateful that Pak Tony and Henry got out, at least.'

'Oh!' she cried in pleasure and surprise.

'You did not know?' Pak Ketut smiled. 'No, of course you couldn't. They escaped. After the blast, they climbed the wall. I tried to help, but . . .' He looked away. 'Henry is badly injured.'

Annie's elation turned to alarm. 'How badly?'

'He showed much courage,' said Pak Ketut, his eyes meeting hers again. 'He saved Pak Tony's life. But then the terrorists shot at him and . . . he had to jump off the wall.'

'Into the car park?' Annie shuddered, recalling the height of the boundary wall.

Pak Ketut nodded. 'The doctors had to put him into a coma. He had a bad skull fracture. There was pressure on his brain and they had to operate.'

'Oh, no.' *Poor Henry.* She shook her head to think that the member of the group whom she'd branded a dithering coward on the first day they met had actually risked his own life to save another's. 'What about Pak Tony? Is he alright?'

'The doctors say he is fine. He has been interviewed by police already, and he is back at Puri Damai.'

'That's good news.'

'Yes.' Ketut seemed to hesitate. 'Pak Tony was not well when Henry was helping him over the wall. I watched them from the car park—Pak Tony could not move. But now Henry is badly injured and Pak Tony is . . . better.'

'Maybe the doctors have missed something?'

'Maybe.' Ketut looked doubtful.

'Can we visit Henry?' asked Annie.

'I will ask the doctor.' Ketut stood up from his chair and went out into the corridor.

Annie lay on her back and stared at the ceiling. She was desperate to see Henry, who was by himself, comatose, and in a different hemisphere to his mother. If Pak Tony was injury-free and had been released from hospital, why wasn't he keeping vigil at the Englishman's bedside? Or hers, for that matter?

Pak Ketut returned shortly, accompanied by a man in a white coat and a nurse pushing a trolley laden with medical equipment.

'So, you have woken up,' the man said jauntily. 'I am Dr Widhi. Nurse Efi will do your obs now.' The young woman set about checking Annie's temperature, pulse, blood pressure and oxygen saturation levels.

While the nurse completed her checks, Doctor Widhi perched on the end of Annie's bed. 'We have given you some intravenous fluids, but you have no major injuries. You were fortunate, I think?' He smiled. 'The police would like to speak to you, if you are ready. The American embassy also.'

Annie digested this. 'Of course,' she said. 'I'll do anything I can to help.'

'I will let them know you are awake,' he said.

'But no media,' said Pak Ketut, in a protective tone.

'No media,' the doctor repeated.

'Can I see my friend Henry?' Annie asked. 'The young Englishman?'

The doctor shook his head. 'Not in his current condition. He is in the high-dependency unit. Only next of kin are allowed.'

Maternal tears welled in her eyes. 'And has his family been contacted?'

'Yes, someone is flying out from England tomorrow.' Dr Widhi touched his hand to his heart. 'Please excuse me. Nurse Efi will take out your cannula, then you will be discharged. I will organise the paperwork. We are preparing for many more casualties.' He hurried out of the room.

Of course, Annie thought. *When the siege finally ends, there may be dozens of dead and injured.* New tears welled up. Ketut reached into the pocket of his batik shirt and passed her a neatly pressed handkerchief.

'Thank you,' she said, dabbing at her eyes. 'I'm very emotional, I'm afraid.'

'I understand.' He held out his mobile phone. 'I could not find your husband's number in the files at Puri Damai. Would you like to call him now?'

She blinked in surprise, and took a second to answer. 'My husband died a long time ago.'

'I am sorry.' Pak Ketut said nothing for a moment. 'I lost my wife eight years ago, too.' Then, after another pause, he asked, 'Why have you not married again?'

'Who would want a fat old woman like me?'

'I do not understand.' Pak Ketut looked genuinely astonished. 'You are so friendly and open, Ibu Annie. Something is wrong with men in America?'

She chuckled, chuffed by Ketut's compliments. 'Maybe.' Then, filled with a sudden yearning, she said, 'But at least I have my dog, Untung, at BAF. I miss her terribly.'

The driver nodded. 'The police and the embassy will want to interview you first, but I can take you to BAF later tonight, if you would like?'

'That's nice of you, Ketut, but I'd like to wait for news of the others.' She looked at him. 'Would you stay with me?'

'Of course.' Pak Ketut glanced at his watch. 'But if you change your mind, I could drive you to Ubud in forty-five minutes. You could visit Untung, then come straight back. We could leave very early tomorrow morning. That way, you would miss no news, I think.'

'Thank you, Ketut.' Annie smiled back at him. 'You're a very kind man.'

⁓

Early the next morning Annie checked her phone, but there was no news from inside the animal sanctuary. She consulted the doctor about Henry, too, but was advised that his condition remained unchanged.

She decided to call Ketut, who answered within three rings.

'Can we get to BAF and back in less than two hours?' she asked hopefully.

'If we leave now, yes,' the driver replied. 'Wait in the foyer, I will be there soon.'

The roads were still quiet so early in the day. Within half an hour of leaving the hospital, they pulled up outside the two-storey building with a sign in the front window that read *Bali Animal Friends (BAF)*. Looking up at the building, Annie felt as if it was the venue of another life, half-remembered in vivid dreams. So much had happened since she'd last set foot inside it, less than a week ago.

'Here we are,' she said, climbing out of the car. 'I wanted to bring the rest of the Fearless group here. Maybe they can visit after . . .' She trailed off, suddenly wracked with guilt. Why *was* she indulging in this visit to BAF while her friends were still being kept as hostages, or possibly worse?

'Don't worry,' said Pak Ketut, perhaps sensing her feelings. 'Take a short break now, Annie. You have been through much.'

They went into the shopfront, already open, where baskets of pet supplies—cans of dog food, collars, and worming medicine—were set out for sale on bamboo racks. A small gold bell, inscribed with the words *Ring for Service*, sat on the unmanned counter.

Annie glanced in surprise at the cages in the window, all of which were empty. 'Usually these cages are full of puppies for sale,' she explained to Pak Ketut. 'Though mostly we just give them away to anyone who can offer a good home. Come through.' She ushered him towards a doorway marked *Staff Only*.

They walked along the hallway, past a series of empty offices, then into the kitchenette. There was nobody around.

'They must be out the back,' Annie said, looking at the kitchen clock. 'It's breakfast time for the dogs.' But oddly, she could hear no barking. It wasn't a public holiday, so where was everyone?

She pushed open the door to the yard, then stood motionless for a moment, her eyes darting from side to side. Cages lay at odd angles, their doors open, as if a small tornado had whipped through the facility.

'Putu?' she called. 'Kadek?'

There was no reply. Feeling rather panicked now, Annie began to pick her way along the path between the cages. Pak Ketut followed not far behind, muttering under his breath, *'Ada apa ini?'*

Coming to a gap in the cages, Annie stopped abruptly. 'Gabriela!'

The Spanish woman sat on the ground with a limpid white puppy in her arms. For a split second, she tried to smile. Then she hung her head and began to sob.

'What's wrong?' Annie crouched down next to her. 'Where *is* everyone?'

Gabriela waved a hand towards the back of the yard, then buried her face in the puppy's fur.

Annie stood up and strode along the path, ignoring Ketut's pleas to slow down and *hati-hati*. At the back fence they found Kadek, the vet nurse, standing alongside a large plot of recently turned earth. The young woman spun around at the sound of footsteps.

'Ibu Annie!' she exclaimed. 'Are you alright?'

'What's happened here, Kadek?' Annie asked, ignoring the question.

Kadek looked frightened. 'They killed the dogs.'

'What?' Annie gasped. 'Who?'

'Men with darts.'

'Darts?' Annie stared around in horrified confusion. 'Where's Putu?'

Just then, Putu and Nathan emerged from the nearby storage shed, each peeling off elbow-length black rubber gloves. With the back of his hand, Nathan wiped beads of sweat from his face—or were they tears?

When he saw Annie, he dropped his gloves and rushed to embrace her. 'Annie—we heard you were at the animal sanctuary. Are you okay?'

She held up a hand to stop him. 'Just tell me now—what in God's name has happened here?'

'I am sorry, Annie.' Putu stepped forward. 'The authorities came two days ago and did a mass rabies culling. We could not stop them.'

She stared at him, unable to comprehend what he was saying.

'They had papers and . . . the police with them,' the vet continued, his shoulders slumped. 'Rabies is increasing in Bali. Sixty people have died of it this year, and it is only March.'

'What? The authorities think killing healthy dogs is a priority, when there's a *terrorist siege* going on?'

'It happened the day before the siege.' Putu shrugged. 'They'd planned it months in advance.'

Annie turned back to Nathan, trembling with anger. 'Were you here when they came?'

The Australian nodded miserably. 'I told them that culling doesn't work. I told them our puppies are vaccinated. But they wouldn't listen. They had orders, they said.'

Annie's hands flew to her mouth. 'How did they . . . ?'

'Strychnine darts,' he said. 'They've been using them on the streets, too. It was awful. They left us to bury them.' He gestured at the turned soil.

'But where is . . . Untung?' Annie whispered. 'Where is *my* dog?'

Pak Ketut began to scout around the yard, looking behind empty cages.

Nathan looked uncertain. 'It was chaos, Annie. I saw her, then she disappeared. There were so many dogs, and at least six men. The animals were suffering, not all of them died quickly.' He looked despairingly at his colleagues. 'Have either of you seen Untung?'

They shook their heads, averting their eyes.

Annie turned and ran, pushing past Pak Ketut. Back along the path, past Gabriela, into the kitchenette, down the hall and up a set of stairs to the second floor. Running into her bedroom, Annie threw herself down on all fours and peered under the bed. The rattan basket beneath was empty.

For a moment she just sat on the floor, next to the bed, shaking uncontrollably. Then she buried her face in the mattress and wailed. A long, mournful howl imbued with every hurt she'd ever sustained over sixty years of life.

After all I've survived, she thought, *I cannot endure this.*

She heard quiet footsteps enter the room. Pak Ketut crouched down beside the bed, gently holding her as she wept. 'Shhh . . .' he said, patting her back.

After a few minutes, Annie's breathing began to stabilise. She sat back on her heels, snivelling. Pak Ketut released her and straightened up. For a moment he stood with his head tipped to one side, as if listening. Annie watched him dully as he looked around the room. And then she heard it, too: a soft, high-pitched whining. Their eyes met.

Annie pushed herself to her feet. She and Pak Ketut tiptoed across the room, following the sound, and stopped in front of a laundry hamper. Pak Ketut removed the lid. Daring to hope, Annie bent down and removed the topmost items: a pair of white trousers, several checked shirts, a dress. A moment later, a small wet nose appeared, followed by a pair of inquisitive eyes, and then two crooked ears. Seeing Annie, the dog leaped out of the basket and into her arms.

'Untung!' Annie wept into the dog's golden fur. 'I thought you were lost.' She looked up at Pak Ketut. 'I thought they'd killed her, or taken her, or . . .' It was as if everything she'd suffered at the animal sanctuary was rendered more tolerable, somehow, by Untung's survival.

'I know,' said Pak Ketut. 'She really is *untung*. A survivor, like you.' He reached down to scratch the dog's ears.

'Or very clever,' said Annie. She tickled the dog's belly and made a general fuss of her, before standing up again. 'We should get back to the hospital. This won't take long.' She reached under her bed for her suitcase. Then she pulled out a drawer, scooped up all of the items inside it, and tossed them into her bag.

'Can I . . . help you?' asked Pak Ketut, watching her in confusion.

She shook her head. 'I don't have much.'

All that work, she thought, *to spay and immunise the dogs, then the government culls them anyway.*

'It's time,' she said.

'For what?' Pak Ketut ventured.

She squared her shoulders. 'To give up. I love Untung, but it's time to let the dogs of BAF go.' She'd made no difference at all, she realised.

The driver nodded slowly. 'Maybe you will focus on . . . people instead? Many are suffering in Bali.'

Annie blinked, stung by the truth in his words. She'd been so busy tending to the dogs of Bali, she'd barely paid attention to the plight of the *people*. She closed her suitcase with a resolute snap, then began dragging it towards the door.

Pak Ketut scrambled to assist her. 'What about those?' He indicated the remaining items in her bedroom: a pile of books, some knickknacks and an empty vase.

'Oh, it's just *stuff*,' Annie replied. 'We fill our lives with it. I don't need it anymore.' She turned and looked him in the eyes. 'But what I *will* need, when all of this terrible business is over, is a driver. One who doesn't mind a dog in his car, who can handle a traveller without a particular destination in mind. One who wants some company, some laughter, and maybe to see a sunset or two. Can *you* help me with that?' She extended her hand hopefully.

Pak Ketut stared at her for a moment, his expression unreadable, then shook her hand. 'Certainly, Ibu Annie.'

She felt herself blush a little. 'Well, then,' she said. 'Let's go back to the hospital and wait for our friends.'

Going ahead of her, Pak Ketut hoisted the suitcase on his shoulder and carried it down the stairs, Untung following at his heels.

Watching them descend, Annie felt slightly lighter of heart. The world was unravelling, but she still had Untung. And now she had Ketut, too.

Gelato. The word blurred before Lorenzo's eyes as he stared at the galley refrigerator positioned directly opposite him. Unable to resist the powerful urge to sleep any longer, his eyelids slipped close. A moment later, he saw the refrigerator door open and the gelato let itself out. Lorenzo leaned forward to catch with his tongue the wispy, sugary puffs that floated beyond his reach. Scoops of cottony vanilla glided past him, round and firm and plump, with little pink bumps for wings. Suggestive, somehow, of the fleshy nipples of his favourite models, wrapped in linen and twill, like dainty sweets in an ornate box. Lorenzo almost groaned with longing. If only he could catch one, take it into his mouth and suck out its sweetness, his hunger might abate.

Lorenzo's head bobbed forward and he whipped it back up, his eyes snapping open. The gelato disappeared. The room was still submerged in semi-darkness, as it had been the previous night, their first in captivity. Two rickety lanterns hung on thin bamboo poles near the entrance to the café, offering some illumination. But their batteries were clearly dying, as the light was growing dimmer.

That morning, the power had been cut to the animal sanctuary, presumably by the police. Without air conditioning or ceiling fans, the café was stiflingly hot. After sunset, Lorenzo had watched from his position near the kitchen, salivating, as the guards gorged on perishables from the refrigerators. They'd left the tinned and packaged supplies untouched for future use. But they'd continued to use their phones and laptops, even in the absence of electricity; they obviously had plentiful supplies of batteries and independent internet access.

But how long can the siege last? Lorenzo wondered. *And, aside from cutting the power, what exactly are the Indonesian and international authorities doing about it?* As each bothersome hostage was escorted away by guards—including Annie, who'd been marched away on the first night—Lorenzo's fear that an orderly resolution was unlikely had only increased.

The captives had eaten nothing for more than twenty-four hours. Many lay weak and unmoving on the floor, stirring only to take an occasional cup of water administered by the guards, scooped out of a bucket. Since he'd seen the guards refilling the bucket from a kitchen tap—reserving the stocks of filtered water for themselves—Lorenzo had reduced his fluid intake. If the time came, he didn't want dysentery impeding his ability to flee. It was the dehydration, no doubt, that had triggered the mirages—the flying marshmallows, vanilla gelato and nonna Marisa's stuffed olives.

He tried to put out of his mind what might have happened to Annie after she was led away. Having seen no sign of Pak Tony or

Henry since the explosion, he could only assume the worst: that they were out there somewhere amid the rank piles of rubble, their bodies swelling in the heat. Contributing to the putrid smell that now assailed the hostages whenever they relieved themselves outside, in the communal trench on the south side of the café.

Janelle was slumped in Remy's lap in the opposite corner of the room, barely conscious and suffering from a head wound. Remy himself was haggard with exhaustion, but continued to tend to her: propping her feet up against the wall, cradling her head, keeping her hydrated. He'd fashioned a bandage from his shirt, which was completely soaked through with blood. Infrequently, Remy would glance in Lorenzo's direction. The Frenchman's eyes were hooded with anxiety, and Lorenzo wished he could offer something more than a discreet nod.

Sitting next to Lorenzo was Cara, still alert, caressing Tito's hair. The little boy lay curled in her arms, sucking his thumb, his eyelids flickering as he slept. After saying nothing for hours, during which time Lorenzo and Cara had worried about possible internal injuries, Tito had finally yielded to Cara's repeated questioning in Indonesian—*Bagaimana adik? Kamu baik-baik aja?*

'*Namaku Tito*,' he'd said at last, his round eyes brimming with tears. '*Di mana ibuku?*'

Cara had translated, her voice tremulous. *My name is Tito. Where is my mother?*

She had pressed the boy to her then, murmuring consoling words that neither Lorenzo nor Annie could understand. Tito had stared up into her face with awe and, sensing perhaps he could trust her, began describing something of his background. He was older than he looked—already five, it turned out—and from Java.

Merely a visitor to Bali, on holidays, like them. His home was in Bogor, south of Jakarta, with his parents, grandmother, two sisters and a caged bird called Budi. His parents and sisters had been sitting next to him at the bird show, he told Cara.

During the long hours of captivity, Lorenzo had watched Cara caring for Tito. Crooning softly to him with unfailing cheerfulness, showering him with hugs and kisses, helping him with his toileting and, perhaps most impressively, repeatedly steering him back from the brink of tears so as not to aggravate the guards. Lorenzo was moved to see such powerful maternal instinct at work. He wondered whether his own mother had related to him in such a way; he couldn't recall much tenderness. And would Lavinia be like this, too, if she had her own child?

Cara's care of the little boy, and her fluency in Indonesian, had not gone unnoticed among the guards either, and they'd started permitting her to take Tito to the toilet block, rather than insist he use the communal pit. One of the guards—a slight man with a lazy eye—had even dropped a handful of prawn crackers into Cara's lap during the first night. Tito had gobbled them up greedily, then nestled himself into Cara's arms again and fallen heavily asleep.

Lorenzo envied the small boy this deep unconsciousness; his own fitful snatches of sleep were filled with tormenting and outlandish dreams. Of grand buffets set with enticing dishes that turned to steaming horse dung when he approached. Of Lavinia, like the dread Medusa, with vipers writhing in her hair. Of a winsome model, standing bare-backed in a field of wheat, who growled like an angry dog at Lorenzo. With sleep offering so little respite, Lorenzo had taken to studying the guards' movements instead. Trying to determine a pattern, or a potential flaw in their security measures.

When they'd first been herded into the café, Lorenzo was certain he'd counted six guards. Since then, four had remained in view. A pair were always stationed inside the café, another two near the bamboo bridge just beyond the entrance. He could only assume the other two were positioned elsewhere in the sanctuary. Perhaps keeping watch—or sleeping—in the owl house, Lorenzo concluded after studying the grubby site map he'd found in his pocket. The map's close-up image showed the owl house to be an elevated structure with no windows—to avoid disturbing its nocturnal inhabitants, presumably—and tall ventilation slits that would be useful for surveillance.

The guards he could see swapped duties at regular intervals—dawn, noon, mid-afternoon, sunset and just before midnight—or whenever a tinny recording of the Muslim call to prayer sounded from the laptop they used near the café's entrance. At each rotation, the two men stationed at the bamboo bridge would take up tasselled prayer mats and disappear down the path signposted *Mushola—50m*, which led behind the café. They would return fifteen minutes later and pass the mats to the other two men inside. Lorenzo had a feeling that those two, after prayers, swapped with the external guards, who would then return to the café and take up position near the bamboo bridge. But it was impossible to confirm this, as it was difficult to differentiate between the guards with their faces partially covered.

In one of their quick, whispered exchanges, Cara had told Lorenzo that she'd tried to eavesdrop on the guards' conversations, but her efforts were thwarted by their use of Javanese, which she didn't speak. However, she'd overheard them listening to Indonesian current affairs coverage of the siege and, once, heard two of them speaking on the phone.

'They're getting instructions from the outside,' she'd whispered furtively to Lorenzo. The idea filled him with foreboding: an authority beyond the animal sanctuary, manipulating the guards like marionettes.

Lorenzo closed his eyes now, wishing it was over. Wishing, too, that he craved more than a mere end to the siege; a loving reunion with Lavinia, for example. She would be beside herself, he knew, not knowing if he was alive or dead. Keeping vigil somewhere, praying for intercession, applying pressure on the Italian authorities. He felt sorry for the pain his predicament would be causing her, but sorrier still for his proclivity that prevented their marriage from thriving.

He sighed, recalling the moment of truth in the Python Pit. How Pak Tony had cupped his ear and asked him to imagine the person he most wished was next to him. To Lorenzo's chagrin, he had not pictured Lavinia. Nor nonna Marisa, nor his ageing mother, nor his estranged father, nor any of his dozens of friends across Europe. Instead, Lorenzo had imagined his favourite young models—Pietro and Valentina—writhing together in the pit, snakes sliding across their naked glistening bodies. And in the centre of that heaving mass, Lorenzo had seen *himself*. Pietro on his left, Valentina on his right, his own tanned skin a foil to their evanescent beauty.

It had been a reflex response to a simple query. But the electric thrill it had elicited in Lorenzo had left him raw and vulnerable, unable to respond properly to Pak Tony; finally, he'd declared he could not answer the question. When Pak Tony had pressed him further, Lorenzo had retreated. For how *could* he explain it to others, when he could barely articulate it to himself? Was it even possible to express, without debasing it, the liminal state in which Lorenzo had lingered for most of his life? His words would be too easily misunderstood, too readily misused by ignorant people who failed to grasp the nuances. Only Lavinia came close to comprehending his infatuation with the sensuality of youth, yet even hers was an imperfect understanding.

The only terms available to Lorenzo were those he refused to use, comprised of coarse syllables and unsavoury connotations. Like *paiderastia* in Greek, evoking the most questionable of social practices in ancient Athens and failing to communicate the wholesome, elevated emotions that characterised *his* friendships with young people. Nor did he acknowledge it as *paedophilia*, a tasteless, modern term. For all the intoxication of proximity with his models, Lorenzo never touched them. He probed them with his photographic lens instead, savouring the intimacy this delivered. But he never, ever, attempted to possess them. Gratification could only demean the relationship, he knew, destroying the delicate erotic frisson engendered by his own unfulfilled desire.

Carnal relations were reserved for Lavinia, therefore. The grunting and groaning of grubby exposure, the power play of command and submission. It was the status quo of most relation-ships between consenting adults, it seemed, each manoeuvring to fulfil their own needs. And Lavinia, without question, knew how to meet hers, guiding his hands and tongue, or grinding away on top of him until her frenzied shrieks made her pleasure apparent to anyone within earshot of their apartment. Yet for all the predictable peaks and release of lovemaking with Lavinia, Lorenzo remained conflicted. The world could not countenance his deepest cravings. And neither, in truth, could he.

For years, the internal discord had been manageable, eclipsed by a thriving career and his easy compatibility with Lavinia. That part of himself he couldn't quite trust—the part that confused and sometimes repulsed Lorenzo—had been compartmentalised. Until recently, when Lavinia started talking about nursery renovations, hypnobirthing and organic vegetable plots, and subconscious fears that might hinder conception.

His fear was *not* subconscious; Lorenzo knew this long before his arrival at the Fearless retreat. Before Monsignor Fattori had laid hands on him in Vatican City, Lorenzo had known exactly what was troubling him. *What if I desire our child as it grows?* The idea was repugnant, making him withdraw even further from Lavinia's inane chatter about pregnancy, birth and babies. But the more he retreated, the more she pursued him. Accusing him of falling out of love with her, of dodging commitment, of selfishness, perfectionism and narcissism. All of which was probably true, Lorenzo decided, unable to explain the real reason behind his reluctance and helpless to appease her.

Their vehement arguments, interspersed with periods of silent attrition, had worn him down. Finally, fatigued and miserable, Lorenzo had acceded to Monsignor Fattori's advice: *Take some time, look within.* What harm could that do? Acquiescing to Lavinia's excitement about the Fearless retreat, Lorenzo had quietly begun to hope—to pray, even—that somehow, on a far-flung tropical island, something might shift for him. But within days of arriving in Bali, Lorenzo had realised that change was not a destination. However many fear safaris, guided meditations or group therapy sessions he completed, one thing remained constant: him. When the Fearless retreat was over, when the memories of Balinese sunsets began to fade, when he and Lavinia returned to their refurbished art deco apartment in a much colder Navigli, *he* would still be there. Janelle had summarised it perfectly in her passion talk gone viral: *Whatever's on the outside, it's always you beneath.* Lorenzo was the permanent, despicable denominator in their lives.

He opened his eyes and turned his head from side to side, rubbing his itchy neck against an exposed wooden beam in the wall behind him. He was covered in mosquito bites; all of the hostages were. If they ever got out alive, they would probably all die of some tropical disease. Lorenzo glanced at Cara, who continued to fan Tito, ceaselessly waving away the insects that encircled him. *That* was selfless love, the likes of which he couldn't comprehend.

Watching Cara care for Tito over the torpid hours of their captivity, he'd been compelled to consider a question he had never asked himself before. In all his interactions with young models over the years, had he ever harmed a child? By legitimising his desire under the guise of photographic composition: *Squat down, open your legs, undo that button. Look at me as if you love me. Like you're scared of me. Like you're hurt.* Letting his eyes linger too long, and always taking a souvenir from the shoot—a soft ballet slipper, a whimsical hair ribbon, a colourful singlet—which he secreted at the bottom of his underwear drawer. But he never touched his models, he told himself, not even once. Surely no harm was done?

Cara looked up and smiled at Lorenzo. It was, he saw now, a beautiful smile. Yet in the early days of the Fearless retreat, he'd been quick to judge the Australian woman. Internally recoiling from her shabby appearance, her severity. Even when he'd learned the reason for it all, at the water cleansing ceremony—how she'd lost her only daughter to drowning—Lorenzo had wondered if perhaps she'd grieved too long.

How wrong he'd been, he realised, closing his eyes in shame.

Lorenzo.

He opened his eyes again.

Lorenzo.

He blinked and looked around. The guards were changing over for the midnight shift, and Cara was leaning towards him. He tilted an ear towards her. 'It's Friday tomorrow,' she said. 'That means longer prayers at lunchtime. That's our chance.'

Lorenzo stared at her.

'Through the bathroom window,' she whispered. 'Annie told me about it, before she . . . went. I checked it when I was there with Tito. We can definitely climb up. There's a gap between the toilet block and the external wall, but it's manageable. We can escape into the car park.'

He frowned, recalling the height of the wall around the perimeter. 'It's too high.'

'Would you rather wait to be shot?'

Lorenzo glanced furtively at the guards. 'But I haven't heard any shots . . . they may not be killing the hostages they're taking away.'

'What else *could* they be doing?' asked Cara. 'Giving them a meal and a hot shower? They're getting rid of the difficult ones, Lorenzo. Just as they did with the staff.'

Lorenzo winced. The group of staff members they'd glimpsed sitting with their hands behind their heads, immediately after the explosion, hadn't been seen since.

'*Cazzo*,' said Lorenzo, losing his cool and raising his voice. He had no prior life experience that could help him make informed judgements now.

Two guards, newly arrived from their posting beyond the café, suddenly turned and looked in their direction. Cara began rocking Tito back and forth, shushing and patting him. The ruse seemed to work, as the guards resumed their conversation.

'We have to escape,' whispered Cara, out of the corner of her mouth.

'But *how*?' Lorenzo whispered back.

Cara focused her gaze on Tito as she spoke quietly. 'At the midday changeover, the guards who finish on the bamboo bridge will go to the *mushola* to pray—for about half an hour, because it's Friday. It's fifty metres away, so there's our chance. During prayers there are just two guards on duty here. We'll have to distract them, then get everyone out through the bathroom.'

'Distract two guards for thirty minutes?' Lorenzo shook his head at the folly of it. 'And what about the owl house guards? There'll be another two guards there—and they must be armed.'

Cara leaned closer. 'I've checked and I can't see the owl house from the toilets. If we can't see them, they can't see us.'

Lorenzo retrieved his site map and studied it in the dim light. Cara was right, the amenities block was a potential blind spot, obscured by the *mushola* and a large Birds of Papua aviary.

'But . . . free *everyone*?' He motioned to the hostages, some of them injured, many seemingly resigned to their fate.

'We've got twelve hours to get the message around the room,' whispered Cara. 'We just have to figure out how to distract the guards.'

'It's a crazy idea,' said Lorenzo sharply.

Cara looked crestfallen. She lowered her head and continued to fan the sleeping Tito.

After a moment, Lorenzo sighed. 'Let me think about it.'

She implored him with her eyes, but said nothing more.

Overwhelmed by the enormity of the task before them, Lorenzo closed his eyes once more.

⁓

Under a groggy blanket of half-sleep, Lorenzo saw himself, four years earlier. Dialling a men's health hotline, six months into his relationship with Lavinia.

'How can I help you, Luigi?' asked the voice at the other end of the line. He'd given a false name and location, fearing he might be traced.

'I think I'm . . . attracted to children,' Lorenzo said. 'Girls and boys. In their early teens.'

The voice hesitated. 'How do you know?'

'I just know.'

'Have you ever hurt any children?'

'No.'

The voice exhaled. 'Is it a fantasy? Many men have sexual fantasies they never enact. Rape, sex with animals, sexual slavery, things that would be illegal if you actually carried them out. Do you have any intention of approaching a child?'

'No.'

'Then it's just a fantasy.'

Lorenzo frowned. 'I don't think so. I've been like this for a long time. I've just . . . never done anything about it.'

It's who I've been forever. A man who loves children, more than I should.

'But from what you've told me, Luigi, you're not a child molester.'

Not yet, he wanted to scream. *I'm calling you now to try to prevent that.*

'Do you know of any . . . support services for people like me?' Lorenzo asked tentatively.

The voice paused. 'Look, there are plenty of services for sex offenders—which you're not. If you have an aberrant sexual fantasy that's concerning you, therapy can help. I'd recommend a clinical psychologist specialising in cognitive behavioural therapy. Sometimes all it simply takes is to change the way you perceive yourself.'

There's nothing 'simple' about it, Lorenzo thought, incredulous. 'Are you saying that I'm misjudging myself?'

'I'm saying that sometimes a fear about ourselves may be inflated—a catastrophic view of ourselves. Maybe that's what's happening here, Luigi?'

Lorenzo felt his chest tightening.

'Would you like me to provide you with some contact details for psychology services in your area?' the counsellor asked.

'Yes, please,' he said robotically.

'Good. Stay on the line.'

Lorenzo listened to the tinny hold music playing in his ear . . . as it gradually morphed into the irritating whine of mosquitos.

He shifted uncomfortably, his body stiff and aching, and surfaced for a moment to bat the insects away. When he remembered where he was—in the bunker at the animal sanctuary—a lump of despair wedged in his throat. He closed his eyes once more, blocking out the bodies prone on the floor, and slipped back into an uneasy sleep.

Nonna.

She was standing directly in front of him, tiny glittery diamonds escaping from her kindly eyes. Tears of joy, he discerned, without having to ask.

'You are a beautiful boy,' she said, 'and so clever. You will know what to do, Lorenzo.'

'But I *don't* know, nonna,' he objected. 'I never have.'

'Come closer,' she said, beckoning to him.

As he walked towards her, padding across the smooth white floorboards of her rustic country kitchen, Lorenzo glanced down at his feet. Pudgy cherub's feet, even at the age of thirty-eight. He watched his toes bend and his heels lift, mesmerised by the leverage and the rhythm, until suddenly he collided with nonna Marisa's shins.

He burst into tears at the shock of it.

She lifted him to her then, making gentle tut-tutting sounds. He laid his cheek against her chest, inhaling her earthy smell, of sage and thyme and rosemary. Every now and then, his snuffling would escalate into a sob, but nonna Marisa would click her tongue and stroke his hair and murmur, '*Non preoccuparti, andrà tutto bene.*'

But how *is everything going to be alright, nonna?* he wanted to demand. He was close to forty, with a life founded on decades of omission.

'I am hopeless, nonna,' he announced, too ashamed to look at her. 'And I am too old to change.'

His grandmother lifted his chin gently with her fingers and looked at him, her eyes quizzical. Then she laughed, mirth bubbling up from within and tumbling out of her body, shaking her jowls and bosom and arms as it exited.

'You are wrong, *ciccino*,' she said, wagging a finger at him. The knuckle was swollen and gnarled, yet as strong and beautiful as the knot of an ancient oak. 'It is never too late, Lorenzo. For you, for me, or for the whole wide world.'

She held his face in her hands. Drinking him in with her eyes, nodding and smiling every now and then as if her greatest hopes had been fulfilled. He squirmed with delight, at her touch, her scent, her confidence in him.

'Surely you must realise by now who you are, Lorenzo?' Nonna Marisa kissed him lightly on both cheeks. 'You are a brave boy. Heroic and fearless.'

Lorenzo opened his eyes and searched the shadows, trying to shake the conviction that nonna Marisa had been here. In the dimness, he peered up at the clock on the café wall. It was two o'clock on Friday morning, the third day of their captivity.

Cara's eyes were closed, but Lorenzo could tell she was awake. They'd been waiting like this forever, their shoulders touching, their stomachs rumbling and their rank breath assaulting each other in clandestine conversations. There was no sign of the guards, as far as Lorenzo could tell, so he leaned towards her. 'We have to use Tito,' he whispered, glancing at the boy lying in Cara's lap. 'It's the only way.'

Cara's eyes flew open and she shook her head.

'Take him to the toilets straight after the midday changeover,' Lorenzo persisted. 'Then call out—say he's sick, that you need help. When a guard goes into the bathroom after you, I will follow him and—'

'I don't want to use Tito.' Cara interrupted. 'It's too risky.'

Lorenzo nodded. 'You're right. But without Tito, the guards will be suspicious.'

Cara's face was ashen, like a weathered statue in a moonlit garden. 'I can't lose him, Lorenzo,' she whispered. 'Not another child.'

'We won't,' he said. 'I promise.'

'What about the other guard?' she asked. 'In the café?'

'Remy will have to handle him, and any others that come running. I'm going to crawl over and talk to him now.'

'Don't, Lorenzo!' Cara looked incredulous. 'They'll see you.'

'Not if I do it slowly,' he said. 'Extremely slowly.'

Cara paused. 'But what if Remy . . . doesn't want to do it?'

Lorenzo looked over at the Frenchman, still cradling Janelle in his arms. He might well refuse, given her condition—and then what? They sat in silence for a while.

One of the guards appeared again at the front of the café and leaned against the rickety railing on the bamboo bridge, gazing at his mobile phone. A hostage cried out and startled him, and he swung around and pointed his rifle at her. The Indonesian woman, whose neck was covered in an angry red rash, promptly burst into tears. She hid her face and sobbed, while her husband frantically tried to shush her. As the guard slowly lowered his rifle, Lorenzo felt his resolve begin to ebb away. The terrorists had supplies, weapons and, in all likelihood, rotations of rest in the owl house. The hostages had only hunger, heat and hopelessness.

Lorenzo glanced at Cara. 'Maybe we'll be rescued soon.'

He'd spent hours imagining the diplomatic upheaval transpiring outside the sanctuary. Foreign governments, concerned for their citizens, expressing their views on negotiation and retrieval, with Indonesia staunchly maintaining its sovereignty. The mounting pressure of media coverage, local and international, and the complexities of negotiations with the captors and, perhaps, whoever was commanding them from the outside. Nothing had happened for two days, but the impasse couldn't continue. Either the Indonesian authorities or the terrorists would have to take decisive action soon.

Cara shrugged. 'But if they try to rescue us, will we survive it?'

Lorenzo looked at her uncertainly.

'The Indonesians aren't used to this kind of situation,' she went on. 'The last major terrorist attack didn't involve hostages. Just bombs, remember?'

She glanced at the guard, who had beckoned to his colleague. The pair of them stood huddled together over their phones.

'If the Indonesian police or the army attempt a rescue, but the guards see them coming, it's over—the guards will try to save face and kill us all.'

Lorenzo hadn't considered that. He scanned the forms of the other captives in the room. Most lay unmoving, immobilised by injury or exhausted by hunger and fear. A young woman in a bright orange bikini top lay nearby, hugging her knees to her chest, groaning intermittently. The injured needed help now, Lorenzo realised. Who knew how long some would last without medical treatment?

'We have to escape,' he said, his resolve hardening once more. 'We can't just sit here waiting to die.'

'But if we use Tito, how do we protect him?' Cara turned to Lorenzo. 'He's an innocent in all of this.'

Lorenzo stared at Cara, the realisation dawning of what he was preparing to do: *to protect the innocents*. 'I will keep him safe,' he whispered. 'I will keep you all safe.'

One of the guards wheeled around. Passing his mobile phone to his partner, he strode across the room towards them. 'Why are you talking?' he demanded.

Lorenzo stared dumbly at him.

'Silence!' the guard bellowed. He raised the butt of his rifle, then brought it down sharply. There was a blinding pain on the bridge of Lorenzo's nose, and the back of his head struck the wall. Stunned, he lifted a hand to his face and felt warm liquid trickling between his fingers.

Cara said something to the guard in a low, cajoling tone. A moment later, the guard crouched down and looked at Tito, who did not stir.

The bikini-clad woman groaned again, louder now, clutching her stomach. The guard stood up, muttered something terse to Cara, then stalked towards the woman. 'Silence,' he said, standing over her. The woman whimpered on the floor.

'I said, silence!' he yelled, kicking her until she cried out.

He dragged her to her feet, then marched her at gunpoint to the café entrance and passed her over to another guard outside. She began to scream—hoarse howls of fear. As the woman's cries receded, a terrified silence settled over the café.

Cara removed the scarf wrapped around her shoulders and folded it into a rectangular wad. Gingerly, she lifted it to Lorenzo's nose. 'Sorry,' she mouthed.

Lorenzo shook his head, trying to communicate: *It's not your fault.*

It was senseless, all of it. Did the woman in the bikini have a partner? Or a child? She almost certainly had a mother and a father, whose lives would never be the same again. Blood trickled down the back of his throat and he gagged. Holding the scarf to his face, Lorenzo suddenly felt supremely thankful that he had only suffered a broken nose. So far.

'I told him Tito was sick,' Cara whispered. 'When the guard hit you. I said he was weak and running a fever.'

So Cara had already set the plan into motion, it seemed. A wave of fear washed over Lorenzo.

'Do we start telling the others?' she whispered.

Lorenzo shook his head. People were unpredictable. The message might get distorted, like Chinese whispers. Or one of the hostages might be overheard telling another.

'Don't tell anyone,' he murmured, from behind the bloody scarf. 'When it's time, let's just hope they follow.'

And what if they don't? his rational mind challenged. Lorenzo closed his eyes, unable to answer. No one else was mounting any resistance; they had to try something. Cara's hand clasped his and Lorenzo opened his eyes again. Her face was frightened.

'I'll go tell Remy now,' he whispered.

Suddenly he remembered the letter, the one he'd scrawled out in the Python Pit after a so-called 'heart-to-heart' with Pak Tony.

Lorenzo had revealed nothing during the snake-holding session and, yet, Pak Tony had seen through him.

'Don't you like yourself, Lorenzo?' Pak Tony had asked quietly, after the other Fearless members had left. 'I think you know who you need to write to, and what you need to say. Remember, there is no greater relief than to tell the truth.'

Lorenzo hesitated. 'But I . . . don't think I can send the letter. Ever.'

'You don't need to make that decision now,' Pak Tony replied. 'Just write it. That in itself is progress. One step at a time.'

And so Lorenzo had complied, penning a cathartic note to Lavinia while Pak Tony lingered nearby. The first words flowed effortlessly:

The pain of pretending is now greater than the pain of disclosure.

Lorenzo pulled the folded letter from his pocket now. 'Pak Tony made me write this,' he said, 'and I think it was a mistake.'

Cara stared down at the note.

'I don't want to carry it with me,' he said. 'It's not who I am.' He recalled his dream of nonna Marisa telling him who he *really* was. 'Can you look after it for me, for now?'

Her eyes welled up with tears, then she nodded. 'What if—?'

He shook his head and passed her the note, then slid away from the wall. Lying on his back, he swallowed the blood that dripped down his throat from his nose. Unobtrusively, he began to inch away from Cara. Pausing every few seconds, before moving off again. Slipping along in increments, like a guerrilla garden snail, the guards oblivious to his progress.

After four hours of edging across a six-metre span, Lorenzo finally slid into the gap next to Remy. The grey dawn announced the changeover of the guards; seizing his chance, Lorenzo prodded Remy's thigh with his forefinger. The Frenchman gasped, as if awoken from a nightmare. He stared at Lorenzo, his eyes wide.

'We are going to escape,' Lorenzo whispered. 'We need your help.'

Clearly this was not what Remy wanted to hear. He glared meaningfully in the direction of the four guards, who stood conversing in low voices just inside the café entrance.

'We have a chance today, because it's Friday prayers,' Lorenzo continued. 'There's a window in the bathroom.'

Remy looked sceptical.

'Hear me out. After the guards' changeover at lunchtime, two of them will go to the *mushola*. Cara will take the boy to the toilet. She'll call for help, and when one of the guards goes to her, I'll follow and disarm him. Your job is to handle the other guard, here in the café. We have to get to them both before they fire a shot, or the guards in the *mushola* and the owl house will hear.'

Remy shook his head.

'What's wrong?' said Lorenzo, his frustration building.

Remy made a gun shape with his hand, and fired it at him.

'They're amateurs. None of them holds a gun like he's used to it.' Lorenzo knew an experienced gunman when he saw one; his father's preoccupation with hunting had educated him in that regard.

Remy still looked unconvinced.

'I know what you're thinking,' whispered Lorenzo. 'But we can't keep waiting to be rescued. The police might bungle it and we'll all get killed in the crossfire. Or the terrorists could panic and shoot us.'

The Frenchman looked pained. He'd clearly considered these possibilities already.

'People are getting sicker here, and they're getting rid of more of us every day, like Annie.'

Remy's mouth began to tremble.

'Cara thinks the Indonesian authorities won't wait much longer. They'll take action soon and who knows how it will end? I want to keep living. I'm sure you do too.'

Remy looked down at Janelle, his eyes bloodshot from sleep deprivation. The other hostages were beginning to rouse, moving stiffly in the early morning light. Two of the guards took up their stations, at either side of the room, to watch the captives. The other two headed away from the café along the path to the *mushola*.

'Remember parasailing?' Lorenzo whispered. 'You had it all inside of you.'

The Frenchman shook his head, and Lorenzo knew the comparison didn't stand. *That* was a trifling fear of heights, unlike the life-and-death predicament they now found themselves in.

'Think of the future, Remy,' Lorenzo urged. He motioned to Janelle, who sported a nasty cut to the base of her scalp. 'That needs medical attention. We could get her out today.'

The Frenchman sat silently for a minute, staring at Janelle. Then he looked back at Lorenzo and, almost imperceptibly, nodded.

The midday air was heavy with humidity, the sun beat down beyond the bamboo screen at the café's entrance, and most of the hostages lay limply on the floor. The changeover guards moved around the room, their rifles slung across their backs. The guards stationed near the bridge had already departed, each carrying a rolled-up prayer mat.

Lorenzo could barely swallow. It wasn't just thirst and his swollen nose. He felt like a fatigued athlete crouched on the starting blocks, poised to commence a race he couldn't win. Wave upon wave of adrenalin surged through his body, enveloping him in a sickening buzz.

Nonna, he thought, raising his eyes heavenward. *Help me, Nonna.*

He looked across the room at Cara, who gazed down at Tito, her expression carefully blank. But Lorenzo could see the tension in her mouth, a slight flush in her cheeks. Beside Lorenzo, Remy sat motionless except for his hands, which he kept wringing. The guards didn't seem to notice anything amiss, accustomed by now to displays of fear and anxiety among their hostages.

Lorenzo waited until Cara raised her eyes to meet his. They stared at each other, poised on the agonising precipice of action. He raised both arms above his head, as if stretching, then awaited her return signal. A few moments later, after watching the guards patrolling—waiting until the guard with the lazy eye was closest to her—she did the same. Lorenzo turned to Remy and whispered, 'Now.'

Cara raised her hand to attract the attention of the approaching guard.

'*Ada apa?*' he asked.

'Tito *mau ke kamar kecil*,' she explained. '*Boleh saya ngantarkan dia lagi?*' Lorenzo knew she was asking to take Tito to the toilet.

The guard gestured impatiently to the entrance and Cara helped Tito up. She picked her way past the other hostages. She was nearing the bridge, ushering the boy along, when the guard hailed her again.

Lorenzo caught his breath as the man walked across to them and bent down to look at Tito, scrutinising him. As Cara spoke in rapid Indonesian, looking increasingly nervous, Lorenzo heard her repeat the word *sakit*—sick. Was the man becoming suspicious?

To Lorenzo's relief, the guard waved Cara on. He trailed her for a short distance, pausing next to the other guard at the café's entrance. They watched as Cara continued over the bridge and down the stairs.

Lorenzo's stomach did several sickening backflips as he observed Cara through the gaps in the façade's bamboo panelling. She walked quickly along the path to the toilet block, then disappeared into the section marked *Wanita*. Any moment now, she would begin calling for assistance, propelling Lorenzo and Remy into action.

Lorenzo looked at Remy, whose face was rigid.

Seconds later, they heard Cara call out, '*Tolong*, Tito *sakit!*'

The guards looked at each other, frowning. '*Ada apa sih?*' the first guard called to Cara, walking in the direction of the amenities block.

She called back immediately, her voice high-pitched and panicked. Lorenzo knew it wasn't all acting.

The guard turned back to his partner and shrugged, then moved further along the path. He stopped near the entrance to the amenities block and called out to Cara. Their exchange continued, until Lorenzo began to fear that the guard would never enter the bathroom. Waiting, Lorenzo shifted his position into a crouch. Remy did the same, visibly shaking as he gingerly shifted Janelle onto the floor.

After what felt like an eternity, the guard seemed to tire of his discussion with Cara. Evidently frustrated, he gesticulated at his colleague standing in the café entrance, then turned and walked into the ladies' room.

Just then, the call to prayer sounded from the laptop at the front of the café. A flock of ducks rose from a nearby pond, squawking loudly.

Taking advantage of the brief flurry of noise, Lorenzo lurched upright and rocketed across the room, his limbs pumping like pistons. His vision seemed enhanced, and he instantly identified the quickest route to the entrance, dodging prone bodies. Shocked hostages gaped at him as he sprinted past. Remy was trailing somewhere behind, his feet slapping on the cold white tiles.

The sound prompted the guard at the entrance to turn around, as if in slow motion, raising his rifle. Remy wasn't close enough, and Lorenzo was already upon him. He slammed his shoulder into the guard's chest, knocking him backwards with such force that they plunged together over the bridge, down the steps and onto the path below. The crack of the man's head against the pavers was decisive. Lorenzo straddled him anyway, watched his eyes roll back in his head as blood pooled beneath his skull. A moment later, the guard's body went limp.

'Stay here,' Lorenzo whispered to Remy, who now stood panting at his side. 'Take this, just in case.' He removed a box cutter from the guard's belt. 'Tell the hostages not to move until we say.'

Remy nodded. Lorenzo yanked the strap of the rifle over the guard's head, then stood up and began moving quickly towards the toilets.

As he approached, he could hear Tito crying, and Cara and the guard continuing to converse, which suggested the guard hadn't heard the commotion outside. Flattening himself against the outside wall of the toilet block, Lorenzo crept to the door, then stole a look around it. Cara was crouched next to the *bak*, a large tub filled with water, with Tito whimpering next to her. The boy's face was blotchy with distress and the guard was bent over him, wiggling his fingers and making *chk-chk-chk* noises, trying to distract him.

Without pausing for thought, Lorenzo rounded the corner and charged at the guard, swinging the butt of the rifle at his head. But the guard caught sight of Lorenzo's reflection in the mirror, and dived aside. Rolling across the slippery floor, the man fumbled for his rifle. Before he could reach the trigger, Lorenzo tackled him.

He rammed the man's head against the *bak*, then hurled him face down into it. He held the man's head beneath the water, pinned by his body weight. The guard moved jerkily, his movements frantic. But Lorenzo held his neck fast, even as the man thrashed about and, finally, began to lose strength.

Suddenly Cara cried out and Lorenzo wheeled around, expecting to see more guards.

'Don't drown him,' she cried. 'Please, don't drown him.' She hugged Tito's face to her chest.

Lorenzo held the guard under for a few seconds longer, until his limbs stopped moving. Then he pulled him out by the back of his shirt and let him slump to the floor, motionless.

'Come on.' He strode into the cubicle with the window above it and climbed onto the toilet seat. Reaching up, he pulled off the window grille and cast it aside. He stepped up onto the cistern and then hoisted himself into the gap. The exterior wall lay less than a metre away, partially obstructed by foliage.

'Give me that,' he said to Cara, nodding at a large drain plunger on the floor beside the toilet. From the corner of the small cubicle, one arm still holding Tito, she grasped it and passed it up to him.

He hacked at the foliage with it, clearing a way through. Then, realising that the exterior wall was slightly higher than the window, he half climbed, half jumped across the gap. The barbed wire on top of the wall scratched at his limbs and he crouched there a moment, peering over the wall. The drop was significant enough to break bones: he and Remy would have to help the hostages across the gap and down the other side.

Someone cried out from the car park below, and Lorenzo realised he'd been spotted. He raised an arm above his head in acknowledgement, then pressed a finger to his lips, trying to communicate the need for silence. But the excitement in the car park grew, and a moment later, a group of uniformed officers rushed towards the wall with two long bamboo ladders. Lorenzo held up his palm to communicate *wait*.

The officer at the front of the group held up his hand too, and the men behind him immediately halted. The leader looked up again. Lorenzo gave him a thumbs-up, then pressed his finger to his lips once more. *Wait,* he mouthed to the man, who nodded.

Lorenzo clambered back across the gap into the window, his breath ragged. 'Stand on the cistern and pass me Tito,' he said.

Cara nodded and coaxed Tito up onto the toilet seat, stepping up beside him. She put one foot on the cistern, but struggled to lift Tito any further.

'I'll take him,' said Lorenzo, leaning down and grasping the boy with both hands.

As Lorenzo pulled him up into the window, Tito began to whimper. Lorenzo hesitated, looking back at the gap. The boy was light, but attempting to jump across while holding him would be risky.

A head appeared above the wall. It was the leader of the uniformed officers.

'Ladder,' whispered Lorenzo.

The leader nodded, disappeared for a moment, then reappeared with one of the bamboo ladders. He pushed it through the gap in the foliage. Lorenzo pulled it across to the window, positioning it as a makeshift bridge. It wasn't secure, but it would do.

Holding Tito in one arm, Lorenzo moved carefully across the ladder, then passed the boy to the officer. At least half a dozen ladders were propped against the external wall now, Lorenzo saw.

Panic gripped him. 'Stay on that side!' he whispered hoarsely. 'We will pass you down the hostages.'

The lead officer looked at him, expressionless. 'I follow my commander's orders,' he said, before carrying Tito down the ladder.

We need to get out now.

Lorenzo turned to help Cara, already climbing through the window. Her feet slipped on the bamboo rungs as she clambered across, almost upsetting the ladder.

'Tell the Indonesians they must wait,' he urged, guiding her down onto an external ladder. 'Tell them we have more than sixty hostages coming *now*.'

She nodded. 'Thank you, Lorenzo,' she said, her eyes filling with tears.

He smiled at her, then turned and hurried across the ladder once more. He slid down into the cubicle, then raced out of the toilet block, looking around. It was only a matter of time before Friday prayers would be over.

At the café entrance, Remy stood by the guard's unmoving body. Relief flooded his face at the sight of Lorenzo.

'We're out,' Lorenzo whispered. 'I need your help on the wall. Get Janelle ready.'

Remy nodded. He ran into the café and swept Janelle over his shoulder in a fireman's lift. As he did, several hostages near the entrance stood up and others began to murmur.

Lorenzo had followed Remy inside. He stood on a chair near the entrance and held up his hands for silence. 'We've found a way out,' he said in a low voice. 'But you *must* stay calm.' He pointed at the amenities block. 'Follow us quietly and we will get you out.'

'No way,' a voice said. A blond-haired man in board shorts and a Bintang singlet stood up. 'They'll be rescuing us soon. I'm staying put.'

'Me too,' said the woman next to him, and others nodded in agreement.

There was no time to attempt to reason with them. 'Go now, Remy,' commanded Lorenzo. The Frenchman strode off towards the toilet block, carrying Janelle across his shoulders. 'Anyone else who wants to come must come now.'

Lorenzo jumped down and ran after Remy as a sudden, undesirable din erupted behind him. Chairs scraped on the café's tiled floor, people urged one another to stand up, or quarrelled about what to do. Others were already following Lorenzo, the sound of their footsteps prompting him to run even faster.

Back in the amenities block, Lorenzo found Remy already standing on the toilet seat, struggling to lift a limp Janelle through the window.

'You go through first,' said Lorenzo. 'Crouch on the ladder and reach back. I will push her out.'

After lowering Janelle into Lorenzo's arms, Remy climbed through the window and onto the bamboo ladder. A moment later, his hands appeared in the gap. With one foot on the cistern, Lorenzo hauled Janelle up under the arms and pushed her upper body through the window. Her head lolled alarmingly. Remy leaned over and grasped her shoulders.

'Okay,' said Lorenzo. 'Go!' Together, they lifted Janelle across the gap.

While Remy carefully lowered her over the outer wall to the waiting officers, Lorenzo turned to find the bathroom filled with panic-stricken hostages. They surged forward, some jostling each other.

'Don't push!' said Lorenzo, and extended a hand to an African woman standing immediately in front of him. She was uninjured and climbed up through the window quickly. A middle-aged

304

Indian man was next, then three frightened Japanese children. The eldest of the trio, a boy of no more than ten, insisted that his two younger sisters go first.

'You're a brave boy,' Lorenzo told him, guiding him over the gap.

As the hostages copied those before them, the process became smoother. The able-bodied moved quickly, with Lorenzo's help inside the bathroom and Remy's assistance on the ladder and at the wall. Lorenzo worked ceaselessly, steadily moving the hostages up and through the window, lifting those who needed more assistance, until sweat drenched his shirt and made his hands slippery.

He'd counted twenty-six hostages crossed to safety when a short, gaunt man appeared in the line holding an elderly woman in his arms. Her skin was ashen and her eyes were closed. The man stumbled and almost dropped the woman, who Lorenzo presumed was his mother.

'Here,' said Lorenzo, reaching for her. 'Let me help.'

Taking the woman in his arms, Lorenzo noticed that she was cool to the touch. He squinted then, observing the set of her jaw and the stiffness of her limbs.

'Sir,' he said cautiously. 'Your mother is . . .'

'Unconscious,' said the man, in a thick Slavic accent.

Lorenzo looked again at the woman. 'Sir,' he repeated. 'Perhaps we can put her—'

'Get her out *now*!' spat the man.

Lorenzo nodded. Arguing would only cause further delays. He stood on the cistern and called for Remy's assistance. 'This one may be hard to move.'

Remy's eyes widened when he saw the woman, but he said nothing. Lorenzo attempted to lift her through the window, but the rigidity of her body made it difficult to manoeuvre.

After several failed attempts, some of the waiting hostages became agitated. A man called out, 'She's dead! Put her down!' and the group surged forward again.

'No!' cried Lorenzo, pushing them back with his foot. 'We are not animals. Help me get this woman out.' He pointed to a strapping man with a ginger beard. 'You—help me.'

Remy had moved into the window, straddling it, his upper body hunched forward. The Indonesian officer had leaped up onto the outside wall and crouched there, waiting.

Lorenzo stood on the toilet seat and turned to the bearded man. 'Okay—lift!'

The man hoisted the woman up and Lorenzo shunted her partially through the window. Remy helped to move her onto the ladder bridge. The Indonesian officer leaned forward from the wall and gripped the woman's shoulders. As he hauled her across, her shoe caught on a rung of the ladder. Remy leaned over to extricate it, and the ladder wobbled and tipped sideways. The woman's body rolled off the ladder and fell between the walls, landing with a thud in the dirt below. The ladder clattered down on top of her.

Remy and the officer stared down, horrified.

'We have to leave her there,' said Lorenzo.

The woman's son barged at Lorenzo then, pummelling his chest. The bearded man pushed him back against the cubicle wall and, without hesitation, slammed his fist into the man's face. The man slid to the floor, unconscious.

'Stop!' gasped Lorenzo. 'Stay calm!'

The anticipated half-hour for Friday prayers was surely over. At any moment, the guards would return and find the café nearly empty.

'Quick,' said Lorenzo, reaching for the next hostage. 'You'll have to jump across. Careful of the gap.'

Four Chinese hostages, an Australian trio, a man with a maple leaf sewn on his cap; Remy and the Indonesian officer reached for them from the wall, helping them across the gap. The bearded man passed his pretty, blonde daughter up to Lorenzo, and then helped two young women from Europe, and a couple who looked Indonesian. Finally, only a handful of hostages remained. As he lifted an older Australian woman through the window to Remy, Lorenzo heard a commotion behind him.

He turned to see the bearded man now standing over the guard still lying on the floor outside the cubicle. The guard was regaining consciousness, spluttering and coughing as his head rolled from side to side. The bearded man held Lorenzo's rifle, waving it near the guard's head.

The guard's eyelids fluttered. The bearded man snarled, his finger hovering over the trigger.

'Don't shoot!' Lorenzo called desperately.

The guard's eyes opened.

An ear-splitting crack rang out, shattering the mirror on the wall, and the guard on the floor tried to roll away. Three more bangs and blood spurted across the tiles. The bearded man dropped the rifle immediately; the guard lay lifeless, and two hostages fell to the floor, hit by stray bullets.

Lorenzo jumped down from the window and bent over the fallen hostages. Both were bleeding and shrieking in pain.

Any moment, Lorenzo thought. 'Go!' he commanded the bearded man. 'Get out!'

The man pushed past him and climbed through the window. Lorenzo helped the two remaining able-bodied hostages up after him.

'Climb up,' Remy urged Lorenzo, from the outer wall. 'Come now!'

'Two more are injured here,' he called back, turning to a woman with a neck wound. He looked around for something to stem the flow of blood. The man punched unconscious was starting to stir, too.

'Leave them!' Remy cried. Lorenzo pressed his bare hand to the wounded woman's neck.

Suddenly there were voices just outside the bathroom. Lorenzo looked towards the door and froze. Two guards came through the doorway and stalked across the tiles, their rifles trained on him. Lorenzo instinctively eyed the rifle on the floor, only a metre away.

'Hands up,' said a guard, following his gaze.

Lorenzo lifted them.

The second guard crouched down next to the dead guard on the floor. He stared for a moment, before looking furiously at Lorenzo. 'Kneel,' he commanded. 'Hands behind your head.'

Lorenzo obeyed, shaking.

The two guards stood in front of him, their rifles raised.

Lorenzo closed his eyes and saw Lavinia's face on their wedding day, radiant with joy.

A breeze whispered beyond the window, a rustling of leaves like a thousand soft footsteps.

This is how it happens.

A curious calm settled upon him. He opened his eyes and looked directly at the guards.

This is how I meet nonna Marisa again.

FAILURE

Remy watched helplessly as two hospital wardsmen pushed Janelle's stretcher towards an opaque sliding door marked *Darurat—Emergency*. Dozens of people lined the waiting room. Some were siege survivors, slumped in chairs or against walls. Others were translators, diplomatic personnel, relatives or friends.

A cordon of police officers was positioned outside the hospital entrance, fending off the media throng. Inside, a triage team of local doctors and international volunteers was reviewing every new arrival and ongoing case. Having sustained only minor lacerations from the barbed wire, Remy had been deemed a low medical priority. He was exhausted, hungry and dehydrated, but all that could be easily fixed; he was soon offered food, drink and a change of clothes by a junior nurse. But given the grave and uncertain nature of her injuries, Janelle had been taken for assessment immediately.

'Please don't die, Janelle,' he murmured, watching the light brown crown of her head disappear behind the emergency doors. 'Not now that I have found you.'

'*Bonjour, Monsieur. Comment allez-vous? Vous avez subi un grand choc, j'imagine.*'

Remy looked up to see a white-haired woman standing beside his chair, a clipboard in her hands. Her impeccable outfit was entirely at odds with the chaotic scene around them.

'I'm Marie, from the French consulate,' she explained, continuing to address him in French. 'What's your name?'

'Remy de Brive.' He stared at his hands, wishing her away.

The woman perched on the seat next to him. 'And where are you from, Remy?'

'Saint-Germain-des-Prés.'

'Oh, I'm from Saint-Sulpice. Small world.' She began scanning a list on her clipboard.

'*Too* small,' muttered Remy. He glanced at an English-language newspaper lying on a waiting room table. *Islamic extremism strikes Bali*, the headline screamed.

'Was that your wife?' Marie asked, motioning to the emergency doors.

'No.' He expelled the syllable with such force that the woman flinched and Remy felt bad. 'I . . . would like her to be,' he explained. 'But I may not get the chance to ask.'

I don't deserve the chance, he thought.

Marie laid a hand on his arm. 'It's hard to wait for news.'

You don't understand. I failed Lorenzo. I let him die.

Remy shook his head, remembering how he'd called out to Lorenzo, urging him to leave while he still had the chance. And then, rather than climbing back into the bathroom and dragging the Italian out, he'd turned and fled himself. He'd slid down the bamboo ladder into the car park and watched dazed from the ground as dozens of uniformed men stormed up over the wall. Seconds later, he'd heard gunfire, and then he was bundled into a waiting emergency vehicle. As he was borne safely away, he looked back and saw that the animal sanctuary was in flames.

Marie looked sympathetic. 'There's a counsellor here from the American consulate. Or a British chaplain, if you would prefer?'

A psychologist or a priest. Remy snorted and shook his head. Neither of those professions could help him. No one could.

'You've been through a lot,' she said, patting his arm now.

'Thank you, Marie,' he said, shrugging her hand away. 'I'd like to be alone, please.'

'I understand. But I am sure you would like to speak to your family in France? Here.' She removed a mobile phone from her pocket. 'It's a free service.'

He stared at the phone, feeling inexplicably empty.

'Or . . . would you like me to call someone for you?' Marie asked gently.

Remy pictured his parents in Paris, anxiously awaiting news. Glued to media updates, imagining all manner of catastrophic scenarios.

'Here.' Marie passed him a notebook and pen. 'Write down a name and number.'

He scrawled down his mother's details, then returned the notebook.

'I will tell her you are safe and well,' said Marie, standing up to go. 'And that you will call very soon.'

Remy nodded, knowing full well that he couldn't talk to his parents, not now. He couldn't possibly explain that he was waiting for news of a woman with whom he'd fallen madly in love. A woman who didn't conform to their vision of a suitable match, who wouldn't embrace their wealth, and who would probably question the inequities of their privileged lifestyle. He couldn't describe how, despite her fundamental foreignness—in culture, class and world view—the possibility of losing Janelle was more painful than the prospect of enduring their disapproval for the rest of his life.

He couldn't tell his parents this, not yet. Not until he knew whether Janelle would survive.

'She's going to be fine,' said the Balinese doctor, jotting notes onto a medical chart.

Remy stared at Janelle, lying pallid against the expanse of white hospital linen, her arm connected to a drip. Her eyes remained closed, even now.

He didn't dare believe it. 'But what about her head?'

The doctor slipped the medical chart back into an opaque folder, then snapped it shut. 'The wound was deep, it needed twenty-two stitches. The good news is that it didn't penetrate the base of the skull. We can remove the stitches in ten to fourteen days.' The doctor motioned at the IV drip. 'We are giving her precautionary antibiotics.'

'Are you sure there is no damage to the brain?'

The doctor looked mildly irked. 'At first we thought she had a coup-contrecoup injury. Which in English is, er . . .'

'I am French,' said Remy. 'I know what it is. Trauma to both sides of the head.'

'My apologies. I assumed you were Australian.' The doctor smiled. 'Foreigners all sound the same to me.'

The doctor's pager vibrated on his belt, but he ignored it. 'We scanned Janelle's brain using an MRI, but there was no evidence of swelling. No sign of white matter lesions or other trauma, only mild contusion, consistent with a localised injury. Something sliced into Janelle's head, probably a piece of metal. But it wasn't an impact blow.'

'But she was barely conscious,' Remy countered.

'Yes, she lost quite a lot of blood and went into mild shock,' the doctor explained. 'Dizziness and weakness, passing out or having trouble standing up—these are all symptoms of shock.'

Remy gestured at Janelle. 'Is she still in shock?'

The doctor's smile was warmer now. 'No, she is just sleeping. Were you the one who helped her at the animal sanctuary?'

'Well, er . . . I tried.' Remy felt suddenly defensive. 'I put pressure on the head wound and tried to wrap it up, but the bandage kept falling open. I elevated her feet, kept her warm, gave her fluids. Just basic first aid.'

'You probably saved her life,' said the doctor. 'Shock can be fatal if left untreated.'

'Oh.' Remy stared in surprise.

'You did very well,' the doctor said. 'Most people cannot think clearly in an emergency, especially when they are under threat themselves.'

Remy nodded, recalling the Australian man who had refused to leave the café. How many hostages had stayed behind with him? And when the guards had returned, what had become of them? His eyes began to smart.

'When will she wake up?'

The doctor shrugged. 'When she is ready. Have you been examined?'

'In triage,' said Remy. 'I am not an urgent case. I will wait here until she wakes up.'

'Alright.' The doctor moved towards the door. 'I will tell my colleagues you are here. Someone will come for you soon.' He pointed to a sleeper chair in the corner. 'Try to get some rest. We may have to bring other patients in here. There aren't many beds left.'

'Of course,' said Remy. 'Thank you, doctor.'

He waited until the doctor had closed the door before pushing the sleeper chair across the room, sliding it next to Janelle's bed. A hand crank allowed him to carefully lower her bed; when the two were level, he stretched out on the chair beside her. Wary of bumping the cannula inserted in the back of her wrist, he reached for her hand.

It was the first time he had lain down in three days, and the sensation was overwhelming. His body felt as if it had been immersed in warm water, and he realised the extent of his physical tension throughout the siege. He watched the rhythmic rise and fall of Janelle's chest, and his eyelids became heavier. His breath became deeper, circular; he'd been breathing rapidly for the past seventy-two hours, he now understood.

I want to spend it with her, he thought. *I want to spend my last breath with her.* It was the only certainty that remained.

Holding fast to Janelle's fingers, and reassured by the knowledge that she *would* survive, Remy succumbed to sleep.

He awoke with a start. For a few horrendous moments he lay stiff and unmoving, his eyes closed, convinced he was still at the animal sanctuary. Then he opened his eyes and saw the IV drip, and realised where he was. A clock on the wall told him it was four-thirty. The same afternoon? He couldn't have slept very long. Wiping a trail of saliva from the corner of his mouth, he pulled himself upright to check on Janelle.

'Hello, sleepyhead,' she said. She was lying on her side, one hand propped beneath her cheek, fully conscious for the first time in days.

Remy beamed, leaned forward and wrapped his arms around her. *You're back.*

He pressed his nose into her hair, letting tears of relief roll down his face.

I love you.

He was desperate to tell her so.

'Ouch,' she said, pulling away. 'My head hurts.'

He slapped his forehead. 'I'm sorry. Your stitches.'

'I'm the one who should be apologising. And thanking you. From what I can remember at the animal park . . .' She smiled wanly. 'You were there for me the whole time.'

He reached for her hand and grinned at her, almost giddy with anticipation.

'Janelle,' he said. 'I have been thinking. Every minute of the siege, I was thinking, if we actually survive this . . .' He squeezed her hand between his. 'I need to tell you something I've never said to anyone else.'

Janelle's face was weary. But he couldn't wait any longer to tell her what was inside him. The siege at the sanctuary had taught him that if he let this opportunity pass, it might never come so perfectly again.

He stood up and pushed the sleeper chair away, then slid down onto his knees next to her bed. 'Janelle, I love you.' He searched her face, awaiting the expression of delight, words of reciprocity, or a passionate kiss.

As she continued to stare at him, Remy waited in an excruciating limbo.

Her lips parted, as if she was on the verge of saying something, but nothing came out.

'What's wrong?' he asked.

'I . . . I'm surprised.'

'Why?'

'Have you seen a doctor yet, Remy?' she asked. 'Are you delirious?'

His mind whirled. 'What do you mean?' He realised suddenly that he had not considered for a moment what Janelle might think. He'd been confident, somehow, that she understood his feelings and shared them, and that his declaration would make as much sense to her as it did to him.

She sighed. 'I remember when we were parasailing. You talked a lot about French women. How they wouldn't wear zinc or rash shirts or . . .'

'*Non, non.* You are so refreshing for me, Janelle,' he said. 'You are not pretentious. I love that.' He gripped her hand. 'Remember the shoulder massage at the intimacy workshop? I touched you and it was like . . . electricity. I had never experienced anything like it. I had to leave the room.'

Janelle looked confused. 'You said you had gastro.'

'I lied,' he confessed. 'I didn't want everyone else to know. But then, at the tooth-filing ceremony, I realised I had to tell you how I felt. The manhood rite showed me that I need to start taking more responsibility for my feelings and actions. But I didn't get the chance to tell you all this . . . before the animal sanctuary.'

She lowered her eyes.

'There is something else, isn't there?' He felt sick to the stomach. 'It is the YouTube clip, yes? I am so sorry for that. It was a stupid mistake.'

Janelle shook her head.

He stared at her. 'You . . . don't feel the same way?' He pulled himself up off his knees and sat awkwardly on the edge of her bed.

'Remy.' Her eyes glistened. 'We've just lived through something dreadful. We're still in *hospital*. We don't even understand what's happened to us. Well, *I* don't. I need to recover. I'm very honoured, Remy, but . . . it feels like an extreme response to an extreme situation.'

'It *is* extreme,' Remy agreed vehemently. 'Because life is so short, we have seen that at the animal sanctuary. Why should I wait? I love you! We love each other, *n'est-ce pas*?'

She looked troubled. 'I . . . I don't know, Remy. It's all happened so fast. We've only just met. We haven't even *kissed*.'

'You're right.' He smiled. 'Would you like to?' He leaned towards her, but she turned her face away.

A curious numbness spread through his chest, a discomfort far greater than anything he'd experienced during the siege. Slowly, he released Janelle's hand.

There was a cautious knock on the door. It swung inward, and three figures appeared in the doorway.

'They're here!' cried a familiar voice. Pak Tony rushed into the room, reaching the bed in several bounds. Tears ran down his cheeks as he hugged Remy first, and then moved to Janelle's side. 'I'm so glad you're okay,' he said, clasping her hand.

'Oh!' Janelle cried, looking behind him. 'Cara, is that you? And *Annie*?' She gasped. 'I thought you were . . .'

'Me too,' said Annie, hurrying to the bedside. Pak Tony stepped aside, beaming, and the American hugged first Janelle, then Remy. 'I didn't think I'd live to see any of you again.'

Cara joined them now, wrapping an arm around Janelle's shoulders, then pulling back. 'You look so much better than you did. Are you alright?'

Janelle nodded, clearly overcome.

'And as for you . . .' Cara turned and smiled at Remy. 'Come here, hero.' She pulled him into a tight hug. He received it numbly.

'Is Tito alright?' he asked, remembering the little boy Cara had cared for throughout the siege.

'They had to operate on his arm, but he's going to be okay. Thanks to you and Lorenzo.' She turned to Pak Tony. 'Do you know, Remy held off the guards while Lorenzo got Tito and me out?'

Remy's face reddened. 'It wasn't like that . . .'

Cara smiled knowingly. 'You won't be able to stay out of the limelight forever, Remy. The world will want to know how you and Lorenzo managed to rescue so many hostages. Where *is* Lorenzo?' She looked around the room.

Remy was stunned into silence. Gradually, the realisation sank in: no one else knew. After their escape, the hostages had been shunted into waiting emergency vehicles and taken away immediately. Remy was the only one who'd been there at the very end.

'He was killed,' he whispered finally. 'I'm so sorry.' Cara seemed to shrink before his eyes. Annie covered her face, and Janelle began to weep quietly. Pak Tony simply gaped, aghast.

'Lorenzo was the hero,' murmured Remy. 'I didn't do anything, apart from what he told me to do. He helped all the hostages get through the bathroom window. But when the guards came, I . . .' He faltered. 'I couldn't help him anymore.'

I didn't *help him*. The silence in the room was censorious, Remy felt.

At length, he wiped his eyes. 'Lorenzo was the true hero.'

'His wife is asking for him,' said Pak Tony, shakily. 'She's waiting outside for some news.'

'Oh, no,' said Annie. 'That poor, poor woman.'

'I'll go to her now,' said Pak Tony. 'She must be told.'

'I'll come with you,' said Annie.

'Thank you.' Pak Tony looked relieved. 'Henry is on the second floor now, too. He came out of a coma this afternoon. They're expecting him to make a full recovery.'

'Oh, thank God.' Janelle smiled through her tears.

Remy felt a rush of relief, too—followed almost instantly by renewed sadness for Lorenzo. Only he had been lost. Brave, clear-thinking Lorenzo.

'Henry's allowed visitors, but he can't move much yet.' Pak Tony looked sheepish. 'He was injured rescuing me. Another tale of bravery. Who would have thought it when we started Fearless?'

He shook his head. 'It was only last Sunday, but it feels like a lifetime ago.'

No wonder Janelle rejected me, Remy thought suddenly. *Who tells someone they love them less than a week after meeting them?*

There was a soft tap at the door and the group turned as one. Remy half expected it to be Henry or, absurdly, Lorenzo. But a Balinese nurse stepped into the room and nodded to the group.

'Mister Remy?' She looked apologetic. 'The doctor has sent me. Please come to consulting room three for your check.'

Remy nodded and stood up from the bed to go.

'Wait a moment, Remy,' said Pak Tony. He turned back to the others. 'I have an idea. What we've been through . . .' he raked a hand through his hair, 'it feels surreal. Maybe we can talk about it a little later this evening? We could share supper together in Henry's room?'

The others nodded.

'Will they . . . let us do that in a hospital?' asked Annie.

'This is Bali, remember,' said Pak Tony wryly. 'But I'll check with the nurses and let you know if there's a problem.'

Remy nodded too. It seemed churlish to do otherwise.

'Alright then,' said Pak Tony, smiling now. 'Let's meet at eight-thirty tonight in Henry's room. I'll bring supper. And if any of you needs to come back to Puri Damai before then, just call Pak Ketut to be picked up.'

'We don't have our phones,' said Janelle. 'They took them at the animal sanctuary.'

'You can use the hospital's, I'm sure,' said Pak Tony. 'Some of the embassy staff have phones available, too. The Australian consulate is one of them. Annie and I will check on that after we've seen Lavinia.'

'Thank you.' Janelle smiled gratefully. 'I'd like to call my family.'

'I'd better go see the doctor now,' said Remy, moving towards the door. He needed to get away from Janelle, and his growing feeling of humiliation, as quickly as possible.

'And I need to check on Tito,' said Cara. 'Are you okay by yourself, Janelle, for a while?'

'I'm fine.' Janelle smiled. 'All thanks to Remy.' He couldn't bring himself to make eye contact with her. 'See you tonight,' she called, as he walked out of the room.

Remy knew he couldn't possibly face her again. It had been presumptuous and foolish of him to declare his love for her, just hours after their escape from a terrorist siege resulting in the death of Lorenzo and so many others. His timing was terrible. He strode down the hallway without waiting for Annie, Cara and Pak Tony. He didn't want to talk to anyone. He didn't want to be in Bali any longer.

As he moved along the hospital corridor, tsunami-mind shadowed him like an assassin. He stared at the grooves in the linoleum, cracking and widening into hungry fissures. Imagining himself plunging into a dark chasm and the earth clamping shut above him, swallowing him whole.

⁓

After a rudimentary medical examination, Remy was escorted into a makeshift interview room off the hospital foyer to speak with two Indonesian police officers. One of the men—clearly the superior—was thin and jittery, with a habit of blinking rapidly as he spoke. His taller, pudgier sidekick remained silent, engrossed in his task of transcribing Remy's every word. Irrespective, it seemed, of the large sign taped to the desk: *Videorecorder in use.*

Remy felt edgy as he recounted the events at the animal sanctuary. The senior officer listened intently, stroking his straggly moustache, then peppered Remy with questions about the guards' movements, behaviour and communication during the siege. After fifteen minutes of questioning, the senior officer closed his black leather notebook.

'Thank you, Mister Remy,' he said. 'Do you have any questions for us?' It was a routine query; he seemed entirely disinclined to further discussion.

'A few, actually,' Remy replied.

The officer frowned. 'How many? We have a large number of interviews to do.'

Remy laughed nervously. 'Three?'

The officer cracked his knuckles with a sharp popping sound. 'Go ahead.'

'Okay, er . . . what happened to the hostages who stayed in the café?'

'You do not know?' asked the officer.

Remy shrugged. 'I haven't had access to the internet.'

'The hostages barricaded themselves in the café kitchen,' the officer said. 'When the tactical response team moved into the bathroom, they killed one of the terrorists. The other three terrorists retreated to the café.'

So there were *six guards in total*, Remy thought. Lorenzo had been right about that, too.

'What happened next is not clear—we are still investigating,' the officer continued. 'The terrorists set off another explosion, or set alight the café. We don't know yet, because the fire damage has destroyed the clues. But all the hostages inside died. There were fifteen we think, but this cannot be confirmed yet because the bodies are badly burned.'

Remy's mouth went dry. With at least a quarter of the hostages dead, how could it be argued that their escape plan had even worked? What would have happened if all the hostages had stayed in the café and waited for the end of the siege? He and Lorenzo were responsible for more than forty people escaping—but fifteen hostages had died as a result of their actions, too. The man in the Bintang singlet who had objected to their plan—he was not responsible for anyone living or dying. It wasn't clear to Remy whose action had been right.

'You have more questions?' prompted the officer.

'Were any of the terrorists arrested?'

The officer looked at Remy, stony-faced. 'They were all killed.'

Remy recalled Lorenzo's warning about what might happen if the police or army stormed the park. 'There can be no trial, then,' he said, thinking now of the victims' families. How could they piece together exactly what had happened to their loved ones during their last moments, without a proper investigation and trial? Remy lowered his eyes, crushed by guilt.

'Not unless we find the mastermind on the outside. We think the gunmen were just following orders, playing at terrorism.'

'*Playing*?' Remy was horrified by the use of the word. 'They knew exactly what they were doing.'

'Not really,' said the officer. 'They used homemade pipe bombs and pressure cookers, only eighty thousand rupiah from Matahari store. Just google the instructions.'

The junior officer sniggered, and Remy couldn't fathom why.

'They hid their weapons in cooler boxes, backpacks and unopened umbrellas,' the senior officer continued. 'They had knowledge about the sanctuary, so they smuggled it in easily. There is no security post at the park, no checking of bags on entry, no metal detector. There is only one way in and one way out, with a big wall around it, easy to patrol. They held all the hostages in the café like cows in a *kandang*. The layout of the sanctuary made it easy for them.' The officer smiled, and it grated on Remy. 'Except for the window in the bathroom. They didn't think of that. Or how brave their hostages would be.'

Brave? Remy blinked. He'd been terrified the whole time.

'They were clever, too, letting some of the hostages go.' The officer leaned back in his chair. 'It gave hope to everyone on the outside and made people listen to them.'

'I'm not sure what you mean,' said Remy.

'They let the staff go just after the bombs went off,' he explained. 'It helped draw attention to their cause—Salihin's release—and then the foreign governments start arguing about what to do. The terrorists got more time and publicity, you know?' The officer folded his hands. 'We must do our next interview, Pak Remy. *Terima kasih.*'

Feeling drained, Remy wandered out into the hospital foyer and stood near the window, thinking. He lost track of time as he stared up at the sky, watching it turn from tropical blue to a hazy blood orange. The media throng remained outside in the waning light. A camera suddenly appeared on the other side of the window and snapped in Remy's face, the flash blinding him momentarily.

Repulsed, he turned away and walked towards the stairwell. He glanced at his watch: Pak Tony had arranged for the Fearless group to meet in Henry's room in roughly two hours, but Remy had other plans. He groped in his pocket for the letter he'd written in the foyer while waiting for the police interview, scrawled on the back of a vomit bag he'd begged from a passing nurse. He checked, too, for the torn-off piece of paper confirming his flight number.

On the second floor, he asked at the nursing station for Henry's room number, then walked to Ward 2A and knocked on the door.

'Come in,' called a female voice, in English.

Remy pushed the door open. There were a dozen patients in the room, most with family members clustered around them. Males and females lay adjacent to each other, reflecting the desperate shortage of hospital beds. The level of noise in the room seemed higher than a hospital would ordinarily allow. Two of the beds were empty, although with rumpled sheets suggestive of recent occupancy, while the bed nearest the window was curtained. In the bed closest to the door lay a young Anglo-Saxon woman, her face bruised and swollen. Remy wondered how she'd sustained such injuries in the siege—a blow to the face, perhaps.

'Excuse me,' he said. 'Is there a man named Henry in this ward?'

'He's over there,' she replied in an Australian accent, motioning to the bed shrouded by a curtain.

'Thank you.' He approached it. 'Henry?'

The curtain parted, and an angular face with earnest grey eyes peered out. 'Hello. I'm Jim.'

'I'm Remy. Henry's friend from Fearless.'

'Oh, right! Come in.' He pulled back the curtain.

'When did you get here?' asked Remy, stepping through.

'Just this morning, actually. He woke up not long afterwards.' Remy nodded, staring at the figure in the bed. Henry lay motionless, his head swathed in bandages. Without his glasses, his face looked vulnerable and rather child-like.

Remy's eyes welled up as Henry smiled at him. It felt as if he was being reunited with a very old friend.

'Henry!' Remy hugged him carefully. 'Thank God you survived!'

'Only just,' Henry replied, smiling. 'I did a job on myself.'

Henry's speech was a little slower than usual, Remy noticed. 'Are you in a lot of pain?'

'The light hurts my eyes.' Henry lifted a finger in the direction of the curtain. 'The drape helps. I've got an almighty headache, too. From the surgery or the fall, I'm not sure which.'

'From both, I'd say,' said Jim. 'Lucky he didn't smash his brains out, the idiot.'

'Jim's my best friend,' said Henry. 'Can you tell? I love you too, mate.'

'You were very lucky.' Remy shook his head in wonder. 'I heard you rescued Pak Tony, too. You were incredibly brave.'

'The British media's got wind of it through the embassy,' said Jim, puffing up with pride. 'He's quite the celebrity.' Henry looked deeply embarrassed.

'You'll probably need a holiday when all of this is over,' said Remy, gently. 'Once you're back in London, make sure you come and visit me in Paris. You too, Jim. I don't know what interesting birds we have in France, but I have enough room for you both in my apartment.'

'Oh, Paris has beautiful woodpeckers and thrushes,' enthused Jim. 'And I've always wanted to visit the Eiffel Tower.'

'You're welcome anytime,' said Remy, smiling. 'But for now, I've come to say goodbye.'

'You're not leaving, are you?' Henry looked confused. 'I thought everyone was meeting up here tonight.'

Remy felt himself redden. 'Yes, but . . . I'm flying out just before midnight. I'm not ready to talk with the group about what happened. Not yet. I just really want to get home and see my family.'

Jim made a sympathetic sound. 'That's understandable. You've lived through a terrorist attack. I'd want to go home, too.'

Remy reached into his pocket and removed the note. 'I have a favour to ask,' he said to Henry. 'Could you give this to Janelle for me?'

Henry eyed the vomit bag without moving his head. 'No points for presentation. Is everything alright?'

Remy folded the note. 'I've failed too many people.'

'Wait a minute,' objected Henry. 'You're busy telling me how great I am, when I only helped Pak Tony. Jim told me how you and Lorenzo rescued almost everyone inside the animal sanctuary. That's not failure. That's a bloody triumph of courage and human spirit.'

'Hear, hear,' said Jim.

'Thank you.' Remy looked at the floor. 'But you're forgetting the fifteen who died. I didn't help *them*. And now I've alienated the woman I love.'

'Janelle?'

Remy nodded.

'Oh, shite.' Henry's face was consoling. 'At least you're in touch with your feelings, mate. Pak Tony would be proud. Don't be so hard on yourself.' Henry lifted his hand and took the note. 'I'll give this to Janelle. You two deserve a happy ending.'

'It's too late for that.' Remy glanced at his watch. 'Pak Ketut is coming to pick me up in ten minutes.'

'Come here and give me a hug, then,' said Henry. 'But you'll have to do all the work, because I can't move.' They laughed, then embraced.

At length, Remy straightened up from the bed and shook Jim's hand. 'The world needs Henry, so make sure he gets better quickly.'

'I will,' said Jim. 'Then we'll come and stay with you in Paris and you'll regret you ever asked us.'

Remy smiled and waved to Henry a final time before turning to leave. He closed the curtain behind him and made his way across the room.

Glancing at the young woman in the bed near the door, he suddenly felt sorry for her. 'You're a siege survivor, too?'

'No.' Her lips hardly moved. 'Facelift.'

Remy stood for a moment, bewildered. A *facelift*, when the whole world was falling apart? Then, remembering Janelle's passion talk, he blurted, 'You don't need plastic surgery to be beautiful.'

'Fuck off,' the woman said. 'It's none of your business.'

Feeling as if he'd been punched, Remy hurried out of the room. It was another failure among a litany of his making. He fled down the fire stairs, two at a time. Nothing had changed; everything was the same as before. Even after the horror of a terrorist attack, the world kept spinning; the petty demands of seven billion lives belied a more complicated global picture. And his own life was part of that arbitrary, nonsensical chaos. After all, wasn't he running away from Bali because a woman he'd only known for a week hadn't told him she loved him back? If that wasn't ridiculous, he didn't know what was.

He burst out into the car park below, almost colliding with Pak Ketut who stood near the stairwell door. The minibus idled nearby, in a patient pick-up zone. The Balinese man steadied him, laying a hand on his arm. For a second, he looked into Remy's face.

'I'll take you to the airport now,' said Pak Ketut, motioning towards the vehicle. 'You need to go home.'

Cara and Annie watched the retreating forms of Henry and Jim disappear behind the frosted glass marked *Keberangkatan— Departures*. Remy had left first, without even saying goodbye, on the same day the siege ended. A few days after him, Janelle had gone too, back to Australia to see her sick niece. This final departure now signalled the end of the group's time at Puri Damai. Pak Tony had been generous in allowing them to stay on at the resort with family members who'd flown in after the siege. But with only Bali-based participants remaining on the island, it was time to return to their ordinary lives.

Cara felt bereft watching the two men leave. The act of standing in an airport departure lounge stirred spectres of other, sadder goodbyes. The vivid memory of her husband, Richard, standing forlorn on a Sydney footpath some four years earlier, watching her taxi leave for the international airport. Saying goodbye to her frail parents, and being unable to tell them when she would return.

More recently, her heartbreaking parting from Tito, who'd flown back to Jakarta accompanied by an uncle.

Cara gratefully accepted another tissue from Annie and blew her nose. Tito's uncle, Om Jono, had only come forward to claim his nephew after Tito's photo was televised. To Cara's dismay, he seemed far more interested in the wad of cash that Cara gave to him to buy essential items for Tito than in his vulnerable nephew. But there was nothing she could do: he was Tito's next of kin, Australia had no adoption arrangements with Indonesia, and Om Jono insisted that Tito would be well cared for alongside his own six children.

Six children? Cara could barely contain her alarm. She'd exchanged contact details with Om Jono, assured him she would visit Jakarta soon, and offered to support Tito's education. '*Untuk selamanya,*' she'd said. *Forever.* The man's continuous polite nodding had done nothing to alleviate her concern.

So she'd stood in the domestic departure lounge, talking and singing to Tito, until his flight's final boarding call. Then she'd kissed his forehead and hugged him one more time. '*Jangan lupakan Cara, sayang,*' she'd whispered. *Don't forget me, darling.* Om Jono had been surprised by this display of affection. Even more so when he went to lead Tito away and the boy had cried out for Cara, his face crumpling. She'd waved and smiled and blown him kisses until he'd vanished down the aerobridge, then she'd put her head in her hands and wept.

Now Annie gave her a hug. 'Are you alright?'

Cara nodded sadly, and they began to make their way back to the car park.

'Only two Fearless crew left.' Cara tried to sound upbeat.

'So, where to now, your place or mine?' Annie smiled. 'Oh, that's right, I don't have a place.'

'You're not thinking about going back to BAF, are you?' asked Cara.

'Lord, no. It was good of Pak Tony to let us stay at Puri Damai as long as he has. Especially with family bunking in and everything. Seeing Natalie was a huge boost for me.' She sighed. 'I miss her already.'

Annie's daughter had flown into Bali within days of the siege. Cara, by contrast, had received no visitors. Her father was too frail to leave Australia, her mother had explained, and Richard had been attending an accountancy conference in Europe. When he'd finally learned of Cara's involvement in the siege, he'd telephoned her immediately. The concern in his voice was palpable, but he hadn't offered to visit. Both of these interactions had left Cara feeling desolate, and more than a little homesick.

'Would you like to stay at my place tonight?' she asked Annie. 'There's a sofa bed in my lounge room.' She wasn't craving solitude anymore, she noticed.

Annie gave her a squeeze. 'No, thanks. I think we'll just overnight it somewhere in Ubud, before we start our trip.'

'*We?*' Cara cocked her head. 'Are you and Pak Ketut . . . ?'

'Going on holiday?' Annie smiled. 'Yes.'

'That's great!' said Cara. She briefly wondered if there was anything more between the pair, but resolved not to pry. 'When do you leave?'

'Tomorrow,' said Annie. 'As Pak Tony says, there's no time like the present.'

'And that's why they call it a gift!' Cara chimed in, and they both laughed. As they continued to walk, Cara said softly, 'But he's right, of course. The siege at the sanctuary showed me that.'

'I know,' agreed Annie. 'When you've lived through something like that, you can't waste another moment, right?'

Reaching the car park, Annie hailed Pak Ketut, who sat crouched against a wall with her dog, Untung. The driver leaped to his feet and opened the hire car door for the women. 'Where to now?' he asked, then added, *'Mau ke mana?'*

'Ketut's teaching me Indonesian,' explained Annie, smiling at the driver.

'Good for you,' said Cara. 'It's a useful language to know.'

'Indeed! You saved us all in that bird park with your fluency.'

Cara shrugged.

'Don't dismiss it,' scolded Annie. 'The media say you were just as important in saving lives as Lorenzo and Remy. By talking to the guards in Indonesian, you made them trust you. The escape couldn't have happened without you.'

'We all played a role, Annie. You found the window and told me about it. It was teamwork.' Cara looked away, embarrassed. 'Could you possibly take me to Penestanan now, Pak Ketut ?' The driver nodded, obliging as ever.

They listened to the radio as they drove. Two weeks on, the media hoopla surrounding the siege continued. After listening to ten minutes of analysis and speculation, Pak Ketut switched it off. 'There is not much music anymore.' He sighed. 'Too much talking now. It does not help the dead.'

Annie pointed out the window. 'What on earth is *that?*'

337

Suspended from the eaves of a hall set back from the road was a papier-mâché giant. The creature was evidently female, with pendulous breasts, a pregnant belly and a hairy maw below. But it was its eyes—the vacant stare of death—that were most unnerving.

'That is *ogoh-ogoh*,' explained Pak Ketut, in a matter-of-fact tone. 'Soon it is Nyepi, the *saka* New Year. We put our sins into the *ogoh-ogoh* and then they are burned away, so we are purified in time for the new year.'

Annie looked disconcerted. 'They seem very . . . oppressive.'

'It's a bit of a shock at first,' agreed Cara. 'But you get used to it after a while.'

'Are they always female?' Annie whispered to Cara.

'No, they can be anything,' she replied. 'It's like the shadow side of the Balinese. Everyone's always smiling here, then once a year, they make these *ogoh-ogoh*. Maybe it's a way of relieving tension in a tight-knit community.'

For the past three years, during the eight weeks preceding Nyepi, Cara had watched the young men of Penestanan designing and building their *ogoh-ogoh*. Chatting and singing and drumming together after dark, constructing monstrous creations of clay and papier-mâché, woodwork and paint, battery-operated lights and moving parts. Their two months of labour culminated on the eve of Nyepi in March, when local priests exorcised the villagers' sins, driving them into the *ogoh-ogoh*. The monsters were then carried—much heavier now, due to the weight of the sins sealed inside—to a local field and set alight. There was a carnival atmosphere to the bonfire, with fireworks and cheering, as the villagers watched their sins being expunged.

They returned home then for Nyepi itself, a twenty-four-hour period of silence spent in quiet reflection. The evil spirits awoken the day before had to be convinced that Bali was uninhabited so they would leave the island in peace for another year. No one was permitted to use electricity, talk, have sex, or leave their home. The provincial government turned off the TV channels and closed the airport. With nothing to stir them or to chase, even the street dogs fell silent.

Pak Ketut pointed out another *ogoh-ogoh* on the roadside, a monstrous lizard man with eight arms, a deformed face and dripping fangs. 'The young men are going to a lot of effort,' he observed. 'But they may be disappointed, if the government bans the parade.'

'Why would it?' asked Cara. As far as she was aware, only once had the *ogoh-ogoh* festival been banned, when it fell during elections.

'To protect Muslims,' said Pak Ketut. 'The government is worried that people might get carried away this year because of the siege, maybe run amok in Muslim villages.' He shook his head. 'But I think cancelling the *ogoh-ogoh* parade is more dangerous than anything else.'

They spent the rest of the trip gawping at the *ogoh-ogoh* they passed: vampire mothers holding their bitten-dead babies; creepy sallow-faced children with knives protruding from their necks; zombie mutants with three heads, exposed brains and gargantuan genitals.

After an hour's drive, they pulled up outside Cara's villa. It was dark and quiet, and Cara felt suddenly reluctant to spend a night there alone. *I'll get used to it again*, she told herself.

They climbed out of the car. Cara found the spare key to her front door concealed beneath a terracotta planter and opened it, turning on all the lights. Indra had prepared nothing for her return, she saw; no small basket of fruit or flowers, no special note or other kindness. She'd tried to contact him from Puri Damai but, with her mobile phone destroyed by fire during the siege, she'd been forced to find the number for his office. She'd called numerous times, but he was never there. Cara wasn't confident that the evasive young woman who took her messages had even conveyed them to Indra.

Pak Ketut carried her bag inside.

'Thank you, Pak Ketut.' Cara shook his hand, then touched hers to her heart. 'It has been a pleasure knowing you. Take care of Annie.'

He grinned. 'I will.'

'I don't need a man to look after me,' said Annie with mock indignation. 'I've managed a long time without one. But it'll be nice to have a travelling companion.'

Pak Ketut bowed and returned to the car, leaving the two women alone.

Cara couldn't help herself from asking again. 'So, are you and Pak Ketut . . . ?'

'We have an arrangement,' said Annie, looking a little flushed. 'Now that the Fearless retreats are on hold, Pak Ketut doesn't have a job anymore. Pak Tony has given him permission to escort me around Bali. I'm paying him; it's convenient for both of us.'

'Oh.' Cara felt a little disappointed. 'I thought there might have been something more to it.'

Annie began to smile. 'Well, I'm not saying there isn't . . . Who knows? We like each other. But for now, we're just friends.'

Cara beamed, encouraged by this. 'How long will you be away?'

'I'm not sure. A few months, maybe. I'm staying deliberately *un*focused and seeing how the spirit moves us.'

Cara laughed. 'Sounds wonderful. And you're really not going back to BAF?'

Annie shook her head. 'Call it an admission of failure. Or maybe it's self-preservation. Either way, sometimes you just have to admit defeat and get out.'

Touché, Cara thought. For the past four years, Bali had been right for her. But now, since surviving a terrorist attack, it was starting to feel all wrong. She'd not stopped thinking about her family in Australia.

They walked back out to the car together, their arms inter-twined. 'I don't know where any of this is going, actually,' Annie whispered, nodding at Ketut. 'I've never felt so adrift in my life. But I've decided to follow my heart, for a change.'

Cara pulled Annie into a hug. 'Good on you,' she said. 'Make sure you take lots of photos and and tell me all about it. Actually . . .' She reconsidered. 'Just relax and enjoy yourself, Annie.'

Annie turned towards Ketut, who opened the car door for her.

'*Selamat jalan!*' Cara called out. 'Enjoy your trip.'

'*Selamat tinggal*, Ibu Cara,' Pak Ketut called back. 'Goodbye.'

It was a polite, formulaic response literally translated as *enjoy staying behind*—but for Cara, it jarred. She didn't want to stay behind anymore, she thought, waving until the car's tail lights faded into the darkness. It was starting to feel as though life itself was leaving her behind.

With a heavy sigh, she turned back to her empty villa.

Remy was surprised by how emotional he felt, walking into the arrivals lounge at Charles de Gaulle airport. Usually a composed, reserved woman, Remy's mother almost deafened him—and the watching crowd—with her weeping. His father simply stood there, tall and dignified, with silent tears coursing down his cheeks. Camille threw herself at Remy, almost knocking him over, before whispering fiercely, *I love you, little brother.* Remy found himself crying and laughing, both thrilled and perplexed by this unprecedented demonstration of familial emotion.

Yet almost as soon as he stepped into the rear of his parents' car and they began the drive back to his former life, a hollow feeling rose within his chest.

And there it remained, despite the dozens of relatives and friends who telephoned and visited him. Not to mention the unsolicited overtures from strangers—prompted by ongoing media coverage of his actions—who felt moved to contact him via social media. It was flattering, but all rather overwhelming.

Remy couldn't shake the sense that it should have been happening to someone else; a stronger, more extroverted person who could savour the attention in ways he couldn't.

A week after his return, Remy received an email from Henry:

Hi Remy,

How are you settling back into life in Paris? You're a bit of a media superstar, I see. Hope it's not too crazy.

I'm feeling a lot better—fewer headaches and not so photosensitive anymore. But my parents want me to get checked out by doctors in England before I do anything else (and they're probably right). So Jim and I are flying back tomorrow—and guess what? We're planning a birdwatching weekend in Paris! Don't worry, we won't land on your door-step, we'll just take an apartment.

Jim's dead keen to do the Eiffel Tower, though—he's booked us in already (tickets are attached). If the time and date suit you, will you meet us at the top? It'll be just like a Fear Safari!

Best,

Henry

P.S. I've got something for you from Janelle.

Remy was relieved to read of Henry's rapid recovery, but his stomach clenched at the reference to Janelle. Not to mention the idea of going up the Eiffel Tower, which had always seemed to him the stuff of nightmares. But he'd just survived a real-life nightmare, and there'd be a reward at the top—something from Janelle.

He checked the tickets, then quickly typed a reply:

Hi Henry,

Great news! So glad you're feeling better now, but it's a good idea to get a second opinion in England.

I'll meet you at the top of La Tour Eiffel at 5pm that Saturday—you have given me a reason to push through the fear!

My number is at the bottom of this email. But don't call me or I might change my mind! See you then.

Cheers,

Remy

He pressed send and, for the first time since leaving Bali, felt marginally more satisfied with life.

⌒

It was a crisp spring day in the off-peak period, and the ticket queue for the Eiffel Tower was short. By arriving at 4.30 pm exactly, the time when Jim and Henry would be starting their own ascent in the lift, Remy left himself no room for procrastination. He had just thirty minutes to get to the top, mostly on foot.

'You know this entry is for the *stairs*?' asked the woman in the ticket booth.

'Yes,' replied Remy, placing his money on the varnished wooden counter. He preferred the honest, steady work of his own legs over the mechanical moving parts of the hydraulic lift. 'How long does it take to climb?'

'Depends how fit you are,' said the woman, her eyes roving over him. 'By the looks of *you*, not too long.'

Embarrassed, Remy thanked her and hurried over to the entrance to the stairs.

The base of the tower was almost empty, except for burly-looking soliders in combat fatigues and green berets carrying Famas assault rifles. There was a dozen of them at least, and their weapons looked like bazookas compared to the thin rifles Remy had seen during the Bali siege. Suddenly, tsunami-mind sprang into combat mode: he imagined the guards opening fire, spraying the tower's steel-grey lattice with scarlet arterial spurts from his own bullet-ridden body.

Remy closed his eyes, attempting to shut down the mental showreel. The strange thing was that tsunami-mind had disappeared entirely during the siege, when the danger was real. But now that he was back on French soil, and there was no obvious threat to his personal safety, the mental scourge had returned. *I can choose to ignore it*, he told himself.

He started climbing the first flight of stairs, striding up them purposefully, counting the steps in his head. His breathing soon quickened, with both the exertion and the sense of increasing distance between himself and the ground. Mercifully, the treads and risers beneath his feet were solid metal, with no gaps he could see through. But the grilles on either side allowed for a view of the tower's surrounds. Remy tried to focus on the stairs and the reassuring rhythm of his breath. But finally, unable to ignore the glint of gold-topped roofs in his peripheral vision, he stopped on a landing and looked out.

The city's iconic structures lay spread out before him—Palais Garnier, Notre-Dame, the Arc de Triomphe—amid the orderly grandeur of Haussmann's boulevards. But to linger too long gazing out was to invite fear into his heart; he pushed on, soon arriving on the first floor. Tourists milled around an exhibition explaining the tower's engineering. Remy removed his anorak but didn't stop. It was 4.55 pm; Henry and Jim were probably already at the top.

He began the trek to the second floor, swinging his arms and increasing his pace. The higher he climbed, the more conscious he became of the tower's inevitable tapering. He could see out the other side of the structure more easily now, and he noticed his body mounting its predictable response; his stomach tightened and he began to gasp for air. He paused for a moment, closing his eyes and deliberately taking longer, deeper breaths. Repeating to himself Pak Tony's advice: *Fear is just excitement without breath.*

He set off again, synchronising his breathing with every step. Deploying another of the Fearless strategies, he focused on the rhythmic alternation from right to left foot, and the rolling sensation from heel to toe. He refused to look beyond the side grilles now, studying instead the metallic nodules embedded in the treads. Just as his calves began to object to the hike, he arrived on the second floor.

It was 5.10 pm and he had climbed as high as any visitor was allowed to reach on foot. Now came the toughest part of the challenge: to reach the very top of the tower, he had to take a glass lift. Avoiding the souvenir shops and cafés thrumming with visitors, he bought a ticket and took his place in the queue for the elevator.

A group of excitable tourists had already gathered outside it. When the doors opened, an attendant ushered the group forward, then motioned to Remy to follow. He obeyed grudgingly, feeling mildly claustrophobic as he pressed himself into a corner of the lift. The doors closed with a hiss and the elevator began moving skyward on a slight diagonal trajectory. The tourists talked eagerly and Remy squeezed his eyes shut, clinging onto a guide rail.

Tsunami-mind delivered its brain-bomb: Remy imagined the elevator's steel cables snapping, the tourists' terrified screams as the glass cube plummeted towards the earth, and the fiery explosion on impact. A surge of nervous perspiration soaked through his shirt. To distract himself, he tried to focus on the Edith Piaf tune being piped through the elevator's speakers, 'Non, Je Ne Regrette Rien'.

A moment later, the elevator came to a stop, and the doors opened onto the top floor. Remy found himself being bustled out by the tourists, some of whom rushed forward immediately and began squealing at the view. He lingered on the landing, staying close to the tower's central pillar. It was much, much higher than even he had imagined.

He began to work his way around the pillar, scanning the faces of passing tourists for those of his friends. Despite the sturdy floor-to-ceiling enclosure, he was loath to approach the edge. But knowing Henry, the Englishman would be standing on the outermost point with his binoculars poised.

Trying to ignore the weak feeling in his knees, Remy noticed a small window set into the tower's central column. Inside were lifelike wax models of Gustave Eiffel and Thomas Edison sitting beside a gramophone. As he paused to read the plaque beneath the window, he fancied he felt a slight vibration pass through the tower. He closed his eyes, fighting off a swamping wave of vertigo.

Paralysed, Remy felt his heart thumping crazily at his chest wall. Where were Henry and Jim? Could they not come and find *him*? He kept his eyes clamped shut, conjuring his go-to relaxation vision of Bordeaux vineyards in the summer. Slowly, he began to count backwards from ten to one, just as Pak Tony had taught him. When he began to feel better, he opened his eyes once more and turned around.

And there she was, standing not a metre in front of him, in a pink coat with a fur-trimmed hood.

'Janelle?' He gaped at her, wondering if this was another product of tsunami-mind. A final, fantastical vision before he fainted on the floor.

The vision stepped forward. 'Henry gave me your note on the day you left Bali,' she said, smiling hopefully at him. 'So here I am.'

Astonished, Remy looked down at the piece of paper in her hand. Glimpsing the words *Dear Janelle* and *Love, Remy* in handwriting other than his own, he stared, confused.

'I wasn't very receptive, after the siege,' Janelle continued, her cheeks flushing. 'But I wanted to show you that I'm open to . . .'

Unable to speak, Remy took the note, his eyes darting over the words, the unfamiliar handwriting. All at once, he understood what Henry had done. It was a blatant, audacious attempt to engineer a happy ending. And—even more astoundingly—Janelle had actually come all the way to Paris, despite her fear of flying.

'You flew . . .' he said weakly.

'Twenty-two hours from Melbourne.' She beamed at him. 'And I didn't even have to drink vodka. I used Pak Tony's magic bottle of love, instead.'

He passed the note back to Janelle and closed his eyes, trying to think.

'What's . . . wrong?' she asked.

Should he reveal that the romantic invitation—to meet in Paris, at the top of the Eiffel Tower—was actually penned by Henry, and that they had both been taken in by the Englishman's plot? Should he tell her that the real note had contained a glum apology and a goodbye?

'I can't believe you're in Paris,' he said at last, keeping his eyes clamped shut. 'Right up here. With me.'

'Oh, yes.' He felt her arms slip around him, her head resting against his chest. He became conscious of her scent, a fragrance burned in his memory from when they'd sat together on the minivan after their parasailing adventure. 'I'm so proud of you, Remy,' she said. 'When we first met, you said you could never do this. And look, here you are.'

He opened his eyes and gazed down at her. In that moment, all the failures of the past receded. The future was what mattered now.

'Remy, there's something I want to say to you.'

She took his hands and tears started into her eyes.

'Wait,' he said. 'There's something I need to say to you first.'

Slowly, he bent down on one knee.

A tourist squealed nearby, but was quickly hushed by her friends.

'Janelle, will you *not* marry me?'

Her eyes widened.

'Not *yet*, I mean,' said Remy. 'Stay here with me in Paris. Get to know me better. We can buy croissants and *café au lait* in the mornings. On the weekends I will take you hiking. We can explore some of Europe. We can just . . . hang out together?'

She nodded, still looking a little uncertain.

'You were right to reject me in Bali,' he continued. 'It was too soon, too rushed, too intense. We'd just been through the most life-changing experience. But . . . I still believe we belong together, despite our differences. Like the sun and the moon, remember?'

She smiled in recognition of their light-hearted exchange on the first day of the Fearless program.

'I believe it, too,' she said, gazing down at him. 'And . . . I love you, Remy.'

He felt as if he could leap off the tower and fly.

Standing up again, he smiled at her and pushed back the hood of her jacket. He brushed her hair away from her cheeks. 'What do you say, Janelle? Do you agree not to marry me—yet?'

'I do,' she breathed.

As their lips touched, Remy felt a vortex of vertigo seizing him.

Only this time, it was pure joy.

Cara had been home for five nights and now it was Nyepi Eve. The *ogoh-ogoh* parade had not been banned, much to the villagers' delight, but she was averse to venturing out. The gruesome creatures lining the roads were unsettling, with their bulbous eyes and bloody mouths and silent screams. Cara couldn't look at them without recalling the siege: the contorted faces and misshapen bodies of the dead, a world out of control.

She sat alone on her balcony instead, watching the villagers gather at sunset and the arrival of the white-clad holy men to pray over the *ogoh-ogoh*. It was a beguiling idea, Cara mused, this magic formula of contrition and combustion. That all human error might be remedied on one cathartic night, with a communal exorcism and purification by fire. But she knew that the ritual only applied to people whose transgressions were inconsequential. Her own failure had been too grievous, the result too horrific, to be absorbed by any *ogoh-ogoh*, no matter how large or repulsive.

The warbling of an ancient Sanskrit hymn rose from the road below, marking the commencement of the ceremony. It was a haunting sound, a recitation sung across continents and centuries. Cara could hear the villagers, too, murmuring their ritual greetings: *For my wrongdoings against you, intentional or unintentional, please forgive me.*

A million failings the world over, Cara reflected, humanity awash in a sea of suffering, trying to make sense of it through rituals and faith. Or, in the world from which she'd fled four years ago, by suppressing it with *more*—more food, more money, more *things*—so that failure and suffering were barely discernible beneath the shiny surface of consumerism and excess.

She watched the villagers shaking hands in the shadows, tacitly acknowledging and accepting each other's fallibility and the imperfection of the world around them. Perhaps theirs was a wiser culture than her own, Cara thought. In the face of human suffering, it was futile—conceited, even—to continue to demand answers. *Why me? Why now? Why my baby?* Or even: *Why you? Why did you do that to me?* Perhaps, like the Balinese, one could only merely accept that this suffering was so, and attempt to forgive oneself and others for contributing to it.

Cara turned her face to the night sky, towards the diamond pinpricks glinting in the inky darkness. Echoing the villagers, she murmured, 'For my wrongdoings, Astrid, intentional and unintentional, please forgive me.'

As the Sanskrit incantation grew louder, Cara's quiet weeping joined with the ceremonial crescendo until finally, it petered out into silence.

At the priest's bidding, groups of young boys moved forward to hoist the *ogoh-ogoh* onto bamboo racks. Drummers gathered alongside them, shouting encouragement, as the boys heaved their burdens onto their shoulders. Cara found herself holding her breath. Was it safe for children to do this? Would they hurt themselves, by dropping an *ogoh-ogoh* or going too close to the flames? The maternal instinct remained, she knew, even when the child was gone.

She watched the boys move down the road with their *ogoh-ogoh*. When she could no longer see them from her seat, she wrapped her hands around a bamboo pillar and pulled herself up onto the balustrade. Her feet wobbled as she balanced precariously on the balcony rail two storeys above the ground, watching the boys' progress all the way to the bonfire.

At the end of the road, she could see lanterns burning. Reaching their destination, the boys began moving their *ogoh-ogoh* into position on the oval. A firefly flew into Cara's line of vision, and for a whimsical moment she fancied it drew Astrid's name against the sky. She craned her neck to watch it, when suddenly a loud cracking noise made her jump with fright. Her left foot slipped off the balustrade and dangled, for a split second, in nothingness. It was a moment of suspension, an invitation to erasure.

She gasped and scrambled back up onto the rail, clinging to the post. Frightened by the part of herself that was tempted to let go and, in one swift second, eradicate four years of pain. It would be harder to stay and live life without her daughter, she knew. But for the first time ever, she wanted to try.

As fireworks whizzed aloft and erupted with further loud cracks, she climbed carefully down onto the balcony, her legs shaking. In the distance, the first *ogoh-ogoh* exploded. A cacophony of whistles, plastic trumpets and beating drums sent the evil spirits skyward with the bonfire's sparks. A cheer rose from the crowd of villagers, celebrating the victory of forgiveness over fear.

Cara's eyes followed the sparks heavenward, as they rose like luminous souls fleeing the earth.

———

On the day she finished packing the final box for freight, a month after Nyepi, there was a subdued tap at her front door. It was Indra, with his blinding smile.

'Oh!' she exclaimed, hugging him. 'Where have you been?'

He held her tightly, without speaking, before pulling away. 'I'm so sorry, Cara. I didn't realise where you were until I saw it on the news. I went straight to the hospital, but they would not let me in. Next of kin only, they said.' He shook his head with frustration. 'The day after that, the . . . unrest started and I had to get out before seeing you. I tried again and again to call your phone—'

'It was destroyed in the siege,' she said.

He groaned. 'You have been through much. Are you alright?'

'I am now.' She exhaled. 'Come in, Indra.'

He followed her inside.

'But where did you go?' she asked, leading him through to the lounge. 'I've been worried about you.'

'Java. People like me are not wanted here,' said Indra, lowering his voice. 'I left ten days before Nyepi. People were getting hurt in Muslim villages. Maybe I shouldn't have come back.'

'I know.' Cara grimaced. 'It's awful.'

The siege had pushed even the Balinese beyond their limits of interfaith tolerance. Anti-Muslim sentiment had been exacerbated by the dwindling number of international visitors to the island. Most incoming tourists had cancelled their travel plans, and many expatriate residents had fled to their home countries. The Balinese economy, so dependent on foreign income, was now in the grip of a steady downturn.

'Would you . . . like some *teh jahe*?' Cara asked feebly. Indra shook his head.

'I'm having some anyway,' she persisted, moving to the kitchen and switching on the kettle.

'*Terima kasih.*'

'Does that mean yes or no?' She smiled at him. 'I always get confused with that kind of thank you.'

'Yes, please,' he said, smiling back.

She pottered around, setting out cups and saucers and steeping slices of fresh ginger in hot water. Spooning six teaspoons of sugar into Indra's mug, just the way he liked it. When the tea was ready, she returned to the lounge.

'I came back to tell you, I have a new job.' Indra sipped from his mug, watching Cara over its rim. 'At a five-star hotel in Yogyakarta. The money is good, and I get a room in the staff quarters. I will be away for a year. Unless you . . .' he paused, picking at the long thumbnail he used for plucking his guitar, 'would like to come with me?' He smiled. 'We could drink ginger tea—we call it *ronde*—in the town square at full moon. It is very romantic.' He looked at her shyly.

In that moment, Cara could imagine a life with him. Of lazy weekend mornings browsing in markets and drinking strong Javanese coffee, and sipping *ronde* in the moonlight. Of endless *jalan-jalan* circuits on the back of his motorbike in Yogyakarta. Of afternoons in bed during the wet season, waiting out the tropical downpours, and cool morning swims in the dry season. But she knew it couldn't happen now.

'I'm sorry, but I have to go away too,' she said.

Indra's face fell. Then, almost instantaneously, he smiled. Cara had never really understood this quirk of Indonesian culture, the sudden smile to conceal pain, fear or sadness.

'So you hate Muslims too, now?' he asked. 'You think extremists are here in Penestanan?'

Cara frowned, disoriented by Indra's uncharacteristically sarcastic tone. She'd seen the sign in the village—*Tolaklah adanya fundamentalisme Islam di Penestanan*—exhorting locals to defend their neighbourhood against Islamic extremists. But she was no more fearful of extremism than she had been before the siege. A terrorist attack was like any other low-likelihood, high-consequence event—akin to a shark attack, or a lightning strike. It rarely happened, but when it did, it was devastating.

'Of course not,' she said softly. 'Many of the victims at the animal sanctuary were Muslims, Indra. We both know that. I just have to go back to Australia and deal with my past.'

Indra considered her. 'But you are separated from your husband.'

'Yes.' Cara sighed, remembering the email, still in her drafts folder, asking for a divorce. 'It's not finalised. We still have contact on financial matters.'

Indra's eyes narrowed. 'Are you going to finalise it?'

Cara reached out and took his hand. 'You're my best friend in Bali, Indra. Maybe more than that. But I have to go back and see my husband and my family.'

He let go of her hand and stared into his mug of tea. The expression on his face pained her and she felt she owed him more. 'I . . . also had a daughter, back in Australia,' she explained. 'Four years ago she died in an accident. I have to go back to where it happened.'

Indra looked up at her, astonished, and then his eyes flashed with hurt. 'You never told me.'

'I didn't know how to, Indra,' she said. 'For years I was numb. It's only now, after everything that's happened, that I've actually started feeling things properly again. I think the siege jolted me out of limbo and . . . I've realised I have to go back.'

The idea had been percolating ever since Nyepi. After that night, she'd detected a subtle shift within herself. Nothing as radical as forgiveness, but a slight distancing from the abhorrence with which she'd regarded herself for so long. A newfound recognition, perhaps, that hers was just a single episode in a vast continuum of human suffering.

'So now that you are feeling things again, you think this is a good time to go away?' Indra still looked wounded. 'Maybe you have never shown me who you really are, Cara.'

'Maybe,' she conceded. 'Maybe I didn't even know it myself. I'm sorry, Indra.'

He stood up and tossed a small bundle of postal items onto the lounge. 'Your mail.'

'Thank you,' she said quietly.

He did not look at her directly. 'When are you going back to Australia?'

'Early June, at the end of the lease.' It was still six weeks away. 'I'm sending off some things by sea freight tomorrow.'

He walked to the door. 'I'll be in Java by June. You have my email, if you need anything.'

'Indra . . .' she began. The wooden door clapped shut behind him. She hadn't even given him her new mobile number.

Cara stared at the slight indentation on the cushion where Indra had sat. The thought that she had lost him, after four years of friendship, alarmed her. She harboured no illusions that returning to Australia would be easy. Indeed, it was entirely possible that when exposed once more to the life that she had left behind, she might turn around and fly straight back to Bali. Then where would she be, without Indra?

She sighed again, and reached for the bundle of mail Indra had delivered. Shuffling through the envelopes, she noticed that the front page of today's *Bali Post* carried yet another siege-related headline—*Staffer accuses Paradise boss.* Cara scanned the article:

An unnamed staff member of Paradise Animal Sanctuary has told police officers that two months before the terrorist attack, an argument broke out between workers and their boss, Diego Schneider.

'The three brothers were not happy with their wage, with no increase for three years,' the source told police. 'They asked for more, but Mister Diego said no. He told them they could only have two days holiday for Ramadan because of tourist high season. The workers were already angry. This made it worse.'

Schneider, a Portuguese property developer with multiple business interests in Bali, co-owns 49 per cent of Paradise Animal Sanctuary with his wife, Dewi Ayusari.

Neither of the owners were available for comment.

Cara tossed the newspaper aside. Even if he was a terrible boss, it didn't justify what happened. A global network of Islamic extremists had already claimed responsibility for the attack, so why were local media fuelling such hearsay? It could only bolster conspiracy theorists. Today, it was the animal sanctuary boss; who would be accused tomorrow?

A hand-addressed silver envelope caught Cara's eye, postmarked Paris. She turned it over and saw the names *Remy and Janelle* embossed on the back. Letting out a little squeal of delight, she tore it open to find an invitation to the commitment ceremony of Janelle Porter and Remy de Brive, to take place in Seminyak, Bali, on 13 June.

Thrilled, Cara seized her mobile phone and messaged Janelle: *I received the invitation—what wonderful news! So happy for you both. In Bali! Where are you now?*

Within seconds, Janelle responded: *Paris . . . I went straight back to Oz after the siege to see my family. Bella was doing better, so after about a week I decided to take a risk . . . like Annie told me at our crazy vagina spa. Remember that?!?*

Cara laughed out loud and typed: *How can I forget?*

A moment later Janelle replied: *We can get the band back together at the wedding! I have never been happier in my life.* ☺

Cara smiled, remembering how she'd watched Janelle and Remy flirting in the early days of the retreat. How their attraction had almost been derailed by the Frenchman's YouTube mistake, and then overshadowed by the siege. Remy and Janelle might well have been Romeo and Juliet, with a modern twist of terrorism overlaying a classic tragedy.

And yet love had prevailed, she thought, as the tears in her eyes blurred the writing on the invitation. In a world tarnished by violence and fear, perhaps fairytale endings were still possible.

⁓

A few weeks later, Cara received an email from Pak Tony.

> Hello dear friends,
> It won't be long until we're celebrating Remy and Janelle's union. What a blessing! It's also a chance for all of us to get together and reflect again on what we went through in March. I am sure we all have much to share.
> So, I'd like to invite you all to breakfast together at Balangan Resort on the day before the ceremony. Lavinia, Lorenzo's wife, will be in Bali—I thought it would be appropriate for her to come too. I'll also invite Pak Ketut, who is part of our Fearless family.
> Please let me know if you can make it.
> Love and light,
> Tony

Lavinia. Cara suddenly remembered the letter that Lorenzo had entrusted to her at the animal sanctuary. In the immediate aftermath of the siege, she'd been too preoccupied with Tito, and with helping Henry and Janelle at the hospital, to consider what to do with it. She'd glimpsed Lavinia at the hospital too—surrounded by consular officials assisting with the repatriation of Lorenzo's body—but before she knew it, she'd flown back to Italy.

Cara had kept tabs on Lavinia from afar, primarily through a Facebook page that she'd set up in Lorenzo's honour. Week after week, Lavinia appeared on every Italian talk show and current affairs program, in magazines and newspapers, extolling her dead husband's heroism and sacrifice. She was glamorous even in grief.

With no clear instructions from Lorenzo, and recalling his ambivalence about its contents, Cara vacillated about what to do with the letter. Destroy it, or send it to Lavinia? Or simply relay her last conversation with Lorenzo, and let his widow decide?

Concluding that this was the right course of action, Cara had messaged Lavinia a month after the siege. *I'd like to discuss something with you,* she wrote, but Lavinia didn't respond. So she'd slipped the note into the top drawer of her bedside table for safekeeping, where it had lain undisturbed since, beneath a growing pile of newspaper clippings.

But the wedding would be her opportunity to give Lavinia the note, she realised. Cara went to her bedside table now, just to be sure, and found the crumpled, stained sheet of paper buried at the bottom. She unfolded it and gazed at Lorenzo's elegant, symmetrical handwriting. It mirrored his personality: stylish, yet controlled. She pictured the distressing task of hand-delivering this posthumous letter to Lavinia and began to have second thoughts.

Who was Lorenzo, really? She wondered. From the way his widow described him, a saint. And yet, Cara had seen the hurt in his eyes when she'd sat with Lorenzo, shivering and vulnerable, after he'd pulled her out of the holy pool. She'd witnessed the darkness that had settled on him in the Python Pit, and sensed an unspeakable private pain as he'd sat alongside her in the Birdsong Café, fingering a letter he didn't care to keep. The very same note in her hands now.

She didn't read Italian, but as her eyes ran over the neat sentences, they were drawn to a recognisable term: *paedophilia*. She stared at the lines of unfamiliar words around it. Had Lorenzo been a victim of abuse himself? Was that the reason behind his fear of fatherhood?

Taking the note to her computer now, Cara opened Google Translate and typed the entire letter into the Italian–English function. She hesitated, her cursor hovering above the words 'Translate Now'.

She pressed the button.

⁓

On a tranquil morning in June, the Fearless group gathered on a rugged escarpment overlooking Balangan Beach. In the absence of Indra's expert escort—and preoccupied by the note she carried in her handbag—Cara got lost en route and arrived twenty minutes late. She felt self-conscious as she jogged towards the group, seated on a large *poleng* picnic rug near the edge of a cliff. A secluded arc of creamy sand stretched behind them, marked with patches of faint green and rusted brown near the shore. At the beach's edge, flanked by sloping rock cliffs, palm trees swayed over a cluster of unoccupied beach recliners. Out in the ocean, surfers teabagged near the left-hand break, their small dark forms barely observable against the sparkling expanse that stretched to the horizon.

Cara could identify almost all of the group, even at a distance. Remy and Janelle reclined on a navy-blue double beanbag. Annie and Ketut sat side by side too, their posture relaxed and intimate. Henry lay on his back, gazing up at the sky, while Pak Tony knelt beside a stunning-looking woman. It was only when she got nearer that Cara recognised the woman as Lavinia. She'd put on a considerable amount of weight—perhaps due to the stress of Lorenzo's death? Cara herself had lost weight after Astrid's death, but everyone responded to tragedy differently.

Laid out on the picnic rug were platters of pastries, ice buckets filled with champagne, pitchers of orange juice, plungers of coffee, and fragrant baskets of frangipanis. A waiter in traditional dress stood back from the group, observing them, poised to act on their every request. He smiled at Cara and called out, '*Selamat pagi, miss!*' as she jogged past him.

I'm hardly a miss anymore, she thought, returning his greeting.

By the time she reached the group, Cara was breathless. 'I'm so sorry I'm late.'

'It so doesn't matter,' said Janelle, the first to leap up. They embraced, and then Remy joined in, lifting Cara off the ground in a giant bear hug.

'Congratulations!' She smiled at them both. 'I can't think of a nicer couple.'

'Isn't it brilliant?' said Henry, standing up to kiss Cara. 'I like to think we can all take some credit.' He looked Cara up and down. 'There's something different about you . . .'

'Oh?' Cara wasn't sure what he could mean. She motioned to his head. 'Is everything alright now?'

'Fighting fit,' he replied. 'Jim and I are heading off on a bird-watching bonanza straight after the wedding.'

'Still chasing the Bali starling, then?'

Henry laughed. 'There's nothing like unfinished business.'

Cara thought instantly of Richard in Sydney. A week after her awkward meeting with Indra, she'd sent an exploratory email to Richard. Tentative, conversational, committing to nothing. And to her surprise, he'd responded warmly. After a further month of lightweight exchanges, Richard had ended an email with *P.S. I don't suppose you'll be in Sydney anytime soon?* and she'd almost wept with relief. After years of sadness and sporadic contact, there was still a connection between them.

In three weeks, she'd replied. *Let's catch up.*

'And here's my other favourite Aussie gal!' Annie called, elbowing her way in to hug Cara. 'I've missed you, hon.'

Cara snorted. 'I bet you've been too busy sightseeing with Pak Ketut to give any of us another thought.'

The driver stood behind Annie, waiting to greet her. 'Ibu Cara,' he said, touching his hand to his heart. 'It is good to see you.'

'You too, Pak Ketut,' she said. 'Haven't you had enough of driving Annie around Bali yet?'

'*Belum*,' he replied. 'She is very good company.'

'Pak Ketut!' Henry called suddenly and the driver turned. 'What bird is that?'

The Englishman pointed at a flash of colour in a nearby hedge and the driver squinted.

'Excuse me, Ibu Cara,' he said with faux seriousness. 'I have important *burung* business.'

'Of course.' She laughed, then turned back to Annie. 'How was your trip?'

'Wonderful,' said Annie, smiling coyly. 'It's not over yet, either. We've volunteered at schools along the way, teaching English here and there. We've still got the whole of the northwest to go.' She leaned towards Cara and whispered, 'But coming back to the south for a wedding like this, it makes me want to get married again.'

After looking to make sure the driver wasn't listening, Cara nudged Annie. 'So, you're in lo—?'

'I'm not sure what you'd call it,' Annie interrupted her. 'I'm still paying him as my driver. Putting labels on relationships doesn't serve anyone. We're very good companions, and it feels wonderful.'

Cara smiled too, even though she wasn't entirely sure what to make of it. 'I'm happy for you, Annie,' she said sincerely.

'Thank you. And if I can find a connection like this at my age,' Annie added, 'then you can too.'

Cara raised a sceptical eyebrow. But today was not a day for cynicism, she reminded herself, gazing out at the glittering blue.

'Isn't this just the perfect place to get married?' said Janelle, joining Cara and Annie. She turned and planted a kiss on Remy's cheek. 'It was *his* idea, of course.'

'Of course.' The Frenchman gazed adoringly at Janelle. 'It had to be high, for you. Close to the angels. Remember the intimacy workshop?'

Henry rejoined them. 'Oh gawd, Remy, do I ever. You said that Janelle's shoulder massage was "like being touched by an angel", and I almost puked on poor Cara here.'

The group laughed.

'I'm glad you didn't,' said Pak Tony, stepping forward to embrace Cara. 'Hello, at last. Henry's right—you do look different. Your face is . . . lighter. Softer, somehow.' He led her towards the Italian woman, who stood up as they approached. 'This is Lavinia, Lorenzo's wife.'

'Hello,' said Cara. She was even more gorgeous up close: the mane of luxuriant hair, the voluptuous curves, the flowing cream-coloured dress that highlighted a flawless tan. Compared to Cara, Lavinia looked positively Amazonian.

The Italian smiled tentatively at her. 'When Pak Tony told me the group was meeting up again, I wanted to join you, because . . . After what happened, I had to get Lorenzo back to Italy quickly, for the funeral.'

'I understand,' said Cara. 'It's good to meet you now.'

'You sent me an email months ago,' said Lavinia. 'I am so sorry I didn't reply. You wanted to discuss something?'

'Oh, yes.' Cara's grip tightened on her bag. 'Actually, Lavinia—'

'Excuse me, everyone.' Pak Tony tapped a champagne glass with a teaspoon. The babble of conversation fell away and they all turned towards him. 'Now that we're all here, let's toast the bride and groom. We'll be doing that a lot over the coming weekend, but this is a very special Fearless moment. Something beautiful has emerged from something terrible.' He raised his glass. 'To Remy and Janelle!'

The group cheered. 'To Remy and Janelle!'

As she sipped her champagne, Cara saw Pak Tony drain his glass. *Hadn't he been a teetotaller before?* she thought, surprised.

'Please sit down, all of you,' he said. 'Let's form a circle of trust, just like we used to.'

They took their places on the picnic rug, and Lavinia sat next to Cara.

'What a serendipitous opportunity this is for us to reflect on what we've been through.' Pak Tony proffered his glass to the waiter, angling for a top-up. 'Some things have changed radically for me since the siege. I'm drinking now, as you can see!' He laughed rather awkwardly, and no one else joined in. Cara and Annie exchanged a glance.

'It's also a great pleasure to have Lavinia Ricci with us this morning,' Pak Tony continued. 'Now . . .' His blue eyes scanned around the group. 'Who would like to start by sharing their reflections?'

No one spoke. *Does Pak Tony expect us to come up with pithy platitudes about surviving a terrorist attack?* Cara wondered.

After a moment, Pak Tony said, 'Then I will share my reflections first. Perhaps that is best, after all.' He looked from one to another, his expression unusually meek. 'You see, I learned something very important at Paradise Animal Sanctuary. I learned how judgemental and unsympathetic I've been with the very people I've claimed to be helping on my Fearless retreats.'

Cara stared at the facilitator in surprise. Had she heard him correctly? In the time she'd known him, Pak Tony had never once confessed to human fallibility. His had always been a rousing refrain of continuous improvement.

'The ugly truth is, before the siege, I considered myself superior to my students. I had my diet, my yoga and meditation practice, my thriving business and my happy personal life. I had made it, I thought. I had fearlessly claimed my divine birthright of success, and I was guiding others towards theirs.' Pak Tony shook his head. 'In reality, I was egocentric. What I called discipline was actually the worst kind of inflexibility. But almost nothing in the course of my ordinary life would have shown me my flaws. Like so many teachers, my pride made me unteachable. It took terrorism to show me.'

He stared out at the sea. 'After the bomb went off, I found myself in the grip of terror. Suddenly I was a child again—being bullied by Rotterdam tough guys and hiding under the bushes. Only the stakes were much higher, and this time I couldn't run. When Henry discovered me, he thought I was wounded. But actually, I was paralysed by fear.'

Pak Tony turned towards the Englishman. 'Henry had to carry me out, at great personal cost to himself. I have said it to you in private, but I'd like to say it again, before everyone—thank you, Henry. When you started the retreat, public speaking made you faint.' He smiled wryly. 'But when faced with a much bigger threat, you showed true valour. I needed you more than you needed me. This was a lesson I had to learn.'

He looked at Annie. 'Do you remember, Annie, asking me what *my* odyssey would be on Fearless?'

She nodded.

'Well, that was it, right there. I had to recognise my own imperfection.' Pak Tony raised his glass. 'So I would like to propose another toast, to the man who helped me to see this. To Henry!'

'To Henry!' the group cheered.

Henry's cheeks had flushed a deep red. 'Those are kind words, Pak Tony, but . . . I just did what felt right.' He looked rather overcome. 'And maybe it wasn't right *enough*. I mean, I helped Pak Tony over the wall. But I . . .' His eyes glistened. 'I often think, I failed to do more. I didn't even consider going back into the park and trying to save anyone else . . .' He swiped at his tears, rather fiercely.

'You saw a woman shot,' said Pak Tony softly. '*Anyone* would have run. I ran, when you were still in hospital. I hid at Puri

Damai and didn't come out until the siege was over. I'm not proud of that.'

'I ran too,' said Remy, his face sombre. 'And fifteen people died because of it. This is what I tell anyone who calls me a "hero". Maybe the people who stayed in the café were actually the most heroic? I don't know. We never will. Just ask the families of the people who died in there.' He glanced at Janelle. 'It still keeps me awake at night, despite all the joy in my life. It could occupy me forever, if I let it.' He fell silent for a moment. 'We all did what we were capable of at the time. Some of us surprised ourselves, some of us didn't. Some did truly superhuman things, like Lorenzo. And like you, Henry.'

The Englishman gave a wobbly smile. 'I was an accidental participant in Fearless, remember? I only ended up at Puri Damai after my taxi driver got lost chasing the wrong type of bird.'

The group laughed again, but it was rather sniffly.

'But one thing I've learned from my time in Bali is that there *are* no accidents.' Henry took a long sip of mineral water to compose himself. 'I've been an atheist for as long as I can remember. Not a campaigning anti-Christian or anything like that, just a non-believer. Then, arriving in Bali, suddenly faith was everywhere. All those offerings on corners, stairs and bridges. Every single Balinese person believes in God, right? Their version of it.'

He closed his eyes for a moment, as if focusing on a memory. 'When the explosion happened, I thought I was going to die. And I just . . . started saying these prayers I hadn't thought about in years.' He opened his eyes. 'Then, one of the terrorists walked right up to me and pointed a gun in my face and . . .' He faltered. 'He *spared* me. Just because I showed him some common human courtesy, maybe. After that, I didn't get shot on the wall. And then I survived the fall. All these things could have killed me. But, by grace, they didn't.

'I know what you're probably all thinking,' Henry continued. 'I've had some sort of near-death experience, right?' His cheeks flushed a deeper red. 'All I know is, I called on God that day and I survived. I'm not exactly sure what God really *is*, but I know I don't believe in some sort of divine headmaster who's keeping score above the clouds. *That* God told the terrorists to blow up Paradise Animal Sanctuary, apparently.'

Henry exhaled. 'Whatever shape my faith takes, I know it's not going to be extreme. And while I'm working it out, I've decided to follow my passion.' He smiled. 'Life's so short. There are ten thousand species of bird on this planet, and I'm going to try to break a world record by spotting seven thousand of them in one year. Jim's coming with me. We're starting right here in Indonesia, next week. We're calling ourselves The Big Bird Nerds, and the birdwatching community seems to like it. We've even got a few sponsors lined up for our trip.'

'Seven *thousand* birds?' Remy's eyes goggled. 'That's . . .'

'Crazy, I know.' Henry laughed. 'But actually, the goal's not as important as the fact that Jim and I are doing it together. Jim is one of the most important people in my life—Fearless taught me that. Maybe Littlefish wasn't the complete nutter I thought he was. Here I am now, planning a boys' own adventure with my best mate. If that's not embracing masculinity, I don't know what is.' He smiled. 'And Littlefish said I'd grasp femininity better afterwards, which is something to look forward to.' He winked.

'Ah, but you should be hunting birds,' Remy called out gleefully. 'Because that is what real men do.'

'I'll be shooting them with my camera,' replied Henry wryly, 'and blogging about the trip, because actually, I love writing. I've always kept a diary, and I'm a much better writer than I am a speaker. Maybe I don't have to face my fear of public speaking at all; maybe I'll accept failure and start playing to my strengths instead. Maybe being awkward, nerdy Henry is actually okay, because masculinity comes in all shapes and sizes.'

He stopped short, looking rather embarrassed. 'Gosh, that was a ramble and a half, wasn't it?'

Pak Tony laughed. 'Especially for someone who hates speaking in public!'

The Englishman smiled. 'It's that bottle of love of yours, Pak Tony. I even used it at a twitcher conference a few months back.'

'How did your speech go?' asked Annie.

'They loved it,' replied Henry.

Pak Tony looked rather emotional.

'Well, I'm accepting failure too,' declared Annie.

Pak Tony composed himself. 'How so, Annie?'

'After the siege, I realised I've spent decades being totally task-focused,' she explained. 'It's been part of my life motto: focus and faith. Truth is, I've hidden behind a rigid set of goals, always trying to make a difference "out there" in my church, my community, with my teaching, and then in Bali, with BAF. But all that activity distracted me from the real issues, in *here*.' She tapped her chest. 'I tried to make myself indispensable, because I'd seen how easily Kevin had been replaced on the farm. It was a rude shock, watching how quickly the world just moves on after death. So you were right, Pak Tony, at the beginning of Fearless.' She nodded at the facilitator. 'All these years, I've been afraid of dying. I made myself ridiculously busy, trying to leave an indelible mark on the world.

'The siege short-circuited that, for the first time in my life. Firstly, I realised I'd failed at BAF. I'm a sixty-one-year-old privileged white American: is it my place to try to overturn hundreds of years of culture and practice? The Balinese didn't invite me to their island. And as Ketut pointed out, although I don't think he meant to,' she smiled at the driver, 'why was I so concerned about Balinese dogs when there's so much pain and suffering among the people here? Talk about an oversight.'

She shook her head. 'So, I decided to embrace my failings and try being *unfocused* for a change. I took the first proper holiday I've had in forty years, travelling around Bali and—' she winked at Pak Tony—'asking questions. You taught me the power of questions, Tony. And when I actually listened to the answers, I started to educate myself. Now I can speak to the Balinese in Indonesian.' She turned to Pak Ketut. '*Saya sudah lebih lancar, ya?*'

Pak Ketut grinned at her proudly. 'Yes, you are more fluent now.'

'As for faith, well . . .' Annie smiled. 'I'm learning to be more flexible. My core beliefs haven't wavered, but I'm much more accommodating of others. I used to think moderation was spineless, but now I realise it's even harder to pull off than extremism. I'm blessed to have a friend like Ketut to come with me on this journey.' She reached out and squeezed Pak Ketut's hand. 'And when we've seen Bali, we're going to Europe. I've got some unfinished business in Paris, an old dream I'm resurrecting.' She smiled at Remy and Janelle. 'You might have some international guests next year.'

'We'd love that,' said Janelle.

Henry wolf-whistled. 'Wedding bells in Paris for Annie and Ketut?'

Annie shook her head. 'I doubt it. We're just living in the moment, not over-engineering life.'

'That's wonderful news.' Pak Tony smiled. 'And I'm so proud of you, Annie, if I may say so.' He looked around the group. 'Who else would like to share?'

Cara took a deep breath and raised her hand. She had always been reluctant to divulge her feelings during the retreat, but now found she wanted to tell these people—her *friends*—exactly what the experience had meant to her.

'I'm the opposite of Annie, actually,' she began. 'I've taken *too much* time out. Four years of hiding is way too long.' She looked down at the carefully manicured grass. 'Bali has been a kind of purgatory for me, a place to just exist. But then being in the animal sanctuary—where we were actually fighting for survival—I realised I didn't want to die.'

Her eyes filled with tears. 'Holding Tito at the sanctuary—being with a child again—it felt like something just thawed inside of me. I have to go back to Australia and reconnect with my husband and my family. I have to learn to be with people again. A bit like the odyssey you set for me, Pak Tony, but for much longer.'

She closed her eyes, imagining seeing Richard again. 'It's not going to be easy. It's going to be very, very complicated.' She opened her eyes once more. 'But at least I know, after everything we've been through, I can cope. I can sit with my fear without feeling like I might not survive it. Of course I will; I can survive anything now. That's quite a gift, and I have Fearless to thank for it.'

Pak Tony smiled. 'Those insights are a gift to us all, Cara. Our individual shifts have been very different, haven't they? For some, they've been internal. For others, the change is explicit, affecting what we do and how we move through the world.'

'That's me,' said Remy. 'There have been many obvious changes. Like asking the woman I love *not* to marry me at the top of the Eiffel Tower.'

Janelle grinned. 'After climbing the stairs, no less.'

Remy gazed ardently at her. 'And then taking her back there again, a month later, with an engagement ring in my pocket.'

The group spontaneously cheered.

Remy smiled. 'Fearless taught me to care more. Meeting all of you, I saw more passion than in a whole restaurant of Michelin chefs. Annie and her dogs, Henry and his birds . . . and I will never forget Janelle's passion talk.'

'Who could?' crowed Henry. 'It went viral. There are millions of men worldwide who envy you, Remy.'

'I know.' The Frenchman reached for Janelle's hand, rather protectively. 'She did that because she cared so much. Without any real consideration of the possible consequences.'

Janelle looked self-conscious. 'And we'll get to those in a moment, believe me.'

'But being here in Bali showed me my own indifference,' Remy continued, 'to how my actions—or failure to act—have repercussions. I've been too comfortable in my little insular world, earning my money and deciding how to spend it.'

'That's too harsh,' objected Janelle. 'You care about a lot of things, Remy.'

'*Pfft!*' It was the Frenchman's turn to look self-conscious now. 'So, I have just started a new job. My parents are not pleased, but I can live with that. I realised something at the tooth-filing ceremony: as an adult, I can choose to care less about my family's opinion and more about the big issues.' He grinned. 'I am working in an impact investing firm. I have finally found a social project, Pak Tony, as you challenged me on Fearless.'

'In La Défense tower?' Henry jibed.

'No, thank God. On the third floor of a very old building.' Remy pulled a face at Henry. 'We invest in companies that offer more than a financial return; they contribute to a sustainable world.' He looked animated. 'We do policy work, too—on climate change, renewable energy, water trading . . .'

'So our blueblooded Frenchman has turned green?' asked Henry. 'That *is* a big change.'

'And you are sounding like my father, Henry,' Remy laughed heartily. 'But if Janelle and I ever have children, at least I can show them that their father tried to improve the world. I'm not wearing a hairshirt and ashes—I'm still very much in financial markets—but it's something more meaningful, at least. It matters.'

'Good for you, Remy,' said Annie. 'If you can make the world a better place *and* get paid for it, that's a lot more sensible than what I tried to do at BAF.' She turned to Janelle. 'Are you a lady of leisure in Paris, then?'

'Hardly.' Janelle smiled ruefully. 'I can certainly relate to what Henry said about coincidental things being part of a greater plan.'

'Oooh, do tell,' said Annie.

'Well, I'm sure everyone can remember how angry I was with Remy for posting my passion talk to YouTube,' Janelle began. 'I totally overreacted to an honest mistake. But then we got caught up in the siege and I forgot all about it.' She looked at Remy, blushing a little. 'Afterwards, when I flew back to Australia, I realised the clip had *really* gone viral.'

She paused to take a deep breath. 'Millions of young women got behind it. Taylor Swift even tweeted about it! Suddenly people started contacting me with offers for interviews, even a book deal. Someone asked me to do a Touchable shampoo commercial. I mean, my hair is *mousy*. Can you imagine it?' She laughed. 'I kept saying no. But then I realised I could actually do something constructive with all the attention.'

She looked nervously around the group. 'So, I've set up the Bella Foundation in Australia to support eating disorder services around the world. I'm going to donate my appearance fees into that. Last week I signed my first product endorsement deal with GoGirlz. They want to use a real woman, rather than an airbrushed model, in their web commercials.'

Even Cara had heard of GoGirlz, a hugely popular global skincare range for young women.

'I don't know how long it will last,' Janelle continued, 'but it beats consumer research. In fact, it's going to pay for me to retrain as a counsellor. That was the only part of my market research job I actually enjoyed—getting inside the heads of my interviewees. Once I've retrained, who knows? Maybe I'll be able to help others to face their fears. Maybe you'll employ me at Fearless one day, Pak Tony?'

The facilitator clapped his hands, grinning.

'Wow,' said Henry. 'That's huge, Janelle! Congratulations.'

'I'm flying to London after our honeymoon for my first photo shoot with GoGirlz. If Lorenzo was here . . .' Janelle's smile wavered as she looked at Lavinia, 'he could have given me some tips.'

Lavinia smiled. 'You will be *bellissima*.'

'You're going to be famous!' squealed Annie.

Janelle lowered her eyes. 'It's a cause close to my heart. GoGirlz is sending a positive message to young women about real beauty.' She looked up again. 'My niece is going to come to London with me for the photo shoot. Arabella told me it's given her a reason to get stronger. And that means more to me than anything else.'

She smiled wryly at Pak Tony. 'Remember how you told me to try something new every day? Well, I've just gone and got myself a completely new life.'

'Hurrah!' said Henry, raising his glass. 'To Janelle, a natural beauty!'

The group cheered again, and Janelle laughed. But her face quickly grew serious again. 'Actually,' she said, 'let's toast Lorenzo. When I was furious about the YouTube clip, he was the one telling me to calm down. He saw its potential. In fact, Lorenzo is why all of us are here together now.'

They all raised their glasses again. No one spoke for a moment.

Pak Tony turned to Lavinia. 'Would you like to say something, Lavinia? Janelle's right. We are here due to Lorenzo's bravery.'

'Yes . . .' Lavinia looked around unsteadily. 'Firstly, I would like to say thank you for the emails about Lorenzo. I am sorry I haven't replied to all of them. I couldn't read them after a while, it made my heart too sick.'

Cara frowned, privately wondering why Lavinia's heart hadn't seemed too sick for media interviews.

'That is understandable,' said Pak Tony. 'Of everyone here, you lost the most in the siege.'

Lavinia sighed. 'Yes, but sometimes even now it doesn't feel real. Sometimes I feel like I'm going to wake up and find Lorenzo next to me. Or I'll smell his shirts in our wardrobe and, for a moment, it's like he's right there. But, of course, he isn't.'

Cara winced, understanding. She'd moved overseas to avoid the many small reminders of Astrid.

'Maybe these things are happening in my mind because I wasn't there when Lorenzo actually . . . died,' said Lavinia. 'All of you shared Lorenzo's last week on earth and—' she looked directly at Remy now—'you were the last to see him alive.'

Remy nodded slowly.

'Can you tell me about it?' Lavinia asked softly.

Remy told her everything. From the moment he'd woken to find Lorenzo sitting next to him in the café with a bold escape plan, to the final moments before Lorenzo's death, when he'd ignored Remy's pleas to abandon the remaining hostages.

'Unlike Lorenzo, some of us were *not* heroes,' said Remy, his eyes watery. 'I helped with the other hostages, but I failed to stay to the end, I was too afraid. But Lorenzo did not falter. It was as if his whole life had led him to that moment. He was like a god, and the rest of us were mortals.' He wiped his eyes with the cuff of his shirt. 'You should be very proud.'

Lavinia stared at Remy. 'That doesn't even sound like Lorenzo,' she murmured. 'He was mostly quiet and reserved. He must have surprised himself, I think.' She smiled faintly. 'He did that a lot, actually. Expecting the worst of himself, then doing much better than he'd imagined.'

Her smile faded. 'He felt that way about fatherhood, too. I think he didn't want a baby because he was afraid he wouldn't be a good father. Probably because his own father had failed him.' Her lower lip trembled. 'That was why we came to Bali, to help him with those subconscious fears. But now . . .' She covered her face with her hands.

Annie moved closer to Lavinia and put an arm around her. 'But now we know he would have made a great father. He was strong and courageous when it counted. He saved all of us—and dozens of people he didn't know. You can carry that with you always, Lavinia.'

Not when she learns the truth, Cara thought, stricken. She'd read the translation only once, but the final sentence remained etched in her mind: *I cannot defend my models—or our future children—from myself.*

'Thank you, Annie,' Lavinia whispered, leaning into the American. 'That is very important to me, because . . .' she cupped a hand under the curve of her belly, 'Lorenzo and I are having a baby anyway. I was already pregnant when Lorenzo joined Fearless, but we didn't know. It was still too early. You can tell now, yes?'

Cara's mouth dropped open. The flowing clothes, the weight gain; it suddenly made sense.

'Oh, bless you.' Annie pulled Lavinia into another hug.

The Italian brushed tears from her eyes. 'That is why I've done so many media interviews, when all I really felt like doing was curling up and dying myself. I want to keep Lorenzo's legacy alive for his daughter.'

Cara felt ashamed of her own uncharitable assumptions. 'You're having a girl?' she said with a wistful smile. 'You're so lucky.'

'Do you think so?' Lavinia looked uneasy. 'I will be a single mother.'

'I know so. A baby changes everything.'

Lavinia looked sightly reassured. 'Was there something you wanted to share earlier, Cara? About Lorenzo?'

Cara held the last of the champagne in her mouth, fighting the urge to spit it out. Her hand rested on her bag, containing the letter from Lorenzo.

But now she was privy to new information: the presence of an unborn child. What good could come of sharing with Lavinia these ugly revelations from beyond the grave? Which was more important—compassion or truth? A long time ago, Cara had sworn a journalistic oath of truth at all costs. But then Astrid had arrived and her world had been turned upside down.

Cara swallowed the champagne. *A baby changes everything.*

'Lavinia,' she said, 'Lorenzo was one of the kindest men I've ever met.' She briefly closed her eyes, remembering his compassion at the water cleansing ceremony. 'The day before we went to the animal sanctuary, he shared something with me. He told me that you would be the best mother in the world.'

'Did he?'

Cara saw the delight in the other woman's eyes, the exquisite relief. 'Those were his exact words, and I wanted you to know.' That much was true, at least.

The Italian woman smiled through her tears and whispered, '*Grazie.*'

Pak Tony reached for Lavinia's hand. 'We are all touched by your story, Lavinia,' he said. 'And thrilled that a new life, testament to the love you shared with Lorenzo, is growing inside of you. Even after death, everyone and everything is connected.'

Often without knowing it, Cara thought. Her decision to withhold the letter had just changed Lavinia's life, and that of her unborn child, and neither would ever be the wiser.

Pak Tony turned to the wider group. 'Listening to your reflections this morning, I am proud and humbled to know you all. So before we disperse for the real celebrations of this weekend, I'd like you to stand with me once more.'

They clambered back to their feet. Cara and Annie stood on either side of Lavinia, their arms around her waist. Henry stood with one arm around Pak Ketut and the other around Remy, who held Janelle's hand in his. All of them connected by human touch.

'Let's make a simple toast.' Pak Tony raised his glass and smiled. 'To fears and failures, faced or embraced. And to strangers we have grown to trust and love. To fearless friends!'

As the group echoed his words, Cara's heart surged with gratitude. For her time in Bali, and the space it had offered her to sit quietly with her grief. For her place in this group, and the uncommon friendships born of quiet reflection and violent chaos. And for the chance to gently probe her own pain, moving towards something more buoyant and hopeful than she'd ever imagined possible.

Cara lifted her face, relishing the sun's warmth upon her skin, listening to the ocean's ebb and flow, inhaling the aroma of damp frangipanis and tasting the invisible salt crust upon her lips.

Amid all this beauty of Bali, she sensed something else. Poignant and comforting, calling her beyond the sea.

Her own homecoming.

Acknowledgements

As always, I'm indebted to the Allen & Unwin team for their expert care during the novel-birthing process. Thanks to Jane Palfreyman, Christa Munns, Clara Finlay, Wenona Byrne, Andy Palmer, Louise Cornegé, Charlotte Bachali, Alissa Dinallo, and to all the unsung heroes of publishing and bookselling of whom authors are largely ignorant.

I am grateful to the many people in my life who are willing to read my early, rambling drafts. For their commitment of time and critical feedback, huge thanks are due to Jan Lingard (several times over), Connie Diakos, Sarah Bramwell, Jodie Thomson, Sarah Barrett, Gaile Pearce, Kim Healey, Michelle Taylor, Natasha Brain, Melissa Attia, Danny Russell, Deborah Carlyon, Tegan Molony and Ewa Wojkowska.

For their assistance with specific cultural, linguistic, technical and other matters, I am grateful to Louise McLeod Tabouis, Erica Pontalti, Pierre-Luigi Balducci, Rachel Glitz, Colin Healey, Virginia Lloyd, Andrew Edwards, Sarah Alderson, Jenny Lalor,

Anna Seassau, Iluh Sudianing, Jennifer Fleming, Luisa Brimble, Don Norris, Rhonda Carpenter, Rachael McLennan, and Sasha and Nathan White.

I'm lucky to have the love and companionship of long-suffering family and friends, especially Stuart Higgins, Lesley Collins, Amanda Collins, John Attia, Tim Haydon, Debra Reed, Amanda Thomas and Judith and Des Huxley.

For their continued cheering from the grandstand of life, thank you to the Jack family, the Jones family, the Bale and Campbell families, Veronica Abolins, Ellen Fanning, Peter Dredge, Peter Kerr, John and Libby Fairfax, Kate and Nathan Fabian, Genevieve Freeman, Suzanne Kent and Bertoes, and Those Who Must Not Be Named.

Special thanks to all my friends in Bali, especially the Pelangi School community, for walking alongside us during our precious years in paradise.

And for their constant inspiration, relentless questioning and daily death-defying acts of fearlessness, all my love and gratitude go to not-so-little Oliver, Skye and Luke. I want to write the world for you.